LUCKY STARS

GHOSTS AND REINCARNATION SERIES
BOOK V

KRISTEN ASHLEY

ROCK CHICK
PRESS

Lucky STARS

❊ GHOSTS AND REINCARNATIONS SERIES ❊

NEW YORK TIMES BESTSELLING AUTHOR

KRISTEN ASHLEY

EXPECTATIONS AND DISASTER

Belle

There came a knock at the door.

Belle Abbot jumped like a frightened cat and whirled away from her reflection in the mirror.

She knew who was there.

She stared at the door thinking, not for the first time, she did not have a good feeling about that night.

She felt both a strange, thrilling expectation and a not-so-strange fear of disaster.

This combination of feelings was very weird.

The former, she had no idea its cause.

The latter, she knew was Miles.

She should have never agreed to come there.

She knew it, she just knew it. She should have never let him talk her into it.

It was too soon.

They'd only been dating a month, which was way too soon for her to meet his mother.

And it was definitely way too soon for her to spend the weekend at the family's ancestral castle in order to attend his mother's posh annual birthday bash, which would be a veritable crush of the rich and famous.

Belle was not comfortable in a crush of people. She'd *definitely* not be comfortable in a crush of the rich and famous.

She walked on leaded feet across the huge expanse of her richly appointed bedroom to the door. She was forty-five minutes late to join the party downstairs, and she wondered what Miles's reaction would be to her tardiness.

She was late partially because it took her *forever* to do her hair.

She was also late because she was purposefully dillydallying in an effort to delay her arrival at the festivities and hysterically considering feigning a headache, or a fast-acting and incapacitating stomach flu.

She pulled open the heavy door.

She was right. There stood Miles Bennett.

He looked, she noticed instantly, very good in his formal attire.

This wasn't the first time she realized how good he looked. Indeed, it wasn't something you could miss.

However, she'd thought he'd looked good before she'd ever met him, considering he was famous because he and his family were extortionately wealthy.

She'd seen his pictures in magazines since she was a young, romantically-minded girl and he was a teen. She (and undoubtedly many other girls around the globe) watched him growing up tall, strong, lean and handsome, living a jet-set lifestyle. The kind of lifestyle that always captivated the press and young, romantically-minded girls. Therefore, the press covered his life regularly and with a great deal of devoted attention. The same devotion that young girls who grew to be young women who grew to be just women without the young attached followed it.

He was blond, blue-eyed, broad-shouldered and had a slim but muscled body that he held with an attractive ease.

Though there was something in his eyes that worried Belle. Something she couldn't quite put her finger on. Something she didn't think she liked.

Those eyes did a sweep of her and she watched as they grew hungry not in an entirely good way. In what Belle thought was a somewhat greedy way,

A way that put her on edge.

Then he muttered, "Jesus."

Belle wasn't certain about his odd response.

She looked down at herself anxiously and asked, "Do I look okay?" before her eyes lifted back to his.

His gaze moved from her chest to her face and he grinned. That look that made her uncomfortable left his face. Another look, a look that made her think maybe she was being a bit crazy, a look filled with warmth and affection, replaced it.

His hand came out and he teasingly flicked the ruffle at her neck.

"Is it one of yours?" he asked.

He meant her dress and he didn't mean to ask if she owned it because, obviously, she did.

She had a small shop in St. Ives, which sold, almost exclusively, a line of clothing creations that she designed and made. She also sold a few friends' jewelry collections and other bits and bobs when the mood struck her, which was often.

The shop had been somewhat hand to mouth until the recent extraordinary events that rocked her life. Now, she had to employ two seamstresses to help her keep on top of stock, and her used-to-be very unusual, personalized orders had quadrupled.

"Yes," she replied to Miles.

Her dress was knee length and form-fitting. It was a beautiful crepe de chine she'd found that she'd fallen in love with instantly and bought yards of it even though the cost was astronomical. It was the color of blush, that was neither peach nor pink nor cream but an elegant mixture of the three.

The back was high. It was sleeveless but there was a deep slash from the throat to the empire waist at her midriff. This was made demure by a delicate, two-inch, complementary blush-colored chiffon ruffle running the length of the slash and around her neck. Nevertheless, it showed the skin of her chest provocatively.

She'd paired the dress with high-heeled pumps that were about three shades darker than the dress (on the pink side). The shoes had peekaboo toes that had a small rosette which flattered the shoes and drew attention to her French-pedicured toenails.

"Gorgeous," Miles murmured, and Belle had to steel herself against that word which he used often in regards to her, even calling her that as an endearment.

She considered any endearments in a month-long relationship way too early but she never said anything, though she had to admit it kind of gave her the creeps.

It was a word her ex-husband, Calvin, had used to describe her, and just as Miles, Calvin had used it as a sweet nothing. Sometimes even saying it when he felt repentant, wiping away the blood from her lip, pressing the ice to her eye after he'd used his fists on her.

"We should join the party, Belle. Mum's asking after you," Miles told her, pulling her out of her thoughts and taking her elbow, forcing her forward, closing the door to her room behind them.

Belle had met Joy Bennett, Miles's mother, that afternoon when they'd arrived at the family castle, called Chy An Als Point. An imposing, rambling, stone structure with an uneven roofline, some of it built hundreds upon hundreds of years before on a jagged Cornish cliff. The winds blew the waters of the sea so they smashed against the rocks at the castle's base, giving the already daunting castle a strangely unsettling atmosphere.

You couldn't say the castle was beautiful. The many different styles of its construction, as it was added onto century after century, clashed weirdly at the same time they managed to mingle.

You *could* say it was spectacular, almost like a living entity, powerful, magnificent and impenetrable, perched for centuries on its cliff.

Regardless of the fact that it was slightly spooky, Belle loved it.

Upon meeting Miles's mum, Joy, Belle liked her without reservation. She was a lovely woman, tall and svelte, sharing the coloring of Miles. She was open, friendly, welcoming and kind, if a bit dramatic. But considering Belle's mother and grandmother, Belle was used to more than a bit of drama.

Joy was also, Belle found (to her surprise), wary of her son. This was something she tried to hide, but Belle, her senses attuned to the strangeness she felt from Miles, read it and worried about it.

Then again, Belle worried about everything.

Belle was, unfortunately, a worrier.

Still, Joy loved him. That was obvious, and she was affectionate toward him. But when her eyes drifted between Miles and Belle, Belle saw the backs of them grow uneasy.

This did not aid in Belle's indecision about how she felt about Miles Bennett.

Not one bit.

Belle walked beside Miles down the thick carpet runner that ran the length of the stone-floored hall. He'd tucked her hand in the crook of his elbow in a way she thought was a tad too possessive but also wondered if her caution had more to do with the lessons she'd learned from Calvin and less to do with the reality of Miles.

She'd only dated two men since divorcing Calvin. She promptly found she couldn't open up to either and realized she was not yet ready to move forward in life romantically.

She should, she knew, be more like her mother and grandmother. Both of them had been handed by God an overabundance of outspokenness, outgoingness and outrageousness. They also had the capacity to plunge themselves, both feet first, eyes open, into cold, shark-infested waters if there was even the slightest possibility that there might be something rich and rewarding to come of this endeavor.

Since she was a little girl, Belle had thought that God had been so generous to her grandmother and mother, he'd not had enough to hand out when Belle came along.

Therefore Belle Abbot had lost out on these qualities and all her life she had been timid, apprehensive and never took an uncalculated risk.

Never.

It was safe to repeat that point...*never*.

"It's too bad your brother couldn't make it to your mother's birthday party," Belle remarked as they made it to the top of a carpet-runnered stone stairwell that she and Miles and four other people could easily walk down, side by side.

Miles's brother, James Bennett was equally (if not more) famous as Miles.

He was also, in looks, the exact opposite.

Miles looked like his mother.

James Bennett looked like his now-deceased father.

Black-haired with startlingly green eyes rimmed with long, black lashes, James Bennett (if the pictures were true) was taller than Miles. He was also lean and broad-shouldered but his muscles were more powerful. And, if Miles held his body with a casual ease, James held his with a fierce command.

James, in the many photos Belle had seen of him (and there were many), was more intense, more masculine, his features bolder and stronger, while Miles's still held a hint of boyishness.

James, being older, (arguably) more attractive and standing to (and unfortunately, three years ago, upon his father's untimely death, actually doing it) inherit the castle, had much more attention on him his whole life.

He, however, had not gone into the family banking business but instead started his own business. He did something complicated Belle didn't understand and did it very, *very* well making him far, *far* richer and increasing the already oppressive attention he had from the media.

He had, however, also inherited the role of CEO of the vast banking conglomerate that extended throughout the European Union and the Americas that the Bennett family had owned for years.

Now he did both, reportedly with great success even if his attention to these two undertakings was rather shocking since only one would tax even the best of men.

This served only to increase public interest.

The fact that he and Miles routinely dated and often had rather public but usually short-lived (though frequently stormy), relationships with every glamorous, beautiful and available model, actress and debutante, squiring them to art openings, charity functions and exclusive restaurants, made it all the worse.

"Oh, he's here," Miles said, and Belle nearly missed a step when Miles made this casual statement.

"He's here?" Belle breathed, unhappy about this news.

Miles had told her James couldn't attend because of some business in Slovakia or Bosnia or some country ending in "ia."

She was already incredibly nervous about the evening. She didn't need another reason to be nervous. And James Bennett was the kind of man who could make even the most beautiful, sophisticated, accomplished, confident person nervous.

And Belle was *none* of those.

"Oh yes, he's here. Arrived as a surprise for Mum a little over an hour ago." Miles looked down at her and smiled. This smile, Belle saw, was not warm and affectionate.

It was strangely...

She stared up at him...

Triumphant.

As if someone had called Miles and told him that he'd won the Nobel Prize for simply existing.

This was so weird it also didn't make Belle happy.

In fact, it kind of freaked her out.

They made it to the bottom of the stairs, and before Belle could process her emotion she heard her name cried.

And it was cried loudly.

She took her eyes from Miles and looked across him to see Joy heading, or more accurately described as *charging* their way.

She was wearing a deep burgundy dress with long sleeves and gathered cross-draping. To Belle's experienced eye, the dress was complicated and stunning.

"I love your hair!" Joy exclaimed when she arrived at Belle and Miles. She leaned in and gave Belle a cheek touch and air kiss, her hands curling on Belle's forearms. She leaned back and cried, "And your *dress*!" She said no more, her tone and emphasis were enough to say what words *simply* did not describe.

Belle fought the urge to touch her hair nervously. She'd pulled it back softly from her face and fixed it in a loose chignon at the side of her nape. It took about twenty tries to get it right but she'd finally done it.

Except one, long, thick tendril that curled down the side of her neck, which would not, no matter what Belle tried to do (and she'd tried everything), stay fixed in the knot.

"Thank you," Belle whispered, her gaze moving to the guests in the vast hall, of which there were a fair few standing about, all of their eyes on her.

After the events of eight months ago, she'd become somewhat accustomed to eyes on her.

That didn't mean she liked it and it always made her feel awkward.

Or, more awkward than she normally felt.

Joy linked her arm through Belle's and announced, "Let's get you a drink, shall we?"

Joy pulled Belle away from Miles and toward the fantastic drawing room, which was decorated in whites, creams, yellows and golds. Miles had given her the full tour of the castle that afternoon. It had taken more than an hour mainly because Belle was enthralled that any family could actually *live* in such historical splendor but also because it was *huge*.

It boggled the mind.

Or, at least, it boggled Belle's mind.

Though, Belle had to admit, her mind was not difficult to boggle.

The drawing room had even more people, and Belle felt her body grow tight as upon their entry many of their eyes moved to her.

Joy didn't seem to notice and leaned close to Belle, not as if they'd met only hours before but as if they were bosom buddies and had been for decades. "Miles delivered your present to me while you were getting ready. I love it, Belle. Thank you."

Belle turned her head to Joy at these genuine and heartfelt words and she smiled.

She didn't know if she should give a woman she'd never met a present but considering she was attending her party and dating her son she figured it would be bad manners if she didn't do something.

It took fifteen calls to her grandmother, mother and a variety of friends before Belle chose a piece of jewelry from her shop. Hammered silver that was cut sharply in places, rolled stylishly in others and liberally sprinkled with freshwater pearls, it had a unique style and Belle thought it was lovely.

Still, what did you get the woman who had or could have everything?

Clearly, Belle hadn't done a bad job of it.

"I'm pleased you like it," Belle murmured, sounding as pleased as she was and Joy squeezed her arm.

"I don't like it, I love it. It's unusual, beautiful and very thoughtful," Joy replied.

For the first time since she arrived at the castle, Belle felt unmitigated happiness and her smile deepened.

They stopped at a small bar set up for the party with a variety of glasses and bottles of liquor with buckets of ice. It was attended by a dark-jacketed, bow-tied bartender.

"Two champagnes please," Miles ordered, coming to stand behind Belle, and she felt his hand move to rest at the small of her back.

She looked over her shoulder at Miles and tried to hide her annoyance.

He did that all the time, ordered for her. And it wasn't like he knew her preferences because he barely knew *her*. He just said things like, "You have to try this," or, "This is the best thing they make," and then he'd order it for her without allowing her to say a word.

She actually didn't want the meals he ordered her and at that moment she also didn't want champagne.

With her nerves, she needed at the very least vodka. If she had the courage of her grandmother and mother, she would have ordered a shot of tequila (or three).

Champagne wasn't even in her top five.

She sighed and let it go.

One thing she'd learned from Calvin was to pick her battles.

And she was not going to have words over champagne.

The bartender held out the glass to her but Miles leaned in and took it, moving it the scant inch between the bartender's hand and Belle's as if Belle was above doing such common things as accepting a glass of champagne from a lowly servant.

This act so surprised and irritated her, she very nearly said something.

Of course, she did not.

Instead, she clenched her teeth a moment before she lifted the glass and sipped.

"Oh there's Adele!" Joy cried suddenly, glancing across the room. "I must go say hello." She turned to Belle. "Now that you have refreshments, I can leave you to it." Her eyes moved upwards to her son. "Now

Miles, don't let Belle get drunk and dance on any tables," she ordered, and the very idea of Belle "Meek and Mild" Abbot dancing on a table made Belle burst out laughing.

When she'd controlled her hilarity and her gaze focused on Joy, the woman's blue eyes were studying Belle and they were shining with an odd, soft light.

Then she leaned toward Belle and whispered. "You should do that more often, darling."

Without another word, she was gone, melting into the crowd.

Miles moved her away from the bar so others could order drinks and Belle braced because she was certain she was going to have to start mingling.

Belle hated to mingle. She had no talent for small talk and found the effort grueling.

They did not, however, sift into the crowd. Instead, Miles's hand at her waist curled her body toward his and then in so they were hips to hips and belly to belly.

Startled, Belle looked up at him.

Firstly, they were too close, loverly close. It wasn't seemly, and furthermore they weren't lovers.

Secondly, they'd shared some kisses but she hadn't even let Miles get to second base and he'd tried on every date they shared, even the first one. She was uncomfortable with this casual but extreme closeness that gave the wrong message.

They certainly were *not* at a point in their relationship where he would hold her that close in public.

In fact, Belle wasn't entirely certain there *ever* would be a time in *any* relationship where she'd allow a man to hold her that close in public.

Not before Calvin.

Not during Calvin (not that he was that way inclined, fortunately).

Not after Calvin.

She put her hand to his bicep and leaned against his arm, tipping her head back to look at him.

She opened her mouth to ask him to move away when she felt it.

A trill shot up her spine causing the small hairs at the hairline of her neck to rise and she felt her belly dip right before it warmed.

Of its own accord, her head turned to the side, her eyes moved instinctively and locked on a man across the room.

He was an unbelievably handsome, green-eyed man who stood straight and tall, his body, even at rest, clearly at his command and his gaze was riveted on her.

Belle's knees went weak, heat hit her cheeks and her fingers clutched Miles's arm as she looked upon the indecently attractive James Bennett, in the flesh, for the very first time.

Jack

Jack was listening to Yasmin talk as he took a sip of champagne before the crowds parted and he saw her wearing a blush-colored dress and pink shoes. Both dress and shoes were feminine and unbelievably sexy in a way they hinted tantalizingly at the charms of the woman wearing them rather than brazenly displaying them.

He was struck by the sight of her. Struck enough for his body to go completely still, his hand holding the glass arrested in its descent from his lips.

Abruptly it hit him who she was.

In the last eight months he'd seen her pictures dozens of times, maybe even scores of times in the media.

Belle Abbot, "The Tiny Dynamo," "The Great American Heroine," and half a dozen other nicknames the press had given her when, eight months ago, she'd witnessed an accident in front of her while driving down the road. A bus carrying school children coming back from an outing had flipped over a bridge into icy waters.

She'd stopped her car, torn out and dove into the freezing sea to save the lives of seven schoolchildren and the bus driver who she'd plunged after, again and again, to pull from the bus.

Two children had swum free themselves, two children had drowned.

Both drown victims Belle had pulled from the watery wreckage, and one she was still giving CPR when the paramedics finally arrived.

This was all caught on other onlookers' phones, both in photos and video.

They did not help Belle Abbot. No. Instead they sold their photos far and wide. Photos of her dripping wet, diving, breaking the surface with a child's arm wrapped around her neck, dragging the child behind her, kicking toward the shore.

The press had made a meal of her, as they would because the story was, frankly, astounding.

They hadn't, however, as the months passed, lost their interest.

Mainly because, when Belle Abbot wasn't cold, wet and saving lives, she was exceptionally pretty.

Not beautiful, her nose was too pert, her skin was peaches and cream, she was not petite but also not tall.

But she was uncommonly pretty with shining, unbelievably thick, dark blonde hair streaked with honeyed highlights. Her body was perfectly proportioned and lusciously curvaceous. Lastly, she had a classic, elegant style, a bearing that was nearly regal and she was way too photogenic for her own good.

Further, she was an enigma.

In a time when instant celebrity was coveted to the point of obsession, she didn't speak to the press. She didn't sell her story. She didn't do television interviews. She didn't pay any attention to the media at all. She kept her eyes averted, head bowed and went about her daily life as if she hadn't committed an act of selfless altruism. An act that had already, without Belle Abbot's input or approval, been made into a television movie.

Her head turned and her gray eyes hit him and Jack felt as if someone had taken a sledgehammer to his gut.

He was wrong.

Perhaps she wasn't as photogenic as he thought.

In the photos, she was not beautiful.

But in the flesh, she was a knockout.

It struck Jack that she was with a man, a man who was holding her close, and Jack's eyes moved to the man.

They did this as Yasmin breathed, "I don't believe it."

When Jack saw his brother Miles holding Belle Abbot, his still body went rock solid.

He felt Yasmin's hand clutch his forearm as Miles turned to look at what had caught Belle's attention.

Jack watched as Miles's face took on an expression Jack knew very well. Indeed, Jack had seen it time and again for as long as he could remember.

It was the look Miles got every time Miles engaged him in a competition, which happened often between the two brothers. Over the years Jack had vigorously participated, until somewhat recently, after their father died (but even before) when Miles's obsessive competitive streak had turned to unhealthy compulsion.

The look on Miles's face was filled with triumph.

Jack knew at that moment that Miles was not with Belle Abbot because she was graceful, stylish and extraordinarily sexy.

He was with her to rub Jack's nose in it.

"Jack, is Miles with Belle Abbot, The Tiny Dynamo?" Yasmin whispered.

"Yes," Jack's deep voice clipped tersely.

"My God." Yasmin was still whispering, this time in shocked horror as Jack watched Miles break away from Belle but he held her close to his side as he guided them their way. "He's going to eat her alive," Yasmin finished.

Her words were Jack's thoughts precisely.

Jack didn't move as Miles and Belle walked the short distance. Only his eyes cut to Belle, who was looking at Yasmin, then she looked away not even sparing Jack a glance.

"Jack!" Miles greeted him with a handshake even though this was rude. Any gentleman knew he should greet Yasmin first.

However, he wouldn't have called Belle's attention immediately to Jack if he had demonstrated good manners.

And called it he did. Jack watched as her head moved and she lifted her eyes to him.

Fifteen feet away, Jack thought she was a knockout.

Two feet away, her stormy gray eyes on his, she was phenomenal.

"Belle, I'd like you to meet my brother, James Bennett. And his girl-friend, Yasmin Delacourt," Miles introduced them.

She lifted her hand for him to shake rather than her cheek for him to kiss.

For some reason this irritated Jack to an irrational extreme. Such an extreme, it brought him to the point of action.

Therefore, when his hand closed around hers, it did it powerfully and he used it to pull her closer to his body. Taken by surprise, she came up to her toes then over, moving toward him and lifting her hand at the last minute, bracing herself by resting the champagne glass she held against his arm.

He put his other hand, which also still held his glass, to her waist and he bent his head. He brushed his lips against her cheek at the same time he smelled her elusive, sophisticated perfume. Instead of releasing her and letting her pull away, he lifted his head and looked into her eyes.

"Belle," he murmured.

"James," she murmured back, her eyes caught on his for the briefest second before they moved over his shoulder, her hand tugging at his, her body tense and trying to move away.

"Jack," he corrected, his hand in hers pulling her closer, his other hand curving slightly around her back so she was, effectively, in the circle of his arm. Their hands held between their bodies, her breasts nearly, but not quite, close enough to brush his chest.

Her remarkable eyes skittered back to his.

"I beg your pardon?" she whispered.

"My friends call me Jack," he told her softly.

Her eyes grew slightly wider and her mouth parted deliciously when she breathed, "Oh."

His eyes locked on her lips.

With an intensity that startled him, Jack felt the urge to kiss her. This urge was so forceful, his hands on her actually tensed as if to pull her closer just as she leaned in slightly.

His gaze moved to hers and he saw she was also staring at his mouth, her face soft, her eyelids heavy, her desire to be kissed was written on her features in unconcealed temptation.

Good fucking God, he thought right before she was pulled away by Miles, and Jack lost hold of her.

Miles positioned her firmly and pointedly at his side.

This sudden movement surprised her and her head came up, her expression cleared of desire and she looked charmingly cross for a moment before she was able to control it.

This almost made Jack laugh, however, the scheming yet annoyed look Jack caught on Miles's face wiped away all thoughts of laughter.

Belle's head turned to Yasmin and she smiled a small smile before she pulled away from Miles to kiss Yasmin's cheek.

"Yasmin," she mumbled.

"I'm not Jack's girlfriend, you know," Yasmin announced, apropos of nothing, instead of greeting Belle in return.

"You're not?" Belle asked, her voice quiet.

Yasmin's eyes were moving between Jack, Belle and Miles, and Jack saw they were scheming as well but in an entirely different way.

"Yasmin," Jack muttered with a warning note in his voice but Yasmin, as usual, ignored it and talked over him.

"We were, ages and ages ago. Now we're just friends. Close friends but just friends. We've been friends for years. But we're only friends." Yasmin made herself perfectly clear and Jack felt Miles's displeasure without having to look at him.

"So, you're friends?" Belle mumbled her dry question and Jack chuckled.

As he did so, he saw her eyes on him held a hint of shocked pleasure before they quickly moved away.

"Yes," Yasmin replied, amusement in her voice, her eyes on Belle. "By the way, Joy showed me the brooch you gave her. It's stunning."

Belle and Jack both looked at Yasmin.

"What brooch?" Jack asked.

"Joy told me that the girl Miles brought with him, Belle, obviously," she nodded her head at Belle and then carried on, "bought her a brooch for her birthday. Very unusual, very gorgeous. I want one," Yasmin replied throwing a smile toward Belle as Jack's eyes moved to her as well.

She was, again, looking anywhere but him.

"You bought Mum a brooch?" he asked her and her eyes went to his ear.

"Yes," she replied.

"It's fantastic," Miles put in, pulling Belle closer to his side and Jack watched her body grow visibly tense. "It's from her shop in St. Ives."

"I'll have to visit your shop," Yasmin told her.

Belle looked relieved to have an opportunity to move her gaze to Yasmin whom she gave a nod and another small smile. "I'd like that."

"She made her dress," Miles declared, and Jack watched a becoming flush creep into Belle's cheek as Miles went on, "The one she's wearing tonight."

"Miles," she whispered, clearly embarrassed and equally clearly wanting him to shut up.

Miles ignored her and kept talking. "She designs clothes." His eyes moved to Jack and his hand not wrapped around Belle's waist came across his body. Holding his champagne glass, he flicked the ruffle at her collarbone with an extended finger. "Sexy little number, isn't it?" he asked Jack.

"Miles!" Belle hissed with now obvious embarrassment as her body went solid.

"It's lovely," Jack murmured, wondering how angry his mother would be if he did physical injury to his brother at her birthday party before turning the conversation off Belle's more than just lovely dress to something else. "Are you spending the weekend?"

Belle's eyes came to his and he thought he saw a hint of gratitude at his change of topic before they moved swiftly away.

"Yes," Miles stated, curling Belle possessively closer, his head bending in an openly intimate way toward hers, both actions gave his words more meaning. "We're staying until Monday."

His insinuation was not lost on anyone and Belle's cheeks flamed.

"Joy tells me you're in separate bedrooms," Yasmin remarked, boldly calling Miles out on his nonverbal lie.

Jack would have laughed but Belle's eyes flew to Yasmin and she looked mortified.

She turned into Miles and tipped her head back. "You know," she said softly but somewhat desperately. "I think I need to go fix my lipstick."

It was clear she was desperate to escape.

Clear to everyone but Miles.

"Your lips are perfect, gorgeous," Miles replied and Jack watched as something crossed her face. Even in profile he could see it and it looked like she flinched as if she'd been struck.

Jack found her look both stirring and upsetting.

He didn't have time to try and understand this reaction, Yasmin moved forward.

"Yes, her lips *are* perfect, Miles. But mine aren't," Yasmin declared and linked an arm through Belle's, forcibly moving her away from Miles before she continued. "Now, as you men know, we ladies have to visit the little girl's room in pairs, so I'm claiming Belle as my second. We'll be back."

Before anyone could say a word, Yasmin led Belle from the room.

Belle, Jack noted, didn't look back.

Both Miles and Jack watched them leave.

"She's something, isn't she?" Miles asked Jack, his eyes still on the door the women had walked through.

Jack clenched his teeth as anger surged inside him.

In a low, displeased voice, Jack demanded, "Give it up, Miles."

Slowly, Miles's head turned and he looked at his brother.

Jack saw a sly look in Miles's eyes, a look that Jack also knew very well as he'd seen it countless times.

It was the look Miles assumed when he knew he was going to lose (which was frequently) and decided to do whatever he had to do to win no matter how devious or underhanded it needed to be.

"Give it up?" Miles repeated, his face changing to false innocence.

"Yes, give it up," Jack returned. "Play your games on the pitch, in the board room and with women who know the score. Belle Abbot clearly doesn't know the score. Fucking with that woman's head, Miles, is lower than you've ever sunk. And you've sunk pretty damned low."

Jack watched the red creep up his brother's neck, signaling his anger.

He leaned toward Jack and clipped, "I saw the way you were with her. You're not asking me to give it up for Belle's sake. You're asking me to step aside because you want a crack at her."

Jack's first response to his brother referring to anyone having "a crack" at Belle was the nearly overwhelming desire to put his fist in his face.

With effort, he quelled this desire and realized what Miles said was both right and wrong.

Jack Bennett did, indeed, want "a crack" at Belle Abbot.

Actually, when it came to Belle Abbot, Jack found he wanted a number of things.

He wanted to see if he could break through her obvious, nearly crippling shyness and get her to respond to him. He wanted to hear her soft, sweet voice utter more than a few words. He wanted to teach her to look in his eyes, not at his ear. He wanted to see what would happen to her timidity when he kissed her. He wanted to know if what he read behind her stormy eyes and if the promise of her tempting body proved true when he had her naked underneath him.

And he decided instantly he was going to do all of those things.

Every last one.

What he would not do was break her in order to do it.

Something which Miles would not hesitate to do.

Therefore, he had no other choice really.

Thinking of Belle's lips parting on her soft "oh," Jack wouldn't have even considered another choice.

But knowing his brother, he definitely had no choice.

And, his decision made, his eyes focused on Miles, Miles read what was in Jack's gaze and then Jack watched his brother smile.

Then Miles's eyes began to burn with an unhealthy fire that made Jack's gut get tight and his brother whispered hungrily, "You're on."

❧ 2 ❧

JAMES'S TOUR

Belle

Belle wandered down the long hall looking for escape.

But escape wasn't easy to find.

There were people *everywhere*.

Joy must be much loved, for the castle was enormous and in every nook and cranny there were people.

And Belle needed to escape people.

She'd just spent the three most excruciatingly uncomfortable hours of her life amongst a stifling clutch of *people* and she needed somewhere where she could be alone and just *breathe*.

Her night was uncomfortable for three reasons.

Firstly, Miles was intent upon being *way* too close at all times and introducing her to everyone who came within shouting distance.

And this he did with alarming zeal.

Secondly, both Joy Bennett and Yasmin Delacourt were acting as if she was a long lost daughter (Joy) and a best friend from high school lost for decades and now joyfully reunited (Yasmin).

Belle already liked Joy but it seemed the lady was protecting her.

More times than Belle could count, Joy materialized at Miles and Belle's side in order to curb Miles's wild enthusiasm at breathing Belle's air. This she did before she had to go off and be the guest of honor that she was, which as the hours passed she seemed to do with more and more trepidation.

With time Belle got over Yasmin's overwhelming friendliness not to mention her startling frankness and began to like her. However, Belle noted, Yasmin seemed to do the same thing as Joy in the same protective way.

The striking, leggy, curly redheaded, barely clothed Yasmin, at first, terrified Belle. She really liked Yasmin's turquoise satin slip dress with the deep cleavage, deeper back and short hem even if it left very little to the imagination. Then again, if Belle had a body like hers, she might consider wearing the same thing (who was she kidding, she'd *never* consider it).

But she was clearly a very nice woman who'd been around the family for some time and also seemed to be regarded as a kind of daughter.

Regardless, Belle thought Yasmin and Joy's behavior was beyond odd. Although, she had to admit, she was grateful for it. Miles was driving Belle up the wall.

Lastly, and most importantly, until about a half an hour ago when he'd thankfully disappeared, James Bennett was always there.

Always.

He wasn't close but he was also never far, and often she'd feel that weird trill up her spine, the hairs on the back of her neck would stand up and her belly would melt. She'd look around and, every time it happened, she'd see that he had his amazing jade-green eyes on her.

She did not understand why he was watching her.

It was simply *bizarre.*

What was more bizarre was Belle's reaction to him.

Okay, so he was the very definition of masculine beauty.

And there was the fact that she was shy and nervous, not just at the worst of times but *all* the time.

But James Bennett utterly and completely *petrified* her.

He was way too attractive. No one should be that attractive.

In fact, Belle thought being that attractive should be against the law.

He should be locked up in order to save all of womankind from his stupefying appeal.

He was, Belle convinced herself, dangerous, he was so darned good-looking.

When he'd first touched her, first spoken to her, she'd actually felt her body moving toward him of its own volition like she was made of metal and he was magnetic.

After that happened, she decided she wanted nothing to do with him.

Indeed, she wanted nothing to do with the entire family no matter how nice they were (except, possibly, Miles in the nice department).

She should have *never* come there.

And she decided she was breaking up with Miles the first chance she got.

If it didn't demonstrate *extremely* bad manners, she would have done it that very night.

She would definitely do it tomorrow.

This was most assuredly *not* a safe place for Belle Abbot to be.

She needed her tranquil, cozy cottage. She needed her tidy sewing room. She needed to be anywhere but there.

On that thought, she saw a closed door and hoped that no one would mind if she opened it and went inside. She didn't care if it was a closet. She'd stand amongst the brooms just to get away for five minutes.

She opened the door and found it wasn't a closet.

Instead, it was James Bennett's study. She remembered it amongst the numerous rooms Miles had shown her that afternoon.

It was, Belle saw with relief, dark and deserted.

She slipped in and quietly closed the door.

This room, like all of the rest in Chy An Als, was huge. It held a gigantic desk with two chairs at angles in front of it, all of which sat in the massive bay window. There was a large, tan-colored, button-backed sofa that was situated facing an enormous, stone mantel fireplace, a heavy, ornate, dark wood, low table between the two. There was another seating area in the corner, two comfy armchairs separated by a round table and sharing an ottoman. The entire room (outside the window) was lined in bookshelves chockablock with books.

Belle didn't see any of that. Instead, as she started to pick her way across the room aided by the bright moonlight shining from the bay window that faced the sea, she heard the telltale jangle of dog tags.

Between the table and fireplace, she stopped and looked down to see a large dog, who appeared in the moonlight to be a German shepherd, standing at attention and staring at her.

Belle smiled.

She *loved* dogs.

Slowly, so as not to alarm him, she crouched low and, just as slowly, lifted her hand toward him.

He came forward cautiously and sniffed her hand.

"Hey there, fella," she whispered and watched his head come up at the sound of her voice.

Then it moved, his snout butting Belle's hand. At his invitation, she shifted forward slowly, shuffling in a crouch, and started to stroke the silky, thick fur at his handsome head.

"Aren't you beautiful?" she asked on a soft coo. He inched toward her as the strokes became her fingernails scratching behind his ear and she let out a soft laugh. "You know it, don't you? Just how beautiful you are," she went on and lifted her other hand to rub his neck as her nails worked behind his ear.

He came closer and sat down, pressing into her hands and she leaned her face toward him carefully not wishing to scare him.

She didn't. He lifted his mouth to her face and licked her jaw.

Belle burst out laughing and framed his doggie neck with her hands, catching his ruff gently in her fists and giving his neck an affectionate shake.

"Now, that's the best kiss I've had in three years," she told him with complete honesty, and she heard his tail sweep the floor at her compliment.

She took her hands away and stood, patting her hip to bring him with her as she made her way to the window.

"Come on, handsome," she invited softly. "Show me the view."

He trotted alongside her as she went to the window, stopped and looked.

All she saw was sea and sky in every direction. Both the waters and the heavens the same rich midnight blue, the white caps of the waves breaking the sea, fluffy white clouds dotting the sky, all of it illuminated by the moonlight.

It was spectacular.

She looked down at the dog, who had sat next to her, and bent slightly to stroke his head.

"I could live here for a thousand years and never get used to this view," she told the dog.

"I'm not sure that's true," the very deep, very masculine, very unmistakable voice of James Bennett said from behind her.

Terror shooting through her, Belle straightened and whirled to face the room. She did this so fast the blood rushed to her head and she swayed slightly while her eyes focused on where the voice had come from.

On the couch she could see long legs covered in dark trousers stretched straight out. There was a white shirted chest, one arm cocked so a shadowy dark head could rest on a hand and the other arm up, looking like it was holding a glass.

Her first petrified thought was to run directly from the room.

This was a good thought, a thought she was ready to go with whole-heartedly.

Unfortunately, Belle's feet had somehow come detached from her brain's commands and didn't move.

"I've lived here thirty-eight years and don't even see it anymore," he continued speaking, not moving from his position, but she knew from her melty stomach and the hairs prickling at her neck that his eyes were on her.

From the silence in the room, she realized something was expected of her and she swallowed.

Finally, she mumbled, "That's kind of sad," because it was.

Her locked body became frozen as she watched the white shirt move, curling into the trousers and she knew he was going to stand.

Now! Her mind screamed at her immobile feet. *Now's the time to run!*

Her feet stayed stubbornly stationary.

She saw James was on his own feet and coming her way.

Belle stared at him, body statue still as he approached then kept approaching then *kept* approaching until he was not even a foot away.

Then he stopped and she nearly let out the breath she was holding but he immediately leaned in close.

Too close.

Magnetically close.

She steeled her body against his pull and her lungs began to burn as she looked up at him to see that he was gazing over her shoulder.

She saw his eyes flick down to hers in the moonlight even though he didn't lean away.

"You're right," he said softly. "It is sad."

Do something! her mind shrieked.

"Um…" her mouth said.

Then she stopped speaking.

"Yes?" James prompted, still not leaning away.

"What?" she asked quickly, mind all of a sudden completely blank.

"You were going to say something," he told her.

Was she?

She was.

What was she going to say?

"Um…" she repeated.

She stopped speaking again.

His entire face, bathed in moonlight, smiled.

Seeing it, Belle's mind went completely blank again as her belly did a weird, not unpleasant in the slightest, flip.

"Why are you here?" he asked quietly.

She felt her head give a tiny jerk and then tilt.

"Here?" she parroted.

"In the study," he explained. "Away from the party." He hesitated and his voice was deeper when he went on, "Away from Miles."

Well, one thing she knew, she couldn't tell him his brother was driving her up the wall and she was breaking up with him that very next day.

"Um..." she said yet again before her mind kicked in gear. "I needed a break. I'm not a people person."

Now why did she tell him that?

It sounded rude and it made her sound like an idiot.

A rude idiot.

Even though it was true.

He seemed to get even closer when he remarked, "I guessed that."

She was stunned and a little disappointed. She thought she'd been pretty good at hiding it.

"You did?"

She heard his soft chuckle. It was a delicious sound. Just as delicious as it was the first time she heard it and that made her belly do a weird, intensely pleasant flip too.

"Yes, Belle. You're definitely not a people person," he told her.

For some reason she didn't like him thinking that so she decided to explain. "No, it's just a lot of people, all together, at once. Normally I'm okay, you know, on a one-on-one basis."

"Like now?" he asked.

No, she was definitely not okay standing in a moonlit room with Magnetic James Bennett chatting one on one.

"Kind of," she semi-fibbed (all right, so it was an out-and-out lie).

He studied her a moment and then moved away. She watched as he put the glass he'd been holding on the desk and turned back to her.

Her body locked as his strong fingers curled just above her elbow. She felt them there, so hot on her skin she thought they were going to leave burn marks.

As she was thinking this, he moved to her side and propelled her forward.

She took two steps and froze, rooted to the spot.

Her head tilted to look at him and she queried, "Where are we going?"

"Don't worry, Belle. We're not rejoining the party. I'm going to show you The Point," he explained.

Belle felt immense relief that she had a ready and truthful excuse to get out of a tour of "The Point" (what they called his enormous, multi-tude-of-rooms-filled castle) with James Bennett.

"That's okay. Miles took me on a tour this afternoon."

She watched as James looked over her shoulder and muttered, "Of course he did."

He moved forward again, his hand firm on her arm so she had no choice but to move with him. As they went toward the door, he grabbed his dinner jacket from the arm of the couch.

"Um, James…" she began to protest but he spoke again.

"Jack," he stated firmly then he let out a low whistle and Belle heard dog tags behind them.

"Okay," she agreed hesitantly and went on, "I should probably find Miles and—"

He cut her off. "I'm betting Miles missed part of the tour."

Belle couldn't imagine that. They'd been wandering around for over an hour.

"I think he was pretty thorough," Belle informed him as he stopped them and put his hand to the doorknob.

He looked down at her before opening the door. "My brother is many things," he said softly and there was a wealth of meaning behind his words, Belle just didn't understand it. "But he is not thorough."

He opened the door and guided her through.

Then he guided her down a deserted hall.

Then he guided her through some busy kitchens.

Finally he took her out a back door.

They stepped into the nippy May evening and Belle shivered.

Upon her shiver, James pulled her to a stop and dropped her arm. She turned to him and saw he was shaking out his dinner jacket. Before her mind registered his intent, he moved close to her front, his hands came up on either side of her and he settled the jacket on her shoulders.

His fingers came to the lapels and pulled them closed at her chest, leaving his hands there.

Throughout this she stood shocked and solid.

It was a kind thing to do.

Immensely kind.

Even gallant.

It was also, the way he did it, casually intimate.

She barely knew the man and yet there she was in the night wearing his jacket, his hands on her and it seemed, unlike when Miles touched her, strangely natural.

"Better?" he murmured and all she could do was nod.

Part of her hoped they could stand like that forever (or at least for a while).

Part of her wanted to run screaming into the night.

Therefore, she felt relief *and* disappointment when his hands moved from the lapels of his jacket.

Her body relaxed then grew stiff again as only one of his hands dropped away.

The other one came up to her neck, sliding against her skin in a barely there touch (but still, she felt it, and his touch affected her *everywhere*). He tugged free her errant lock of hair from where it was caught under his jacket.

She felt rather than saw him twist it around his finger, his eyes on this movement, his expression thoughtful, his face beautiful and all she could do was stand there and stare.

Suddenly his finger released her hair and he dropped his hand.

That was when Belle realized her lungs were burning again due to lack of oxygen because she wasn't breathing.

"I think you'll like the part of the tour that Miles missed," he told her and she nodded because she couldn't think what else to do.

He turned and put a hand to the small of her back, moving her forward, walking beside her, his hand never leaving her (and it burned there too).

He glanced behind them as they walked and called, "Baron," and the German shepherd jogged up to his side.

They walked silently along a stone path that led around the castle and up a small hill. Some of it was uneven though not treacherous. But James obviously knew this path like the back of his hand because before they hit the rough patches his arm would slide around her, fingers curving at her waist to pull her protectively to his side.

Belle didn't think much about this because her mind was in a perpetual horrified whirl.

How she was going to make it through whatever he was going to show her, she had no clue.

However, their silent, moonlit stroll was weirding her out even more.

It wasn't like this was the first time they walked close by each other's sides but as if they'd done it countless times before. And because of that, it seemed even more personal than Miles holding her close in the drawing room.

She had to break the silence and the strange, innate intimacy.

"Is he yours?" she blurted.

"Excuse me?" he asked.

"The dog, Baron. Is he yours or is he a family dog?" Belle clarified.

"He's mine," James stated in a way that made it clear the dog was definitely his.

Something about the way he said this gave Belle a melty belly too.

Therefore she decided to stop talking.

Finally they approached a building set some distance away from the castle and James stopped Belle at a wooden door. He opened it, gently pushed her ahead of him and then stopped her again. His torso twisted, his hand still on the small of her back, and light flooded the room.

It was stables.

Belle immediately emitted an unabashed cry of delight.

She *loved* horses.

She turned and smiled up at James.

"I *love* horses," she told him, but even seeing his eyes were on her, something which normally would terrify her, she was too excited to be scared of him. That was how much she loved horses.

Therefore she turned away and instantly moved toward the steeds.

There were ten stalls, eight of them filled, the heads of the horses hanging over the doors as they looked to see what was happening.

Belle slowly approached the first horse and put her hand under the horse's nose. The beast sniffed and snorted at her hand and she laughed softly at the tickling sensation. Once the mare had given her permission, Belle moved closer and stroked her muzzle.

"She's beautiful," Belle breathed as she felt James arrive at her side.

"You like animals," James commented.

Belle kept stroking.

"Yes," she replied quietly, her eyes never leaving the animal.

She gave the horse one last rub then moved around James, not looking at him, to the next, giving him a nuzzle. She went to the next then the next.

At the last stall, she saw a huge gray, his smoky mane sleek and long, his body bigger, muscles more defined and powerful than any of the other horses.

He was pure equine beauty.

James was again at her side as she stroked the steed's nose.

"He's my favorite," she whispered, and as if the horse understood her words, he moved his nose to her neck and blew, causing Belle to let out a short, startled giggle.

"He's mine," James said and Belle moved her head away from the horse, her hands still on his powerful jaws, and looked up at James.

"I'm thinking you have good taste," she told him.

His eyes locked on hers and they went strange like they were amused and something else. Something she couldn't read. Something that made her belly feel warm again.

"I definitely have good taste," he replied without a shred of humility.

Belle didn't know what to say to that so she didn't say anything.

With one last pat, she stepped away from his animal and said, "You were right. Miles didn't show me the stables but I'm glad you did. Thank you."

She started to move by him in the direction of the door but he caught her by the elbow, that strange heat coming from his touch again, searing into her skin.

She tipped her head back to look up at him and saw his chin was dipped to look down at her, his intense green eyes staring into hers.

Instantly, her breathing became labored.

"You haven't seen all I wanted to show you," he said.

"I haven't?" she asked.

He shook his head and moved her around, drawing her to a room at the end the stables. Baron came with them and he was dancing around James's long legs as they made it to the door.

James opened the door and Baron pushed through them to get inside. James leaned in, switched on a light and then pressed Belle inside.

On the floor ensconced on a huge dog bed with warm rugs all around was another German shepherd. Her head came up but her body didn't, likely because there were several little German shepherd puppies nestled and asleep at her belly.

Without thinking, Belle clapped her hands in front of her and shouted, "Puppies!" and immediately she moved toward the dogs.

Baron gave her an excited bark, obviously feeling pleased with himself as father of this brood, and Belle gave his head a rub before she dropped to her knees on the rug.

"Who's the proud papa?" she asked and Baron gave her another happy bark and licked her hand.

Belle turned her attention to the mama shepherd.

"And who are you?" she asked as she let the female dog smell her hand before Belle stroked her.

"Her name is Gretl," James replied, and Belle looked up and gave him a smile.

"They're beautiful," she told him, turning her attention back to the doggie family, and she saw some of the puppies waking, blinking and fumbling toward her.

She caught the closest one and picked her up, cuddling the puppy to her face. The puppy sniffed, squirmed and finally licked Belle's face and Belle nuzzled the writhing little one to her neck, that unmistakable puppy scent enveloping her senses.

"I just love the smell of puppy," she murmured into soft fur, gave her another squeeze then set her down and grabbed the next one to approach.

As she did, she saw James's hand reach out and nab a puppy who was climbing up the expensive fabric at Belle's thigh. She turned her eyes to him as she snuggled her newest bundle.

He was in a crouch close by her side and working at containing the six, now awake bundles of energy who all wanted to play with Belle.

"Are you keeping them?" she asked and watched him shake his head as he pulled back another pup from her knee. Her voice held a hint of a surprise when she went on to inquire, "You're not?"

He and his big, huge castle could easily harbor eight dogs.

No sweat.

"They're all sold," James said. "Baron and Gretl are both champions. Their litters are popular."

Belle looked down at the happy, floppy-eared puppies, both Gretl and Baron nosing them as James kept at his containment efforts and Belle exchanged her puppy for a new one to snuggle.

She couldn't imagine for one moment letting go of a single pup.

"You won't even keep just one?" Belle queried.

His eyes turned to her and she realized belatedly how close he was. The room was lit and she could see, like she did when he first greeted her back in the drawing room, how thick, black and long his lashes were.

Women paid good money for someone to glue lashes that beautiful on their eyelids. Looking at his, surrounding those green eyes, eyes a color she couldn't believe was from nature, she was, put simply, entranced.

"Pick one," he said and, at his surprising words, she blinked out of her trance.

"Sorry?"

"Pick one," he repeated and she tore her gaze from his and looked down at the adorable, happy, fidgeting puppies.

Her shocked eyes went back to James.

"I thought you said they're all sold."

"They are," he replied. "I'll return the fee of the one you've chosen."

She stared at him in shock.

Was he for real?

"You can't do that," Belle protested.

His lips tipped up slightly at the ends and she watched them as if this small movement was the most fascinating thing she ever beheld.

And she thought maybe it was.

Then she watched his lips form the words, "I can."

She moved her eyes to his. "So, what you're saying is, you're giving me a dog."

It was then his mouth formed a full-fledged grin. "That's what I'm saying."

Yes, he was for real.

Her eyes skittered away and she quickly exchanged her puppy for a new one.

Her nerves, which had disappeared for several glorious moments, returned and she felt an overpowering, nearly paralyzing self-consciousness.

Cuddling her new puppy, she mumbled, "I can't accept a champion litter dog."

"You can," he returned.

Her eyes moved to him but this time she looked over his shoulder.

"I can't," she repeated.

"Belle," he said her name softly, his deep voice wrapping around it like an embrace, and the effect made her shiver. He sounded like he was calling out to her even though she was on her knees right beside him.

She moved her eyes to the vicinity of his though she didn't look in them. She looked mostly at his nose.

He had, she thought somewhat agitatedly, a very nice nose.

When she did this, she heard his delicious chuckle.

"Belle," he repeated and, against its will, her gaze finally lifted to his eyes and when it did, he repeated, "Pick one."

"I can't have a German shepherd," she told him.

"Do you have another dog?" he asked, and she shook her head, looking away and dropping her puppy to give belly rubs to two bundles who were happily squirming on their backs on the floor. "Do you have a cat?" he went on and she shook her head again. "Do you let your house and they don't allow animals?" he pressed.

She finally spoke. "I own my place. It's just that I don't have a garden and my cottage isn't very big. German shepherds are large dogs. They need room to move." She scooted closer and stroked Gretl's head, continuing in a near whisper. "It's nice of you to offer anyway. Very generous." Her voice went even quieter before she murmured, "Thank you."

With that, she stood.

She could take no more. She would prefer Miles's stifling attention at a shoulder-to-shoulder crowded party (her definition of torture) to playing with puppies in a warm room in a stable with criminally handsome, seemingly very sweet James Bennett.

She took a backward step to the door as he straightened from his crouch.

"I should really be getting back," she told him, looking behind her toward the door.

It was only a few feet away but the distance yawned behind her like it was a million miles.

The puppies jumped at her ankles.

James spoke and what he said made her head twist around to look at him.

"We haven't finished the tour."

"We haven't?" she asked, wondering what he'd show her next.

Kittens?

Lambs?

An adorable baby rhinoceros?

He shook his head, moved forward, bending low to control the puppies at the same time his hand came to her hip, fingers hot through the fabric as he expertly maneuvered her out of the room. Baron came with him. Gretl stayed put and James managed to get her and his dog out without any of the puppies escaping.

It was a minor miracle.

However, instinctively, Belle thought he was the kind of man who wrought minor miracles on a daily basis.

Once he'd turned out the light and closed the door, he took her elbow again and led her along the stalls toward the door they entered. But he didn't take them to the door. He took them to a ladder that led up to what looked like a hayloft.

When he had her facing it, she heard him say, "Up."

Fear seized her and Belle stared at the ladder. Then her head tipped back to examine the open floor of the hayloft facing the stable. She looked at the ladder again.

And panic coursed through her.

She didn't do ladders.

She also didn't do heights.

And she *certainly* didn't do one full side of the floor opened to a neck-breaking fall haylofts.

She turned and nearly collided with him, he was standing so close behind her.

"I can't go up there," she breathed.

He was looking down at her. "Why not?"

She blinked and looked over his shoulder. "I just can't."

"It's safe, Belle. I wouldn't take you up there if it wasn't," he replied.

Her eyes went to his ear. "I'm sure it is. I just don't do ladders," she admitted, paused then continued, "or heights."

Or out of the way, scary haylofts with unbearably handsome men, she thought. A thought that she would never, even if paid, speak aloud.

"You'll be fine," he assured her, his voice deeper and gentler, and somewhere in her panic-stricken brain it registered that he was genuinely trying to assure her rather than force her to do something against her will.

"I—" she started but before she could say more, his hands came to her waist, he got close and all panicked thoughts (indeed, all thoughts, panicked or not) flew from her head.

She looked up at him to see his face was close.

Very close.

Magnetically close.

She held her breath and barely controlled an impulse to lean toward him.

"I'll take care of you," he murmured and then his fingers tightened at her waist.

He turned her to face the ladder and before she knew what he was about, he actually *lifted* her clean off her feet. Reflexively her hands shot out to grab the sides of the ladder and her feet found the rungs. His hands slid down to her hips and he put pressure there, urging her to climb.

And she did.

Instantly, she felt him come up after her.

Not a few rungs after her but *right* after her, his arms around her body, hands moving along the ladder sides just under hers and his body warm against her back. She was sheltered from danger by his big, strong frame and her fear of heights (and ladders and haylofts, but not him) completely melted away.

She made it to the floor of the hayloft and stepped in, James coming right after.

Without hesitation, she moved to the safest area available, the center of the loft, as he strode to its outer wall. She watched as he unlatched a pair of doors and slid one to the side then the other.

He turned to her and ordered quietly, "Come here."

She didn't want to.

She *really* didn't want to.

The doors were open to the night. She could easily fall out them and crack her head open. Or break her arm. Or sprain her ankle. None of which she wanted to do.

Even though she didn't want to, she pulled his jacket closer about her and walked slowly to his side, stopping several feet from the edge.

"Belle," he called again and she tilted her head back to look at him, her mind filled with thoughts of her broken body at the base of the stables, her knees feeling spongy, like they couldn't hold her weight. "Look," he urged and she watched him turn his head.

Her gaze went in the same direction and she caught her breath.

Spread out before her was his castle, huge and imposing on its cliff, many of its windows shown with bright lights, the sea and sky beyond it inky black. The white caps broke the waters and against the sprawling shoreline you could see the foamy surf pounding against the rocks.

It was magnificent.

It was *way* better than the view from the study.

It was even worth the torment of being in the company of wickedly handsome James Bennett.

Without thinking, Belle took a step closer to the edge and breathed, "I wish my grandmother was here."

"What?" James asked, his voice holding more than a little amusement mingled with surprise.

She looked up at him and repeated, "I wish my grandmother was here. She's a painter. She could paint this for you." Belle looked back at the view and went on, "She might even *pay* you for the opportunity to paint this."

Belle felt him get close to her side. "You're grandmother's a painter?"

"Yes," Belle answered not taking her eyes from the vista. "She's kind of well-known. You might have heard of her. Lila Cavendish?"

Something emotive stirred the air, emanating from James. It was strong enough for Belle to tear her gaze away from the seascape to look up at him again.

"Your grandmother is Lila Cavendish?" he asked when her eyes hit his face.

Belle nodded. "Do you know her?"

"I have one of her pieces in my office in London," he replied. "She's extremely talented."

Belle felt a sudden, warm burst of pride and murmured, "She is."

"So you come from a talented family," he remarked, and she kept staring at him and shook her head.

"No, it's just Gram that's talented," she told him.

He got closer, his chin dipping down further to look at her and he asked, "I thought Miles said you made your dress?"

Immediately, Belle looked away.

"Belle," he called again but she didn't look back.

Instead she answered the sea, "Yes, I made the dress."

"It's beautiful," he complimented her and she felt that trill go up her spine again. So strong it not only raised the hairs on the back of her neck, it tingled all along her scalp.

"Thank you," she whispered then sought to find another subject, any subject and luckily her mind found one. "Which piece of Gram's do you have?"

He thankfully allowed the subject change and replied, "It's called 'Sedona Bloom.'"

Belle smiled at the sea and nodded. "I think I remember that one. She did a Sedona series when we lived there. The Arizona desert is remarkable in bloom."

"So, you're from Arizona," he noted and she shook her head, crossing her arms on her chest under his jacket.

"We're from everywhere." She kept speaking to the view, finding it easier to hold this conversation when she could pretend he wasn't there and so damned close. "Mom and Dad got divorced when I was six and

Mom and I followed Gram wherever she went. Which was a lot of places."

"Like where?" James asked.

It was at that moment that it occurred to her that James had known her for barely an evening and Miles had known her for a month. And Miles didn't know her grandmother was Lila Cavendish or that her parents were divorced or that she'd moved around a lot.

He didn't know any of this because he'd never asked.

"Arizona, California, Colorado, New Mexico," Belle answered. "Gram went through a New Orleans phase so we stayed there for a school year. And she became infatuated with Savannah so we were there for an entire summer." She stopped and when he didn't speak she decided she should go on, so she noted inanely, "It was very humid."

"Interesting life for a child," James muttered. "What did your father think of this?"

Belle's hand came out from under the jacket and she waved it in front of her. "Oh, he didn't mind. He was a wanderer too. I never saw much of him, really."

"You don't sound like you find that upsetting," he observed.

Belle shook her head. "I didn't have much of him but he's a big personality. When I did have him, I had all of him and that was better than most kids have."

She felt his heat and knew he'd drawn closer.

She tried to pretend that didn't happen too.

"I hear Lila Cavendish is a bit of a character as well."

She knew what he meant.

If her father was a big personality and Gram was a character, what had happened to her?

She didn't know why she said what she said next. Maybe it was the sea, the puppies, the several glasses of champagne she had at the party.

Or maybe it was just him.

But she said it.

"I used to wish I was like her," Belle confided softly. "She and my mom are cut from the same cloth. They light up a room."

Forgetting her fear of heights, she walked to the edge and leaned her shoulder against the door, losing herself in the view, and kept talking.

"Once when I was young, we visited my great-grandmother in a retirement home. It was the first time Gram and I visited her after Gram moved her in there. We walked in and it was dreary. Depressing." Her voice dropped even lower. "You wouldn't believe it."

Belle shut her eyes against the memory, opened them and forged on.

"I remember Gram taking one look at all those old people in their bleak rec room and muttering, 'This will *not* do.' Then she dug in her purse and pulled out her bag of lemon drops. To this day, she always carries a bag of lemon drops." This last came out in a barely there whisper.

She twisted her head to look at him and saw he was watching her, his arms crossed on his chest, his face so gentle and striking she had to look away so she'd have the courage to continue.

Belle pulled in a breath and watched a wave break against the jagged rocks of the shore before she went on.

"Anyway," she said in a brighter voice, "she went around the whole room offering the old folks lemon drops, telling jokes, laughing and talking and livening up the room. That's all it took. Gram and a bag of lemon drops."

When he spoke, his voice was closer and her body jerked in surprise as she turned to see he was again at her side.

"There are many ways to light up a room."

He would, she thought, know all about that. His magnetic beam probably entered a room ten minutes before he got to the door.

"Some women," he continued, "light up a room just wearing an extraordinary dress."

She looked away and nodded in agreement. "Like Yasmin."

"Yes, like Yasmin. Though Yasmin's dress tonight doesn't come close to the one you're wearing."

Belle's body jerked again and her head twisted around to look at him. It did this so quickly she thought she might have pulled something.

Before she could assess if she needed medical attention, he finished softly, "And she didn't design hers."

Something was happening.

She knew this because he was getting even closer.

Panic ensued, quickly chased by hysteria. She moved back but her shoulders were against the door and one side fell away to nothing so she froze in sheer terror.

His hands came to her waist and he moved directly into her space. So into it, *her* space evaporated and *their* space took its place.

"James—" she began in a warning protest, her voice trembling.

"Jack," he muttered as his head bent, his hands sliding around her waist to her back, his fingers putting pressure there so her body touched his.

And then he kissed her.

Kissed her.

Belle couldn't believe it.

His mouth on hers was firm and warm and his hands at her back were burning into her flesh. She felt the trill up her spine, the tingle along her scalp, her belly flipping then warming.

All this felt good. It felt thrilling. It felt like something she wanted more of (a lot more).

Still, she put her hands to his arms, gave a good shove and pulled her mouth away from his.

"We can't," she told him but her voice was oddly breathy.

"We can," he replied instantly.

"No," she said.

"Yes," he returned then his arms tightened around her so her body wasn't touching his. It was plastered against it.

His head slanted and his mouth came down on hers again this time harder, warmer. Insistent.

She opened her mouth to protest, her fingers curling at his arms and his tongue slid inside.

The minute his tongue touched hers, her entire body responded. Heat shot through it and her knees went weak then buckled. She felt her belly plummet, a quiver of excitement shot between her legs and her body melted into his.

Without thought to anything, not Miles, Joy, good manners or her own sanity, Belle kissed him back. Her hands slid up and around his neck and she pressed closer to the heat of his hard body.

He felt her response immediately (he couldn't exactly miss it) and he pushed his advantage, deepening the kiss, tightening his arms, one hand sliding up her side and stopping then his fingers began to stroke the side of her breast.

That, Belle thought hazily, felt good.

Very good.

So good, Belle felt her breasts swell, her nipples harden and she moaned right into his mouth.

It was then she realized that he'd been controlling the kiss.

She knew this because it was also then when he lost control of it.

His head came up and before she could think, he stepped back twice, dragging her with him.

When he stopped them, his head came back down, their mouths collided and this kiss was wild. It was coupled with bodies pressing closer, hands gliding. His jacket fell from her shoulders and Belle didn't even notice.

The world had dissolved.

Nothing existed but James, his mouth, his hands, his body and all the unbelievable things he was making her feel.

Things she'd never felt in her whole life, not with Calvin, not with Miles, not *ever*.

She was not Belle "Meek and Mild" Abbot.

She was another being entirely.

A being who would neck in the hayloft with a rich, famous, entirely too handsome man, even when she was dating his brother.

She was Wicked Belle. Risk-Taker Belle. A Heretofore Unknown Belle who jumped into shark-infested waters with both feet, her eyes open because she knew something rich and rewarding would come of it.

She tugged at his shirt at the back, pulling it out of his trousers and her hands went up, gliding across his hot skin, feeling the hard muscle of his back and she loved it.

No.

She *adored* it.

She pressed in, wanting him closer, wanting him to absorb her.

Suddenly, his mouth tore from hers and his body was gone. Belle felt a rush of cold and a sense of confusion, but before she could gather her thoughts and return to her shy, timid reality, his hand grabbed hers in a vicelike grip.

Then he dragged her to the ladder.

"Down," he growled, his voice strangely rough.

"What?" she whispered, her eyes flitting to his, her mind in a turmoil, her body on fire.

"Go down," he repeated.

She looked stupidly at the ladder. Then she was forced to look back at him.

She was forced because his hand wrapped around her neck and he yanked her to him, their bodies crashing together and his mouth crushed down on hers in another wet, wild, open-mouthed kiss that sent her senses reeling.

He lifted his head and demanded in a voice now so beyond rough it was hoarse and just the sound of it sent a luscious quiver shooting between her legs, "Poppet, climb down."

Without hesitation, Belle climbed down.

James came after her.

He grabbed her hand and pulled her out of the stables not even bothering to turn out the light.

She had no time to think mainly because her mind was occupied with keeping up with him and not tripping. He was walking quickly, his long legs eating the distance, dragging her by the hand in a half run behind him.

"James," she called, feeling the need to take a moment, take a breath and get her head together.

"Jack," he clipped.

She saw they were quickly approaching the castle.

"Where are we going?" she asked, rushing behind him.

"My room."

"Your *what*?" she cried, reality crashing in, her mind asking her what in the holy heck was she doing and her hand pulled at his.

The instant she did this, he stopped, turned and Belle ran right into him.

His arms went around her and he hauled her to his body.

"My room, Belle," he told her. "I'm taking you to my room."

She stared up at him in stupefaction. "I can't go to your room."

"Not only can you, you're going to," he declared.

Belle blinked, beyond stupefied, straight to staggered.

"I—" she started but he cut her off.

"You can go with me or I can carry you. Choose. Now."

"James—" she started to protest but stopped when his fingers wrapped around the back of her head at the same time his arm grew tight, molding her to his body.

"I'm not going to say it again, Belle. I want you to call me Jack," he demanded and then his mouth came down on hers.

He gave her another kiss. Meek and Mild Belle disappeared and when he lifted his head, she walked or, more accurately ran to keep up with his long strides, with him to his room.

3

JACK'S PROMISE

Jack

Jack woke to a dark room.

In the moonlight he saw beside him a vast expanse of white-sheeted bed with Belle's naked body not occupying it.

Instantly alert, he came up on an elbow thinking she'd gone to her room or even left the house.

Instead he saw her sitting in the window seat, knees to her chest, her glorious hair falling down her back. She was wearing his dress shirt and gazing out to sea.

Baron was sitting at her side and Belle's hand was absentmindedly stroking the dog's head.

Jack settled, his eyes never leaving her, and he gave himself a moment to consider his behavior of earlier that night.

After he'd dragged her to his room like a Neanderthal, he'd not taken her to his bed. He'd not disrobed her or himself. He'd not even let her kick off her shoes.

Instead, he'd pinned her against the wall, captured her mouth with his, yanked up the skirt of her dress and pulled down her panties. Hands to her ass, their lips still locked, tongues sparring, he'd lifted her and without hesitation she'd wrapped her arms and legs tightly around him.

Then he'd taken her against the wall, rough, fierce and completely uncontrolled.

She came within minutes, hard and intense, the soft, sexy noises she made quickening his own need. For a moment, with a deep satisfaction that felt almost primal, he'd watched her face in climax before his own staggering orgasm wiped everything from his mind.

It had been utterly magnificent.

He'd never experienced anything like it.

Nothing even came close.

After they'd finished, she kept her tight hold on him, her face pressed to his neck, the fingers of one of her hands in his hair.

And, holding Belle against the wall, Jack memorized every inch of her that he could feel, her breath on his neck, legs around his hips, fingers in his hair and the sweet, wet tightness between her legs.

She moved her head, put her mouth to his ear and whispered in her soft, honeyed voice, "Jack."

He knew what she was thinking.

Therefore he turned his own head and kissed her.

Jack didn't want her thinking and questioning.

He wanted her focused solely on him.

He pulled out of her gently, catching her gasp in his mouth as he did so, and carried her to the side of the bed, kissing her the entire way. There he set her on her feet, took off their clothes and fell with her on the bed.

The second time, he savored her and her delectable body, using his mouth and hands, patiently coaxing her out of her timidity, urging her to do the same to him.

She did, shyly at first, becoming bolder and finally, with a mixture of the two, she achieved wildly successful results.

The second time ended like the first. Rough, fierce and completely uncontrolled.

Although his orgasm was not as staggering as the first, he did have the delightful opportunity to watch hers from start to finish.

Without a word and definitely not allowing Belle to utter one, he'd shifted their bodies under the covers, pulled her in his arms and held her tight with one arm while stroking her spine with the tips of his fingers.

Shortly after, he felt her weight settle into him and he knew she was asleep.

Shortly after that, he allowed himself to sleep as well.

Now, watching her study the sea, Jack considered his actions.

He had no idea why he behaved the way he'd behaved. He'd never done anything of the like in his life.

He also had no idea why Belle brought this out in him.

Although it likely had something to do with the fact that she was the first woman he'd encountered who made it clear she'd rather be anywhere but with him.

It also likely had something to do with Baron's acceptance of her. Jack's dog was usually wary and protective, especially when Jack was close. Baron didn't give his trust or affection easily. One sniff at her hand and her soft coo was all it took for Belle to win Jack's dog which, to Jack, spoke volumes.

Further, it likely had something to do with watching her open, unguarded delight when she was with the animals.

And probably it had something to do with the sound of her sweet, soft laughter.

It also could have to do with her story about her grandmother and the lemon drops.

Undoubtedly, it had to do with the depth in her eyes that said there was something there. Something he wanted, even so far as needed, but he wasn't allowed to see. Something he couldn't have nor could he take.

Something he'd have to earn.

Lastly, it most assuredly had something to do with that lock of thick, shining hair that fell against her neck, adorably revealing her imperfection.

Jack, however, was not the kind of man who spent a great deal of time considering his actions.

So he didn't.

She simply was who she was, *all* of who she was.

And Jack liked it, *all* of it.

And he wanted it.

So he took it.

But also, he was going to keep it because now it was his.

On that thought, he threw the bedclothes aside. He went to his dresser, pulled out a pair of pajama bottoms and tugged them on. Baron trotted to him while he did this and Jack lifted his head to see Belle was watching him, head twisted to look over her shoulder, her arms wrapped around her calves.

Jack walked across the room to join her.

As he walked, she moved jerkily as if she'd been torn from a trance or had a layer of ice wrapped around her that had been shattered.

She released her legs and stood, her head tilting back, her hand coming up as if to ward him off, and she whispered, "Jack—"

His chest came up against her hand, his hands went to her waist and he turned her so her back was to his front, his movements cutting off whatever she intended to say. He moved and sat in the window seat, taking her with him, lifting his legs bent at the knees and positioning her between them. He rested his back against the wall, Belle's back against his chest and he wrapped his arms around her, one about her stomach, the other about her chest.

Instinctively Jack felt containment was key. Given the opportunity, Belle would retreat either physically or emotionally and after what they'd just shared, he wasn't going to allow that.

Even so, she held her body stiffly in his arms.

"Jack—" she began again.

"Belle," he interrupted her with a squeeze, his voice low and quiet. "Not tonight. We'll talk about it tomorrow."

Although he would not have thought it was possible, he felt her body grow even stiffer.

Baron settled in beside them, resting his head on the window seat by Jack's hip as Belle turned in his arms so she was facing him.

At the same time she tried to pull away.

Jack's arms tensed and she was forced to put her hands on his chest to push back but he kept her close, not allowing escape.

She gave up pushing and her eyes lifted to look in his.

He could see her face in the moonlight but he couldn't read her eyes and he wished he'd thought to turn on a light.

She hesitated before speaking, and with embarrassment dripping from her voice, she whispered. "I've never done anything like that before in my life."

"I know," he replied softly and understood he'd scored a point when her stiff body relaxed somewhat in his arms.

"I don't want you to think—" she started, he gave her a gentle shake and his head bent so his face was closer to hers.

"Poppet, get that out of your head. I don't think anything except what we shared earlier was unbelievably, fucking magnificent."

Even in the dark, he could see her lips part in surprise and her eyes widened in wonder seconds before she found something else to be embarrassed about. "Your mum—"

There was no way Jack was going to explain the intricate history of competition between the Bennett brothers, Miles's taking sibling rivalry to a compulsive extreme and Joy's total understanding of it (and incessant worry about it) when Belle was in his shirt, in his arms, in his room, in the moonlight.

He'd do it tomorrow morning when she was eating breakfast in his bed after he'd made love to her again.

"She won't mind," Jack said and he felt Belle's body jerk.

"She won't mind?" Belle's sweet voice had grown louder. "She's your *mum*. How could she not mind that I came to her birthday party with one brother and spent the night with the other?"

"Belle—" Jack tried to break in but she was struggling again in his arms.

"She's going to think I'm a slut." Belle's eyes had left his and she was muttering with agitation as she fought his hold on her. "And rude," she added and then finished with hilarious melodrama. "*Oh my God. She's going to think I'm a rude slut!*"

Jack bit back laughter and began again, "Belle—"

But she kept talking and fighting.

"I have to go. Tonight. I should have left when you were asleep. I don't know what I was thinking. Why didn't I go? I should have gone. I should—"

Jack silenced her by wrapping a fist in her thick, soft hair and gently tugging.

Her body stilled and her head tipped back. He seized his opportunity, his mouth descended to hers and he kissed her quiet.

He took his time and he made certain to do a thorough job of it.

When he lifted his head, her body had melted into his, her face was soft and her eyes had no trouble holding his.

Jack noted this achievement for future reference.

"Now, listen to me," Jack ordered softly when he had her undivided attention. "I'll explain things to Mum. I'll explain things to Miles." He watched her wince when he said Miles's name but he kept talking. "Trust me, they'll understand."

"What can you possibly say that will make them understand?" she whispered, her voice horrified.

"You haven't been dating Miles long, have you?" he asked, and she hesitated at his change of subject before she shook her head. "Was it serious?" he went on, and she shook her head again. "Was it going to get serious?" he pressed gently, and he felt her take in a breath and then sigh.

"I was going to break up with him tomorrow. I—"

Jack suppressed the sense of elation her words caused and cut her off by saying, "I'll make him understand."

"I should talk to him," she replied swiftly.

His hand left her hair and came to her face, his thumb stroking her cheekbone.

"You can talk to him after I talk to him. There are things you don't understand. Things that I'll explain." She opened her mouth to speak but Jack kept talking, "Not now, in the morning." He dipped his face closer and touched his mouth to hers then left it there. "You can trust me, Belle. I'll take care of it."

She pulled slightly away, her eyes left his and he felt her body start to stiffen again so he ran his hand down her spine, something that caused her to stop bracing and start to tremble.

He noted this for future reference too.

"Belle," he called.

She didn't look at him when she asked quietly, "Why?"

"Why what?"

Her gaze moved to his nose and she replied, "Why everything? Me, tonight, what happened. All of it."

His hand went back to the side of her face and he demanded quietly, "Look at me, poppet."

After a brief hesitation, she lifted her eyes to his and only then did he speak.

"I'm not going to explain why. I'm going to take the time and show you why." His hand moved down to her jaw and his voice got deeper when he went on, "And I'll do it until you get it. Until you understand how lovely you are." His thumb moved along her lower lip as he continued, "Until you understand how interesting you are." His thumb left her lip and his mouth replaced it. "Until you understand why I'd drag you to my room to fuck you. And until you understand why I want to do it again." He brushed his mouth against hers before he murmured, "And again."

As he spoke, her body became soft and yielding in his arms, her hands slid from his chest and her own arms curved around him.

When he finished, she dropped down and rested her cheek against his chest, her forehead pressed to his neck and she whispered, "You have to know, this isn't me. I don't know who this is. I don't behave like this," she paused then, for emphasis, she added, "ever."

"Like what?"

She replied in a barely there voice. "What we did tonight. I don't do things like that. I know you want me to think it's all right, but what we did was wrong."

Her long hair was spread across his forearms and he gathered it in a hand to twist it softly in his fist before he replied, "There was nothing wrong about what we did."

He felt her shake her head against his chest but even as she disagreed with him, her arms grew tighter.

"Jack—" she started to protest.

"Belle," he cut her off. "What I saw of you tonight with Miles was wrong. Very wrong. What we have is *not*."

"Jack—" she began again but he gave her hair a gentle tug, she stopped speaking and tilted her head back to look at him as he dipped his chin down.

When he caught her eyes, he spoke. "If you let me in, poppet, even a little bit, I'll prove it to you. I promise you, I'll make you understand. This, whatever it is, and we both feel it, is right."

He felt her grow still and watched her tongue wet her lips before she said words in an awful voice that left no doubt how much it cost her to say them or, indeed, the terrible feeling behind them. "I've done that before, with a man, let him in. It wasn't smart."

It was Jack's turn to grow still.

He wanted to know what she meant but understood intuitively that conversation was also not for the moonlight but for the daylight when she was eating breakfast in his bed after he'd made her come and after she'd done the same to him.

"I'm not that man," Jack returned firmly.

She started to pull away but his arm around her grew tight and she stopped.

"Jack, you have to listen to me," she demanded, a hint of desperation in her voice.

"No." He slid her back up his chest so they were face to face and went on, his voice turning fierce. "Tonight is ours. Tomorrow morning, I'll explain how it is, and if you'll share it with me, you'll explain. Then I'll take care of everything." She shook her head and his fingers holding her hair wrapped around the back of her head to stop her movement. "Belle, you can trust me." He dropped his forehead to hers and repeated his oath in a forceful murmur. "I promise you, you can trust me."

He watched close up as her eyes squeezed tightly shut.

They opened and focused on him.

Then she whispered in an aching voice that registered painfully somewhere deep in his gut, "You promise?"

That was when he thought her part of the conversation might not be best left until the morning.

"Belle, perhaps you should tell me—"

It was Belle's turn to interrupt Jack.

"You have to promise," she demanded.

Jack's hand left her hair and both his arms wrapped around her.

"I promise," he muttered and started to ask. "Now—"

But she shook her head. "In the morning."

"Belle—" Jack began but she cut him off.

"In the morning." she repeated.

Jack's voice dipped lower in warning. "Belle—"

She completely ignored his warning.

Before he could say more, she pulled slightly away and said, "Let's go to bed."

Jack didn't move.

Belle put her hands to his chest, pushed up, broke through his arms and scooted from between his legs. She came to her feet beside him next to Baron and, one hand scratching behind Baron's ears, she bent and grabbed Jack's hand with the other.

"Come to bed," she whispered.

For a brief moment, Jack Bennett sat in the window of his room looking at his woman in his shirt standing next to his dog.

After that moment was over, he didn't need to be asked a third time to go to bed.

4

SIBLING RIVALRY

Belle

Belle woke tucked in the curve of Jack's warm, hard body, his heavy arm resting on her waist.

The sunlight was shining in her face.

The events of the night before hit her in a happy rush. Thinking about them, she snuggled into Jack and felt his arm tighten in his sleep.

This made her smile.

She shouldn't be smiling. She should be embarrassed at how she'd behaved, what she'd done.

Belle "Meek and Mild" Abbot would be embarrassed.

No, Belle "Meek and Mild" Abbot wouldn't be embarrassed, she'd be mortified.

But this Belle, whoever she was, wasn't.

She wasn't because Jack Bennett didn't take her back to the party.

In the dark, in his study, he saw her pet his dog and look out his window.

Then he spent the next hour showing her things *she'd* want to see not things *he* wanted her to see.

And he knew straight away she wasn't a people person and didn't judge her. Nor did he force her to stand at his side while he introduced her to person after person necessitating that she make small talk, her most hated thing in the world (outside of the media and their microphones and cameras, she hated them more than small talk, loads more).

Instead, he protected her, took her away from the crush to someplace safe. Someplace she liked to be.

And he asked her questions and listened to her answers like not only was he interested in her responses but as if he cared.

And he'd given her three orgasms.

Three unbelievable orgasms.

She'd never had one induced by a partner.

Not a single one.

And in one night, Jack had given her *three*.

Belle read romance novels but she always thought all that rigmarole about passionate, mind-boggling sex that could sweep you away on a fiery hot wave was all fiction made up by extremely imaginative women.

But it wasn't.

It was *real*.

And it was *fantastic*.

And she wanted more of it, *lots* more (if it was with Jack that was).

Furthermore, he said she could trust him.

And she believed him.

There was no way *not* to believe him, the way he made his promise. His voice was all low and rumbly, his arm was tight around her, his eyes were looking straight into hers.

After Calvin, Belle knew better than to trust anyone ever again, or at least not a man.

But she couldn't help it, she trusted Jack.

It was a risk. An uncalculated, spur of the moment, outrageous risk, but for the first time in her life Belle wasn't the least bit frightened.

Because somewhere during their middle of the night, moonlit talk she realized she was safe with him. She could be herself with him and he actually *liked* it.

Criminally Handsome James Bennett liked her, Belle "Meek and Mild" Abbot.

He liked her a lot.

She could tell. It was hard to miss with all of the sex and cuddling and moonlit conversations full of promises.

Lastly, he called her "poppet" and it wasn't like Miles calling her "gorgeous."

Belle understood why she wasn't fond of endearments uttered early in a relationship.

Because they were empty and meaningless.

When Jack called her "poppet" it was different. It wasn't empty nor was it meaningless.

It was warm and full of the possibility of something rich and rewarding.

She finally knew why she had that strange, thrilling feeling of expectation before she joined the party last night.

She had her very first premonition. Her mother, who had them all the time (practically hourly) would be in fits of delight when Belle told her.

She'd had the premonition that she'd meet Jack and it would be as wonderful as it was.

On that thought, she heard the jangle of dog tags and saw Baron sit up from his place on the floor at her side of the bed. His head swung toward Belle and he rested it on the mattress, his doggie eyes blinking at her.

Belle stretched out a hand to stroke his soft head and whispered to the dog, "Morning handsome."

She heard Baron's tail thump on the floor as the arm around her waist moved, curling up to become what she knew was a strong, long-fingered hand curving around her breast.

Belle felt a tingle slide up her spine as Jack's body pressed forward.

His chin moved the hair at the back of her neck and then he said in a just waking up growl, "I take it you aren't talking to me."

Belle smiled at Baron and shook her head, saying, "No."

Jack kissed the back of her neck then its side. His body and hand disappeared but only to press her to her back. He got up on an elbow and loomed over her.

She looked at him in the daylight.

He looked slightly sleepy but no less handsome.

In fact, he looked better than ever.

Really, it should be against the law (but she wasn't going to turn him in, no way).

She smiled again, Jack's eyes moved to her mouth and his hand came up to frame the side of her face.

"Sleep well, poppet?" he murmured.

Belle nodded and his gaze moved from her mouth to her eyes.

"Good," he muttered, his head descended, his mouth touched hers in a sweet, effective, barely there, morning kiss. When he lifted it again, his gaze turned toward Baron and he remarked, "You've stolen my dog."

Belle let out a surprised giggle and asked, "What?"

Jack's eyes came back to hers and she saw they were smiling even though his mouth was not.

It registered somewhere in the depths of her soul that this was the most beautiful sight she ever beheld about a nanosecond before he repeated, "You've stolen my dog. He always sleeps on the floor on the other side. *My* side. He never sleeps on this side."

Belle's head tilted inquiringly on the pillow. "You have a side?"

Jack studied her face a moment before asking, "You don't?"

She shook her head. "No, I sleep in the middle."

He kept watching her before his face went soft and he said quietly, "That's good news, poppet."

"Why?" Belle asked, confused at his statement.

His head descended again, this time to bury his face in her neck where he muttered, "No reason." Then he went on to say, "Feel free to sleep in the middle with me."

Belle let out another giggle and she slid her arms around his back, curling toward him as she informed him unnecessarily, "I did, last night. You did too. We're in the middle now."

"Mm," he replied, mouth against her neck, and Belle felt a shiver slide through her right before she felt his tongue touch her neck which made the shiver turn into a full-blown, luscious tremble.

"Jack," she called before things got out of hand, which if their experiences of last night were anything to go by (both times before their talk *and* the time after) they could do.

And fast.

"Hmm?" Jack mumbled as he slid his mouth to her ear.

"I have to go to my room," Belle told him and instantly his head came up.

"What?" he asked.

"I have to go to my room," she repeated.

His brows drew together and he queried gently, "Do you want to tell me why?"

She slid her hands up the hard muscle of his back and answered, "I need to go and get my toothbrush."

His brows unknitted, his face relaxed and he kissed her nose, then for some unknown reason he declared, "I've got an electric toothbrush."

His face disappeared in her neck again.

Belle stared at the canopy of the four-poster and tried not to think about how nice his lips felt on her neck.

Jack's room was larger than hers and this was saying something since hers was enormous. His was decorated in rich browns, dark blues and mustardy golds. The canopy, curtains and coverlet were a subtle, swirling, paisley mixture of the three.

It was lush.

"Um, I'm glad," Belle mumbled and went on uncertainly as his mouth worked at the sensitive skin at her neck. "My dentist tells me every time I visit him to get one. They're supposed to be the thing. It's good you take care of your teeth. That's important."

His head came up and he studied her again, his green eyes shining and his mouth twitching like he was trying to control laughter.

She had no idea what was funny except maybe him telling her he had an electric toothbrush. But *he* wouldn't think that was funny as, apparently, he thought that was the most natural thing in the world to share while having a morning cuddle.

When he succeeded in this task, he said, "Belle, what I meant was, I have an electric toothbrush with separate heads. You can have an unused one."

"Oh," Belle breathed, feeling like a complete idiot, and his eyes watched her mouth form that one syllable like it was mesmerizing.

Then he muttered, "God, you're sweet."

She completely forgot she was an idiot, a trill shot up her spine straight into her scalp, her belly melted and Belle's head tilted again when she asked, "I am?"

His eyes came back to hers.

"Yes, poppet," he replied softly. "You are." His voice dropped even lower when he finished, "Unbelievably sweet."

For a second, she couldn't speak mainly because she couldn't breathe.

Then she didn't know what to say but she felt she should say something. He'd just given her a lovely compliment. The best she'd ever had (by a mile). It would be rude to let it pass without comment.

So she whispered, "Thank you."

For some reason her response made him roar with laughter. His body collapsed on hers but she took his weight for only a moment before his arms curled around her. He rolled to his back taking her with him so she was on top.

She lifted up with her forearms on his broad chest. He held her closely and she watched as he got control of his hilarity.

He was, if it could be believed, even more handsome when he was laughing.

"I still need to go to my room," she told him and his hand came up to pull her hair away from her the side of her face to hold it at her back.

"Why?" he asked, still smiling.

"I need a change of clothes," she told him.

He shook his head. "No you don't."

Belle blinked. "What am I supposed to wear?"

His fingers slid through her hair at her back, came up then plunged in for another pass (and she distractedly registered she liked his hands sifting through her hair, quite a lot) as he answered, "If you need clothes, I'll get you another shirt."

Belle didn't mind wearing his shirts. In fact, she liked it.

Still, for some reason only known to someplace deep in the back of her anxious mind, she knew she needed her stuff. She didn't know why but she felt somehow exposed without it. Not to Jack but to everyone else in the castle.

She didn't want to emerge from Jack's room sometime in the afternoon with the remnants of her makeup from the night before on her face and either Jack's shirt or her dress on her body.

The very idea was the definition of mortifying.

Therefore she kept trying to find a way to get to her room. "I need underwear."

His smile turned wicked as his eyes caught hers. "No you don't."

Her belly did a flip before it dipped at his words (and his smile) but she kept trying. "I need something to pull my hair back."

He moved a thick tress over her shoulder and twisted it around his fingers against her chest. "I like your hair down."

"Jack!" she exclaimed in frustration.

"Belle." He grinned, totally disregarding her frustration and seemingly having the time of his life.

Belle tried yet again. "I need my cleanser, moisturizer. I need my *stuff*."

The amusement in his gaze gentled, he lifted his head and touched his mouth to hers again. "All right, poppet. I'll call Elaine and get her to move your things in here."

Belle's body went solid and almost at the same instant she felt Jack brace under her but she didn't pay any attention even as his hand left her hair so his arm could wrap tightly around her back.

"You can't call Elaine," Belle declared even though she had no idea who Elaine was. But she didn't want *anyone* to know she was moving into Jack's room except her and Jack.

"Why not?" Jack asked.

"Because she, whoever she is, will know I'm with you."

"And?" Belle felt her eyes grow wide at that question, thinking the "and" was obvious but Jack kept talking. "Belle, people are going to know, very soon."

"They're going to think—" Belle started but Jack cut her off with a squeeze of his arms.

"I don't give a fuck what they think."

"Well, I do," Belle told him.

"You shouldn't."

He was right. She shouldn't.

Perhaps there was still some Old Belle hanging around.

"I know," she admitted softly. "I still do."

He studied her face and then he sighed.

Belle instinctively felt she'd forged an advantage so she took it.

"Can we please have a little time?" she asked quietly. "Just for, you know, ourselves?"

She watched his face grow soft before he replied, "Of course," and Belle relaxed on top of him for half a second before he spoke again. "I'll go get your things."

She went solid in horror before declaring, "You can't get my stuff."

His mouth did that twitching thing again before he asked, "Why not?"

She had no ready answer. She just didn't like the idea of Jack gathering her stuff, of which there was a lot. She was very girlie. There were tons of bottles and tubs and *things*.

He might think she was high maintenance.

She didn't want him to think she was high maintenance (even though she was).

And worse, what if he missed something?

"You just can't," she returned.

This, bizarrely, made him start chuckling. She felt the sound in her belly and the feeling had nothing to do with his body shaking with laughter beneath hers.

"Poppet," he said. "If you don't like the idea of people knowing about us yet then I don't like the idea of you roaming the halls in the morning looking like you've been thoroughly fucked."

Belle gasped and her hand flew to her hair.

Was that what she looked like?

What did that even look like?

Oh goodness gracious! Her mind breathed in horror.

"It's a good look," Jack went on, his eyes smiling again as he watched her face. "But it's *my* look. I gave it to you. I'm the only one who gets to see it."

He had a point.

And what he said made her feel all warm and squishy inside.

She still didn't want him to go get her stuff.

Belle looked to his bedside table and saw it was early. The party undoubtedly went late. Belle knew a bunch of people were spending the night (they had, like, a gazillion bedrooms). Still, she couldn't imagine anyone was up yet. Belle was an early riser. By his instantly alert behavior, she could tell Jack was too.

She looked back at Jack. "It's early. No one will be up yet. I'll hurry."

"Belle—" Jack started to protest.

She broke in, "I promise, I'll be really fast."

"I'd prefer—" he began again but Belle leaned closer to him.

"Please, Jack. I'll be quick." When he seemed unrelenting, she got even closer and repeated, "Please?"

At her plea, he lifted a hand to the side of her face, his thumb moving to slide along her cheekbone and she knew she'd won.

Therefore, she smiled.

His eyes dropped to her mouth right before he smiled back.

At the sight, she knew she'd been wrong.

The smile in his eyes that didn't reach his mouth wasn't the most beautiful thing she ever beheld.

His returning her smile while giving into her crazy, neurotic wishes was.

"All right," he muttered and she couldn't help it (and didn't try), she got even closer and brushed his mouth with her own before starting to push away but his arms tightened. He brought her back so she was crushed to him.

Then his hand sifted into her hair at the back of her head and he put pressure there until her mouth was on his. When it was he gave her an open-mouthed kiss that was hot and wet and sweet and very, very long. So long, he curved her body around so she was on the bottom again, her arms wrapped around him and he was on top.

When his head lifted, she was in a daze. Not only her spine and scalp were tingling but other places where tingling besides and she forgot all about going to her room.

"Hurry," he muttered his demand in a growl against her mouth, her desire (now significantly muted) to get her things came back to her and she nodded.

She scooted out from under him and got out of bed, all of a sudden distressingly mindful of her nudity. She grabbed the first thing she could find, which was his shirt. It was still partially buttoned so she quickly pulled it over her head and shoved her arms through. She then snatched up her panties and, back to him, slid them on under the voluminous folds of his shirt.

Her eyes went to the bed, and as she feared, he was up on an elbow. The sheets were down to his waist. His broad, hard-muscled chest was on display.

His chest was one of the myriad things she liked most about him. In fact, he had a great body which he did, indeed, have entirely at his command, in very delicious ways.

His gaze was on her.

She felt heat in her cheeks and she dashed to nab her dress and shoes.

She walked swiftly to the door and heard dog tags behind her.

Then she heard Jack demand, "Take Baron."

She stopped at the door, hand on the knob and looked at Jack then at Baron who was standing halfway between the bed and the door. His head was swinging between them both looking doggie confused.

"He wants to stay with you," Belle told Jack.

"He wants to go with you," Jack told Belle.

"No, he doesn't," Belle returned.

"Belle, he does," Jack retorted and went on, "Take him."

Dress under her arm and shoes dangling from her fingers, Belle still managed to put an affronted feminine hand to her hip.

"You're very bossy, do you know that?" she asked him.

"I have one hundred and eleven thousand, nine hundred and fifty-three employees. I have to be bossy," he answered.

Belle's mouth dropped open in astonishment at that impossible-to-believe fact.

Belle had only three and they were always driving her straight up the wall (or, at least, Belinda, her young, starry-eyed shop assistant did).

Therefore she asked on a whisper, "Really?"

He grinned but didn't respond to her question.

Instead, he ordered, "Go get your things."

She turned to the door because standing in his shirt across the room and not in his arms in his bed, she was losing the courage to banter with Jack, and she muttered, "I'm not taking Baron."

She heard him chuckle before he let out a sharp, short whistle, giving in and calling his dog.

She opened the door, stepped into the hall and started to close it behind her but threw him a grin of gratitude.

Baron was at the side of the bed, tail wagging, getting a head rub from Jack, but Jack's eyes were on her.

He smiled back.

Her belly did a flip, she licked her lips and closed the door.

Then she hurried down the hall.

As she did this, even though it was daylight, she thanked her lucky stars.

Belle had many lucky stars and she thanked them often.

She had a loving family even if she didn't see her dad very much and her mom and Gram were a little nuts. She'd had an interesting childhood, seen many places, met nice people. She had a small cadre of good friends she cared about deeply. She owned her own business and did something she loved. She had a gorgeous cottage that was cozy, inviting, safe and very close to the sea, the sea being something that always made her feel happy and at peace.

Only once in her life had her stars turned. That was when she met, fell in love with and married Calvin.

But now, somehow she knew, with Jack those stars shone brighter than ever before. She also knew in her heart even after only one night that what she and Jack had was good, it was natural and it was right.

It could even be destiny or, at least, that was what her mom would call it.

And she was ready to throw caution to the wind in order to have it, to hold it and keep it forever.

She was so caught in these happy thoughts she almost missed the murmuring voices as she made to turn from the wing Jack's room was in to the one where hers was located.

She stopped just in time, took several steps back, away from the voices, hiding herself, and she plastered her back against the wall.

"...seen Belle?" Belle heard the final words of the question uttered quietly by Joy.

"No," Yasmin answered. "She disappeared shortly after Jack."

Belle bit her lip with concern that they were talking about her and she was eavesdropping, which was beyond rude, as Joy mumbled, "Oh dear."

"Oh dear is right. Miles is livid. He was looking for her all night," Yasmin carried on.

Belle's stomach pitched and she wondered if she could get back to Jack's room without them noticing, but before she could make a decision Joy started talking.

"I know. He must have asked me if I'd seen her a dozen times," Joy told Yasmin.

Belle wasn't surprised about that (though she *was* worried).

"He asked me too," Yasmin replied.

Belle wasn't surprised about that either.

"Do you think she just went to her room? She looked very uncomfortable. I don't think she's a party person," Joy commented wisely.

"She didn't go to her room," Yasmin answered and Belle held her breath in an effort not to gasp.

"How do you know?" Joy asked the question in Belle's head.

"Because Miles told me some of the staff saw her and Jack walking through the kitchens and out the back door," Yasmin answered, and in an effort not to suffocate herself Belle forced her breath out silently and took another short, silent (yet fearful), intake of lifesaving oxygen.

Miles knew she was with Jack.

So did Yasmin.

And now Joy.

This was not good.

"Oh dear," Joy repeated but this time she sounded worried.

"When I see Jack, I'm going to wring his neck. He should know better," Yasmin declared fiercely, and Belle thought this was odd.

So odd she forgot about how rude it was to eavesdrop and she leaned closer to the corner.

"You're right, darling, he should," Joy muttered.

"It's worse than you think," Yasmin said in a soft voice and Belle inched even closer to the corner so she could hear better.

"I don't think I want to know," Joy replied and she sounded like she didn't want to know. In fact, she sounded like she *really* didn't want to know.

Even so, Yasmin told her and what she said made the floor lurch crazily under Belle's bare feet.

"Miles told me Jack told him to back off from Belle," Yasmin confided, and Belle felt her eyes widen in surprise, wondering why Jack would do such a thing.

"I'm not sure that's a bad thing," Joy remarked and Belle wondered anew why Miles's mother would agree.

"No, except Miles told me that Jack said this because he told Miles he wanted a crack at her," Yasmin returned.

Belle's hand went to the wall as her weight pressed into it because her knees had buckled.

A crack at her?

What did that mean?

She didn't have to wait long to find out.

"Jack wouldn't say that," Joy defended.

"Normally, I wouldn't think so either but you didn't see Jack when he first met her. As they were being introduced, right in front of Miles, he made a play for her," Yasmin said.

"He didn't," Joy whispered in horror.

"He did," Yasmin returned. "He knew who she was the minute he saw her. The gorgeous, enigmatic Tiny Dynamo, the ultimate challenge for the Bennett brothers. And he knew why Miles brought her here, to throw down the gauntlet, to shove her in Jack's face. And Jack took up the challenge immediately. I saw it with my own eyes. Miles told me Jack threw down when they were talking about her. Miles informed me Jack even said, 'You're on.'"

Belle's heart started racing so fast she felt her pulse beating in her neck *and* her wrists and she thought surely the two women could hear it.

But she was too astounded to care.

You're on?

A crack at her?

Her mind flew from memory to memory of the night before, wickedly handsome, outrageously famous, incomprehensibly rich James Bennett determinedly wooing her.

Her, Belle "Meek and Mild" Abbot.

Not because he liked her.

Not because he thought she was interesting.

But because he was competing with his brother to win a prize.

She should have known she'd never capture the attention of a man like that.

She should have *known*.

She didn't want to wish that she'd never saved that school bus driver or the children from drowning, but in her darkest moments of the last eight months (for instance, *now*) she had to admit that she sometimes did.

She felt bile slide up her throat and tears stinging the backs of her eyes. She swallowed painfully and blinked back the wetness as the women kept talking.

"I don't know what I'm going to do with those two," Joy's voice was filled with angry frustration. "This constant rivalry, it's driving me mad. It started practically the day Miles was born and it just gets worse and worse. But I thought Jack..." She paused for a moment before she continued, "Poor Belle, caught in the middle. She's such a sweet girl. I should never have left her side. I knew it. I just *knew it*." She sounded like she *knew it* and her certainty made Belle's heart lurch.

"She is," Yasmin agreed. "But if I know Jack, it's too late. He doesn't often take Miles up on one of his challenges, but when he does he stops at nothing to win. I think he thinks eventually Miles will tire of losing."

"Yes, but this has gone too far. I'm going to have to have a word with the two of them the first chance I get," Joy replied with resolve.

"I'm sorry, Joy, but you're right," Yasmin gently concurred. "I don't care if they're grown men, something must be said. Playing with Belle like that, it's just cruel."

"Yasmin, darling, if this hasn't gone past the point of redemption and you see Belle, you'll have to look after her. I'll do the same. She isn't leaving until tomorrow. We *have* to protect her from this," Joy declared.

"Of course," Yasmin murmured and Belle knew by their voices they were moving down the hall.

As their conversation trailed away, Belle stood plastered against the wall feeling utterly, devastatingly, *irreparably* humiliated.

The handsome, legendary, born-in-a-castle-with-a-silver-spoon-in-their-mouths Bennett brothers had competed to win her, a human being.

And she'd fallen for it. Not only with James but also, if not to the same extent, with Miles, even though she'd always known something was off about him.

Now she knew exactly what it was and, in hindsight, it was glaringly obvious.

Worse, Joy and Yasmin felt they needed to protect her like she was some naïve idiot unable to look out for herself.

Worse than that, they were right.

She *was* a stupid, silly, foolish, naïve *idiot*.

Belle choked back tears as she peeked around the corner and saw the hall deserted. Joy and Yasmin had disappeared.

Then she ran to her room like the very devil was at her back.

She had to get out of there.

Immediately.

She knew all along this wasn't a safe place.

And she'd been right.

She should have listened to herself.

She now understood the reason she wrapped herself in cotton wool. To protect herself from this kind of irrevocable damage because it hurt worse than anything she could ever imagine. Worse than a broken arm. Worse than a sprained ankle. Worse than *anything*.

She threw open the door to her room and charged in only to come to an immediate, rocking halt.

And this was because Miles was lying on her bed clothed in his tuxedo without the jacket or tie but still wearing his shoes. He had his arms lifted, his head resting on his hands. He looked, for all the world, like a man in thoughtful repose.

When she arrived, his eyes turned to her, they took in her face, her hair, James's shirt and they narrowed dangerously.

Then his voice, low and trembling with fury, came at her, lacerating her frayed nerves and exacerbating her already overwhelming humiliation.

"He fucked you," Miles declared.

At his awful but very true words, Belle jolted out of her horrified stance and ran to her handbag. Throwing her dress and shoes in the direction of her suitcase, she turned and dug in her purse to find her phone.

"You let him fuck you," Miles's voice said from behind her.

She pulled out her mobile and bent her head to it, her mind racing, her thumb touching the screen, her shaky hand making her call nearly impossible.

"Belle," Miles called.

He was closer. She could hear it and she could feel it and it terrified her.

She hit the call button and put the phone to her ear.

"Belle, I'm talking to you."

Miles's voice was changing, his tone had turned biting. She didn't have to look at him to know his anger was fierce.

She'd heard that tone before, dozens of times, and her fear escalated alarmingly.

The call connected and she asked to be put through to a taxi service.

"Belle, put down the fucking phone," Miles demanded, but the call went through and Belle moved. Digging in her bag, she pulled out a pair of jeans.

"Belle, I said put down the *fucking* phone."

Miles's voice was getting louder, but Belle, beginning to panic and almost unable to cope with her stifling humiliation, ignored him, focusing solely on escape.

The taxi service picked up and Belle said in a tremulous voice, "I need a taxi at Chy An Als Point. Immediately. It's an emergency," she semi-lied.

It wasn't a true emergency, just an emergency to her.

But in order to get away, she was willing to lie.

She'd worry about the black mark against her soul later.

A lot later.

"Belle." Miles's voice was an ugly warning.

"What's the name?" the lady at the taxi service asked in her ear.

"Belle Abbot," Belle answered.

There was a brief pause then a breathy, "The Tiny Dynamo?"

Belle shut her eyes tight at the hated, ridiculous title the papers had given her as she felt the fury emanating from Miles hitting her.

"Yes," she replied, not willing to extend the energy to fight it.

"And it's an emergency?" the lady asked.

"Yes," Belle semi-lied again.

"Someone will be right there, love. Don't you worry," the lady assured her and Belle felt immense relief mingled with guilt for leading the nice taxi lady on.

"Thank you," Belle whispered, only the relief evident in her voice then she touched the screen to end the call.

She threw her mobile on top of her purse and shook out the jeans, still ignoring Miles.

"So, you think you can come to my home, meet my mother, spend the night fucking my brother while I'm at the party searching for you, half mad with worry and then just *go home*?" Miles's dangerous voice asked.

"Go away, Miles." Belle sounded exactly as frightened as she felt and she didn't care.

She yanked up the jeans, fastened the button fly and then dashed around the room, gathering her things and running back to the bag, shoving them in.

"Go away?" Miles asked quietly as she did this.

"Yes. Go away," Belle repeated, rushing around the room, blindly grabbing her belongings, not looking at him.

"Go away," Miles whispered and it was a sinister whisper. A whisper that sent shivers of fear up her spine.

Belle didn't respond, she pushed her hand into her bag, found her flip-flops and pulled them out, dropping them to the floor.

She felt him get close when she shoved her feet into the shoes.

"Look at me," he demanded.

"Go away," she whispered, thrusting her stuff into the bag so she could do the zip.

She felt fingers tighten brutally around her upper arm and with an instinct borne of experience, she braced minutes before he shook her by her arm savagely so she turned to him.

His face was frighteningly red with clearly evident wrath and Belle sucked in a terrified breath at the sight right before he roared, "You fucking *whore!*"

She flinched and belatedly tried to jerk her arm out of his grip.

This didn't work.

Fear spiraled through her belly as he took her other arm in his grasp and shook her so hard her head snapped back.

He was shouting loudly when he said, "A *month* I've been taking you to the finest restaurants, feeding you the best food, dancing *fucking* attendance on you like an absolute jackass and you barely let me put my tongue in that sweet mouth of yours. Yet, in one fucking *night* you open your legs for my fucking *brother* when I'm under the same goddamned *roof*." He shook her roughly again and yelled, "You *fucking* whore!"

"Let her go, Miles."

Belle and Miles's eyes swung to the voice that came from the door.

There stood James wearing faded jeans and a black T-shirt that fit snug on his chest and stomach. His black hair was tousled. His feet were bare. His powerful body was held stiff and the expression on his face was downright scary.

At the sight of James in all his angry beauty, Belle forgot her current physical predicament and tears crawled up her throat, stung her eyes and she didn't have the strength to hold them back.

They spilled down her cheeks.

James's angry gaze swung to her face, he took one look at her and the obvious anger turned to even more obvious fury and he strode purposefully into the room.

"Take your hands off her," he demanded.

"Fuck you," Miles returned viciously.

James got close, his eyes locked on his brother and he warned softly, "I'm not going to ask again."

James and Miles glared at each other and Belle stood frozen watching them as the white-hot current of what seemed to be hatred crackled between them.

Suddenly Miles moved. He tossed Belle toward James with great force, sending her flying across the short expanse and colliding into James's body.

James's arms immediately folded around her to hold her close.

"Have her," Miles snapped, sounding like she wasn't a she but an it.

A toy, a plaything, something you could blithely toss around and throw away.

"We'll talk later," James said in a way it was clear anyone in their right mind wouldn't want to be present at that particular chat, and Miles's ugly expression turned uglier.

"No, Jack, we won't. Fuck that," Miles clipped.

"We're going to have words," James demanded.

"We're done talking," Miles retorted.

"What's going on?" Joy asked, her concerned voice coming from the door and Belle had had enough.

She yanked out of James's arms and ran to her bag.

There was stuff in the bathroom but she didn't care. She'd buy more. She was leaving, immediately, even if she had to walk halfway to town to meet the taxi.

She started to zip her bag but felt the hot touch of James's hand at the small of her back.

"What's going on?" Joy repeated in a motherly demand at the exact same moment James murmured, "Poppet."

At that word, Belle zipped her bag with a sharp movement and whirled around, dislodging his hand, her eyes shooting up to lock on his.

"Don't touch me," she whispered, her voice thick with tears.

His hand came up and toward her face as he said gently, "Belle."

She lifted her own hand, knocking his aside. It registered somewhere that her action made his body jerk and his brows drew together.

"I said, *don't touch me,*" she repeated and turned away. Grabbing her suitcase by the handles, she moved to get her purse. "I never want to see you again." She turned, her gaze sweeping the room to see Miles was still there, Joy was at the door and Yasmin had joined her.

The women looked pale. Miles looked furious. James looked concerned.

All of them were watching her.

"*Any* of you," Belle declared then grabbed her purse, hitched it on her shoulder and started to march to the door but James brought her up short with a hand at her wrist.

She stopped and looked up at him.

"Poppet—" he started, and at his repeated endearment something fundamental inside her that was holding together by a miracle broke apart.

"Don't you dare," she hissed, the tears clearing from her voice and eyes. "Don't you *dare*. You wanted a crack at me?" she asked, and James flinched, his eyes shot to his brother in what Belle read as guilt causing her heart to flutter in an altogether too painful way before they came back to her on her next words. "You got it. Three of them if I'm counting right. You won, James," she told him and his eyes narrowed when she used his real name. "You can stop playing the game. Just note your hash mark on the board, move on to your next victim and leave me alone."

She yanked from his hold and started to walk away but he caught her by the wrist again.

"Belle, listen to me—" he began when her eyes moved to his.

"No, I listened to you last night when you told me I could trust you," Belle shot back. "You lied. I'm not listening to you again."

James's face changed. It took on a look of frustrated but controlled anger and he used his hand to bring her closer as he looked to the door.

"Get out and close the door behind you," he ordered.

"Don't bother," Belle said immediately to the women who hesitated at the door. "I'm leaving."

"Belle, we're talking," James told her.

That something that was broken inside her started cutting deep, the jagged ends tearing at her insides. The pain was immense and she couldn't hold on much longer.

"Take your hand off me," she demanded.

"Belle, we're talking," James repeated.

Belle leaned in, overcome by hurt and humiliation, and she screeched into his face. "I said, *take your hand off me!*"

With force, she pulled free and started running.

He caught her just feet from the door with an arm around her waist. Joy and Yasmin had begun to move aside but stopped when he swung her around.

"Get out and close the goddamned door," James clipped harshly.

Belle twisted around in his arm to look at Joy. "Don't close that door!"

"Belle, darling…" Joy started but Belle didn't listen.

She'd dropped her suitcase somewhere along the line and was struggling in earnest to break free of James's arm that was held tight around her waist.

"Go and close the *fucking* door!" James shouted, and Belle heard everyone move around her, including Miles. Someone closed the door but she was still pushing against his arm with her hands and her weight.

Once the door closed, James used his arm to shake her gently.

"Calm down," he ordered, his mouth at her ear, the heat of his body pressed against her back.

"Let me go," she demanded.

"Belle, I don't know what Miles said to you—"

"Miles didn't say much of anything except he called me a fucking whore," Belle snapped, gained an inch but only so James could turn her to face him then both his arms locked around her. She stopped struggling, looked up at him and added, "Twice."

"That's unfortunate, love, but—" he began but she cut in.

"*Unfortunate?* You call that *unfortunate*? I've never been called a whore *in my life*!" she screamed.

"Belle—" he started again but she kept talking.

"And I deserved it. He was right. I know it, you know it. That's *exactly* how I acted."

He gave her another gentle shake as she watched his face grow hard. "Don't say that."

She changed themes and accused, "You said you'd take care of everything."

"It wasn't me who wanted you to go to your room," he shot back.

He was right.

So right.

She was *such* an idiot.

Then again, if she hadn't, she wouldn't have known who he was. He would have kept using her and lying to her to rub his brother's nose in it.

Until he lost interest.

And she would have loved every second of it.

Until he broke her heart.

"You're right," she told him. "It's my fault."

"That's not what I meant."

She was losing the will to fight so again she switched themes.

"Let me go," she demanded.

That earned her another gentle shake. "I'm not letting you go."

"Let me go!" she shouted.

"You have to give me the chance to explain."

"I don't have to do anything, James," she retorted.

At the sound of his name, his arms tightened and she knew he was getting angry with her.

"Stop calling me that," he warned.

"Okay, I will. Gladly. I'll stop calling you *anything*," she returned.

"Cut the crap, poppet, you know, between us, it's bullshit."

She was right, he was angry with her, she could tell.

And for some reason, she didn't care.

And furthermore, she didn't know anything.

Except there was no "us." There was a one night stand, something else she'd never done in her life and something else that caused her extreme humiliation.

"I don't know anything of the sort except you and Miles take sibling rivalry to unprecedented extremes and I got caught in the middle."

"That isn't fucking true," he snapped.

"No? So you're saying me and my winning personality knocked you clean off your feet?" she asked sarcastically.

His eyes narrowed even as he admitted, "Something like that."

She felt anger tear through her at his lie and got up on tiptoe to hiss, "You are so full of it."

He glared at her a moment before his gaze moved to the ceiling as his hand slid up her back and tangled in her hair.

She steeled herself against how good his touch felt, how sweetly familiar it was even though she'd only had it for one night.

When his gaze came back to hold hers, his anger had disappeared and with one look at his gentle face, she had to *re*-steel herself.

"You're full of surprises," he murmured.

"Funny, I was thinking the same about you," she snapped back and this, for some insane reason, made him grin.

His head dipped closer and her body froze.

"Who would have thought the woman I met last night who could barely bring herself to look in my eyes could stand here this morning in my arms arguing with me?" he asked a question to which he didn't want the answer and he did it in a voice that said this no longer annoyed him. Instead, it said he found it adorably entertaining.

It occurred to her what he was doing and she felt tears sting her eyes yet again.

"Don't," she whispered.

His face got even closer, so close their foreheads were nearly touching.

"Don't what?" he asked softly.

"Don't do this," she told him. "You don't have to worry. I won't go flying into Miles's arms. That ship has sailed."

She watched his eyes flare before he lowered his head so their foreheads were now actually touching.

It hit her in a way that wounded her deeply that she liked that.

It felt nice.

Calvin had never done that to her. Calvin's intimacy and affection began and ended in bed.

"Poppet," he muttered. "That's not what I'm doing."

"Don't, James. Just stop it."

"Belle."

"You played your game, you won. Just score your point and let me be."

"That isn't what's happening here."

"I'm not stupid," she whispered. "I know who you are. I know who I am. The man you are can't possibly want the woman I am. You can't think I'm that stupid."

His arms gave her a squeeze. "I don't think you're stupid and I don't want to hear you talk about yourself like that. You need to give me the chance to explain."

"I need to leave."

"You don't want to leave."

"I do."

"You don't."

"Trust me," Belle returned with feeling. "*I do.*"

She felt his body go still and his face moved away from hers.

"You mean it," he stated quietly, something weird in his voice. Something that sounded like surprise and maybe affront.

She didn't reply. She just nodded.

He stared at her a moment before asking in soft, awful voice, "You're telling me you think what happened last night was all an act so I could best my *fucking brother*?"

The way he said it made it sound ludicrous.

Then again, it was.

"Wasn't it?" she inquired and went on, even though his face now held an expression that made him look like he'd been struck and hard, and it hurt her to say what she said next but she did it anyway (self-defense, as it were). "You should feel proud, James. You did a bang-up job. I'd convinced myself you were half in love with me."

At that, he let her go and took a step back. He did this so swiftly she swayed for a moment without his arms around her.

She righted herself even as she felt that maybe, just maybe, she'd made a colossal mistake.

She stared at him for one hopeful second, trying to read his face.

It was hard and it was cold.

"You want to go, Belle?" he asked. She kept quiet and he finished, "Then go."

Belle studied him, suddenly unsure. He was holding his body stiffly as if he was stopping himself from doing something, what, she couldn't imagine.

She looked into his eyes. Usually warm and gentle or soft and amused, now they were blank.

She waited for a sign, any sign, that she hadn't misread her lucky stars.

He gave her none.

Nothing.

Just stared at her, his face hard, his eyes void.

That was it then. He was done.

Challenge accepted, mission accomplished and he was through.

She swallowed the lump that formed suddenly in her throat and turned. She reached down to grab her bag and walked to the door. She felt his eyes on her but she didn't look back even as she hoped she'd feel his hand on her wrist, his arm hooking about her waist, making an effort, any effort, to stop her.

She opened the door and walked through.

James (as far as she could tell), didn't move.

Joy and Yasmin were in the hall but they weren't far away. Miles had disappeared. There were others there, people she'd met at the party, just a few of them likely woken by the shouting, moving slowly down the hall, pretending to be on their way somewhere but looking curious.

She ignored them and kept walking even as both Joy and Yasmin called her name.

She just kept going, head bowed, eyes to the floor. She moved as swiftly as she could down the stairs, across the massive hall, through the huge, studded wooden doors, which took all her strength to shift even a few feet so she could slide through.

The taxi was waiting and only when she saw it did she start running.

Lewis and Myrtle

At the top window of the eastern-most turret, two children, a black-headed boy and a fair-haired girl, stood holding hands and looking out the window at the pretty woman wearing jeans, a man's shirt that was way too big on her and funny-looking shoes that weren't really shoes but they also were. They were something they heard people in these times call "flip-flops," which they both thought was very funny and they'd made a game of the words. Hiding themselves, closing their eyes and one calling "flip" and the other calling "flop" until they found themselves again.

They watched as she ran to the black taxi shining in the sun like a rabid dog was close at her heels.

The taxi driver barely had a chance to get out before she had the back door open. She threw her bag in then she did the same with her body and slammed the door.

The driver wasted no time and drove off with a squeal of wheels.

The little girl, named Myrtle, turned to the little boy, named Lewis, and dropped his hand.

"She doesn't look very happy," Lewis remarked.

Myrtle wrinkled her nose. "If Miles was my boyfriend, I'd run from the castle too."

Lewis grinned. "Only because you *love* Jack." He put great emphasis on the world "love" and Myrtle punched him in the arm and looked back out the window.

"She looked sweet with Jack last night when we saw them walking to the stables," Myrtle commented.

"Yes," Lewis unusually concurred with his sister. Then again, he liked the look of the blonde lady, she was very pretty and she reminded him vaguely of his long since dead mum. "Though, maybe something happened because when they came back, they were walking really quickly."

Myrtle giggled. "I know! He was practically *dragging* her."

"I wonder why they were in such a hurry?" Lewis asked and Myrtle bit her lip.

"Did you see them kissing?" Myrtle whispered.

Lewis didn't look at his sister when he answered back in a whisper, "Yes."

Myrtle's voice was worried when she asked, "Do you think Miles found out Jack kissed his girlfriend?"

Lewis's eyes moved to the window and he looked down the road, the taxi long gone.

"I hope not. He can be not very nice and I don't think he'd like Jack kissing his girlfriend," Lewis replied and felt his sister shiver beside him.

As he'd been doing for quite a number of years (over two hundred of them), he tried to protect his sister from anything that might distress her.

So he leaned in, bumped her with his shoulder and shouted, "Flip-flop!"

Myrtle needed no further encouragement. She shot up several inches from the floor and darted across the room, her ghostly body melting through the wall. She did a forward spin and headed down and through the stairs.

Then, when she found her hidey-hole, she shouted, "Flip!"

And some ways away, she heard her brother's ghostly, "Flop!"

Eyes firmly shut, Myrtle floated in his direction.

5

JACK MEETS LILA AND RACHEL

Jack

Three months later...

Jack saw movement out of the corner of his eye.

He turned his head to see his assistant, Olive, and her short, squat body. She was wearing a heavy tweed skirt even though it was the middle of a very warm summer. One tail of her blouse had come untucked. And her short, naturally gray but dyed peach (for some reason unknown to him) hair was spiked as if she'd been running her hands through it with severe agitation.

Olive Mayfair could singlehandedly plan a successful war with multiple fronts but she wouldn't be able to do it without displaying a great deal of tremendously disorganized, blatantly obvious stress.

She stood at the windows to the conference room where Jack was sitting in a meeting and she was gesticulating wildly, like she was guiding a plane in to land and didn't quite know what signals to make so she was making it up as she went along.

Her eyes were wild.

With one look at her Jack knew either the world was coming to an end or there was a toilet backed up in the branch of his bank located in Iowa City, Iowa.

He looked back at the conference table at which he was sitting at the head.

The ten people in the room with him were all watching Olive.

"Excuse me," Jack muttered, put his hands to the arms of his chair and pushed up. He grabbed his Mont Blanc pen, a present his father gave him when he graduated from Oxford, and his wildly expensive phone that could, if he'd take the time to program it, likely call Mars, a present from Yasmin.

He pushed through the door, Olive lunged forward immediately, grabbed his arm and dragged him away from the windows.

She tugged him to a stop, looked up at him and, with a grave expression on her face, declared, "We have a problem."

"You don't say," Jack muttered dryly.

"This is Code One!" she announced on a whispered screech.

Jack crossed his arms on his chest and regarded her silently.

"Lila Cavendish and her daughter, Rachel Abbot, are here," she told him.

Jack felt her words like a sharp, strong jab direct to the gut.

"Excuse me?" Jack asked, hoping he hadn't heard what he thought he'd heard.

"Lila Cavendish and Rachel Abbot, grandmother and mother to Belle Abbot, are here. In your office. Right now."

Jack's eyes narrowed as his temper flared.

Why Belle's mother and grandmother would be in his offices in London, he could not fathom.

He also didn't care.

"Get rid of them," he demanded and Olive threw her hands out at the sides.

"I knew you'd say that and I tried. They won't go."

This surprised him. "They won't go?"

"No. I didn't even let them into your office. They marched right in. Lila actually made herself a cappuccino with your espresso maker." She paused. "And your milk! Straight from your fridge!" She said this last like it was a crime punishable by death.

"Why are they here?" Jack asked.

"I don't know. They won't tell me. They're demanding to speak to you," Olive replied.

"Tell them I'm in a meeting and they'll need to make an appointment," Jack said.

"I did that already. They don't care. They said they'd wait 'until the cows come home,' whatever that means. We don't have cows in London," Olive noted unnecessarily.

Jack made a decision and turned toward his office. "I'll take care of them. Go back to the meeting. Tell them I'll be five minutes."

He watched Olive nod and walked to his office trying, not entirely successfully, to control his anger.

The debacle with Belle at The Point had made the papers. How, Jack didn't know. But considering the number of people who saw Miles prominently displaying Belle on his arm at the party then the next morning all the shouting, and finally they watched Belle fleeing the castle, it could be anyone.

Including Miles, a maneuver, which if his brother arranged it, backfired.

For an entire month, the media was in fits of glee. They picked every possibility of the Bennett brothers' love triangle with an adopted national treasure apart, and Jack had to admit they did a splendid job of it.

The Bennett brothers' rivalry wasn't a secret and many people who only remotely knew Jack or Miles were more than happy to discuss it.

Jack and Miles had been depicted as lascivious libertines, targeting a media darling as the spoils of a heinous contest, playing with her affections and using her body for their immoral pleasure.

Belle had been depicted as a fragile, not entirely clever, lamb at the slaughter who fell headlong in love with Miles then Jack or both of them at the same time, depending on the story.

At first, it had been a feeding frenzy, all three of them caught in it. No matter where they went, there were cameras, microphones and prying, insulting questions hurled in their direction.

Jack, Belle and Miles had all kept silent. Jack, because if he let himself react, he'd likely do bodily harm. Belle, because she never spoke to the press. Miles, because he'd drawn the short straw. The press, latching on to his loss in the "competition" for Belle, rubbed his face in it constantly, something he detested.

Miles had finally lost his patience and disappeared, not telling anyone, not even Joy, where he'd gone.

Belle, Jack noted with vague concern he would not allow to form fully, seemed to get paler and thinner by the day, and she too eventually disappeared, which was a mistake as that led to a week of the media speculating that she was with Miles.

Jack didn't change his behavior in any way.

Miles had returned six weeks ago when the story was well and truly dead.

Belle, Jack noted distantly (but the press noted it far more assertively), emerged two weeks ago looking paler, thinner and far more fragile.

Jack would not allow himself to care.

Whatever romantic idiocy that had him in its clutches and led him to behave like a besotted fool at her merest smile, her softest giggle, the depth he'd convinced himself was in her eyes, was gone.

Completely.

Time, distance, absence and Belle herself had swept it away.

If his mind turned to his behavior that night or her unshakable belief that he would abuse her so monstrously, especially after what he thought they'd shared, or her refusal to allow him to explain, or the memory of her walking away from him without even glancing back, the fury would begin.

But he'd learned to control it like everything else in his life.

And he did control it. To the point where he barely thought of her anymore unless she was thrust into his consciousness.

Like now.

He arrived at his outer office, his gaze slicing to his secretary, Gillie, who stared at him wide eyed and opened her mouth to speak.

Jack cut her off before she could utter a word. "Don't. It's not your fault."

"Do you want me to call security?" Gillie asked as Jack strode to the door of his office.

"No. This is not going to make the papers. Leave it," Jack ordered and pushed open the door.

Two women were in his office. One he could imagine was Belle's mother. The other looked more like her older sister.

The elder woman was dressed all in dove gray, a flowing, light, ankle-length skirt, silk woven tunic and stylish flats. Her hair was a shining mixture of both blonde and white, as if the white that would declare her age to the world was trying to win but the blonde of her youth refused to let go.

She had very unhappy, stormy gray eyes.

The other one was also blonde, with Belle's thick, long hair untethered and falling in a wild mass of waves down her back. She also had gray eyes, which, turned to him, weren't stormy but surprised and a little curious. She was wearing jeans, cowboy boots, so much silver at her fingers, wrists, neck and all along the curves of her ears it was a minor miracle she could hold herself upright and a purple T-shirt that asked, bizarrely Mummy, where's Fluffy? across the chest in glittery, green script.

Jack closed the door behind him, put his shoulders to it, crossed his arms on his chest and regarded both women.

"You've got five minutes," he announced.

Lila, who he assumed was the older one unless Belle did have a sister, which could well be as Jack knew her about as far as he could throw her, said with grave affront, "Well, that's a fine how-do-you-do."

"Mom…" the younger one mumbled softly, her voice, Jack noted even on that one word, was the same as Belle's, sweet and musical.

At the sound of it, Jack clenched his teeth.

"Ladies, I'm busy," he told them. "You're losing time."

Lila's back straightened, her eyes shot daggers at him and she opened her mouth to speak but Rachel got there before her.

"We agreed I'd do the talking," Rachel said to Lila.

Lila turned her murderous glare to her daughter and announced, "I've changed my mind."

"Mom, seriously, let me do the talking."

"No, I've got a few things to say to this...this..." Lila stuttered but was so caught up in anger she couldn't find an appropriate word.

"Say them," Jack clipped his invitation. "Then go. I have things to do."

"All right then..." Lila started, leaning forward, clearly ready to let loose a stream of invective, but it was what Rachel said at the same time that caused Jack's body to go rock solid.

"Belle's pregnant."

Jack stood motionless at the door, his mind completely blank as the two women ignored his stunned reaction and bickered in front of him.

"I can't believe you just blurted it out like that!" Lila snapped.

"Well, it's not news you can easily cushion," Rachel returned.

"He doesn't deserve *cushioning* but you didn't have to just...*blurt it out*," Lila fired back.

Rachel put her hands to her hips. "How would *you* have done it?"

Lila put her hands to her hips as well. "I don't know but I wouldn't have blurted it out."

"You're just mad you didn't get to tell him and be all," she raised her be-ringed hands to either side of her head and shook them, "*drama.*"

Before Lila could respond, Jack's voice hit the room and they both jumped when he said, "Excuse me."

They turned to him and stared as if they were surprised he was even there.

Yes, he thought, they were both very like Belle.

"Let's go back to Belle being pregnant," Jack suggested in a deceptively soft voice.

His mind, unusually slow, still not wrapped around this fact, however, he did recognize one of the feelings he was feeling.

It was anger.

"Well, she's pregnant. That's it. That's what we came to say," Rachel told him as if she did this every day, forced her way into men's offices and informed them the one night stand they'd had months ago was pregnant.

"And you're saying you think it's mine," Jack stated, and the air in the room changed drastically.

It was not friendly before, but after he uttered his words, words he knew were unnecessary, words he also knew were a serious insult, the air became sluggish and suffocating.

Rachel, the more pleasant one, lost all vestiges of pleasant. Her eyes narrowed and her cheeks went pink.

As becoming as this was (the same as when her daughter blushed), Jack's gaze moved to Lila and he saw she stood straight and still, hands clenched into fists at her sides, the daggers in her eyes had turned to deadly spears.

"We shouldn't have come here," Rachel muttered furiously. "Belle told us but did we listen? No, we did...not...*listen*. Do we ever listen to Belle? No, we never...listen...*to Belle*. Do we always get in trouble? Yes! We do!"

Jack, instinctively knowing Lila was the more worthy opponent, didn't take his eyes from her as Rachel ranted. Therefore he saw immediately when her expression cleared, the anger cooled and she looked at her daughter.

"This is good," Lila told Rachel.

"How is this good?" Rachel returned sharply.

"Belle didn't want him to have anything to do with the baby. He doesn't think it's his. Belle gets what she wants." Lila clapped her hands together like she was wiping away dust and declared, "*Fin.*"

Jack watched Lila walk to his couch and pick up a sleek, expensive purse.

Then her gaze went to the painting over the couch. A painting that had been moved from his old office to this office three years ago upon his father's death. A painting Jack had owned for twelve years. It was the first painting Jack had ever invested that kind of significant money in. His own money. Money that *he'd* earned.

Her painting.

"You know, Belle told me you owned one of my pieces and I gotta say, it goads me you have it but I'll let it be," she said to the painting and then looked at him, eyes unfriendly, face unhappy. "We walk out of this room, you cease to exist. And good riddance," she finished as her daughter walked up beside her and grabbed a square, battered, woven, tan leather handbag with a long strap from the couch.

They both walked toward him but he didn't move.

When they were forced to stop in front of him, he still didn't move.

"We're leaving now," Lila announced.

"I'll want to speak to Belle," Jack returned and he watched with some surprise as both women grew pale.

Therefore he knew without asking that not only had Belle told them not to come there, she didn't know they *were* there.

Lila rallied first. "That's not going to happen."

"She's carrying my child. I'll want to speak to her," Jack retorted.

"Well, since we don't know *if* it's your child, that's unnecessary," Lila shot back.

"It's mine," Jack said with soft meaning and watched the women exchange nervous glances.

"We thought," Rachel started, but when Jack's eyes cut to her, she stopped. He watched her swallow then she pressed on, "We thought it was only fair you knew. Belle doesn't want anything, not your money or anything. She didn't even want you to know she was carrying your child. But she's keeping it and it's yours too and we thought it was only fair," she finished, but when Jack didn't speak she continued. "Please don't make us regret this gesture."

Belle, Jack noted, was very like her mother.

This did not make him waver mainly because Belle was pregnant with his child and fully intended to keep it from him.

And that was not going to happen.

"I'll want to speak to her," he repeated.

"Damn it, man!" Lila burst out.

"Either you arrange it or my solicitors will," Jack warned. "And I don't think you want solicitors involved."

Lila made an angry noise but it was again Rachel who captured Jack's attention.

"Why?" Rachel asked softly, her voice trembling with an emotion he couldn't quite read. Hurt or anger, he wasn't sure. "She doesn't want to see you. Why put her through this?"

"It's my child," was all Jack said to explain, which he thought was quite enough.

"I beg to differ. It's *Belle's* child too, not just yours," Lila snapped.

"Then Belle and I, as the child's mother and father, will speak like civilized people about what will happen during its gestation, birth and continued existence."

"Oh lordy," Rachel muttered.

"It's *gestation*?" Lila breathed in a furious whisper.

"I'll choose the obstetrician, the best, who will see to Belle's care while the baby's developing. I'll choose the hospital, the best, so I can be assured of a successful outcome during delivery. And Belle and I'll discuss what arrangements will be made after its birth."

"Belle's already got an obstetrician," Rachel noted.

Jack's eyes cut to Rachel. "Unless he's the best, Belle will have another one."

"*She* is lovely and Belle likes her," Lila informed him.

Jack moved from the door and walked to his desk while saying, "This isn't something we're discussing. It's something I'll discuss with Belle." He paused, put his phone and pen on the desk and turned, leaning a thigh against the side, his hand on the top. "Or my solicitors will discuss it with hers."

"I knew by the way you and your brother behaved you were a bastard but *nobody* is *this* much of a bastard," Lila snapped then clamped her mouth shut when Jack's lethal gaze sliced to her.

"This conversation is over," Jack announced.

"Please don't do this," Rachel begged and Lila shot her a furious look but Rachel ignored it. "Belle's under enough stress as it is."

"Then I suggest you encourage her to speak with me," Jack replied instantly regardless of the fact that he felt more than a vague sense of disquiet at Rachel's earnest words. "Tell her Saturday afternoon, three o'clock at The Point."

"*If* she decides to come, and that's a big 'if,'" Lila proclaimed, "then we'll be with her."

Jack extended his head and murmured, "By all means."

Rachel and Lila glanced at each other before Lila declared, "I do *not* have a good feeling about this and usually my feelings are *spot on*."

Jack didn't comment.

Neither did Rachel.

The two women stood staring at him, perhaps hoping he'd relent.

He didn't.

Lila put her hand to the doorknob saying, "We've done enough damage to Bellerina. Let's go, Rachel, before we do any more."

"This wasn't my idea," Rachel replied.

"Well, it wasn't mine," Lila retorted.

"If I remember correctly, it was," Rachel said.

They kept squabbling as Lila led the way out but Jack saw Rachel turn at the door and call, "We'll see you Saturday."

Then Rachel closed the door behind them.

Jack stared at it.

Belle Abbot was pregnant with his child.

One of the three indisputably magnificent times he'd fucked her (Jack knew he couldn't put that down to romantic idiocy), he'd made her pregnant.

Belle, thin and wan, if the pictures in the paper were anything to go by, had been pregnant with his child for three months.

And she wasn't going to tell him.

She was going to keep his child from him.

If her mother and grandmother hadn't intervened, he might never have learned not only that he was going to be a father but that his child existed on the planet.

On this thought, it took an extreme effort of will not to pick up the expensive phone Yasmin had given him and throw it across the room.

Instead, he picked up the desk phone and dialed Olive's extension.

He put it to his ear, and when she answered, he said, "Get me everything you can on Belle Abbot. I want her home address, phone numbers, e-mail and work address by the end of the day. You have two weeks to compile a complete history."

"What's going on?" Olive asked in his ear but he didn't reply.

He put the phone down, put Belle and her family out of his mind and went back to his meeting.

✾ *6* ✾

ALL FREAKING DAY LONG
SICKNESS

Belle

As her mother drove Belle's car, Belle watched The Point get closer and closer.

She felt like throwing up.

This was not unusual. For the past six weeks she'd been throwing up a lot.

Morning sickness was a misnomer. All Freaking Day Long Sickness was more like it.

She hoped she got through this—whatever it was—with James without vomiting on some priceless rug.

That would be beyond humiliating. Not that he could humiliate her any more than he already had, both privately and very, very publicly.

Still, she hoped it didn't happen.

It had been three days but Belle was still angry with her mom and Gram.

She could not *believe* they'd gone to see James.

In all their crazy schemes, that was the craziest.

She had no idea what they were thinking (then again, she never did).

Six weeks ago, after finding out she was pregnant and allowing herself a week of temporary insanity (intensified by the lessening, but still present, media scrutiny), Belle had decided to keep the baby.

She was thirty-five and she was never, but *never*, going to get in another relationship, even under torture.

She'd die before she let another man muck up her life.

So she decided this would be her only chance. Unless she was artificially inseminated. Or she adopted, which would be difficult as she was single and although currently wildly famous (not for all good reasons), she wasn't wildly rich and successful, like a pop star or an actress who could mosey down to Africa with her army of attorneys and have her pick of children on whom she could lavish her attention.

She'd gone home to tell her family and, like an idiot, in a misguided attempt at acquiring moral (and other) support, she'd brought them back.

She should have never done that.

She knew better.

Therefore for the first time in her life (or, since she'd become involved with Miles, *then* James), she had no idea what *she* was thinking.

With her behavior of the last three plus months, she seriously needed to get her head examined.

Like today, letting her mom (her Gram was staunchly against it) talk her into going to speak with James.

She knew she should just hire a solicitor and plan, fight, hope and do anything else she had to do to bring about the best for her child.

But no.

There she was in her car, her mother driving, and The Point was looming huge and daunting in front of them.

She just hoped she didn't look as bad as she felt.

She'd decided to wear jeans because she didn't want to make it look as if she cared overly much about her appearance when seeing James again. Then she'd decided to wear slightly faded but not excessively faded jeans because she didn't want James to think she was being in his face with her casual attire.

She'd paired this with a white camisole over which she wore a very feminine blouse she'd designed herself. White. Nearly see-through. Delicate pin-tucks at the front. Girlie gathered cap sleeves with a tiny ruffle at the edges. Buttons open enough to show some cleavage but not enough cleavage to make her look like the hussy she felt she was the last time she'd visited The Point.

She'd put on a pair of silver ballet-toe flats. Carried a big, poochy, black, expensive designer handbag that she'd purchased in a wild flight of fancy at duty-free shopping on her way home to tell her family she was pregnant (this, she excused as still being in the throes of temporary insanity). And, last, she'd donned a black belt with enormous, square, silver rivets in it.

She'd worn silver hoops in her ears, a dozen silver bangles at her wrist and put her hair in a ponytail at the back of her head because James told her he liked her hair down. *That* she knew was being in his face but she didn't think it was obvious so she cut herself some slack.

She looked like an innocent rock 'n' roll virgin.

Albeit a pregnant one.

She sat as her mother parked the car at the base of the sweeping, wide, stone stairwell that led to the arched, fifteen-foot tall, studded, wooden double doors.

Belle felt a wave of nausea and swallowed it down.

Her grandmother, sitting in the back seat, leaned forward and rested her hand on Belle's shoulder. "You okay, Bellerina?"

No, she was definitely not okay.

But she didn't admit that.

"Let's just get this done," Belle muttered instead, threw open her door and stepped out.

No sooner had she done this than one of the double doors swung open and Joy, wearing an elegant, blue dress the likes of which one would don to meet The Queen, came flying out.

She was wearing the brooch Belle had given her.

"Belle!" she cried, rushing down the steps, throwing her arms wide, and Belle braced just as Joy reached her and gave her a warm, friendly hug. "Oh darling, I'm so pleased to hear your and Jack's news. So, so, so, so, so, so, *so* pleased," she chanted, her arms still tight around Belle, and Joy was swinging her side to side with abandoned delight.

Joy moved a bit away but held Belle by the forearms so she could look into Belle's eyes with a friendly smile.

As if the last time Belle saw her, Belle wasn't dashing out of her house in humiliation after loudly fighting with *both* her sons because she'd been dating one and slept with the other.

As if, for a month after that, Belle's sordid relationship with her sons hadn't been written about in detail (not all of them correct, but they were correct enough) in every newspaper on three continents (maybe seven, Belle had no friends in South America, Asia, Africa or Antarctica so who knew).

Joy gave Belle's arms a squeeze and repeated on a whisper, "So pleased." Her head jerked around and she shrieked, "My *God*! You are *not* Belle's mother!" And she rushed to Rachel and embraced her too.

"Is James Bennett adopted?" Gram asked, *sotto voce*, in Belle's ear and Belle choked back a wave of hysterical laughter.

This was not hard to do. While swallowing her laughter, she saw movement at the door and her mirth and hysteria died.

She looked up and there stood James, arms crossed on his chest, legs set wide. He was wearing jeans and an untucked, tailored, black shirt. He was looking even more beautiful than she remembered him and she thought she'd remembered every single detail of him in glaring clarity but, apparently, she had not.

His gaze was on her and she felt the trill go up her spine as her belly did a flip that had nothing to do with nausea.

Quickly she turned away and watched Joy introduce herself to Gram with another welcoming hug.

Joy disengaged from Gram and linked arms with Belle, leading her up the steps.

"I've ordered high tea and we've made sure we have plenty for dinner if you all decide to stay, which I think would be lovely," Joy wittered on as she firmly guided Belle up the steps even though Belle tried very hard to drag her feet.

They nearly made it to the top and Belle didn't look up but she saw James's thighs, hips then stomach and none of them moved out of the way of the door.

She ignored this by turning to Joy and saying, "I'm sorry you went to all that trouble, Joy, but I'm not very hungry."

The forceful, no-nonsense words uttered in James's unmistakable, deep voice brought Belle to a stop.

"You'll eat."

Her gaze skittered to his still unfairly beautiful eyes and she saw he was staring at her.

"I'm not hungry," Belle repeated.

"You're eating for two so you'll eat," James returned, and Belle felt the heat sting her cheeks at his nearly instant reference to their unborn child.

She also felt like running back down the steps to her car or avoiding it altogether, jumping into the sea and swimming to France.

At the same time she felt like kicking him in the shin.

No, "Hello." No, "How are you?" No, "I'm so sorry I broke your heart and devastated your life, all in one night, how will you ever forgive me?"

Just, "You'll eat."

Belle didn't know what to say so she looked away and said nothing at all.

Luckily Joy knew exactly what to do in intensely uncomfortable situations and she guided Belle into the house and to the sitting room, a room Belle especially liked, decorated in warm greens and bright yellows. She chatted the whole time making them all at ease (or as at ease as they could be under the circumstances) and then rushed out to order the refreshments.

Belle, Mom and Gram all had taken seats.

James stood leaning against the mantel of the fireplace, arms still crossed on his chest.

Belle wished he would sit. He was tall and he seemed even taller (for obvious reasons) when she was seated.

She, however, didn't tell him this.

In fact, except for a quick glance, she didn't look at him at all.

"What a, erm, lovely room," Mom commented nervously.

James didn't reply.

They waited.

James still didn't reply.

"Can we get on with this?" Gram asked impatiently.

James spoke but Belle still didn't look at him. "We'll wait until Mum returns."

"Whyever would we do that?" Gram snapped.

"Do you expect the have the right to speak about the future of your unborn great-grandchild during these discussions?" James asked.

"Of course I do," Gram returned, unusually not quick enough to catch his meaning.

"Then we'll wait until Mum returns," James stated firmly and Gram clamped her mouth shut and glared at Belle.

She did this as if it was all Belle's fault when it wasn't *Belle* who'd shot off to London and forced herself into James Bennett's office and announced he'd gotten someone pregnant.

Belle returned her grandmother's glare.

Gram's eyes grew narrow, something which, when Belle was a child, would frighten the dickens out of her. Something which, when Belle was a pregnant thirty-five-year-old woman sorting through the mess Gram had made for her (well, kind of), Belle didn't react to at all.

Gram let out an annoyed sigh and looked away just as Joy re-entered the room.

"Tea, cakes, sandwiches, everything, coming right up," Joy announced and at the very thought of food, Belle felt bile slide up her throat.

She put her hand to her chest and swallowed. She felt her mother's eyes move to her in question and Belle spared her a glance and gave her a short shake of the head.

When she looked away from Rachel, her eyes slid past James then came jerking back when she saw his gaze was narrowed on her hand at her chest.

She dropped it and looked away.

"All right," Joy clapped happily as she sat down, "let's talk baby. Belle, darling, are you taking vitamins?"

She was, however most of them ended up in the toilet.

She didn't tell Joy this. She just smiled and said, "Yes. Everything, so far, is healthy and happy."

"Except those headaches you get," Mom put in.

"And the morning sickness," Gram added.

"Oh dear, are you getting headaches and nausea?" Joy asked with concern.

"It's not that bad," Belle assured her on a total lie.

She was going to hell with a number of black marks on her soul, she just knew it. And most of them could be attributed to her behavior around the Bennett family.

"Who's your doctor?" James asked suddenly and Belle's eyes went to his shoulder.

"Dr. Flanagan. She's an obstetrician in Penzance."

"I'll want to check her credentials," James declared and Belle felt extreme irritation but she bit it back.

"Of course," she murmured and heard her grandmother emit an angry noise, but Belle gave Lila a look and Lila bit her tongue.

"Where are you planning the delivery?" James asked and Belle looked back at his shoulder.

"I haven't gotten that far yet," she told his shoulder.

"Belle," he called even though he obviously had her attention.

She kept staring at his shoulder. "What?"

"Look at me," he demanded, no warmth or amusement in his tone as he called her on not meeting his eyes and her body jolted unpleasantly as her gaze jerked to his and, once he held her eyes, he declared, "You'll have our child in theater."

"Dr. Flanagan is going to refer me to a midwife," Belle told him, with effort keeping her eyes locked on his.

"You'll deliver with qualified doctors present," he replied.

"But—" Belle started.

"This isn't up for discussion," James stated and Belle heard her mother make a small, surprised squeak as her grandmother made a not-so-small, annoyed grunt.

Joy, however, said quietly, "Jack—"

But James ignored his mother, his eyes holding Belle's, he decreed, "You'll move into The Point within the month."

Belle's heart stopped beating at the same time her mouth dropped open.

"Now, see here—" Gram began, coming out of her seat but James's eyes cut to her.

"Sit down, Lila," he ordered and Gram sputtered in nonverbal outrage but James ignored her too and his gaze came back to Belle. "If you want your mother and grandmother here, that's fine. But you're moving in at your earliest convenience but within the month."

Belle felt the nausea roiling in her belly and she wasn't certain it had to do with All Freaking Day Long Sickness.

"I can't move in here," she whispered.

"You can and you will," James stated.

"I can't," Belle breathed.

"If it's a financial difficulty then I'll arrange for you to be moved," James told her.

"It's not a financial difficulty!" Belle cried, beginning to panic.

"Good, then you'll tell Mum when we can expect you," James returned.

Belle stared at him a moment before asking, "Are you mad?"

"No, not in the slightest. You're carrying my child. That means something to me. I've missed three months of its development. I don't intend to miss any more." He stopped speaking. His eyes changed to something she'd never seen on him before. Something frightening and not very nice. Something that made her even more nervous than normal and more than a little bit scared before he spoke, saying words that explained his look. "And you won't keep it from me."

"It's a child in a womb," Mom spoke up.

"It's *my* child in a womb," James retorted.

"You can't see anything or feel anything or—" Mom kept at it.

"It'll grow. It'll kick. It'll move. There are theories that a developing child hears voices, music, even understands and connects with the beings around it as it grows. Belle doesn't get to keep that to herself. She'll share it...with me," James stated implacably.

"I can't live with you," Belle spoke on a horrified whisper.

"You can," James returned.

"James, you know I can't," Belle said softly but she'd made a mistake.

She'd called him James.

If the look on his face just moments before was frightening and not very nice, this one was downright terrifying and filled with borderline loathing.

"I'm not giving you a choice," he said low, his voice full of the dangerous menace apparent in his eyes.

"And what will you do if she refuses?" Gram asked.

"I'll fight Belle for full custody once the baby is born," James answered coldly and this announcement was met with all around shocked gasps.

Except Joy, who exclaimed. "Jack!"

And Belle, who could no longer fight back the nausea.

It was coming, no amount of swallowing was going to stop it and if she didn't find a bathroom and soon, it would be all over the dainty coffee table.

So she shot up from the couch and ran from the room, heading from memory to the bathroom Yasmin took her to when she was at the party.

She barely made it. Falling to her knees on a sliding skid and putting her face in the toilet, she gave up the small lunch of tuna salad sandwich her mother made her eat.

Tuna, she realized too late, was no fun re-experiencing.

When she was done, she rested her hot forehead against the toilet seat, wrapping her arms around the back of her head.

Belle really hated vomiting.

She'd avoided doing it for years and was glad she'd never have another child because, after this, she was hoping she'd avoid it for many years to come.

Her eyes opened and she looked at her belly. "You're already causing trouble you know," she told her belly softly. "I'm kind of not enjoying this throwing up business. So, if you could tone it down, I'd appreciate it." Her still (almost) flat stomach didn't reply so she went on, "Or, at least wait until I've had a hot fudge sundae and wouldn't mind a second taste."

At her final word, she felt a hot hand on her back.

She'd know the feel of that hand anywhere, anytime. If she had to walk blindfolded through a million hands, she could source it and if she lived to be a hundred years old, she'd remember it.

Her head shot up and to the side and she saw James crouched close beside her.

He wasn't looking at her, though his hand was still on her back. He was reaching out and flushing the toilet.

Okay, so, she'd been pretty humiliated by this man but this was the icing on the cake.

His eyes came to her and she wished she wasn't so slow. She should have got up and walked out. Just like that gloriously awful night when she'd woken and he'd still been asleep, she should have left then too.

Instead, she was in close quarters with James after having just vomited, feeling like an idiot and she could see his lushly lashed eyes close up.

Something she never wanted to do again in her life.

Something she relived in her dreams every night.

"Does this happen often?" he asked quietly using a voice she was far more familiar with.

"About twenty times a day," Belle tried to reply matter-of-factly but, she had to admit, it took effort not to lean toward him. His internal magnet, in this mood, was full force.

"Have you told Dr. Flanagan?" he went on and she nodded but didn't speak. "And?" James prompted.

"I'm drinking stuff she gave me. It's okay, James. You don't have to worry. The baby is getting nourished."

Something she couldn't read flashed in his eyes but before she could decipher it, he continued, "And you?"

"Me what?" Belle asked, confused.

"Are you getting nourished?"

On that, she broke from his magnetic beam and stood.

She could, surprisingly, cope with him being a jerk (just barely) but his fake concern was something she couldn't bear.

He stood with her and she walked around him to the basin saying, "I'm fine."

She leaned into the basin and rinsed her mouth, hoping he'd leave, something he did not do.

When she was done, she grabbed a towel and wiped her mouth. Then she pulled the now ever present roll of mints from her back pocket and put two in her mouth before returning the pack to her pocket.

With that she moved toward the door.

James brought her up short with a hand on her arm.

She looked at his hand then at him. "We should join the others."

He ignored her remark, didn't remove his hand (which felt, by the way, like it was burning her skin) and said, "You're too thin."

"I'm told that happens," she informed him.

"It's my understanding women gain weight while pregnant," he replied.

"Not in the first trimester."

"You're completing the first trimester," he reminded her.

"This will pass," she assured him.

"I'd like to attend an appointment with you and your obstetrician."

"I'll arrange that," she agreed but she'd agree to anything to get away from him.

She tried to pull her arm from his grasp to get out of the close confines of the bathroom as soon as humanly possible but he didn't let go.

"Next week," he demanded and her eyes flew to his.

"Dr. Flanagan is very busy," Belle told him.

"I'm sure I can convince her to find an appointment for us in her diary," James returned.

With the way he said it, who he was and the mountains of money he had, Belle was sure too.

"Fine," she gritted between her teeth and looked away.

"Belle," he called and her eyes snapped back to him. "I want you moving to The Point."

"You've made that clear," Belle assured him.

"I want your verbal agreement, right now."

She shook her head and pulled at her arm but he still didn't let go so she gave up.

"Belle, we're agreeing this now," he demanded.

She looked at his ear. "Give me some time to think about it."

"No."

Her eyes moved back to his and she asked on a whisper, "Why?"

"You know why."

"No," she said with complete honesty. "I don't."

He regarded her a moment as if to assess her truthfulness then he moved closer even though he was already close.

Belle backed away but she had nowhere to retreat and came up against the door.

When she did, he put his hand not already on her to the door by her waist and got even closer.

"You want to know why?" he asked quietly and she nodded, at his proximity unable to speak. Feeling the heat from his body, feeling overwhelmed by his large frame in a way she'd not felt when she was with him before, and he continued, "All right, I'll tell you why."

The way he said that made her think she didn't actually want to know why.

She didn't get a chance to stop him.

"Because, three months ago, you walked away from me without looking back. Now you're carrying my child and therefore, out of necessity as we're sharing parentage of that child, I'm not giving you the opportunity to do it again. Because you found out you were pregnant and you didn't intend to tell me. Because you're obviously having a difficult pregnancy and I intend to make certain it goes as smoothly as possible and ends successfully."

There was a lot there, most of it Belle had no intention of addressing.

So she addressed the only thing she could.

"I'm not having a difficult pregnancy. I'm told what I'm experiencing is entirely natural," she told him.

"I'd like to be assured of that by a qualified doctor," he replied.

"My mother went through the same thing with me," Belle pushed.

"That may be but I still want an expert opinion."

Belle looked away, not willing to fight it. Especially when he was that close and muttered again, "Fine."

"You'll move in?" he asked and her eyes darted back to his.

"That's not what I meant," she answered.

"That's what we're talking about."

She swallowed then took in a deep breath, looked at his nose and admitted, "I don't want to live here. I don't feel safe here. I feel safe at home. I want to stay there. I promise to keep you informed and involved however you like that to be."

"If you don't feel safe here then I'll move in with you at your home."

At these words, Belle's body locked and her gaze jerked from his nose to his eyes.

"You can't move in with me," she breathed.

"Why not?" he inquired.

"Because I own a two-bedroom cottage. With Mom and Gram there, I have a full house. Mom's already sleeping on the couch. There's nowhere for you to sleep."

"I'll sleep with you."

Belle felt her lips part and her eyes went wide as shock reverberated through her system.

"You *are* mad," she said on a barely there whisper.

"I'll do what I have to do to be close to this child," he replied on a not-at-all barely there decree.

"I'll move to The Point," she blurted, then thought better of it immediately and was about to take it back but he saw his advantage and he was a heck of a lot quicker.

He pushed in closer, so close her head had to tilt back but she was against the door. She felt the wood against her head and had to shift toward him to give it room to move so she could look up at him. She felt his chest brushing her breasts and even his hips brushing her belly.

Her mind blanked of everything but his nearness which suffused her senses.

"So, we're agreed, you're moving in," he declared, his voice low and rumbly.

She blinked, trying to catch a thought and stall for time so she murmured, "James—"

"We're agreed," he pressed ruthlessly, dipping his head further so his face was an inch away and all she could see were his beautiful eyes.

"Yes," she whispered.

"You won't renege?" he demanded.

"No."

"Make that a promise, Belle," he ordered and she blinked again.

"What?"

"Promise me, right here, you'll move in and you won't renege."

Belatedly she realized her heart was hammering in her chest and she was finding it difficult to breathe.

Something about this cleared her mind and she was able to focus.

Therefore, with some effort, she plucked up the courage to negotiate.

"I'll promise you I'll move in if you promise never to fight for custody. We'll determine arrangements that will be best for the baby, just you and I, without dragging him or her through that kind of mess."

"Agreed," he said instantly.

At this she relaxed, which was a mistake because it pressed her body closer to the heat and hardness of his.

She tensed again and looked at his ear. "Move back."

She felt him hesitate before he did as he was asked.

The moment he did, Belle turned to the door and put her hand on the knob but she stopped and was forced to look at him again when he spoke.

"I need to ask something more."

Belle didn't speak. She just kept looking at him.

He continued, "Mum is excited about this. She wants to be involved and she—"

Belle cut him off. "I'm happy for Joy to be as involved as she wants. She's a lovely woman and she's the baby's grandma."

The air in the room changed. It turned unpleasant and Belle saw his face had again grown hard.

"You seem to have forgotten that when you decided to keep this from me," he told her, his voice as hard as his face.

Something inside her, a bit of her grandmother coming out for once, made her lift her chin, look him in the eye and defend herself.

Mainly because, she thought, she had every bloody right to do what she did.

"You're absolutely correct," she agreed. "I did. I completely forgot about Joy and the fact that she's a lovely woman. My only thought was to stay well away from you and your brother."

She watched his jaw tense. It frightened her a little bit but she sallied forth anyway because this was her child she was talking about, and when you had a child, you had no choice but to develop a backbone.

"And James, as the years pass, if I get even a suspicion our child is learning to behave in the ways demonstrated during my encounters with you and Miles then we have a problem."

She didn't give him the chance to retort. She turned the knob and got the heck out of there, nearly running back to the sitting room.

James didn't follow.

In fact, he didn't join them for tea.

In fact, she didn't see him again until Joy was walking them out to the car, chattering happily with Mom and Gram (there was, Belle was both pleased and weirded out to note, serious bonding going on between her family and James's).

They were all giving hugs good-bye when, out of nowhere, James appeared at her side.

He handed her his business card.

"I'll expect a call about the doctor's appointment next week," he stated.

Belle took the card, looked at his ear and nodded.

"If you have trouble with the appointment, you tell me and I'll arrange it," he continued.

Belle's eyes didn't leave his ear when she continued nodding.

"I'll expect news about your planned arrival at The Point next week as well," he went on.

Belle licked her lips and nodded again.

She saw his head jerk toward Mom and Gram, and without another word, he strode away.

The Cavendish-Abbot family were silent in the car for several very long minutes as they drove from Chy An Als Point.

Finally, Gram (as usual) broke the silence by grandly declaring, "I do *not* like that man."

This was not a surprise.

The surprise was Mom's verbally stated opinion. An opinion that made Belle's head twist toward her mother, her mouth open, her mind thinking that maybe Mom had finally jumped straight into the deep end.

"I do. I like him a lot."

"*What?*" Gram shouted.

"You do?" Belle breathed.

"He may be a jerk in a lot of ways—" Mom began.

"*May* be?" Gram demanded.

"Yes, he *may* be," Mom returned. "We don't know him all that well and these are emotional times."

"Um, were you *not* present when I explained what happened with James and his brother?" Belle asked incredulously.

"And were you temporarily blind when your daughter poured out her story through fits of tears?" Gram snapped.

"And do you *not* hear the reporters' rude questions shouted at me practically every day?" Belle didn't let up.

"I hear them, Bellerina. Still, I can't help but like him," Mom replied softly.

"She thinks he's sexy," Gram said on an annoyed sigh. "Her brain always gets addled around sexy men."

This, unfortunately, was true.

"Well, he *is* sexy," Mom admitted.

This, unfortunately, was true too.

"But that's not it," Mom continued.

"What is it, then?" Gram demanded to know.

"I don't know. I have a theory," Mom replied and Belle rolled her eyes and turned away.

Her mother had a lot of theories and they were usually daft at best, preposterous at worst and they were mostly at worst.

"Would you like to share your theory?" Gram asked, sounding like she'd rather not hear it but curiosity was getting the better of her.

For her part, Belle didn't want to know.

She didn't want to think of James at all.

Pretty soon, she'd be living in his house and therefore likely having to think about him all the time.

Then she'd have their baby and she'd have to see him far more than she wanted to.

For the rest of her life.

Therefore, she would have preferred a brief respite from James Bennett.

And she *always* preferred a respite from her mother's theories.

"I don't want to share it, not yet. It isn't fully formed," Mom said and Belle sighed in relief.

Finally, something went her way.

"I still can't help but like him," Mom muttered stubbornly.

Well, not *entirely* her way.

"Can we stop talking about this?" Belle asked.

"Of course, Bellerina," Gram stated inflexibly, her meaning clear to everyone in the car, most especially Mom.

Mom drove and they were all silent.

Then Mom's hand came out and squeezed Belle's knee.

"Everything's going to be fine, Bellerina. I feel it in my bones," she whispered.

Hearing these words from her mother on many occasions in her life, Belle knew that Rachel Abbot felt a lot in her bones. Her bones were very busy sensing intuitive communications other mere mortals could not interpret.

However, unlike much of what Rachel Abbot did and said, when her bones spoke, they were rarely wrong.

Belle didn't know what to make of that.

But since it was her Mom's bones speaking, for the first time in a long time, Belle felt a very tiny, nearly imperceptible but still there, smidgeon of hope.

7

SHREDDED

Olive

Olive Mayfair closed her office door on the private investigator and turned back to her cluttered desk.

It was after eight o'clock in the evening and even though she had two days before the deadline Jack gave her on the Abbot report, she wanted to get it done so she could get what she'd learned out of her mind and move on.

She could, of course, simply give him the files but that wasn't Olive's way of doing things.

Jack was a tremendously busy man, indeed, *impossibly* busy.

Therefore, even though she knew he would read every single page of the investigator's file after he read Olive's synopsis of its contents, she was still going to write her summary.

She sat at her desk and stared at the thick file with distaste.

Then she opened it to the first page, a copy of a divorce decree, which she flipped over and saw the first of many medical reports.

Olive turned to her computer and started typing.

Belle Abbot's divorce from Calvin Cole had been granted under what amounted to irreconcilable differences.

Olive was not surprised Cole had divorced his very clumsy, accident-prone wife.

Indeed, according to the reports that Olive carefully studied with growing disgust, Belle "slipped" in her kitchen twice, the bathroom four times, in the garden thankfully only once and she'd fallen down the stairs alarmingly often.

During these "accidents," she'd suffered cuts, contusions, concussions, a sprained wrist and several broken ribs.

Olive thought, sarcastically, that it was abundantly clear that Belle was a danger to herself and Calvin Cole was well quit of her.

Surprisingly, Olive thought with cynicism, Belle Abbot had not visited a hospital even once before her marriage to Cole. In fact, she'd lived a carefree, accident-free, hospital- and doctor-free, albeit active and far wandering life.

She'd even climbed to Machu Picchu with her mother when she was eighteen without managing, in her extreme clumsiness, to tumble down the narrow, treacherous mountain paths.

At a quarter to ten, Olive closed down her computer and walked the short distance from her office to Jack's carrying the file with her report in, all of it in a large, sealed envelope marked URGENT. PRIVATE AND CONFIDENTIAL., like it was a piece of putrid rubbish.

She had never met Belle Abbot but Olive liked her all the same. Firstly, she'd selflessly saved the lives of many children and their bus driver. Secondly, she'd not talked to the press about this act of heroism or the recent business with Jack and his brother at all.

Not one word.

Even when she was painted as a somewhat dim bulb manipulated at the hands of the Bennett brothers, she did not speak. Instead, she kept her silence and her considerable (to Olive's way of thinking) dignity.

Therefore, it rankled even deeper than it would naturally that Belle Abbot had endured a four-year marriage to an abusive husband.

Olive set the report, front and center, on Jack's desk. He was spending more than his normal amount of time in Cornwall but Gillie would have the file couriered to him the next day.

Considering its contents, Olive would usually hand deliver it to him even in Cornwall.

However, in an uncustomary display of cowardice, Olive wanted to be *nowhere near* Jack Bennett when he read that report.

She left the report on his desk and flicked off the light, her mind resolutely moving to the very large glass of wine she would consume before going to bed.

Gillie and Deborah

Gillie Matthews saw the large file marked, URGENT. PRIVATE AND CONFIDENTIAL. that Olive put on Jack's desk sometime in the night.

This was a common occurrence.

It was also common for Olive to put the most important papers front and center on Jack's desk, indicating they needed his immediate attention.

Therefore, Gillie, preparing a packet of things to be couriered to Jack at his office at The Point in Cornwall, set the file on the floor so she wouldn't forget it. She started to rifle through his desk to add other papers that needed his attention but her phone rang.

She ran from the room to get the phone and it was Jack, who spent ten minutes giving her a list of directives through which she took careful and copious notes.

While she was doing this, she was meticulously concentrating and thus missed Deborah from the administrative pool who wandered through the outer office and into Jack's.

It was part of Deborah's daily tasks to enter Jack's office and see to any filing and various and sundry other things that were slightly less important than Gillie's responsibilities.

As Jack always did, anything confidential that needed to be shredded he tossed on the floor by his desk.

Deborah found the file, not unusually stamped, URGENT. PRIVATE AND CONFIDENTIAL. She picked it up and took it to the shredder.

Without reading it (something which was not her place in any way), she shredded every last document.

In the meantime, Gillie had spent a goodly amount of her morning seeing to the priority tasks Jack had assigned her.

By the time she re-entered his office to ready his packet for the courier, she'd forgotten all about the file she'd left on the floor.

Mickey

Mickey Dempsey watched the man walk out of the hospital with his wife.

She'd slipped and fallen down the stairs.

Mickey knew this because, even though he wasn't a qualified doctor, he had a lab coat and more than a dozen different badges proclaiming his right to be in more than a dozen different places, including University College Hospital, London.

Therefore he'd snuck in and read her file.

Mickey looked at the woman whose eye was swollen shut and an ugly shade of purply-blue. She also had a cut on her lip. Furthermore, she was holding her body like it was made of glass.

Mickey had never known anyone who fell down the stairs but unless the woman had fallen down the stairs on her face, he could not imagine how she'd acquired those injuries.

Mickey *had* known a number of people (including himself, on occasion), who had been in bust-ups at pubs and footy matches. He'd even seen himself in the mirror when a fist had hit his face more than once, looking *exactly* like the woman who walked out of the hospital.

He'd also seen his own mother looking like her.

Mickey turned his attention to the man with her.

He was lean, tall and handsome, with light-brown hair and blue eyes.

His name, Mickey knew, was Calvin Cole.

He was once, Mickey knew, married to Belle Abbot, The Tiny Dynamo.

Mickey, who was a freelance investigative journalist putting together an article for whoever would buy it, knew Cole had abused his first wife rather viciously for four years.

Mickey, whose own mother suffered at the hands of Mickey's father in much the same way, knew Cole would pay for what he did to the women in his life.

The public would eat him alive at the very thought of his lifting his hand to Belle "The Tiny Dynamo" Abbot.

Much less him doing it repeatedly for four years.

And no woman in her right mind would ever get near him again.

Mickey would make absolutely certain of that.

This thought made Mickey smile to himself as he started his car to follow them.

❧ 8 ❧

ALL AN ACT

Jack

Jack strode swiftly up the path to the stables where Rachel had told him Belle was with her grandmother.

It was fair to say Jack was not very happy.

Indeed, one could even say he was incensed.

Three weeks ago Belle had, as she'd agreed, arranged for Jack to attend an appointment with her at her obstetrician.

This was not what made him angry.

Her obstetrician was quite qualified (Jack had checked) and seemed confident, knowledgeable and self-assured.

She had also told Jack that Belle's continuing morning sickness, weight loss, pallor and head pain were all quite natural.

Jack didn't believe her.

Two weeks ago, Belle had traveled all the way up to London with his mother in order that she could accompany him to a second opinion appointment with an eminent obstetrician in Harley Street.

During the second opinion with the eminent Harley Street obstetrician, Jack was told the precise same thing.

Jack didn't like it but he believed him.

This, as well, was not what made him angry.

One week ago, Belle, her mother and her grandmother had, as promised, moved into his home.

Upon her arrival, he was pleased both to note and be told by Rachel that Belle was feeling much better. The head pain was gone as was the morning sickness.

Jack saw with his own eyes that the color had come back to her face. She'd even seemed to gain weight and was beginning to form a small baby bump.

However, since she'd moved in, even though she was living under the same roof as him, Jack had barely seen her. Furthermore, the two weeks prior, he'd found it difficult to contact her.

Although he owned and ran two large conglomerates that necessitated him having a personal assistant, a personal secretary and a four-person administrative pool at his command, Belle was busier than he.

If she was not at her shop in St. Ives, she was in the workshop above her shop in St. Ives.

If she was not in her shop or workshop, she was off having coffee or shopping with her mother, grandmother or his mother or a combination of the three or, indeed, the whole lot of them.

If she was not in her shop or workshop or with any of the women, she was out on a walk and over the past week, she took Baron and Gretl.

Belle, Jack noted, walked a good deal.

If she was not in her shop, workshop, with the women or walking with his dogs, he could often see her from countless windows in the house sitting on one of the rocks by the sea surrounding The Point. She did not read. She did not write. She did not sew. She just sat, staring out to sea like not only could it speak to her but it was explaining the meaning of life and she was serenely accepting this knowledge as if it was her due.

If she was not in any of those places, she was asleep.

Belle, Jack noted as well in the last three weeks, slept a good deal.

So much so, yesterday, he'd phoned Dr. Flanagan with no small concern and asked why on earth that was happening.

He was assured this was entirely natural.

Then he'd called the eminent obstetrician in Harley Street who also assured Jack this was entirely natural.

Pregnant women, apparently, slept.

Quite a bit.

Therefore, Jack's goal of spending time with her while his child was developing in her womb was not coming to fruition.

This made Jack angry.

For he knew, without doubt, regardless of how much pregnant women slept, she was avoiding him on purpose.

That made Jack incensed.

And he would not allow it.

Not for another day.

Therefore, he and his dogs were walking to the stables to confront Belle.

Both of his dogs, incidentally, had defected to Belle without the least indication of the years of loyalty they'd offered Jack.

Jack had even caught Baron being shooed out of Belle's room last night.

He'd been walking to his own room and seen her door open. She'd actually had to scoot the dog out with her hands on his rump, so resistant was Baron to her efforts to remove him from her room.

She'd caught sight of Jack, her cheeks went pink, she'd given him a barely there wave, called goodnight and closed her door before he'd had a chance to open his mouth.

Baron, for his part, had the grace to look ashamed.

If Jack had been in any other mood he might find this amusing.

In his current mood, he did not.

He opened the door to the stables not caring that Lila was with Belle.

Although Rachel seemed to be friendly and gracious (albeit a bit strange) both to Jack's mother and to Jack, Lila was not.

Lila obviously liked his mum.

Lila just as obviously detested Jack.

And she made this abundantly clear any chance she got, which, as she was living with him, was rather a lot.

Jack had over one hundred thousand employees and day to day

(even hour to hour), he made decisions for the betterment of the business that angered many of them. Some of them he angered enough that they wrote Jack very scathing letters or sent equally scathing e-mails. Usually this was right before they resigned, if not, it was before they were sacked.

However, he didn't have to live with any of them.

At that moment, he would happily take on Lila Cavendish. He didn't care if she was going to be great-grandmother to his child.

He didn't have to wait for this opportunity, though it would not come to fruition.

As he entered the stables, Lila was climbing down the ladder to the loft wearing jeans and a chambray shirt, both of them old, worn and covered in paint.

A quick glance around showed Belle was nowhere to be found.

"She's in the loft," Lila said quietly and Jack's eyes went to her and then to the seemingly empty loft.

Lila's announcement that Belle was in the loft surprised him. When he'd taken her up there, she'd acted frightened as a rabbit.

"She's sleeping," Lila went on and Jack's gaze went back to her. "I'm glad you're here," she further surprised Jack by announcing. "I have to go to the house to call New York. I didn't want to leave her up there because when she wakes she'll go nuts and won't be able to get down without me with her. It was an actual miracle I got her to go up there in the first place. But I have to make this call. Now, you can hang out and help her down if she wakes before I return." She gave Jack a look that he couldn't read and finished, "I'll probably be a while."

With that and without another word or inviting Jack to say one, she walked by Jack and his dogs and left the stables, quietly closing the door behind her.

Jack looked back to the loft.

Then he went to the ladder and climbed up.

Once there he saw Belle was sleeping on her side on a pile of old blankets. She had one hand under her cheek, the other arm curved around her face, palm up and resting by her forehead. Her legs were curled into her stomach and her face was soft in sleep. Some of her hair was spread on the blankets but mostly it was bunched against her neck and falling in her face.

He had, he realized, never seen her sleep.

She looked about twelve years old.

With some ease, he quelled the desire to bend and pull her hair away from her face and neck.

The desire to settle in behind her and draw her sleeping body into his took much more effort to subdue.

Nevertheless, he did it.

To take his mind off Belle, he looked to the sliding doors.

They'd been opened, an easel set in front of them, a large working canvas on the easel, a small wooden table next to it covered in a mess of tubes and brushes.

Lila was painting the view he'd shown Belle.

Likely Belle had shown Lila the view to paint.

This made Jack contradictorily pleased and annoyed.

He decided to go with annoyed.

He walked to the canvas and studied it, unable to suppress his fascination at seeing a Cavendish landscape in its early phases.

Lila had a tremendous following, many museum pieces, her work was coveted by galleries worldwide and she'd been written about in a variety of art books. She'd been deemed a living, contemporary master.

Many would pay for the opportunity he had at that very moment to see her art in process and it was not lost on Jack that this was one of those rare gifts life let fall in your lap.

"James?" He heard Belle's honeyed, drowsy voice call his name and he had to stifle unwelcome desire at the sound of her drowsy voice just as he clenched his teeth in order not to correct her.

He despised it when she called him James. It was his name and there were people who called him that therefore he knew it was an irrational reaction.

He also could care less.

His eyes went to her and she was up on an arm, pulling her hair away from her face at the same time she was watching him, her face flushed with sleep.

She was wearing a red camisole top and a dark brown skirt that hit her knees and had cream and red patterns in it. The camisole and skirt showed a goodly amount of skin, now tanned from her many excursions with his dogs and her quiet, seaside reveries in the sun.

She had, quite clearly, entered the phase of pregnancy where she'd taken on what many referred to as "the glow."

For Belle, since her natural glow was considerable, the additional element was spectacular.

"Where's Gram?" she asked, pushing up to her feet which were bare, a pair of muted bronze flip-flops were lying by the blankets.

Her toes, Jack noted, were also painted a very bright red.

He took his eyes from her toes and looked into hers.

"She went to the house. She had a call to make," Jack informed her.

"Oh crap!" Belle cried, looking at the ladder, her anxiety immediately evident. "It's already time for that call? I must have been asleep *ages*. I can't *believe* it's that late and I can't *believe* I fell asleep again."

Jack watched her face work through her fear, his mind focused on the fact that he had words to say to her. They were words he'd rather not say in the hayloft where he'd become absurdly enchanted with her four months ago.

The stable floor, he could do.

He'd prefer the house.

But not the loft.

"I'll help you down," he offered as she continued to stare at the ladder at the same time she pushed her feet into her shoes, but when he made his offer, her eyes shot to him.

"I'm okay, actually," she said, throwing out an arm in a false casual gesture, an effort to hide her discomfort. "I'll just hang out and wait for Gram."

"She gave the impression she might be a while," Jack replied and he watched her wet her lips nervously but then she nodded.

"That's okay too," she lied. "I'll just, um—"

Jack cut her off, "Belle, I'll help you down."

"No, really. I'm all right up here until she gets back."

The last time she climbed down the ladder, she did it unaided.

She was also ordered by Jack to do so and she'd done it as they'd both been in the grip of a consuming passion that, looking back, seemed ludicrous.

Even so, it wasn't and Jack knew it.

However Jack had no intention of recreating that event in order to assist her now.

"Lila asked me to look after you. I'll help you down," Jack pushed and her eyes went to his shoulder, something else he once found endearing and now he loathed. He decided not to call her on it and went on, "We'll go down like the time we came up together. I'll go first and you come down right after me."

As he spoke, he watched her tanned face grow pale at the memory he too wished he didn't have to share.

"No," she whispered. "Really, I'm all right to wait for Gram."

Jack was losing patience. He had things to do, the priority being his child and getting things straight with Belle. Then he had other pressing items on his day's agenda.

He didn't have time for her phobias.

"Belle, it's a one-story ladder," he stated wearily. "If I go down first and you fall, I'll be in the position to catch you."

"I know that," she lied, still looking at his shoulder.

He walked to the ladder and swung his arm toward it. "Then let's go."

She shook her head and took a step back.

"Belle," Jack said in warning.

"Why can't you just leave me up here?" she asked, her eyes moving to his ear.

"Because we have to talk and we can't do it up here."

"I'm okay to talk up here," Belle replied instantly, latching on to an excuse to remain in the loft.

"I'm not," Jack returned.

She tilted her head and asked, "Why?"

He'd seen her tilt her head before.

Twice.

Both times it had been lying on his pillow.

He controlled his need to clench his teeth at the memory and instead replied, "I don't have time to explain. I have things to do and I'd like to have our chat and then do them."

"Okay, what do you want to talk about?" she invited.

"Not here."

"I don't under—"

Jack's patience, already wearing thin, snapped and he strode across the loft to her. She had only the chance to back up two steps before he bent at the waist and put a shoulder to her hips.

She let out a small cry but he ignored it, lifted her on his shoulder and walked back across the loft as he felt her arms wrap tightly around his waist from the back.

"What are you—?" she started to ask but her words halted as her body stilled when he turned and executed a one-armed descent of the ladder, Belle over his shoulder, his other arm wrapped firmly around her thighs.

By the time his feet hit the stable floor, her arms were so tight around him they were causing pain, her body was stiff as a board and she was completely silent except for very heavy breathing.

He walked from the ladder, bent again and set her on her feet.

When he straightened, stepped away from her and took one look at her face, it was his turn to go still.

Her fear was so stark, she actually looked in pain. So much in pain, she completely ignored Baron and Gretl who were both clamoring around her legs for attention.

Then her expression changed, the pain didn't go away, in fact, it got worse.

Far worse.

"I can't believe you just did that," she whispered, sounding like she'd just witnessed him hacking away at a body with an ax.

"I climbed down a ladder, Belle, you were safe the entire time," he told her.

She looked away, seemingly trying to compose herself.

And failing.

She pulled her hair from her face with a shaky hand and muttered, "I thought...I'd hoped..." She dropped her hand, her eyes came directly to his with no evasion and she declared, "It's true."

He ignored the unease he felt at her reaction and stated, "Belle, I don't have time for this. Say what's on your mind so I can explain why I need to speak with you and then get on with my day."

She stared at him a moment as if she'd never seen him before then he watched her squeeze her eyes shut and turn her face away.

She took in a deep breath and her gaze came back to his face. This time, she focused on his nose.

"Of course, James. You're very busy," she said softly. "What did you need to speak with me about?"

He ignored her question and asked his own, "You said, 'It's true.' What's true?"

"Nothing," she muttered. "What did you want to talk about?"

Without a reserve of patience to draw on, Jack quickly lost his again.

This made his tone sharp when he demanded, "Belle, just answer the fucking question."

He watched her body jerk and after a moment's hesitation, her chin lifted, her eyes caught his and she spoke.

"I never liked Miles," she announced and Jack braced, instinctively knowing he would not like where this was going before she continued. "I'm sorry. I know he's your brother but it's true. I don't know why I went out with him in the first place. Even after considering this question for four months, I still don't have an answer. He showed no regard for me, or my wishes, ever."

She stopped speaking and Jack waited.

Then she started speaking again.

"You did."

This time, he felt his body jerk and watched as her arms moved to wrap around her midriff in a way that looked protective before she kept speaking.

"You seemed to know I was different, I had phobias, I was neurotic and you didn't care. You acted like you *liked* it, like you thought it was cute." She threw out a hand. "Or something." She paused as she wrapped her arm back around her. "Now I know."

Jack crossed his own arms on his chest, not really feeling like getting into this, talking about Miles or her time with Jack and definitely not how she felt about it.

Even so, he found himself asking, "Now you know what?"

When she spoke again, her voice was quiet and unbelievably sad. "Now I know that night was an act. It was all an act because the Jack I met that night would never have carried me down the ladder like that, knowing he'd frighten me the way you just did."

She couldn't have scored a better hit if she'd pulled a trigger at point blank range.

Before Jack could form a reply, she kept going, softly, her voice now devoid of emotion sounding like it came from an entirely different being, not Belle.

"Now, James, what did you need to speak to me about?"

"It wasn't an act," Jack stated, again ignoring her question.

Belle didn't reply.

She just stared at him, right in the eyes as if she had no neuroses, no phobias, no anxiety, no self-consciousness and lastly, no fear of him.

At this, his unease grew.

"It wasn't an act," he repeated.

She sighed and requested quietly, "James, just tell me what you need to tell me."

He covered the two steps distance between them in an instant.

She didn't flinch or back away.

His unease shifted to something that felt a great deal like alarm. This alarm drove him to do something about her mistaken impression. Something which he found he couldn't abide, not for another second.

She was carrying his child and she thought he was a heartless bastard.

Because of this, he found he was willing to do whatever he had to do to disabuse her of that mistaken impression once and for all.

Jack looked down at her as she tipped her head back to regard him and his course, already started, became clear.

"Would you like me to prove it to you?" he asked softly.

He saw anger cross her expression before she said, "The papers think I'm a moron, I know. But you shouldn't make the same mistake because I'm not. I won't fall for your game twice."

"No, you won't," Jack agreed. "Mainly because you didn't fall for anything the first time."

"Honestly, James, I thought you were busy—" she began and may have intended to say more.

Jack would never know.

Because his hands shot out, closed at her waist and he yanked her body to his.

Then his head descended and his mouth crushed down on hers.

Her hips pulled at his hands but his arms wrapped around her and he held her tight against him.

She felt, he noted immediately, better than he remembered.

But he couldn't taste her.

She wouldn't open her mouth and she was pressing at his shoulders at the same time she was pushing her weight against his arms.

She tore her mouth from his and snapped, "What do you think you're doing?"

"Proving it wasn't an act," Jack replied calmly as she squirmed, her soft body moving against his and Jack remembered how good that felt too.

"By *kissing* me?" she screeched.

"Poppet," Jack murmured and when he did, she stilled in his arms. "That wasn't a kiss." His hand slid up her spine, her neck and into her hair, holding her head steady. "This," he muttered, "will be a kiss."

Then his mouth captured hers again.

She resisted.

He coaxed.

She kept resisting and his arm at her waist slid up her back, his fingers curling around and the tips started to stroke the side of her breast. He felt her stiff body begin to melt at his touch, he knew he was making progress and his lips moved a breath away from hers.

"Open your mouth," he demanded softly.

She shook her head and he wrapped his fist in her hair, pulling her head back gently.

"Open your mouth," he repeated against her lips.

She again shook her head.

"Poppet—" he started.

But she interrupted by whispering, "Don't call me—"

She didn't finish, as she was speaking, he muttered, "There it is."

And his parted lips took hers, his tongue sliding inside her mouth.

Jack tasted her and remembered just exactly how much he liked that as well.

Like the first time he kissed her, she responded the minute his tongue touched hers.

Her body melted into his, her hands glided up his arms, one arm wrapped around his neck, the fingers of her other hand slid into his hair.

He felt triumph shoot through him at her response and as a reward to himself, and Belle, he slanted his head and deepened the kiss.

She welcomed it, a soft, sexy noise coming from the back of her throat and filling his mouth.

At the sound of it, the feel of it, the taste of it, the memory of how much he liked the noises she made nearly four months before when he was driving deep inside her, he groaned into her mouth in return as his arm left her back.

His hand went under her camisole, slid across the silken skin at her waist and up.

His body gladly absorbed the shiver his hand caused just as one of her hands yanked his shirt free of his trousers and he felt her soft, sweet, shy touch trailing along his own skin.

His fist in her hair tightened as he felt his need for her quicken and he knew in a moment he'd carry her back up the ladder and take her on the blankets where she'd slept.

And he was looking forward to it.

He was actually *aching* to do it.

"That didn't take long."

Jack's body froze and he felt Belle's do the same when they both heard Miles's voice.

"This is a record for Belle. It's been a whole week since you two have been under the same roof," Miles carried on as Jack lifted his head and looked into the somewhat dazed but also now frightened eyes of Belle.

She pulled at his hold but his arm grew tighter as he released her hair and contained her retreat by wrapping that arm around her as well.

Miles came to stand at their sides and Jack turned his head to his brother seeing Belle do the same.

"Unless, of course, she's been sneaking to your room at night, Jack,"

Miles noted with a sneer on his mouth, addressing Jack but his eyes were glued on Belle. "But Mum wouldn't know about that, would she? She just got finished telling me it was all good, all platonic, everything was just *swell*. Even though she didn't look like it was swell. She looked like she'd rather you two were going at it like rabbits." His sneer deepened when he continued, "She'll be so pleased."

When Miles stopped speaking, his gaze moved to Jack, and Jack clipped, "Are you finished?"

"Want me to leave so you can fuck Belle in the hayloft?" Miles returned, his voice coated with derision.

"Actually, yes," Jack replied and he felt Belle's body jolt but he kept firm hold of her as he watched his hit score and Miles flinched.

Then Miles recovered. "Don't mind me. I just came to ride." His head jerked to a stall and he went on crudely, "A different kind of riding than you're about to do, of course."

Jack barely restrained an urge to shift Belle aside and do bodily harm to his brother.

Instead, he let Belle have some space but kept her in his arms and turned partially toward Miles who was moving toward the tack room.

"I believe I left a message with your assistant asking you to avoid The Point for the next six months," Jack called to his brother.

"I got the message," Miles replied carelessly.

Jack felt Belle tremble in his arms, he took away the space he'd just given her and pulled her deeper into his body.

When Miles spoke again, he sounded like a spoiled child, "However, it *is* my home and I'll come whenever I want."

"It's my home, Miles," Jack noted with quiet meaning, and he watched Miles's torso twist so he could look at his brother.

"After Dad died, your name may have been transferred to the deed but it's still my fucking home," Miles fired back.

"After Dad died, my name was transferred to the deed, making it *my* home and I let you stay here when I please," Jack returned and Miles moved to face him fully as Jack kept talking. "When I don't, you stay away. And for the next six months, you'll stay away."

Miles stared at Jack in incredulity for a moment before he spat, "You must be joking."

"No," Jack replied immediately. "I'm quite serious."

Miles's eyes shifted to Belle and they narrowed as his face filled with scorn.

"So you're saying you're kicking out your own brother so your latest fuck won't feel uncomfortable?" he asked, his voice snide.

"I wouldn't put it that way, however, Belle and her family are here, this is their home now and I intend them to feel safe and comfortable. I can imagine by your behavior four months ago and just now that Belle isn't feeling exactly safe at the moment. So yes, in essence, what you say is true." Miles opened his mouth but Jack got there before him and when he spoke his voice was low and vibrating with fury. "And, I swear to God Miles, if you call Belle my 'fuck' again or utter one more vulgar statement alluding to her, I'll rip your goddamned head off."

Jack felt Belle's stiff body go solid before it began to relax at his side but he didn't take his eyes off his brother.

Miles glared at Jack, and Jack calmly held his glare.

Though Jack did not feel calm.

He was even more incensed than he'd been when he arrived at the stables.

He was no longer angry at Belle, but at his fucking brother and, more importantly, at what his fucking brother had interrupted.

When Miles didn't move or speak, Jack did the latter. "You're still standing in my stables."

"My horse happens to be stabled here," Miles returned.

"Call Olive. Tell her where you want Mystery stabled and I'll have her transported," Jack replied.

Miles's eyes grew wide. "So now you're kicking out my horse too?"

Jack turned fully to his brother but held Belle closely at his side with an arm tight around her waist.

"I'd like to take the time to explain things to you fully, Miles, so you'll understand precisely how I feel about you right now and my intent that you and anything of yours you need is gone as soon as possible. But it's more important I have the opportunity to speak with Belle. So I'm asking you nicely to go, call Olive, tell her what you need and where you want it to be. She'll arrange everything," Jack said to his brother.

"You're asking me nicely?" Miles queried spitefully.

Jack's voice dipped low with warning when he returned, "If you'd prefer, I'll make my wishes clear *not* nicely. However, as I mentioned, I need to speak to Belle and, to make my wishes clear to you, I'd have to ask her to leave."

Without delay, Miles started to roll up the sleeves of his shirt, his eyes glued to Jack, and he challenged, "Then ask her to leave, Jack. I'd vastly prefer you make your wishes clear not nicely."

For the first time since Miles arrived, Belle spoke, she did it softly and with a good deal of disgust obvious in her tone, "I don't believe this is happening."

Jack looked down to see she was staring at Miles with unhappy astonishment.

Before Jack could speak, she said to Miles, "You need to grow up."

"Run along, Belle. Jack and I have things to discuss," Miles returned, his eyes not leaving Jack.

"I won't *run along* while you two beat each other to a pulp. What's the matter with you?" Belle snapped and Miles's eyes cut to her.

"Oh, I don't know," he drawled sarcastically. "Maybe it's the fact that my brother, who owns my fucking house and the stables where my fucking horse is housed, is standing with his arm around the woman I used to fucking date. A woman who had his fucking tongue in her fucking mouth not five minutes ago. And who's also carrying his bastard fucking child, because, within hours of meeting her, she was so gagging for him she opened her fucking legs, *that* brother is telling me to get the fuck out. Don't you think that might make you a bit peeved, gorgeous?"

Jack heard Belle gasp but it didn't register.

He'd heard enough and it had all poured forth from his brother's mouth.

He was done.

He pushed Belle behind him, his eyes locked on Miles and he muttered, "Go to the house, Belle."

He felt her hands wrap around his forearm in a firm grip.

"Don't let him—"

But Jack turned, his eyes pinned her to the spot and he repeated, "Poppet, go to the house. I'll be there shortly."

She stared at him a moment, her gaze soft and pleading, and she whispered, "Don't do this, Jack."

He felt Belle's use of his nickname slice straight through his gut.

For some irrational reason he didn't have the time to process, he realized the feeling was fierce and intensely satisfying.

He still didn't change his mind.

Instead his hand went to her jaw and his thumb slid along her cheekbone.

"Go to the house, love."

Her eyes moved to Miles then back to Jack.

She nodded, turned on her heel and ran out of the stables.

She stopped at the door and cooed at his dogs, patting her thigh. They ran to her and out the door she closed behind them.

Jack faced his brother.

"I'm going to enjoy this," Miles sneered, slowly advancing.

Jack very much doubted it.

And, in the end, Jack was right.

❦ 9 ❦

MULTIPLE PERSONALITIES

Belle

Belle woke on her side in her big, soft bed at The Point feeling for the first time in her week of living there, strangely pleasant, cozy and safe.

Then it registered there was warmth at her back and a heavy weight on her waist.

She opened her eyes and looked down to see a man's hand (not *any* man's hand, she'd know that strong, long-fingered hand anywhere, it was James's) dangling at her waist. She saw in the sunlight streaming through her windows that the knuckles were raw and torn, painful-looking scabs forming at the splits.

She no sooner processed this disturbing fact when she heard dog tags and two canine heads popped up on her side of the bed.

One darker (Baron), one blonder (Gretl).

She had not gone to sleep last night with the dogs in her room.

She had also not gone to sleep with James in her bed.

Indeed, she had only seen James once after she ran from the stables to tell Joy her two sons were fighting.

Yes, she told on two grown men, what else was she going to do?

Half an hour after she'd run from the stables, Belle, Rachel and Lila stood on the front steps and watched James load a far worse for the wear Miles into Joy's Mercedes. When he'd accomplished that, James left Joy to drive Miles to the hospital, Rachel running down to the car to accompany her.

James had walked slowly up the steps, fury in his gaze, as Lila and Belle watched him in open-mouthed shock.

He hadn't said a word but his glittering eyes sliced through them making them both take a *large* step away from the door.

He'd then locked himself in his study.

Several hours later, Joy and Rachel had come back.

Miles had not.

Joy had gone directly to her room.

Lila made Rachel and Belle leave her alone. A half an hour later, Lila herself went up, taking a tray of soup, sandwiches and a bottle of wine with her.

By the time Rachel and Belle went to bed, Lila nor Joy nor James had emerged.

Now, somehow, James was in bed with her.

Belle reached out an arm, curled her fingers around the edge of the mattress, preparing to catapult herself from the bed.

Before she could succeed in this endeavor, James's arm, resting lightly at her waist, became an iron band, hauling her into his hard body.

Belle froze and felt his face burrowing into her hair.

"We have to talk," he growled.

Holy heck, her mind breathed.

"What are you doing in my bed?" her mouth asked.

"Containment," he answered.

"What?"

"Containment," he repeated. "Given the chance, you'll escape. I'm not going to let that happen."

Holy heck, her mind breathed again.

Belle had dealt with a number of different James Bennetts in the last three weeks. The jerky one (at their first meeting, post-fling). The demanding one (at the doctor appointments). The broody one (the times he wasn't being something else). The impatient one, which was a variation of the jerky one (at the stables). The sexy one (also at the stables). And the loving one (again, at the stables).

This, she could tell, was an all-new James Bennett.

Therefore she thought it best to proceed with caution.

"Can I please get out of bed?" she inquired.

His body moved away and she thought that was an affirmative response.

She was wrong.

His hand pressed her so her back was to the bed and he loomed over her, up on an elbow, his other arm resting on her midriff.

"No," he replied unnecessarily.

She looked in his eyes to see they were still slightly heavy with sleep but nonetheless alert. She couldn't read them but she felt a curl of fear all the same.

So her attention moved to his ear.

When it did, he murmured, "That's a good sign."

She didn't know what he meant but she also was *not* going to ask.

"Um, I'm finding this a bit weird," she confided to his ear.

"Too bad. I have three things to say to you and you're going to listen. Only then can you get out of bed and start your day."

"Oh...kay," she replied hesitantly, hoping with all her heart this would be fast and relatively painless.

He was weirding her out!

"First, if you even see Miles, you get away from him and you call me immediately."

That curl of fear did an ugly little twist.

"What does that mean?" Belle asked.

"This isn't question time, Belle. This is me talking to you, you listening and giving a definitive indication that you understand *exactly* what I'm saying to you."

Belle went silent and just stared.

Definitely weirding her out.

"Do you understand what I just said to you?" he inquired.

She understood.

Oh boy, did she.

All she could do was nod.

"Good. Second, you're avoiding me and it's pissing me off. I didn't ask you to move here so you could enjoy the seaside. I asked you to move here so I could share in the experience of your pregnancy."

"Actually, you didn't *ask* at all. You *told*—" Belle started to correct him but then clamped her mouth shut when his brows drew together in a scary way.

When he was assured she wouldn't be foolish enough to utter another word, he continued.

"You'll spend time with me. You'll eat breakfast with me. You'll eat dinner with me. If you're in the mood for a walk and I'm in the house, you'll find me and, if I can, I'll go with you. I'll take you to your shop. When you're finished, you'll phone and I'll come and pick you up."

As he spoke, Belle realized she was having difficulty breathing.

"Now, is *that* understood?" he finished.

"James—" she whispered, and his eyes started glittering with anger so she stopped speaking (she didn't know what she was going to say anyway).

"You called me Jack yesterday," he informed her tersely.

Did she?

She didn't remember that.

"I did?" she was still whispering.

"Yes, you did," he returned.

"Oh," she breathed, his gaze cut to her mouth and for some strange reason, his face darkened (this, she found, his face did a lot at the weirdest times) before his eyes came back to hers.

"Apparently, if I kiss you, you'll call me by my fucking name."

She didn't want to be reminded of that kiss.

In fact, last night, when her mind wasn't occupied with worrying about Joy (and, she had to admit, James, and, she further had to admit, Miles), it had been occupied with doing anything *but* thinking about that incredibly delicious, mind-blowing kiss.

Therefore, in an attempt not to discuss the kiss, she did something unwise.

"I thought your name was James," she said and she was *still* whispering but, even so, she'd forgotten to keep quiet because his eyes narrowed unhappily.

Therefore, she again clamped her mouth shut.

"I'll bear that in mind," he muttered.

She knew he was ignoring her idiot comment and talking about his kissing her causing her to call him Jack and her eyes grew round at what *that* might mean.

She vowed (silently) never to call him James again and kept her peace.

"Now, give me some indication that you understand the second point," he demanded.

Belle nodded again.

"Excellent," he clipped, sounding like it was not "excellent" at all and then he kept talking. "My last point stems from our discussion yesterday. Regardless of what you witnessed between Miles and I in the stables, what happened between you and I four months ago was *not* an act. Miles may have been competing for you but I wasn't. You clearly don't realize how offensive your accusation was when you made it the morning after the night we shared. If you did realize, you wouldn't speak of it as it's no less offensive now. You won't speak of it again."

Belle was finding it hard not to pant at the low and rumbly tone of his voice.

It was a variation on the voice he'd used when he'd promised her she could trust him.

It was also very like the voice he'd used when he'd threatened his brother right before he beat the crap out of him.

This suggested to her there was not only feeling behind his words but deep emotion.

And she didn't know how to take that.

She had no chance to figure it out, he spoke again.

"Do I make myself understood?" he asked.

Without hesitation, she nodded again.

"I'll be unhappy if we have to discuss any of this again," he told her and she wondered what he meant by "unhappy" considering he seemed *very* unhappy at that precise moment.

"We won't have to discuss it again," she promised.

He stared at her so hard, even though she wanted to, she couldn't move her eyes from his.

Then she felt him relax beside her.

"Good," he murmured.

She was about to ask him if she could get out of bed but his chin dipped down, his eyes trailing her body and he shifted slightly back. His gaze stopped at the small bump at her belly and his hand went to rest there, heavy and hot.

Belle caught her breath at the intimacy of this gesture and fought against the return of pleasant, cozy, safe feeling she had when she'd woken.

"Does he move?" Jack asked gently.

Belle knew instantly she had a new Jack and this one sounded like the loving one.

She steeled herself against how much she liked the gentle, loving James Bennett *and* she steeled herself against the magnetic pull he emitted when he was in this mood.

"No, he hasn't moved yet," she answered and Jack's eyes came back to hers but his hand didn't leave her belly.

"You think he's a he?" Jack asked and she nodded.

"But I don't want to know. I want to be surprised," she told him. "You can know if you want."

His gaze moved back to her belly as he murmured, "I don't want to know."

Belle swallowed at the sweet sensation his murmur caused and was about to ask if she could get out of bed again mainly because she *really* needed to get out of bed.

And away from him.

She was finding this taxing.

Why she seemed to be able to handle herself more assuredly when Jack was being terrible and why she seemed entirely unable to cope when Jack was being anything but terrible, she had no idea.

She just couldn't.

She wanted to cover his hand with hers.

She wanted to lean up and kiss his strong, dark-stubbled jaw.

She wanted to run her hand down his bare chest.

No, she wanted to run her tongue down his bare chest.

While she was thinking these thoughts (and staring at his chest), Jack's eyes came back to her face.

"Have you thought of any names?" he asked, her gaze jerked to his collarbone as her thoughts, with some effort, focused on his question and she licked her lips.

She didn't want to talk about baby names with Jack while they were in bed together.

How she *was* talking about baby names while they were in bed together, she had no idea.

She'd much prefer to write her list down in an e-mail and send it to him.

"Belle," Jack called and she knew the e-mail name exchange idea was out.

Her eyes rose from their mindless study of his collarbone to his face and she blurted, "Lucas for a boy, Olivia for a girl." Then, worried he wouldn't like those names, she went on, "I also like Harry." When he showed no response, just watched her face silently, she kept going, "And Noah." He again didn't speak so she carried on, "And Nathan."

"Nathan," he murmured and the way he said that name, the way it sounded with his deep voice wrapped around it, she knew she'd battle to the death to give her child that name.

"Nathan," she whispered and watched his eyes drop to her mouth.

Then she watched his face grow soft and gentle, a look she hadn't seen in four months.

There was something profound happening. The kind of profound something that happened when a mother and father decided what to name their child.

She felt it slide warmly through her, taking over, taking control, and before she knew it (or could stop herself), her hand moved to cover his on her belly.

His gaze lifted to hers and her hand kept going, sliding up his forearm.

"Belle," he muttered and her hand glided up his bicep.

"Jack," she whispered, and as she was studying his mouth she missed the flash in his eyes and her fingers curled around his shoulder.

Still controlled by the moment and not her own neurotic mind, she lifted up and put her mouth on his.

And she kissed him.

Kissed him.

She didn't know what she was doing. She wasn't herself and she had no idea what this New Belle intended to get from her behavior.

But Jack knew exactly what he wanted and the minute her lips touched his, he took it.

His torso pressed hers into the bed, his arm wrapped around her waist and he rolled to his back, taking her with him, his mouth locked on hers, his tongue sliding inside.

His hands drove into the hair on either side of her head and held her to him as she tilted her head, her tongue dancing wildly with his.

This felt so good, her belly flipped then melted and her body molded to his. Her arm wrapped around him and she moved to her side, urging him to come with her (and he did) so her hands could roam the skin and muscle of his back.

He felt good.

Actually, he felt *great*.

As she touched him, the kiss, mildly controlled, went out of control.

She had invited it and when it came she welcomed it and gave back as much as she got, loving every second.

Only when Jack's hand yanked up her nightgown and slid into her panties at her behind did sanity return in an ice-cold, *what-on-earth-are-you-doing* rush.

She pulled from his arms, scrambled from the bed and stood at its side staring at Jack, who'd come up on a forearm but his body had gone still.

"I'm sorry," she mumbled. "So, so sorry. I'm sorry." He just stared at her, she could see his chest rising and falling, his defined stomach muscles contracting with his deep breathing, and she kept talking, "Hormones. It's hormones. I'm so sorry."

She stood there feeling like an idiot and her gaze went from his passion-filled eyes to his chest which was something she liked. So it skittered to his nose which was something else she liked. So it went to his shoulder which was safe when he was wearing clothes, when he wasn't it was all sinewy and luscious so she settled on his ear.

"Belle—" he started but she blathered on.

"Okay, so, this is obviously going to be weird, considering our brief history. So, for this to work, um...me being here, living with you, maybe we should have rules."

"Belle—" he repeated, and she still didn't look at him when she kept talking.

"Like, you know, maybe you shouldn't be allowed to sleep with me, or, um, wake up with me, or, um...both. That's a good rule."

"Belle—" he said yet again but she kept right on talking.

"And, maybe you're not allowed to kiss me anymore."

"Are you allowed to kiss me?" he asked and she heard it, plain as day, there was amusement in his voice.

Her eyes flew to his face and she saw it plain as day there too.

"No," she answered. "No kissing. None at all. Either you or me."

"I don't agree to that rule," he retorted, throwing back the covers.

Her body went solid in fear and she realized, again too late, that she should have run from the room or locked herself in the bathroom or thrown herself out of a window or *something*.

She still had time but her feet refused to move.

She watched him get out of bed. She noted he was wearing a pair of dark-gray, drawstring pajama bottoms that looked *way too good* on his behind and then he started walking around it, toward her.

"Either me not kissing you or you not kissing me. *Especially* you not kissing me," he stressed and stopped in front of her, his hand coming to her jaw, his voice dipping low and rumbly. "You've never kissed me like that before. That was nice, poppet."

"Another rule!" Belle announced way too loudly, taking a step back and away from his hand, which dropped to his side. "You can't call me 'poppet' anymore."

He grinned. "I don't agree to that, either."

She blinked at him. "Well, do you agree to the first one, the no sleeping together?"

"Certainly," he replied without hesitation and her body relaxed only to go ramrod straight again when he continued, "Unless I'm in the mood."

"The mood?" she whispered and he took the step toward her that she'd taken back and both his hands came to her jaw, holding her captive.

"The mood," he repeated and went on terrifyingly. "And you should know, I'm guessing I'll be in the mood quite a bit, poppet."

"This isn't funny," she whispered, her heart in her voice, but even though she knew he could hear it (he *had* to be able to hear it), he smiled.

"You're right, it isn't funny. I'm also not laughing."

"You're smiling," she accused.

"That I am," he agreed.

"Stop doing it," she demanded.

"I can't."

"Why not?" she asked in a voice edged with hysteria.

"Because now I know," he answered.

Her body stiffened to the consistency of marble but her mouth still was able to form the words. "You know what?"

"I know why you're avoiding me," he replied.

"I'm not avoiding you," she semi-lied.

She kind of was.

Heck, who was she kidding? She definitely was and had been doing it for three weeks.

"You're avoiding me, Belle. And you're doing it because you want what we started in the stables, what we started in that bed, what we had four months ago. You want it just as badly as you're terrified of it."

"It's hormones," she semi-lied again.

It *could* be hormones, what did she know? She was no pregnancy expert (although she was learning).

"It wasn't hormones four months ago."

He had her there.

"I have another rule," she began, jerking her face from his hands and taking another step back, running into Baron, stopping and lifting her chin to Jack. "No talking about four months ago."

"Yesterday, I would have agreed to that." He took another step toward her, negating the distance she'd gained, and leaned in. "Today. No fucking way."

"Why?" she fairly shouted.

"Because now I want to know, when we both know how good it was then, how good it can be again, why you're so damned scared of it. So scared of it, you'd latch on to any excuse you could find and walk away from it, and me, without looking back."

She lifted her chin further and lied, yet again (she was seriously going to hell), "I'm not scared of it."

"You bloody well are. You're scared out of your skin."

"Am not," she snapped.

"Oh yes you are."

"No...I...am...not!" she shouted.

He got even closer, his hands coming to her hips and dared, "Then kiss me."

Her body did a little jerk and she stammered, "Wh-what?"

"If you're so in control then kiss me. Prove to me you can take it or leave it."

She shook her head. "I'm not going to kiss you."

"Scared?" he taunted.

"No!" she snapped.

She saw his eyes smile even though his mouth did not. She remembered the first time she'd seen him do that and just how beautiful she thought it was then.

It was no less beautiful now.

"Liar," he muttered, breaking into her thoughts.

"I'm not lying," she lied.

He didn't reply.

She watched him warily.

He studied her with amusement dancing in his green eyes.

Finally he whispered, "This is going to be interesting."

Belle didn't like the sound of that.

Before she could find something, *anything* to say to convince him he was wrong, he bent his neck and kissed her forehead.

But he only moved away a scant inch when he said softly, "All right, poppet, I'll let you off the hook for now."

"What does that mean?" she asked in a shaky voice.

His hand moved from her hip to cup her jaw and his thumb slid along her cheekbone. "That means I'll see you at breakfast."

He bent again to touch his mouth to her trembling lips and, once he'd done that, his thumb trailed along her lower one.

Without another word, he turned and walked to the door.

Hand on the knob, he looked at her.

"Do you want the dogs?" he asked.

Belle, standing like a statue, tilted her head down to look at Baron and Gretl who were both sitting at her sides, tongues lolling happily, grinning up at her, tails sweeping the floor.

She mutely looked back to Jack.

He'd asked if she wanted the dogs like he asked it every morning during their years-long relationship before popping off to get ready for breakfast.

Not like they'd had their first ever Jack's Multiple Personalities Melodrama in her bedroom.

She wondered to herself if he was mad.

Then, for some bizarre reason, she answered him out loud, "Yes."

At her answer, he gave her a sexy grin, one she'd never seen before, one that looked almost playful.

Her belly did a delightful dip.

"See you at breakfast, poppet."

He closed the door.

She stared at it.

Then she looked down at Baron.

Then at Gretl.

When Belle's attention turned away from him, Baron woofed.

When Belle's attention turned away from her, Gretl licked her hand.

"For some reason," she told the dogs, her voice still tremulous, her fingers moving to scratch behind their ears, "I think I'm in trouble."

Baron woofed again and Belle could swear he was agreeing with her.

❦ ❦ ❦

Belle walked on leaded feet to the breakfast table, dillydallying in the hopes that she'd sit down just in time for Jack to eat his last bite of toast. That way she could keep her promise without actually keeping her promise.

This was a risky endeavor.

The downside was Jack cottoning on to her game and getting scary angry.

The upside was Belle keeping her sanity.

For some reason, she lost it when she was with Jack.

All her life, she'd been a sane person. Very sane. In fact, her mother and grandmother might even say *too* sane.

With Jack, she was *not*.

Considering she'd soon be responsible for another living being, she thought it important to behave like a sensible adult, not a brazen hussy.

She was already losing the Mother of the Year award and she hadn't even had her child.

She'd done everything she could to delay her arrival at the breakfast table.

She'd showered, done her makeup and styled her hair all twisted softly back in a big bun at her nape, a few tiny braids blended in, some wispy hairs here and there at her face and neck. Very romantic and inno-cent-virgin looking.

She then spent a good deal of time deciding what to wear.

Since the weather had been quite warm and sunny, she decided on a violet-colored cotton sundress that she'd designed. It had an empire waist, a deep V-neck with a ruffled trim and a slight A-lined skirt that hit a couple of inches above the knee. She paired this with silver, flat Capri sandals with a rose at the toe.

Although the deep V-neck was *slightly* risqué, it was a sweet Audrey Hepburn type of outfit and everyone knew Audrey Hepburn was no hussy.

As she approached the door to the dining room, she saw movement down the hall and stopped in the door to watch Jack walking toward her.

Clearly her efforts at dillydallying had all been for naught.

He had a sleek, black mobile phone to his ear that looked like something George Jetson might own. He was wearing charcoal-gray trousers with an elegant pinstripe, a crisp, light-blue shirt and a black, midnight-blue and gray patterned tie was hanging loose from his open collar.

His eyes were on her.

She felt a trill race up her spine that ran along her scalp and made her shiver.

She realized she'd frozen when he stopped close and put a hand lightly to her waist.

Only then did she understand her mistake. She should have been cool, calm and casual and given him a jaunty wave before entering the dining room.

Instead, she'd stood gawking at him like a lovesick teenager.

Proof positive that she lost her sanity around Jack.

"Right," he said into his phone, his eyes never leaving hers. "E-mail it. I'll be in the office this afternoon and we'll discuss it then."

He disconnected without saying good-bye and his gaze traveled the length of her.

When they came back to her face, he asked softly. "One of yours?"

Belle, who had fallen into a Gentle Jack Trance, nodded.

"It's lovely," he murmured on a small smile.

"Thank you," she murmured back and saw his smile deepen.

She was staring at his mouth, her own lips parted, her eyes glazing over, her body starting to lean into his magnetic pull when she heard her grandmother's call.

"Morning, kids!"

Belle's body jerked and she snapped out of the trance. As she did this, she saw Jack's mouth go tight and his head turned to look in the dining room.

Belle turned too and she saw everyone there, including Yasmin. And all of them were watching Jack and Belle like they were viewing an awe-inspiring, award-winning play.

"Yasmin." Belle smiled at the other woman shyly. She hadn't seen her since that awful morning and she hoped her reaction to Belle being pregnant with Jack's child and living at The Point would be a far sight better than Miles's had been. "It's lovely to see you."

Yasmin responded as Jack's hand moved to the small of Belle's back and he guided her into the room.

"Not as lovely as it is to see you. After the drama and the resulting media brouhaha, I thought I might be *persona non grata* at your shop. Now, seeing as Jack got you up the duff, I can come shopping anytime."

Belle did a little stutter step at her words and heard Joy emit a soft giggle, her mother laughed outright but her grandmother was glowering at Jack's hand at Belle's back.

Jack pressed more firmly into her back, his warm body got protectively closer and he led her to the empty chair to the right hand side of the head of the table. He pulled it back for her and she sat in it, looking up and over her shoulder at him as he assisted her with pushing it back in.

Then she watched him seat himself at the head of the table.

She recognized she was falling into another trance so she shook herself out of it and looked at the table.

Everyone was watching her again.

She realized she didn't reply to Yasmin and belatedly, she said softly, "You're always welcome at the shop."

"Goody," Yasmin smiled. "I'm coming today. I hope you're stocked up because I got my allowance from my trust fund last week and I can't ask Daddy for a supplement unless I use every last penny." She turned to Gram. "I do that every month. It drives Daddy insane."

"I bet it does," Gram mumbled but she was grinning.

"Well, he was practically absent during my childhood. He was two hours late to my first wedding because of some urgent meeting. And he didn't show *at all* at my second wedding because someone was doing something in Geneva that he had to sort. A monthly supplement soothes the pain," Yasmin blithely replied, her words meant to be amusing but Belle heard the hurt under them and her gaze slid to Jack.

Jack was watching Yasmin, a look of tender concern on his handsome face and at the sight of it, Belle's stomach did another sweet, little dip.

His head turned, he caught her gazing at him, she felt the warmth hit her cheeks and she immediately looked down at her place setting.

"Belle," he called and her eyes went to his ear.

"Yes?" she asked.

He didn't speak for a moment before he said quietly, "Poppet, look at me."

With some effort, her eyes met his.

And he didn't look annoyed or impatient.

He looked amused and affectionate.

It was a good look.

She licked her lips.

He inquired. "What did you do with my dogs?"

"Your dogs?" she asked, forgetting entirely that he had dogs, that she liked his dogs, that she spent a good deal of time with his dogs, and she also forgot her first name.

"Baron and Gretl?" he prompted, his mouth twitching. "I left them in your room this morning."

She gave herself a mini-mental shake and told herself to pull it together.

"Yes, of course, um...I let them out."

"Did they eat?"

"Eat?" she parroted stupidly as she'd again lost the thread of the conversation because she'd become fascinated with watching his mouth form words.

"Yes, eat," his mouth said then he grinned.

She tore her eyes from his mouth and muttered, "No, I didn't think of that." Her gaze lifted to his eyes. "Do you want me to go do that now?"

He shook his head but looked like he was trying not to laugh. "No, love, you don't have to feed my dogs."

"Okay," she whispered and for some reason this made him chuckle.

Belle hadn't heard his chuckle in a long time and she forgot how very much she liked it.

Elaine, the housekeeper, came in at that point and as Belle and Jack ordered their breakfasts, Belle decided it was a much better plan to engage someone else in conversation before she made an even bigger idiot out of herself.

However, when her eyes moved to the others at the table, they were all again watching her and Jack. Yasmin was doing it with a broad smile. Joy was pressing her lips together but you could see her eyes dancing. Mom was looking at Jack in a way that Belle just knew she was getting a feeling in her bones. Gram was glaring at Jack *and* Belle with a look on her face that heralded Belle, at some point during the day, being given the third degree.

And therefore Belle decided instantly the table was no safer than Jack.

Though, Belle had been wrong about the third degree coming from Gram at some point during the day.

She'd decided to dish it out right then.

"Can I ask, at this juncture, what you were doing in Belle's room this morning?" Gram demanded of Jack.

Belle felt her heart sink and she knew it was only courtesy that drove Jack to answer her grandmother.

"We had a chat."

"I can *see* you had a *chat*. Everyone can *see* you had a *chat*," Gram snapped. "Yesterday, you two were entirely different beings than you are right now. *If* you were in each other's presence, which was rare, the animosity veritably crackled. At least it did from *you*." Her eyes narrowed on Jack. "Today you two are all sweetness and light. What gives?"

"Mom, cut it out." Belle's mother, as usual, unwisely decided to go head to head with Gram and entered the conversation.

Gram glared at Mom. "Don't tell me to cut it out."

"I'm telling you to cut it out," Mom returned. "Leave them be."

"I won't *leave them be*. Leaving them be got Belle knocked up!" Gram's voice was rising.

Belle put her elbow to the table and rested the side of her head in her hand.

Regardless of her embarrassed posture, her family didn't let up.

"In her current condition that can hardly happen again," Mom returned, Gram's eyes bugged out and Belle closed her own eyes before opening them again when her grandmother retorted.

"That's not the point!" Gram snapped.

"Then what *is* the point?" Mom snapped back.

"I don't know!" Gram shouted and looked at Jack. "*You* were present at this *chat*. Maybe *you* can tell us the blasted point!"

"Oh lordy," Mom muttered at the same time Yasmin giggled and Joy mumbled, "Oh dear."

Belle wished silently for the floor to open up and swallow her just as Jack spoke.

"I think the point, right now, Lila, is that you're embarrassing your granddaughter and I'll ask you to stop doing it."

Belle's head snapped up and her neck twisted so fast it made her dizzy.

The air in the room took on an edge.

"Jack…" Belle whispered.

His eyes moved to hers and he said gently, "I'm speaking to Lila now, poppet."

"You shouldn't rile her," Belle advised.

He turned his torso toward her and asked, "Are you enjoying this conversation?"

She hesitated before responding honestly, "Not really, no."

He turned back to the table, his gaze moving in the direction of her grandmother and stated firmly, "Then this conversation is over."

Belle chanced a glance at the table and saw Gram looked fit to be tied but Mom was grinning ear to ear.

"Told you!" Mom announced, pointing at Gram then her finger moved to Belle. "Told you too."

"Told them what?" Joy asked and Belle saw her mother's body give a small twitch as her face lost a goodly amount of color.

She dropped her hand and muttered, "Nothing."

Everyone at the table was silent for several long moments.

The only one who moved was Jack and this was so he could pour Belle some coffee.

Belle plucked up the courage to break the silence and said in a quiet voice to Jack, "I don't drink coffee because of the baby."

He stopped himself from filling his own cup and replied, "Of course."

He put down the silver service and took her cup from her place, lifted it to his lips and took a sip.

Belle watched Jack sip from a cup she didn't even use but was somehow still hers and felt, weirdly, the intimacy of this act almost equaled him putting his hand on her pregnant belly for the first time.

The pleasant feeling this gave her was so overpowering it scared her half to death.

She tore her attention from Jack drinking coffee and caught Yasmin openly staring at her with a huge grin on her face.

Then Yasmin declared, "I'm coming to breakfast every day. This is fun!"

Belle didn't think it was fun. Belle thought it was torture.

She didn't share this.

Instead, she caught Joy gazing at her with a bright but pensive look on her face.

"I must say," Joy added, not moving her gaze from Belle. "I agree. I'm glad you're all here. It definitely livens up the place."

Belle knew Joy liked her mom and Gram, like, a lot.

Belle also knew she wasn't really referring to them.

She felt a warm rush slide through her system and she smiled at Jack's mum.

Joy smiled back.

❧ 10 ❧

BELLE AND JACK AND THE SEA

Belle

Belle sat on a thick, woolen rug on the rocks outside The Point watching and listening to the waves smashing against the cliffs.

She was silently asking the sea for peace.

Unusually, the sea wasn't giving it to her.

That was because her life had again turned on its head.

And it was all Jack's fault.

After breakfast two days before, he had, as he'd told her he would do, driven her to her shop in St. Ives.

She didn't understand *why* he needed to drive her to her shop. She was temporarily pregnant, not temporarily blind.

However, she did not ask him this.

The drive had been silent which made Belle intensely uncomfortable. What made her more uncomfortable was that it appeared *not* to make Jack uncomfortable in the slightest.

He'd pulled his sleek, maroon Jaguar around the cobbled street that lined the sea, and without her giving him the first direction, stopped at the winding path that led to her shop in town.

She'd turned to him to offer her gratitude for the ride and saw he was already turned toward her.

Before she could speak, he did. "I'm going to London now, poppet. I'll be home late. Rachel's picking you up."

Belle nodded, a little surprised he was driving to London and back in a day (it was over five hours away) but she wasn't going to comment.

She was about to twist away to exit the car when his hand came up, his fingers curled around her neck and he pulled her close as he leaned in.

He touched his mouth to hers and when his head moved back a half inch, he murmured, "Have a good day."

She nodded again and replied, "You too," but her reply came out all breathy like she'd just run the two hundred yard dash in record time.

This made him grin which made a trill slide up her spine which made her shiver, which she knew he felt because his grin deepened to a smile.

Then he'd slanted his head and kissed her again.

This kiss was not a touch of the lips but harder and longer. If not an open-mouthed, make-out fest, it still worked on her. By the time he lifted his head, she wasn't breathing.

"Go to work," he muttered.

She nodded and with all due haste exited the car.

She knew, as she walked around the hood of the Jag, along the sidewalk and up the winding, cobbled alley that he watched her. She knew this because, the entire time, her scalp was tingling.

Her day was uneventful except for Yasmin, who came and spent an unbelievable amount of money on clothes and jewelry. Then she spent an even more unbelievable amount of time hanging out with Belle and chatting like they'd known each other for years. She eventually left because, she told Belle, she had a meeting with her divorce attorney. Belle had learned during the chatting that marriage number two was even worse than marriage number one and marriage number one had been *nothing* to write home about.

By the time Belle went to bed that night, Jack hadn't returned.

By the time Belle woke up the next morning, she knew he had.

She knew this because the front of his body was pressed into the back of hers, his arm was around her waist, his hand resting on the bump of her belly.

She might have been idiotically slow on numerous occasions with Jack that led to life-altering circumstances, but she was learning.

Although she allowed herself a very brief moment to enjoy his warmth and, most especially, his hand resting protectively against their child (and she allowed their child a moment to feel that protection too), she went into action.

Carefully but swiftly, she exited the bed and walked directly to the bathroom not looking back to see if he woke and only cursorily patting Baron's and Gretl's heads as she went.

Then she spent an inordinate amount of time in the bathroom. Brushing her teeth far longer than necessary. Flossing with obsessive precision. Washing her face and slathering it with a masque. Sitting on the toilet seat (fretting) for ten minutes to let the masque work. And taking the longest shower in history.

All of this was in hopes that Jack would leave before she was done in the bathroom.

When she could delay no more, she walked out to see the bed was empty.

She felt a wave of relief which was followed immediately by a surge of intense disappointment.

She tamped down this insane reaction and got ready for her day.

As it was too early for her mother and grandmother (both late risers) and Joy (also, Belle learned, not exactly a morning person), Belle ate breakfast alone.

Jack joined her when she was sipping a decaf coffee, staring out the windows to the sea and attempting to keep her mind completely blank (although this wasn't working, as such).

His hair was slightly damp, he was wearing jeans, a snug-fitting, long-sleeved, dark gray T-shirt and carrying a newspaper.

He looked really good (criminally good) in his T-shirt and she noted dazedly he obviously liked dark gray and black because, outside of blue jeans, that was nearly all she'd seen him wear.

As she was making this insignificant mental note and staring at him, he got close and bent down, kissing her upturned nose.

"Morning, poppet," he said softly when his face moved away.

"Morning," she whispered, feeling like an idiot even as she made an additional mental note that she liked him kissing her nose and she watched his eyes slide to her coffee cup.

"I thought you didn't drink coffee," he remarked.

"Decaf," she replied, his lips curled up in a barely there but still unfairly attractive grin and he moved to his seat and threw the paper by his place setting as he settled in.

Elaine came in, took his breakfast order and Belle resumed her contemplation of the sea, trying to still her racing heart and her equally racing thoughts.

"Belle," Jack called and her gaze moved to his ear but she forced herself to look into his eyes before he called her on it, something she knew he'd do. "I need to show you something and I don't want you to get upset."

She braced and kept silent. His voice was gentle, not impatient, but still, she couldn't help but worry.

"It's going to happen quite a bit and you're going to have to learn to ignore it," he continued.

"What's going to happen?" she asked, and he flipped open the paper and showed it to her.

She stared in horror at what she saw.

There was a full-color picture of her and Jack taken through the windshield of his car, his fingers wrapped around her neck, their bodies close, their faces even closer because they were kissing.

Goodness gracious!

The whole world was going to see a picture of her kissing Jack!

Her eyes skittered to the caption and it read, *Making Up, Britain's Sexiest Tycoon Wins Back The Tiny Dynamo.*

"Holy heck," she breathed and Jack flipped the paper shut and threw it to the side.

"Ignore it," he commanded.

Her eyes lifted to his. "We were kissing."

"Ignore it."

"In your car," she continued.

"Belle, ignore it."

"I can't ignore it!" she cried. "Everyone's going to know! They're going to know I'm pregnant. They're going to know we're living together. They're going to—"

Jack cut her off, "Yes, they are, and you've got to learn not to care, love."

Her eyes grew wide and she asked, "How? How do you learn not to care about *that*?"

"You just do," he replied calmly and she made a noise that sounded like she was being strangled so he leaned toward her. "Poppet, they're not going to stop. I hate to tell you this but they're *never* going to stop. I know. They've been at me all my life. And you're too damned beautiful and way too photogenic for your own good. So they won't leave you alone either. Once we have our child, they'll go after him too. You need to learn to ignore it and get on with your life."

For a moment, she forgot about her new dire predicament mainly because he'd called her "too damned beautiful."

James Bennett thought *she*, Belle "Meek and Mild" Abbot was "too damned beautiful?"

She couldn't believe it.

"Belle," he called again and she realized her eyes had glazed over so she focused on him, and once she did, he asked, "Are you going to be all right?"

She stared at him a moment and gave her body a shake before she sat back and resumed sipping her coffee.

Her attention went to the sea and she answered on a mini-lie, "Yes. I'm not all right now but I will be."

This was a mini-lie because she had no idea how to make herself "all right" with this latest mess. But she felt a trill race up her spine so her eyes slid to Jack to see he was smiling at her with an expression on his face that looked a whole lot like pride.

"Good," he murmured.

A warm feeling slid into the pit of her belly and settled.

There it was. She'd found a way to make herself "all right" and it wasn't difficult at all.

Jack had eaten his breakfast while Belle sipped her coffee and they did this in silence, Jack again acting as if this was the most natural thing in the world. He'd simply eaten and read through the paper while Belle sat silent and contemplative beside him.

When he was done, he took her to work again and she knew, even before Jack parked (he didn't stop and idle on the street this time), that it was going to be a feeding frenzy.

And it was.

The minute Jack stopped, the paparazzi surrounded the car.

Jack turned to Belle instantly.

She couldn't read his eyes through the green tinted lenses of his gold-framed aviator sunglasses, but she *could* see his jaw was tight right before he ordered, "Do not get out of the car until I open your door."

She nodded, slid her enormous, black framed and lensed designer sunglasses more firmly up the bridge of her nose and did what she was told.

When she cleared the door, Jack's arm slid around her shoulders. He slammed the door, bleeped the car locked and strode forward confidently, taking her right along with him.

As they walked, she kept her head bowed and her body turned slightly into his.

Jack didn't bow his head. He walked like normal (albeit with Belle plastered to his side). He faced forward, his strides wide as if there weren't photographers taking pictures and reporters shouting questions.

Without her giving him directions, he guided her directly to her shop and took the keys out of her hands to let them in.

She took off her glasses and moved to the alarm panel as he closed and locked the door.

The flashes from the cameras were coming through her shop windows as she turned from the alarm and found Jack right there.

As if they weren't the focus of a dozen prying eyes, he got close, his hands came to her jaw and tipped her face up to his.

"Explain your average day," he demanded apropos of nothing, and even though she thought this was a weird question, without hesitation she did.

When she was done, he informed her, "I want you off the shop floor. You can work in your workshop but, until this dies down, I want you off the shop floor."

She stared at him like he'd grown three heads. "I can't be off the shop floor. I only have Belinda helping me in the shop and she's not even full-time."

"Hire a new shop assistant," he replied instantly.

"I can't hire a new assistant. I just hired two new seamstresses. I can't afford—"

He interrupted her by stating in a voice not to be denied, "Then I'll hire a new assistant."

"Jack!" she cried, shocked.

His thumb moved to stroke her cheekbone and his face got close.

"You've been facing this alone for a year. I'll not have you face it alone any longer."

His voice was low and rumbly so she knew this statement meant something more to him than the something it meant to her, and the something it meant to her made her heart lurch and her belly warm.

He went on and his tone had gentled.

"Now, poppet, hire the assistant and I'll pay her salary. If you don't have time, I'll get Olive to do it."

Even though she had no clue who Olive was, all she could do was nod.

He kissed her forehead, his hands tensed on her jaw then he left.

That night after the whole family had dinner together, Jack disappeared with the dogs, Belle and Mom watched a movie then Belle had gone to bed alone.

She woke up in the middle of the night to a dark room.

She then mentally scanned her immediate environment and she felt no warmth, no arm at her waist, no additional presence in the room and she heard no dog tags.

She should have been happy that Jack hadn't slid into bed beside her. This was something she should not be allowing and something that she was, without a fight. Therefore this was something she didn't understand but was also someplace she was not letting her mind go. Even with all that, she turned and checked the bed.

No Jack.

There was no relief this time, only disappointment.

She was battling with this, what it might mean, how she'd be able to carry on for the next five months with her brain so addled, and slowly falling back to sleep, when she heard the door open and the jangle of dog tags.

Seconds later, Jack settled behind her, drawing her body immediately into his as she heard the dogs move around and then finally find their resting places.

"Jack?" she whispered.

"Go back to sleep, love," he whispered back.

Surprisingly, in mere minutes, she did.

He was gone when she woke.

Incidentally, they had an entire *spread* in the next day's paper. This included Belle walking close to Jack's side, his arm around her shoulders. Jack standing in her shop, his hands on her jaw tipping up her face to his as they talked. Jack kissing her forehead. *And* Jack coming to collect her in the evening, them walking back to his car the exact way they'd walked away from it that morning.

Not incidentally, Gram had blown her stack when she saw it.

"You *must* do something about this!" she demanded of Jack, waving the paper in the air when she arrived at the Saturday breakfast table where Jack and Belle had long since eaten. Rachel had just joined them and Yasmin and Joy had been with them for the last ten minutes.

"What do you propose I do, Lila?" Jack asked calmly.

"I don't know and I don't care. Fix it!" Gram retorted hotly.

"Gram—" Belle started.

Gram cut her off while throwing the paper down and seating herself at the table, "Bellerina, you're pregnant. You already have enough stress to deal with without this in your face every morning, noon and night."

"I know I'm pregnant, Gram, but I'm also used to this. It'll die down, trust me," Belle replied.

"When?" Gram shot back.

"Soon," Belle told her.

"Jeez, Mom, take a chill pill. I think it's sweet," Mom recklessly informed them, ignored Gram's eyes nearly popping out of her head and turned to Yasmin adding chattily, "I like the kissing picture best. In the car. But the one where Jack and Belle are talking and he's got his hands on her face is nice too."

"Rachel Leonora Abbot!" Gram shouted.

"What?" Mom asked.

"Have you lost your *mind*?" Gram yelled.

"Quit yelling at the breakfast table. I haven't lost my mind." Then Mom turned to Jack and she smiled. "Looks like you're a good kisser." Belle's breath caught in her throat mainly because her heart had lodged there and Mom, not done, turned to Belle. "That's lucky for you, honeypot."

"Oh my goodness gracious," Belle breathed in horror.

"I think the stress your grandmother is talking about, poppet, begins and ends at the breakfast table," Jack murmured dryly and Belle's eyes flew to him.

He was gazing at her with an expression on his face that said he didn't know whether to laugh or yell and Belle couldn't have helped it if she tried (which she didn't), she burst into uncontrollable giggles.

When she stopped giggling, she wiped her eyes and saw Jack watching her, a look on his face so tender it was nearly raw. She felt her entire system shut down as she stared back with what she knew was unconcealed wonder.

"Jack, you get top prize for the day," Mom butted in to their very public moment. "Bellerina doesn't giggle much so when she does, it's a gift."

Belle turned her head to look at her mother and saw Rachel had a look on her face that was tender too and it was directed at Jack.

"Thank you," she said softly to finish.

It appeared then that Jack and Rachel were having a moment but it was the look on Gram's face that caught Belle's attention.

She was looking pleased with herself.

It was then Belle knew Gram was working a scheme. She just didn't know what it was and she also didn't like it. Her grandmother's schemes were always harebrained and half-witted and, when they bumbled clumsily to fruition, usually heralded the time for them to move to a new town.

Belle didn't have time to question her grandmother. It was time for Jack to take her to work.

Which he did.

And the media frenzy was reaching its zenith, Belle knew this by experience.

There were more of them when they surrounded Jack's car thus Jack did not leave her in the shop.

He took her there, let her in, left her there (locking up behind him) and went to get her a decaf caramel latte (after he asked her preference). He brought back her coffee and one for him. Then he sat on the sales counter, sipping his coffee while she prepared to open. When she opened the store, he got off the counter and mingled and chatted (more like charmed) her many, many, *many* customers like this was not only his job but his calling.

Not to mention Belinda, her twenty-year-old, starry-eyed shop assistant who Belle was certain was going to throw herself bodily at Jack's feet and declare her undying love for him when he told them at lunchtime he was going to go out and buy them a sandwich.

When the door closed on Jack as he went to get their lunch, Belinda stared at it but asked Belle, "Can I have his baby too?"

"No," Belle answered instantly.

"I wouldn't share either, luvie," a woman stated, standing across the store and staring at the door as well.

It was then, out the windows of her shop, that Belle saw the man.

He had dark-brown hair, a rugged but handsome face and a tall, muscled body.

He was watching her through the windows and normally this would give her the creeps. But there was something kindly in his expression that didn't alarm Belle in the slightest.

After he'd caught her attention, he gave her a small smile, turned and walked away, giving her the impression it was just a chance moment of eye contact.

She put him out of her mind and got on with her day.

Jack had spent the day in St. Ives in her shop or with her when she was in her workshop, alternately talking on his phone or talking to Belinda and her customers, and then he took her home.

She escaped him the first moment she could, running to her room and changing into her Fat Day Jeans. She was going to have to buy new jeans soon, she'd already begun to design her maternity wardrobe and had even made a few pieces.

She took the rug and went out to the sea, trying to understand her behavior, Jack's behavior and wondering about her future.

Because *this* Jack, who seemed a permanent fixture (the multiple personalities had totally disappeared), was the Jack who had slipped into her heart that night four months ago in a way she thought he'd never leave.

And this would mean she'd been wrong when she'd accused him of using her as a prize in a competition with his brother.

And that would mean that she'd thrown their night in his face, a night to her that was so magical she thanked her lucky stars for it. A night about which, at the time, she thought he'd felt the same thing.

Which would mean what she'd done was beyond rude. It was insulting and even unforgiveable.

But she couldn't ignore the conversation she'd heard Joy and Yasmin having. And she couldn't ignore the behavior of Jack and Miles in the stables, which proved true their obnoxious rivalry. And lastly she couldn't ignore the way Jack himself had treated her when he was one of the different Jacks.

And she knew better not to proceed with caution.

She'd been hurt before, again and again (and again) in ways many women (luckily) never endured.

Belle knew the pain of a betrayal of trust hurt far worse than a fist slammed into your cheekbone or an arm twisting yours excruciatingly painfully up your back.

Therefore she knew better than to let anyone have that opportunity again.

On this thought, either her mind was so engrossed or the sound of the sea swallowed all other noises, because she missed the auditory warning of someone approaching and felt movement right at her back.

Before she knew what was happening, Jack settled behind her as she saw his legs surround her body, bent at the knees.

Then his arms slid around her at her waist and he pulled her back into his chest.

Belle's body went still at both the memory of when he held her this way before and the beauty of being held that way now.

His mouth came to her ear and he whispered, "I see you out here and wonder what's on your mind, poppet."

"I come out here to clear my mind," she told him honestly.

"Is it working?" he asked.

She shook her head so she heard his chuckle, up close, right in her ear, and the sound of it made her tremble.

She felt his hand's slight movement and it came to rest on the baby while his other arm stayed wrapped loosely, but strangely possessively, around her.

Belle had the sudden wish that this was them, sitting by the sea next to his daunting but beautiful castle after sharing a Saturday together, quietly and patiently waiting for their baby to arrive. A baby whose arrival would not mean the end of what they had now, but would be the beginning of something even more wonderful.

As she had this thought, Jack asked, "Do you want to share what's on your mind?"

She shook her head again instantly.

No, it was safe to say she did *not* want to share.

He didn't speak.

She looked down at her belly and her hand, as if it had a mind of its own, moved to touch the healing scabs at his knuckles.

"Do you want to tell me about Miles?" she asked, also as if her mouth had a mind of its own.

"No," he replied in a way she wished she could take the words back but his hand left her belly, twisted and caught hers. He lifted it, up and over her shoulder, where he brought it to his mouth and touched his lips to it.

Belle's lungs compressed all the air out of her body as he dropped both their hands and positioned them, hers flat against the baby, his on top.

"Let's just say Miles was far more polite when you were there than he was after you left," he told her, and Belle couldn't imagine that as Miles had been well beyond rude when she was there.

Jack kept talking.

"It was coming for a long time, Belle. He'd been pushing for it for years. It was what he wanted and, finally, I gave it to him."

"You didn't want to," she made a guess and his hand twisted again.

His fingers lacing with hers, he moved their hands to rest on his hard thigh.

"No, I didn't want to," he agreed.

"I don't know if Joy is okay with it. Gram won't let us talk to her about it," Belle informed him.

"She's not okay with it but she's lived with it all our lives. She'll cope," Jack replied.

Belle turned her head to look at him and he lifted his chin from where he'd been resting it on her shoulder so he could meet her eyes.

"He's been that way all your life?"

Jack nodded and said, "Not that bad but he's always been competitive. When Dad got sick, it changed, degenerated, got compulsive and became all constant." He stopped and there was something so sad, so resigned in the tone of his voice that Belle had the urge to comfort him. To touch her lips to his or turn in his arms and give him a fierce hug.

Or both.

She did not do either, of course.

Instead she whispered, "I'm sorry. You said you didn't want to talk about it." She looked away and stated firmly, "We'll stop talking about it."

"We have to talk about something else," he told her and the way he said that made her brace. And her bracing made her realize she'd relaxed into his arms and had been resting her weight into his like it was the most natural thing in the world.

This made her brace even more.

"Maybe we can just watch the sea?" she suggested, terrified that he was going to bring something up she didn't want to talk about.

Like agreeing a visitation schedule after the baby was born. Like discussing child support payments. Like a number of things that didn't go along with sitting in his arms and watching the sea.

"No, this needs to be said."

She held her breath a moment then sighed.

"Okay," she relented and his hand gave hers a squeeze.

"We need to talk about what happened in the stables."

She didn't know which time they were in the stables that he wanted to talk about. The first time, which was marvelous and she didn't want to talk about it. Or the second time, which was terrible yet also, in the end, marvelous, and she didn't want to talk about that either.

Nevertheless, talking about either time was better than child support or visitation schedules.

"What about it?" Belle asked.

"I need to apologize."

Her head twisted around as his turned and she looked into his eyes.

"Apologize?" she asked, confused.

"For carrying you down the ladder." She felt her lips part in surprise as he kept speaking. "I was angry at you for avoiding me. I had residual anger at you for keeping the pregnancy from me. And I had a number of things on my mind, many of them needing my attention. This made me impatient. But none of that excused what I did."

"Jack—" she whispered, but he interrupted her and now his voice was fierce.

"I frightened you. The look on your face, I'll never fucking forget it."

"Jack—" she tried to cut in again and failed.

His hand in hers moved to wrap around her body, taking hers with it and he gave her a squeeze before he stated, his voice low and rumbly, "It won't ever happen again."

"Jack—" she said yet again and yet again he kept talking.

"And, you should know, you were right. It was exactly your imperfections that drew me to you."

Belle stopped trying to interrupt and her parted lips became a mouth dropping wide open in complete and total shock.

His eyes dropped to her mouth hanging open and his lips twitched before his gaze rose to her eyes again. "That and your hair."

She kept staring at him.

"And your dress," he continued.

She didn't utter a word, just kept staring at him.

"And your eyes," he went on, the grin turned playful, his eyes went wicked and his voice dropped deeper when he finished, "And, a lot later, those unbelievably sexy noises you made while I was fucking you."

She felt her belly dip and her breasts swell and both felt too darned good for her peace of mind.

Therefore, in a belated attempt at self-protection, her body moved to bolt out of his arms. Where she was going, she had no clue but she was going there, and fast.

The problem was, he'd prepared for it and his arms went tight the minute her body prepared for action and he held her in place.

Her gaze flew to him in alarm even as her skin tingled in anticipation.

"Jack—" she started *yet again* but he talked over her.

"Now, should I kiss you or are you going to kiss me?" he asked and her mouth dropped open and his attention moved to it again. "I'd prefer you kiss me but that doesn't look like it's going to happen, so..."

He let that dangle in the air only the merest moment before he bent his head and kissed her.

His tongue slid inside her mouth and even though she really, really, really, *really* wanted to resist, she didn't.

Not even for a second.

So maybe she didn't really, really, really, *really* want to resist.

Instead, her head tilted, her torso twisted, he let go of her hand and she wrapped her arms around him as he pulled her up his chest and deepened the kiss.

It felt good.

No, it felt *perfect*, kissing Jack on the rocks by the sea. It was the best moment in her life (barring the other best moments she had with Jack) and she never wanted it to end.

His mouth broke from hers, trailed down her cheek to her ear and he whispered, "So fucking sweet."

She trembled in his arms, felt his hand glide up her spine and trembled again.

She was about to twist her head to invite another kiss when her eyes fluttered open, they caught on something odd, she focused on that something and she went completely still.

She stared and terror raced through her, so strong, she didn't feel Jack's body responding to her withdrawal nor did she hear him call her name.

Instead she stared at the two children standing in the window looking down at them. A boy and a girl. The boy was black-headed, the girl was fair. They couldn't be more than eight and ten or even younger.

And, even though Belle could see them plain as day, she could also see *through* them.

"Jesus, Belle, what is it?" Jack's voice was harsh and it snapped her out of her terrified shock, she jerked from his arms and got to her feet.

Her eyes never leaving the window, she retreated, walking backwards.

Then, the little girl waved at her.

Waved at her!

Belle let out a strangled scream just as Jack's arm hooked around her waist, pulled her to his body and dragged her back several wide steps.

"What the fuck are you doing?" he clipped and her eyes flew to him. "You nearly fell over the cliff."

She looked around her dazedly, not having time for the possibility that she nearly did herself, and their child, bodily harm.

She looked back at Jack and said in an urgent, frightened voice, "Jack, there are children in the turret."

Jack's head whipped around and up and when Belle's eyes moved back to the window, the child ghosts were gone.

Jack turned back to her and Belle's gaze met his. "They were there. I swear. I saw both of them!"

"Myrtle and Lewis," Jack said and Belle's mouth dropped open.

"Myrtle and Lewis?" she whispered.

"Who told you the story?" Jack asked.

"The story?" Belle repeated stupidly.

"Was it Yasmin?"

"Yasmin?" Belle parroted again.

His hand came to her jaw. "You can't let it get to you, love. It's just a ghost story. They aren't real."

"Ghost story?" Belle breathed in horror.

He grinned and she was certain at that point he was definitely mad. Mad enough to be locked up because there was *nothing* to grin about when there were *ghosts haunting his castle.*

"Trust me, I've lived here all my life and I've heard that story dozens of times and I've never seen them," he assured her, still grinning like he thought she was hilarious.

"I just saw them," Belle told him.

"No, you didn't."

"Yes, I did."

He looked over his shoulder and up at the turret again then back at her.

"Are they there now?" he asked, and hesitantly she glanced up but there were no ghostly children in the window.

"No," she told him when she was looking at him again.

"Belle—"

It was her turn to talk over him. "I can't live here when there are ghosts in the castle."

"Belle—" he said again and this time his tone had changed significantly. It had grown slightly dangerous.

She put her hands on his chest and fisted his shirt in her fingers. "We have to move to the cottage," she announced then added hysterically, "this *instant.*"

"Poppet—" he began but she kept talking.

"You can sleep with me," she blurted then went on, "And you can bring the dogs."

His arms slid around her and drew her to his body. She could feel his shaking, not with terror, but with laughter.

She tipped her head back to look at him and saw it was true.

He was *laughing.*

"*This isn't funny!*" she screeched.

"It's hilarious," he contradicted, still laughing.

"There are *ghosts* in your *house,*" she cried. "*Child* ghosts. There's nothing creepier than child ghosts. Everyone knows that!" she yelled.

His face dipped close to hers.

"Everyone?" he teased.

"James Bennett, I do *not* find this amusing!" she was still yelling.

Then again, there were *ghosts* in his *castle*.

"Well," he started as one arm dropped, the other one shifted up to wrap around her shoulders and he guided her toward the rug. "That decides it," he finished and bent to nab the rug before moving her toward the castle.

She looked up at him as they were walking. "Decides what?"

"Considering there are creepy child ghosts haunting the castle, even when I'm not in the mood to sleep with you, if that mood should ever strike me, which so far it hasn't, then I'll have to sleep with you anyway." His arm gave her a squeeze. "Protection."

He was still teasing.

She pulled out of his arm, planted her feet and gave his bicep a light smack, shouting, "This is serious!"

He threw his head back and roared with laughter at the same time his hand shot out and wrapped around the back of her neck, playfully yanking her face first into his chest.

His other arm holding the rug came about her and held her to his shaking-with-mirth frame.

Even before he'd completely quit laughing, he looked down at her upturned face and said, "I'll have to have a word with Myrtle and Lewis. They've supposedly been around for two hundred years without causing the least harm but I'd prefer it if they wouldn't appear and scare you silly when I'm kissing you."

"I *do not* find you funny," Belle snapped.

He bent his neck to touch his lips to hers, and after he lifted his head, he remarked, "That's all right, poppet, I do."

He moved to her side, arm still around her shoulders, and guided her resistant body to the castle while she muttered, "I'm *so* pleased you amuse yourself."

He stopped at the foot of the steps and turned her to his front.

She looked up at him to see his eyes still smiling but his voice was serious when he said, "I'll not let anything harm you."

Since he sounded serious, she did too when she told him, "I saw those ghosts, Jack."

"I believe you," he replied instantly, and she was so relieved he didn't think she was a raving lunatic, she relaxed into his body as his hand came to her jaw. "I don't believe in them but I believe you think you saw them. But Belle, even if they do exist, they won't hurt you and I wouldn't let them. I promise."

She just stared at him and made no reply.

"You're safe in my home. You'll always be safe in my home," he told her.

She swallowed because his eyes had lost their smile and had become as serious as his voice.

She still made no reply.

"All right?" he asked when she didn't speak.

She nodded but indicated her understanding of his serious words by letting her body rest deeper against his.

"Can we go inside now?" he inquired, his tone lightening back to teasing.

She looked up at the big castle behind him then at him.

Even though she believed Jack would keep her safe (or, at least, wanted to), she still did *not* want to go into his castle.

"I hope so," she sighed dramatically.

When they walked inside his haunted castle, Jack was still chuckling.

COMPLICATED

Jack

Jack lounged diagonal on the couch in his study, his feet up on the coffee table.

Belle was asleep, curled into his side, arm resting lightly across his stomach, cheek to his chest. Jack had a book he was not reading in his hand which he held against his thigh, his thumb holding his place.

He was looking out the window at the sea stretched out to the horizon.

Things had definitely changed with Belle.

Not much but he was making progress.

And he had Myrtle and Lewis to thank for it.

The evening before when they'd walked into the house after their time on the cliffs, Belle hadn't left his presence.

He knew this was not because she wanted to be in his company but because she was frightened of the ghosts she thought she saw.

He'd explained to her she had nothing to be frightened about. There was nothing more he could do.

Except take advantage of her fear.

This he did without a shred of remorse.

Jack had been correct those months before, Belle was not someone he could take or he could win.

He had to earn his place in her heart.

And he was going to do this.

Not for the sake of his child but because he wanted Belle.

But she clearly was not going to make it easy for him. She'd proved this in many ways, starting with finding an excuse at her earliest opportunity to walk away from him without looking back that morning after the night they'd shared.

And she'd do it again. This he knew for she was, for some reason, absurdly terrified of him and also what they'd shared.

Therefore Jack had to do whatever he had to do to earn his place in her heart and that included entangling her in his life.

To do this, first, he had to win her trust. He'd had it once but she'd taken it from him.

Although he felt he was justified in his anger when she came back to him, that didn't change the fact that he hadn't done himself any favors with his behavior.

Regardless, inherently Jack understood it was essential he conquer the obstacle of repairing the damage he caused and earning her trust before anything else.

And he had little time to do it.

In fact, he had around five months.

At the outside.

He'd prefer to have this accomplished far sooner.

His preference being that very day.

If not, the next day, if he could manage it.

Obviously, Myrtle and Lewis making an appearance worked in his favor. And Jack Bennett was not one to waste an opportunity.

So he didn't.

The night before, Belle had sat at his side at dinner, and before they left the table, she'd turned her head to him and timidly asked if she could join him during his nightly walk with the dogs or, more precisely, she'd asked his shoulder.

He'd agreed and they'd taken their silent but peaceful stroll.

When they came back, he went to his study and she went in search of her grandmother.

Not long later, a soft knock came at the door.

When he called, he was surprised to see Belle put her head through and even more shyly ask him if it would be too much bother if she sat with him.

He knew this mortified her on about the same significantly elevated level as it pleased him.

What he didn't know was how to make something that was clearly difficult for her, easier on her.

He decided simply to nod. She'd scooted in with her sketchpad and a box of colored pencils, head bowed, cheeks pink, and without a word sat in the armchair across the room from him.

Then she'd spent the evening in his study while he worked at his desk.

This, too, they did silently until it was late and she was so drowsy, he saw her head was nodding in an effort to stay awake.

Although Jack very much liked Belle sitting, feet tucked underneath her, silent and busy while he worked, the only noise being the scratching of her pencils on her sketch pad, and he wished this to continue, he'd taken pity on her.

He'd finished with his work and escorted her to her room. There, he lifted her face to his with a hand at her jaw and touched her lips with his own.

Then he left her at her door.

He had every intention of going to his room, preparing for bed and joining her in hers but he'd had a call come just as he was about to leave his room.

Five minutes into his call, there was a knock on the door.

Still talking, he opened it.

Belle stood there wearing a cream-colored silk nightgown with thin straps, a chiffon ruffle at the hem at her knees as well as around the neckline. Although it exposed a good deal of skin, it was not overtly tempting. It was simple, delicate, intensely feminine and, because of all of this, very sexy.

He knew instantly she'd designed it.

Her eyes went to his phone and Jack said into it, "A minute."

He took it from his ear and Belle, a hint of accusation mingling with the embarrassment in her voice, didn't hesitate in saying, "I thought you said you were sleeping with me."

Jack controlled his desire to laugh at her disgruntled discomfiture at the same time he fought against catching her in his arms and kissing her breathless.

"I did," he replied.

She looked down the hall then at him and asked, "Well?"

"I've got a call, poppet," he told her unnecessarily.

Baron and Gretl were pressing for her attention and she bent to give them pats while looking down the hall again.

He watched her wet her lips.

She looked at his shoulder then his nose then his ear.

After all that, she took in a deep breath and what she did next stunned him to immobility.

She pushed through him and his dogs, walked into his room and around his bed to what had become her side. Once there, she pulled back the covers and slid between them.

With some effort, Jack forced himself out of his frozen stance, put the phone to his ear and shut his door.

He talked on the phone while she hung over the side of his bed, petted his dogs and then cooed to them to lie down, which they did.

He finished his call while she settled in, facing the windows.

He turned out the lights, slid in behind her and pulled her to him.

When her body relaxed, Jack thought it only fair to try one more time to calm her fears. "Love, you do know there are no such things as ghosts."

"I know," she lied and he bit back his laughter but not his smile.

The smile died when her arm came to rest on his at her waist, her hand over his at her belly.

He closed his eyes and pressed his face into her hair.

Minutes later, he felt her drift into sleep.

Minutes after that, he did the same.

He knew the minute she woke.

He waited while she hesitated for long moments, lying awake in the curve of his body, and it cost him to let her go when she eventually slid out of bed and left the room.

But Jack was not going to move too quickly and make the same mistake twice.

This time he was going to earn her trust and, when he knew he had it irrevocably, only then would he make her understand she was his.

For he already knew it.

He'd known it since their first night.

She appeared at the breakfast table five minutes after him.

After breakfast, she caught him and his dogs on the way to the stables and told him (or, more to the point, she told his ear) that she was taking a walk.

Jack had intended to ride.

He allowed himself a moment to consider taking Belle with him.

Jack would very much enjoy riding with her in front of him, taking her along the coastline he knew she loved for she walked it nearly every day. His horse, Shadow, could take her farther than she could walk, showing her more than she'd seen, and Jack knew Belle would like that.

As pleasant as this thought was, he didn't want her riding while pregnant even on Shadow who he knew would take care of her. So he changed his morning plans and walked with her.

This did not go exactly well.

His first mistake was to explain to her, when she'd quietly asked about him driving to and from London in a day, that he didn't drive.

He told her that he flew.

That didn't garner a reaction until he further explained that he not only flew, he piloted the plane.

This garnered a response.

She stopped, frozen, and stared, open-mouthed.

Then she asked in a voice dripping with horror, "*You* flew the plane?"

Understanding her reaction, Jack got close to reassure her. "Belle, I earned my pilot's license when I was twenty. I've been flying for eighteen years."

She blinked then repeated, "You flew the plane?"

"Belle—"

She cut him off. "Do you have, um…a qualified pilot with you?"

Jack again bit back laughter and explained, "I *am* a qualified pilot."

"Yes, okay," she replied swiftly. "But, when you fly, do you have another one, in case of emergencies?"

To win her trust, unfortunately, he had to be honest.

Therefore he answered, "No."

"Oh goodness gracious," she breathed.

"Belle—"

To his amused surprise, she shook her head sharply, put her hands over her ears and chanted. "La la la, not listening. This conversation didn't happen. La la la."

He noticed she had pink to her cheeks, either a reaction to her embarrassment at their conversation or her chanting of denial or both.

She dropped her hands and started walking again, her pace picking up significantly, her bearing stiff and uncomfortable looking.

He lengthened his strides to keep up thinking not only that he thoroughly enjoyed seeing her blush, he'd never forget how adorable she was when she let her fear break down her guard.

His second mistake was only ten minutes later when he took her hand, slowed their pace and asked, "Have you hired another shop assistant?"

He felt her hand jerk in his and she looked up at him in surprise. "No, I haven't had time."

Jack looked down at her and inquired with what he thought was a good deal of patience, "I thought I explained I want you off the shop floor."

Her eyes widened the moment before she bowed her head to study the rocky path they were traversing.

"You can't hire a shop assistant in two days."

"Yes, you can," Jack replied because he knew you could.

She looked at him again, her eyes now narrowed with either annoyed confusion or confused annoyance, he couldn't decide which.

Either one, Jack thought, on Belle was cute.

"No, you can't," she told him.

"I can," he told her.

She stopped walking and started speaking. "Jack—"

He pulled at her hand and kept walking, taking her with him and, he thought, ending this particular conversation by saying, "I'll call Olive. She'll have someone at the shop tomorrow."

She tugged at his hand to halt him but he ignored it and kept them moving.

"Jack," she called, her voice definitely moving toward annoyed rather than confused. "You can't call Olive. It's Sunday."

"I can. She's available twenty-four, seven."

Belle's hand tugged his with a force he couldn't ignore. He stopped and looked down at her.

"She's available twenty-four, seven?" Belle asked with obvious disbelief and possible accusation as if he was a slave driver cracking a nasty whip.

"Of course," Jack replied with casual patience.

"Who is Olive, anyway?" she queried, not quite recovered from her shock.

"My PA," Jack answered.

"And she's available at all times?" Belle went on, still, for some reason, not processing this information.

Jack lost his casual patience and slid into amused impatience.

Therefore his lips were twitching when he said. "Yes, Belle, and she gets paid well into six figures to be available at all times. She's not an indentured servant. She's a highly experienced, intensely skilled, extremely loyal, very valued employee who can find a way, on a Sunday afternoon, to hire the best shop assistant in the UK and have her in your store by tomorrow, end of business."

She stared at him a moment and then breathed, "Oh."

And while Jack was watching her parted lips at the same time fighting a nearly overwhelming urge to put his own against her mouth, slide his tongue inside and taste her, Belle continued on a whisper.

"Wow."

Jack won his battle, lifted a hand to her jaw and smiled down at her as he leaned closer. "Wait until you meet her, poppet. Olive is definitely an 'oh wow.'"

At his words, for some reason, something in Belle's face shifted, it softened and a fetching radiance came into her eyes.

He understood he scored a point. He just didn't understand how.

Then she said softly, "I'll look forward to that."

She turned and started walking again but he knew, somehow, her mood had lifted considerably, lightening in a way he'd never experienced from her before.

It was as charming as it was surprising.

Therefore ten minutes later (when he made his third mistake), it should not have taken him off-guard when she threw a carefree smile over her shoulder at him and announced, "I'll show you my new favorite place."

However, this did take Jack off-guard.

Completely.

He had an excuse for not controlling his reaction.

A smile from Belle was infrequent and it was enchanting. A carefree one, though, was something he'd never seen and that was enthralling.

When she started to scramble onto a dangerous outcropping of rock at a cliff face, Baron and Gretl protectively close to her but also alighting the outcrop with practiced ease as if they'd done it every day of their lives, Jack overreacted.

Strike that, it was when Belle, the woman he considered *his* woman and the woman who was carrying *his* child, a woman who was scared of practically everything *but* that dangerous outcropping of rock, started to scramble onto it that he overreacted.

He followed her quickly, caught her with an arm around her midriff and lifted her off her feet. Her back to his front, he carried her off the outcrop to the far safer cliff path and set her on her feet.

When she whirled around to face him, he demanded curtly, "What did you think you were doing?"

She'd stared at him a second then asked what he thought was bizarrely, "Oh no, you're not going back to the jerky one, are you?"

Jack decided to ignore her question, focusing instead on his far more important, and sensible one.

"Belle," he'd clipped. "That outcrop is dangerous. What were you thinking?"

She looked at the rock then at him and stated, "No it isn't. I go there a lot. It's where I do my best non-thinking."

"So you're telling me you won't climb a ladder but you'll scale a cliff?" he inquired with annoyed surprise.

She looked back at the rock then at him. "It's not a cliff."

He looked behind him and back at her. "Belle, it's a cliff. A rocky cliff. A *dangerous* rocky cliff."

She turned to the cliff and studied it as if seeing it for the first time.

Attention still aimed there, she muttered, "It *is* a cliff."

He didn't know whether to burst out laughing or shake some sense into her.

He did neither.

Instead he ordered, "I don't want you to go out there again." When her gaze moved to his face, he asked, "Do you understand?"

She regarded him a moment and said nonsensically, "No, it's the bossy one."

He ignored her again and repeated, "Am I understood?"

"You're understood," she replied quietly, turned back toward the house, patted her thigh to call the dogs and started forward.

Their walk, apparently, was over.

As they had moved away from the house, she had not only attempted conversation, she'd freely engaged in it.

As they moved back to the house, she remained thoughtfully and somewhat disturbingly quiet and her lightened mood had vanished.

Therefore when The Point was in view, Jack got close to her side, slid an arm around her shoulders and halted her. He curled her to face him and she tilted her head back to look at him.

"Don't be cross, poppet," he demanded softly when her eyes caught his, going on to explain. "I acted out of concern."

To this she oddly announced, "I hiked the Inca Trail."

Jack stared at her a moment before asking, "What?"

She put her hands to his waist and repeated, "I hiked the Inca Trail with my mom. We hiked to Machu Picchu." When he didn't speak, she went on, "Which is amazing, by the way."

He was surprised at this news but also uncertain why she was sharing it.

"That may be so but you weren't pregnant nor were you alone when you did it. I'd rather you not climb out onto a cliff outcrop when you're out walking alone."

He'd also rather she not do it when she was with someone, for instance himself, but he didn't say that.

She moved a hint closer to him, tilting her head back further. "No. That's not what I mean. I've been trying to decide why I'm not scared of that cliff, which I'm not. I never thought about it but it's weird." Again when he didn't respond, she continued, informing him, "I think it's the sea."

Although this made no sense to Jack, he didn't tell her that, he remained silent.

When he didn't speak, Belle went on, "I feel safe around the sea. And I feel safe around my mom, which was why I wasn't scared on the Inca Trail. So I tried to find times when I wasn't afraid of something I'm normally afraid of to see if my theory is right. I remembered that, after a while, when we were up in the hayloft that first time, I leaned against the sliding doors that you opened which is something I wouldn't normally do and…"

She stopped talking abruptly and her eyes grew wide as she realized what she was giving away. Her body went solid, she tore her gaze from his and looked at his ear.

Then belatedly she tried to pull away.

Jack's arms slid around her, containing her retreat.

She gave up immediately but held her body stiffly in his hold.

She'd felt safe with him.

This was a highly welcome revelation.

At least it was to Jack.

Belle looked like the very thought terrified her to an irrational extreme.

"Look at me," he commanded gently, and her gaze went from his ear to his far more rapidly than normal, which was also highly welcome. She was looking in his eyes more often, holding his gaze easier and meeting his eyes more swiftly at his command.

Jack decided to confront her directly, not giving her time to retreat emotionally either. "I'm pleased you feel safe with me, love, but I still don't want you out on that cliff."

"Okay," she replied readily and he knew she was agreeing in order to end the conversation, not that she actually agreed.

He knew this because she made a move to pull away but his arms tightened. He gave her a gentle shake when her eyes started to slide away again and he held her gaze.

"You'll always be safe with me, Belle," he told her.

She wet her lips nervously and hastily changed the subject by requesting, "Can we go back to the house?"

"No," he answered instantly.

"Why not?" Her voice was beginning to rise with anxiety but he ignored it.

A breeze slid through the air, taking with it some tendrils of hair that had escaped her ponytail. They caught on her wetted lips and Jack lifted a hand to slide his fingers along her hairline, tucking the tendrils behind her ear as he held her to him with his other arm. He felt her body tremble at his touch with a resultant, vastly pleasant, clutch in his gut.

"A number of reasons," he answered as his hand wrapped around her ponytail, his other arm pulled her even closer, and when he had her affectionately imprisoned he continued. "Firstly, because I'd like a moment to savor the knowledge that you felt safe with me regardless of the fact that I lost that gift through no fault of my own."

He heard and felt her draw in a quick breath but he kept talking.

"Secondly, I'd like to know that you understand you were mistaken when you withdrew that gift, and further that you understand now that I'll always keep you safe."

At these words her body locked and he saw the color leave her face, but relentless he carried on.

"Thirdly, I'm considering kissing you, I haven't decided yet but I'm definitely leaning toward it."

He watched her lips part, color again suffused her cheeks before she informed him, the anxiety in her voice increasing, "I think we should stop kissing."

Jack grinned at her. "Now why would we do that?"

She looked away but he gave her ponytail a soft tug and she looked back, saying, "I don't know. We just should."

"Should we stop sleeping together?" he asked.

"Probably," she answered hesitantly, no resolve whatsoever underlying that word, telling him she not only liked his presence in bed but she wanted it.

The sharp sense of triumph he felt, mingled with the sweet way she'd made this admission, made him chuckle.

Her eyes dropped to his mouth, Jack liked her eyes on his mouth so he dipped his face closer to hers.

"Poppet, I'm not going to stop kissing you and I'm not going to stop sleeping with you. In fact, the minute you give me the first indication I can take it further, I'm going to do more than kiss you." His face got even closer and he went on, "A lot more."

He felt her body jerk and her startled gaze shifted to his eyes.

"We shouldn't complicate things," she told him in a tremulous voice and he couldn't help it, he pulled her closer but threw his head back and laughed. Her hands at his waist tensed as she protested, "I wasn't being funny."

He looked down at her again, still laughing. "Don't you think things are already complicated?"

"Well, yes," she replied. "That's why we shouldn't let them get *more* complicated."

His face got close to hers again and he returned, "I like them complicated and I'll like them even better when they're *more* complicated."

He saw she was having trouble breathing and he knew this reaction directly corresponded with the fear, desire and wonder he read in her eyes.

"Maybe we should talk," she whispered in a way that said she most definitely did *not* want to talk. In fact, she'd rather have her fingernails ripped out at the roots, but she thought it imperative that they do so.

Even though Jack wanted to kiss her, he felt she'd had enough. Instead he moved away from her body but placed an arm around her shoulders, keeping her close to his side as he guided her toward The Point.

"We'll talk later," he promised.

She kept moving forward but her head tilted up to look at him. "When?"

He looked down at her. "When you tell me you feel safe with me again." He bent his face closer to hers and grinned before he went on, "And after things get far more complicated."

He watched her swallow and her head jerked to look forward.

He knew she wanted to say more. He also knew she didn't have the courage.

Taking advantage of that, he pulled her deeper into his side.

They arrived back at The Point only to learn his mother, Lila and Rachel were out somewhere together doing something they hadn't shared with Elaine.

This meant that Belle, who he knew wanted to escape him but he also knew did not want to be left alone to face the possibility of whatever might befall her at the hands of Myrtle and Lewis, was forced to go with him to his study.

He went to his desk to see to some work and call Olive about Belle's new employee.

Belle sat on the couch and gazed out the window.

This was something she seemed to be able to do for hours, mutely, peacefully, as if drawing strength from the view.

This was also something he very much liked about her. It was inscrutable but tranquil and he found it unbelievably appealing.

Within a half an hour, she was curled in the corner of his couch, asleep.

Jack watched her in sleep for long moments, made a decision, left his work, got his book and went to the couch.

With gentle but determined movements should she wake and withdraw, he shifted her sleeping body so he could join her.

She did wake and her sleepy gaze drifted to his face. Her nap, however, was nowhere near complete and he knew instantly her guard was down.

He knew this because, as he tucked her into his side, she awarded him with a small, sweet smile instead of pulling away or going stiff. Without hesitation, she put her cheek to his chest, wrapped her arm around his stomach, curled into him and fell directly back to sleep.

His attention turned to his book but he couldn't focus on it. He found he preferred staring out the window to the sea, feeling Belle's warmth at his side, listening to her soft breathing and contemplating their day.

Therefore when he heard a knock on the door, he ignored it. He had no intention of letting anyone disturb them.

Unfortunately, it was Lila at the door and even though he did not ask her to enter, she did.

He bit back his impatience and the sharp words he would very much liked to have said. Instead, he watched her gaze at them a moment before she walked across the room, took a chair from the front of his desk and dragged it to the side of the couch.

As she settled herself in the chair, Jack spoke quietly but pointedly. "Belle's sleeping."

Lila's eyes went to her granddaughter then to Jack.

"I can see that," she replied as she leaned back in the chair as if she was going to spend the afternoon there. Then she said, "We need to talk."

She was right, they did need to talk. He had a few things he wished to say to her, most of them having to do with how she regularly embarrassed her granddaughter, but some of them having to do with how she treated Jack thus, he sensed, distressing her granddaughter.

However, they didn't need to talk with Belle in the room, asleep or not.

"I would enjoy that, Lila, but not now," Jack returned, his voice still low, guarded and quiet.

"Now," she retorted, also speaking softly. "It's clear things have changed between you two and I need some assurances."

Jack clenched his jaw and remained silent.

Lila either ignored it or didn't see it (likely the first) and continued, "Considering your mother's disposition, her assertion that you are not, in fact, adopted, and your recent behavior, I can assume that things went horribly awry the first time you were with Belle. Or, considering your behavior when I met you and the penchant toward violence you and your brother demonstrated, I can assume that you're setting her up to take a gigantic fall once the baby's born. I'd like you to tell me, honestly, which one it is."

Jack's body clenched as stiffly as his jaw.

For Belle's sake, he forced his body to relax and with as much politeness as he could muster, he murmured, "Please leave, Lila."

"I'll leave when you tell me which one it is," she returned stubbornly.

He regarded her a moment and then said in a low, very unhappy voice, "I'll tell you that you don't know me well enough to make assumptions about me. I'll also tell you that I'm not pleased at your display of judgement when you've no idea what has passed between Belle and I, or my brother and I. I'll further tell you that if you behave this way around our child, I'll not be happy. Without the facts at your command or often with them, standing in judgement of another is a revolting trait and I'll not tolerate it around my child. And lastly, I'll tell you that it's commendable you wish to protect your granddaughter but you aren't doing a very good job of it, insulting the father of her child while she's asleep in his arms."

Jack could swear he saw a light come to her eyes. A light that looked quite a bit like approval.

He also didn't care.

Lila's approval didn't matter to him, Belle's did. He'd earn it with Lila's assent or not.

"I don't think you understand that I've had a goodly number of heart to hearts with your mother," Lila told him.

"You've known her a month," Jack returned.

"What I'm saying is, I know more than you think I do," Lila replied.

"I know what you're saying," Jack explained. "But my mother wasn't present during the time I shared with Belle. She doesn't know what transpired."

Lila gave him a small, all-knowing grin. "*Belle* told me that part."

"Belle may have been there but Belle wasn't in my head. She clearly had no idea what I was thinking or she would never have left this house."

Jack knew exactly what he'd given away and he'd intended to do it. Not because he wished to assuage Lila's concern but because he wanted her to leave before they woke Belle, which was something they courted the longer their conversation lasted.

"So things went horribly awry," Lila muttered, watching him closely.

Jack didn't bother to reply.

They studied each other for long moments before Lila's face changed in a way he couldn't read but he knew did not bode well.

"There are things you need to know about Belle," she whispered.

He didn't like the tone of her voice or the grave look on her face.

Nevertheless he replied, "Let's let Belle share them with me, shall we?"

Lila gave him an unusually hesitant look. "I think you should know them sooner rather than later."

"What I think is that it's clear Belle has trust issues. If she knew I was discussing her secrets with her grandmother it would be detrimental to me winning that trust. Therefore it's best she confide them to me when the time is right for her."

Jack waited for Lila to argue, finding he was increasingly frustrated and thus annoyed that they were having this conversation with Belle present, asleep or not. He was further frustrated that Lila tied his hands because he couldn't communicate the intensity of his anger, nor could he even physically move.

She was, he thought with irritation, very clever.

Her gaze shifted to her granddaughter, her face cleared and for a moment, it gentled.

She hid this look when her eyes returned to him.

"So be it," she declared, stood and looked down on him.

This he also found irritating.

"Handle her with care, Jack," she warned softly. "Belle deserves that."

Jack's jaw clenched yet again at her imparting this unnecessary piece of advice before she continued, and what she said made his gut clench.

"You see, there were those before you who didn't, so it's essential you do."

Before he could utter a word, she swiftly and silently swept from the room.

Her parting words obliterated the serenity he'd felt minutes before.

His mind turned to Belle and his first night together, her earnest demand that he promise she could trust him and the conversation they never had the next morning where she was going to share her secrets.

Perhaps, he thought with no small amount of uneasiness, they should talk before he'd fully earned her trust and made their relationship far more pleasantly complicated.

His arm tightened and he shifted her closer, deciding to clear the foreboding from his mind by reading.

He was engrossed in his book when she woke.

Her cheek gliding on his chest, her eyes opening and focusing fuzzily on his book, Jack watched her blink a couple of times. Then her head tipped up and her gray eyes, still groggy, were soft and had no trouble catching his.

"Hi," she whispered and Jack felt that one word, uttered in her sweet voice, drift across his skin like it was a physical touch.

"Welcome back from dreamland, poppet," he murmured, closing his book and dropping it to the floor.

He pulled her up his chest as he twisted her torso more fully on top of his.

She did not struggle as he did this. Instead, she lifted a hand to pull the wisps of hair away from her face and her eyes dropped to his mouth.

When he'd positioned her so their faces were close, before he knew or, he imagined, *she* knew what she was about, her lips curled into a small smile. She rested her hand on his chest, leaned in and touched her mouth to his.

At this light touch, he felt a surge of warmth through his body but, mouth still on his, Belle froze then jerked back.

Swiftly, his arms closed around her, containing her retreat.

She'd given him his opening.

It was time, Jack decided as the warmth remained in his body, to make things considerably more complicated.

Decision made, Jack didn't delay.

"No, love," he murmured. "Don't be afraid, finish what you start."

"Jack—"

He cut her off by demanding in a low voice, "Belle, kiss me."

He felt her melting, her fingers curling into his shirt but, still, she resisted.

"Jack—"

One of his hands slid up her spine and, as it always did, this caused her to shiver. His body absorbed it as his fingers sifted into her hair at the back of her head.

He angled his own head forward and, lips against hers, he repeated softly, "Kiss me, poppet."

"Please—" she begged even as he felt her body molding to his.

He should put her out of her misery but he needed her to kiss him. He needed her to make that first move of her own volition (albeit with his coaxing). He needed the statement of what such an act would mean, to her as well as to him.

However, if she didn't do this soon, he'd do it. With her body pressed to his, her thick hair falling through is fingers, he was losing control and he was losing it irritatingly fast.

Therefore, his voice was rough when he urged, "Belle, I want you to kiss me."

Her eyes looked into his, he saw the struggle she was waging with her mind then her lids grew heavy, her stormy gaze grew dazed and he knew he had her.

Her head tilted and she pressed her parted lips against his.

That was all he made her do. Jack gladly took it from there.

He knew his end game before she put her mouth to his.

He had no intention of fucking her on the couch as much as he wanted to do so.

He had every intention of making her desire spin out of control.

He was going to make her want him so badly she couldn't hide it from him or, more importantly, herself. She couldn't deny it and she definitely couldn't walk away from it.

He was not, however, going to leave her wanting.

Using his hands and mouth, his vivid memories of the delicious places where she was most vulnerable and the innate understanding that she'd been abstinent the last four months, relentlessly Jack took her to the edge in very little time.

They were facing each other on the couch, side by side, his mouth was on hers, their tongues dancing, her hand was up his shirt at the back, fingers digging into his flesh. He'd pulled her skirt up around her hips, his hand was in her panties, fingers pressing into a place that forced those sweet, husky, unbelievably sexy noises from her throat.

This was when Jack, somewhat vaguely, recognized the flaw in his plan.

For he might have no intention of fucking her on the couch, he had the forceful desire to do just that.

He controlled his craving with an iron will and, when she pressed her hips into his hand, he ended their kiss and murmured against her lips, "Tell me what you want, poppet."

He thought this would take some effort.

He was, with masochistic indulgence, looking forward to it.

Therefore he found it surprising, and infinitely satisfying, when it took no effort at all.

She pressed her torso to his and her free hand slid into his hair as her hips ground down on his hand.

Then she lifted beautiful, dazed eyes to his and whispered, "You."

At her easy but delightful capitulation, he slid his finger inside her and watched her lips part and her neck arch as his hand moved.

Jack loved the sleek, wet feel of her and the sound of the noises she made. He'd only had them for a night, four months ago, but having them again made him realize the raw intensity with which he missed them.

As her reward for giving them to him again so freely, he pressed his thumb to the heat of her and circled.

The noises she made quickened. He knew she was close and his mouth came down on hers and absorbed the soft, sweet mew of her climax.

He broke his mouth from hers and tucked her face in his neck as he coaxed the final tremors from her body, her breath coming fast against the skin at his throat.

When she was finished, gently, he pulled his hand away from her. When he felt the swift intake of breath between her lips, he decided that instead of righting her skirt as he'd intended, he'd slide his hand over her bottom and press her soft hips to his hard ones.

And this was what he did.

She remained pleasantly docile in his arms and only when he felt the stiffness of embarrassment creeping in did he speak.

"Don't," he ordered gently.

"I can't believe—" she whispered against his throat.

"Don't, Belle," he repeated on a squeeze of his arms.

She grew silent.

Then, hesitantly and very softly, she said, "You didn't—"

Jack cut her off again, "When I have you again, poppet, it'll be in my bed." He paused. "Or yours."

"But why—?" she began again and he interrupted her again.

"I was impatient to make things more complicated."

He felt her tip her head back to look at him, and when he dipped his chin to meet her eyes he noted she hadn't moved her arm from around his back and the fingers of her other hand were still in his hair.

This made him inordinately glad.

As this feeling stole over him, he watched her expression change, that radiance from earlier in the day came over it but she remarked, "You get impatient a lot."

"This is probably true," he agreed.

"It's definitely true," she whispered shyly and he grinned.

His head bent further and he touched his mouth to hers.

He only moved away an inch to say, "Then it's only fair to warn you, after that magnificent display, I'm feeling even more impatient to make things vastly more complicated."

"Jack—"

He cut her off again by saying simply, "Belle."

Her eyes skittered to his ear. He felt a mild annoyance that he lost her even for a moment before what she said next, in a voice that was so quiet it was nearly imperceptible, made this annoyance melt away.

"You don't think I'm a brazen hussy?"

He stared at her long enough for her eyes to come back to his in anxious inquiry and when they did, he burst out laughing.

Her body went stiff but he knew it wasn't in embarrassment. It was irritation.

Even so, his arm tightened around her, his hand at her ass pressing her hips deeper into his and he held her close to him until he controlled his amusement.

When he dipped down his chin to look at her, it was not difficult in the slightest to read that she was cross.

Her next words and the way she uttered them, including using his full name, proved her expression true.

"You laugh at very strange things, James Bennett."

"I'm not sure you realize how amusing you are, poppet," he returned.

"I wasn't meaning to be amusing. In fact, nearly every time you've laughed I wasn't meaning to be amusing," she shot back.

He loved it as well when her shyness disappeared and her spirit emerged (but not nearly as much as the noises she made when she was reaching orgasm).

He decided for her sake to try to be serious although he found this difficult considering the subject matter.

"All right, love, obviously this means something to you so perhaps you can explain to me how exactly you've behaved like a brazen hussy."

He could barely say the last two words without chuckling but he managed it.

Just.

Her mouth dropped open before she said tartly, "Well, let me see. I had sex with you within hours of meeting you."

His head dipped close and he brushed his lips against hers before muttering, "Yes, that was nice."

Her hand left his hair and she slapped his bicep.

"Jack, I'm being serious," she snapped.

He moved his face away from hers and fought back a grin. "Of course, my apologies. Carry on."

Her eyes widened at his invitation then they narrowed then she hissed, "Carry on? Do I need to remind you that I also spent the night with you, I was dating your brother at the time and, icing on the cake, I got pregnant. Now, I'm adding ice cream, whipped cream *and* sprinkles by fooling around with you *on your couch*." She emphasized the last three words then, as if his study was open to the public and they were on view, further stressed, "*In your study*." She waited for his response to this damning information and when there wasn't one she finished, "If that doesn't define *brazen hussy*, nothing does."

Jack made a guess and knew, intuitively, it was no risk.

"Have you ever had sex with someone the first night you met?" he asked.

"No," she answered instantly.

"Have you ever had sex with someone when you were dating someone else?" he went on.

"No!" she responded rather more forcefully.

His hand drifted up her spine and he continued light-heartedly, "Have you ever fooled around on a couch in a study with the father of your child?"

He felt her body tense then relax before she said, "Jack—"

He didn't let her carry on.

"What that means is you aren't a brazen hussy." His face got closer to hers and his voice dipped lower. "What it means, my love, is that I'm a very lucky man."

"Jack—" she began again, he had no idea what she intended to say but he didn't care.

He again didn't let her finish.

Instead, he changed the subject by saying, "Thank you, poppet."

He watched her head jerk and her face grow confused before she asked hesitantly, "For what?"

He moved, using his body to push hers back into the couch so he was mostly on top of her, tangling his legs with hers but protectively avoiding resting any of his weight against their child in her belly.

His lips went to her neck as he tugged down her skirt.

"For letting me make you come," he answered on a murmur.

Her hands moved to rest against his chest and, even as he felt her tremble, she suggested, "Maybe we should have that talk now."

His head came up and his hand moved to frame the side of her face.

He watched her a moment and then asked softly, "Do you feel safe with me?"

She blinked then wet her lips but she did not answer.

His thumb traced her lower lip while he muttered, "That's all right, it'll come."

"Jack—" she started yet again but he dipped his head and kissed her, thoroughly.

And he didn't break from her mouth until her hands slid from his chest, her arms were tight around him, her body was pliant under his and he knew, at least for that moment, she was his.

Then he rested his forehead to hers, his thumb stroking her cheekbone and he commented, "I think I'm going to very much like Sunday afternoons."

She tipped her chin up, pressing her own mouth against his.

Jack smiled in triumph against her lips and slanted his head to deepen the kiss when a sharp, urgent knock came at the door.

Both of them froze. Jack with extreme irritation. Belle, he suspected, with something else entirely.

Jack moved first, knifing away from her. He leaned down, pulled her to sitting and fully righted her skirt.

Then he turned to the door, wondering with unamused annoyance if he needed to resort to placing a do not disturb sign on the knob.

He pulled open the door to see his mother standing outside and this surprised him.

She knew better.

"What's—?" Jack started but Joy talked over him.

"Darling, we have a wee problem."

"And that would be?" Jack asked impatiently as he felt Belle arrive at his side.

Jack looked down at Belle to see she'd tidied her ponytail and was wearing an inquiring expression but her mouth was swollen from his kisses and her gray eyes were soft and languid.

She looked, exactly, like she'd just had an immensely pleasurable orgasm.

Jack had seen that look before. He very much liked it and it gratified him that he'd given it to her.

However, he didn't like sharing it.

Especially with his mother.

Joy looked at Belle then at Jack and she bit her lip before she said, "I'm sorry to interrupt."

Jack was sorry too.

More than he could say.

However, nonverbally he spoke volumes and he knew Joy read his face because she nervously kept biting her lip.

Jack slid an arm along Belle's shoulders and pulled her close, suggesting to his mother, "All right Mum, maybe you'd care to explain *why* you've interrupted."

"Well, see...erm..." she stammered.

"Mum," Jack warned.

Quickly, not looking at Belle, she whispered, "Rachel's seen Myrtle and Lewis and she's a bit..." her eyes slid to Belle then back to Jack, "*upset.*"

Jack sighed and asked a question to which he already knew the answer, "You explained they don't exist, didn't you?"

Joy Bennett had been "seeing" Myrtle and Lewis for forty years. It was sporadic and infrequent but she claimed the first time she saw them was within days of moving to The Point after she'd married Jack's father.

Therefore Jack was relatively certain, since Joy believed they existed, that she wouldn't explain to Rachel, who was a sight more odd, loud, if not more dramatic than his mother, that she didn't.

"Erm..." she mumbled, answering without actually answering and Jack clenched his teeth.

Then he looked down at Belle. "Did you tell your mother you'd seen them?"

Belle shook her head as Joy asked in a breathy voice, "You've seen them?"

Belle nodded at Joy. "Yesterday." When Joy didn't respond, Belle added, "They weirded me out."

"Oh dear. They usually aren't this active. Sometimes its years between times I see them and I saw them only the other day, *twice*. And they're pretty choosy who they show themselves to." Joy's eyes moved to Jack. "What do you think this means?"

"I think it means I need to hire a counsellor to come to The Point for a group session," Jack answered dryly.

"Jack!" both Belle and his mother cried.

"There are no such things as ghosts, Mum, and I'd appreciate it if you didn't fill Belle's head with that rubbish," Jack returned.

Joy gave him her patented affronted mother look. "I haven't uttered a word."

Jack was about to speak when Belle put in, "She hasn't."

Jack looked down at Belle to assess if she was lying in a misguided attempt to assist his mother or if she was serious.

With one look, he knew she was serious.

He found this mildly surprising.

However, considering the sum total of melodramatic femininity that was currently housed under his roof, he didn't find it troubling.

"I didn't say anything to Rachel or Lila either," Joy added. "You, and your father before you I might add, always get so foul tempered when I even mention it. So I usually don't bother." She turned to Belle and added conversationally, "Though, it's a fascinating story."

"Mum," Jack warned when he felt Belle's body tense at his side.

"Well, it is," Joy defended.

"It doesn't matter. They scare Belle and I don't want you saying another word," Jack asserted.

Joy turned to Belle. "Oh darling, there's nothing to be scared of. I promise, they're actually quite—"

"Mum!" Jack clipped sharply and Joy jumped.

"Um, I hate to interrupt your chitchat but my daughter is *freaking out*!" Lila called from down the hall while walking toward them. Her eyes were on Jack. "And you better do something about it, my man, because she's upstairs, in Belle's room, packing her things, mumbling about haunted houses and how her *pregnant daughter* was getting *as far as she could* from *this creepy place*."

"Fucking hell," Jack muttered.

At the same time, Belle mumbled an alarmingly experienced, "Uh-oh."

When Lila arrived at their group, Jack made a swift, acutely irritating but necessary decision and asked, "What does she drink?"

Lila blinked up at him and parroted, "Drink?"

"Rachel," Jack went on with slipping patience. "What does she drink?"

Lila looked at Belle and mumbled, "Better question is what *doesn't* she drink?"

Belle giggled, it wasn't with humor but also with nervousness and Jack's patience slipped further.

"Lila," he said low and her gaze snapped to him.

"I'd say this was a tequila moment," Lila answered.

"I think we have tequila," his mother informed them quickly.

"Get it," Jack ordered and looked at Lila. "You get Rachel." Then he told them both. "Meet us back here in the study."

"Gotcha, big man," Lila said breezily and moved down the hall.

Joy looked at Jack and asked, "What are you going to do?"

Jack pulled Belle closer to his side and answered, "I'm going to do nothing. *You're* going to tell the story of Myrtle and Lewis."

Before she could think better of it even in the face of Jack's visibly slipping patience, Joy exclaimed excitedly, "Oh goody, I'm going to call Yasmin."

"If you call Yasmin, I'll break your fingers," Jack clipped out his empty threat with as much menace as he could muster, which was rather a lot at that juncture.

Joy ignored the considerable menace and smiled radiantly at him. "No you won't, darling." Then she looked at Belle and confided, "Yasmin *loves* this story. She's never seen Myrtle and Lewis but she's *dying* to. She'll be *so jealous*."

With that Joy hurried away in search of tequila.

Jack looked down at Belle and saw her face was pale and her eyes were locked on his mother's departing back.

"Poppet," Jack called and her head tipped to look up at him.

"Do you think the baby could withstand a shot of tequila?" She paused briefly before finishing, "Or three?"

"No," Jack replied instantly.

Belle's gaze dropped to his throat.

"I didn't think so," she muttered with disappointment.

In any other mood, Jack would find this amusing.

Considering he'd just been interrupted in his continuing efforts to win Belle's trust at the same time making their situation significantly more complicated, so complicated it was a knotted mess from which she could never extract herself, he was not in such a mood.

Therefore Jack guided Belle back into the study wondering if he could politely rid The Point of his mother, Lila and Rachel without overly upsetting Belle.

At the very least for Sunday afternoons.

12

THE THUNDERSTORM

Belle

Belle stared out the window of Jack's study, both her hands resting on her baby bump.

The white-capped waves were rolling out as far as the eye could see and the wind had picked up. Even though there were only fluffy, white clouds in the sky, Belle knew from ten years of living in England, five of those in Cornwall, that the weather was going to turn.

Jack had gone somewhere. He told her he'd return shortly but didn't tell her where he was going.

Belle only hoped it wasn't to break his mother's fingers though she couldn't imagine Jack would do that even though he sounded like he very much wanted to.

She was contemplating how she felt about her day with Jack (indeed, her last *three* days with Jack) and everything that had happened.

In other words, she was trying to figure out how she felt about the fact that Jack clearly didn't dislike her frequent, quiet reveries. This was something Calvin hated and thought was weird and shared these thoughts frequently. Frequently enough for Belle to stop doing it when he was around.

In fact, Jack seemed not only to accept them but, on some strange level, *enjoy* them. After Calvin's persistent avowals of hatred for them, Belle couldn't believe this was true. Nevertheless, the more she fell into them around Jack, the more she sensed Jack's contentment when they happened.

She was also trying to figure out how she felt about Jack hiring a shop assistant for her, driving her to work and spending a day in her store not because he wanted to but because (she was certain) he was protecting her from the media.

This was beyond nice, polite, simply-protecting-the-mother-of-my-unborn-child thoughtfulness. It was something else, something more.

Much more.

Additionally, she was trying to figure out how she felt about the fact that it was very clear...

No.

It was *vehemently* clear that Jack was thrilled he had fathered a child during a one night stand. Belle thought that was every man's worst nightmare.

Not Jack's.

But further, he seemed just as thrilled (if not more so) that he'd fathered that child through Belle.

Most men would *not* be thrilled about this in any way, shape or form.

Jack seemed delighted.

Belle found this weird though, she had to admit, it also made her secretly happy. Not only for herself but also for their child.

And she was trying to figure out what Jack meant when he told her she'd meet his PA, Olive, saying this in a way that inferred Belle would be around for a while. Not the while it would take for her successfully to birth their child but the kind of while that said she'd not only meet Olive, she'd get to know her.

Which would mean Belle would be a fixture in Jack's life and not the kind of fixture that he'd see when dropping off their son at her cottage or picking him up or speaking with her on the phone to discuss his grades.

A different, extremely more fixed, fixture.

She was also trying to figure out how she felt about the fact that she was letting him sleep with her and she'd allowed him to do the delicious things he'd done to her on the couch.

But mostly, she was trying to figure out how she felt about him *not* thinking she was the brazen hussy she thought she was behaving like but instead that he was a "very lucky man" that she behaved this way with him.

The memory of him saying that (and calling her "my love" while doing it), made her scalp tingle and her belly curl in a way that was nearly (but not quite) as nice as the amazing orgasm he'd given her. Something which didn't embarrass her in the least (well, not after he'd said the things he'd said and held her so tenderly after she'd had it).

She was further trying to figure out how she felt about living in a haunted castle. Something that seriously weirded her out but something she seemed to be able to do (with Jack around, that was).

And, lastly, Belle was trying to figure out what her next move was.

She could either trust Jack would keep her safe and believe in all the things he was saying, not to mention the way he was behaving.

Or she could flee to the wilds of South America and live in a tree house in the rainforest.

She was coming to no conclusions, but considering the many dramas that seemed to befall her moment to moment and thus befall the baby she was carrying, she felt it important to reassure her child.

So she pressed her hands closer to her belly, looked down and said, with more hope than certainty, "Okay, sweets, it all seems very crazy right now, there's a lot happening but I promise it won't be like this forever. It'll calm down and life will be normal and boring."

On her last word, her body gave a small jolt and her head came up as she felt Jack behind her.

His arms went around her, one hand joining hers at her belly, his other arm wrapping around her upper chest to pull her against his tall, hard body.

She was so engrossed in her thoughts she hadn't heard him approach and was completely still when his mouth went to her ear and he said low, "I'm not sure it's a good idea to start lying to our child at this early stage. With your mother and grandmother, I doubt things will ever be normal and boring."

Belle turned her head to look at him, he lifted his own and their eyes caught.

"*Your* mother isn't exactly sedate and unassuming," Belle reminded him with no disapproval in her tone whatsoever.

Jack grinned and Belle's belly did a flip.

"This is true," he agreed good-naturedly.

As if to prove this fact to them, Joy swept into the room, a bottle of tequila held aloft, announcing grandly, "I've got the tequila!"

Jack and Belle shifted slightly to watch her entrance.

Though Jack turned them, he hadn't let Belle go.

Joy slammed the bottle down on the coffee table, straightened and looked at the couple in the window.

Her eyes did a sweep of them, they got bright then she went on, "I've called Yasmin. She says she's dropping everything and will be here in ten minutes. That was five minutes ago."

"Mum," Jack's voice was low and rumbly. Not the happy shiver causing low and rumbly but the oh so scary low and rumbly.

Joy ignored him. "I've ordered a late lunch to be brought in so we can all have a bite to eat while we're chatting."

"This isn't a party," Jack informed his mother, turning Belle fully to face Joy but still not letting her go. His hand moved from her belly and both arms wrapped around Belle's upper chest, keeping her back close to the heat of his front.

She'd never been held that way in her life.

It felt nice.

So nice, of their own volition, her hands lifted to curve her fingers around one of his strong forearms and she held on.

"With a little effort, *anything* can be made into a party," Joy replied breezily, her eyes dropped to Jack's arms and Belle's hands and she continued in a softer voice, "And these days, it seems we have more and more to celebrate."

Before Belle could process this statement, Yasmin stormed in and Belle stared.

She looked entirely normal except for the fact that she was barefoot, there were toe separators between her toes and three toes on her left foot had not been coated with the bright, iridescent tangerine the others sported.

She looked around and then her eyes locked on Joy. "Did I miss it?"

"No, darling, you didn't miss it," Joy assured her, her eyes on Yasmin's toes. "Did I catch you in the middle of a pedicure?"

Yasmin walked into the room, toes curled to the ceiling, her gaze moving to Jack and Belle. "I dropped everything and got in the car. I think I may have broken the land speed record to get here." She looked to Belle. "I've been waiting *years* to see Myrtle and Lewis. If they're appearing more often, I'm considering moving in."

Belle began to wonder if maybe Yasmin wasn't a little mad too but she didn't get to process this either.

Suddenly, Yasmin rocked back on her heels, her arms crossed on her chest and she grinned a mischievous grin. "You two look cozy. We know we'll soon be hearing the pitter-patter of little feet but are we expecting wedding bells too?"

Belle's body went statue still.

So did Jack's.

Belle wanted to run from the room, from the castle, maybe even find a spaceship and ask the astronauts to take her to the moon.

Jack, as if sensing this, tensed his arms.

"Yasmin," he said in that oh so scary low and rumbly voice that was even *more* oh so scary than ever before.

"What?" Yasmin asked with feigned innocence, her grin never slipping. "I need to be prepared. I have to have an outfit and a big hat. *Huge*," she emphasized. "The hat has to be enormous." Her gaze shifted to Belle. "Do you design hats?"

"No," Belle replied in a small voice.

"You should," Yasmin told her. "I bet you'd be good at it."

Before any more could be said, Gram and Mom entered the room and, not surprisingly, they did it far more flamboyantly than either Joy or Yasmin.

Or at least Mom did.

"You!" Mom shouted, clearly in a state, her hand up, finger pointing at Jack then she demanded, "How dare you move my daughter into a haunted castle?"

"Oh dear," Joy muttered.

"Oh dear is *right*," Mom yelled at Joy. "I *do not* believe this. Ghosts. Creepy child ghosts. *See-through* creepy child ghosts." Her eyes shifted to Jack and she screeched, "Child ghosts! *Everyone* knows nothing is creepier than *child ghosts*!"

Although Belle found nothing whatsoever funny about the current moment, Jack, of course, did. She knew this because she not only heard his chuckle but she felt his body shaking with laughter.

"*This is not funny!*" Rachel shrieked.

"Rachel Leonora, calm down," Gram demanded.

Mom turned on Gram. "I will not calm down. We're moving out, this *instant*."

"You're not moving out," Jack stated, all humor gone from his voice, and Mom whirled back to him.

She opened her mouth to speak then she stopped and her eyes moved over Jack and Belle. They rested on Jack's arms and Belle's hands then they lifted to Belle's face.

And they narrowed.

Belle didn't know why they narrowed. All she knew, through a vast amount of experience, was this was not good.

"Oh my *God*!" Rachel shouted. "You two have been fooling around!"

Belle's body gave a surprised jerk as she felt Jack's go solid behind her.

Mom wasn't finished.

"You're fooling around with my daughter while there are ghosts in the house!" she accused Jack as if this was an act akin to rounding up innocent citizens randomly in order to torture them just for kicks. Then, bizarrely, she backtracked, "Not that I frown on fooling around, because, you know, everyone needs a bit of nookie. Especially on a Sunday afternoon." Mom turned to Yasmin and shared, "Best time of the week, Sunday afternoon."

Mortified beyond any mortification Belle had felt *in her life* (and that was saying something), Belle found her voice and snapped, "Mom! Shut *up*!"

Her mother looked back at Belle. "I'm just saying."

Lila started laughing, Joy was biting her lip and Yasmin was grinning ear to ear but, although she couldn't see Jack, Belle knew he was done.

She knew this because, in his oh so scary low and rumbly voice, he declared, "Enough."

Belle saw Mom's body give a small twitch and her eyes went to Jack.

Jack went on and she realized he was not just done, he was *done* and he was *angry*.

"Rachel, enough," Jack repeated, the words vibrating with fury. "I cannot imagine, since you bore and raised Belle, that you and your mother have no idea how much you embarrass her. You are who you are and you behave as you behave, which is a credit to you both as you clearly don't give a damn what people think of you and that's commendable. Further, your behavior is mostly interesting and often quite humorous. That said, from this point forward, you'll consider your daughter's feelings and control it when it might cause her discomfort."

While Jack was making this speech, Mom's mouth had dropped open as had Gram's but Jack wasn't quite done.

"Am I understood?" he asked.

"See here—" Gram snapped, moving forward.

Jack's arms tensed on Belle's chest and he leaned forward, only slightly, but very threateningly (she didn't see it, she *felt* it), taking Belle with him and Gram halted.

"Am I understood?" he demanded, his tone so far past low and rumbly, it was not funny.

"She's my daughter," Mom noted in a far quieter tone.

"She is," Jack replied, his voice less menacing. "But there's a time to discuss personal things and Belle isn't comfortable doing it with an audience. I'm simply asking that you consider her feelings. Something I'm sure you'll have every desire to do."

Belle decided it was time to intervene and she looked up at Jack's jaw.

"I really don't mind," she lied softly.

Jack moved back a few inches so he could catch her eyes.

"You do, poppet. I feel it, I see it but you're too kind to say it."

He was right.

"Is this true?" Mom asked, and Belle looked at her as Jack shifted to her side, his arm around her waist keeping her close.

"Kind of," Belle answered.

"Honeypot, you should have said something," Mom said softly.

Belle shrugged, about as comfortable having this conversation as she was when her mom was announcing to everyone that she and Jack had been fooling around (okay, so she was more comfortable with this conversation, but still).

Jack, somehow, felt that too and announced, "We're moving on."

Then Jack led Belle toward the couch and Belle saw Gram was studying Jack, a thoughtful look on her face, but there was a smile playing about her lips.

Belle thought this was slightly more ominous than Jack's tone earlier (and this was also saying something) but she decided to ignore it.

She had other things to worry about.

Lots of them.

Jack sat in the corner of the couch bringing Belle down by his side. His arm curved around her shoulders and he tucked her body into his.

The others settled too. Mom and Yasmin dragging chairs across the room and, Belle noticed belatedly, one of the chairs from in front of Jack's desk somewhere between her falling asleep and waking up had been angled toward the couch.

Belle had no time to question this. Joy sat on the opposite end of the couch to Jack and Belle and Jack spoke.

"Lila tells us you drink tequila," Jack said to Mom, and Mom looked at him.

"I drink everything," she replied honestly.

"I recommend you take something to calm your nerves," Jack suggested. "At Lila's advice, Mum has brought tequila."

"Oo, I love tequila, especially at two o'clock in the afternoon. I'll get the glasses," Yasmin offered, jumped up and walked to a standing chest, the top of which she opened and there unfolded a veritable bar, including decanters filled with different colored liquors and shiny, expensive-looking glasses of all shapes and sizes.

"Cool," Belle whispered and felt Jack's fingers give her shoulder a squeeze.

She decided not to look at him.

He would probably be smiling at her, which would make her scalp tingle or her belly dip, and Belle was pretty sure she'd had her quota of both of those for one day (in spades).

As Yasmin was pouring tequilas all around, though she poured something else for Joy, Jack declined and Belle, obviously, couldn't partake, Elaine came in. She was rolling a tray filled with sandwiches, bowls of potato chips, another bowl of salad, small glass pitchers filled with dressing, a large glass pitcher filled with iced water, a teapot, a coffeepot and a tray of cakes.

Belle was slowly but uncomfortably getting used to being waited on hand and foot. It made her feel weird especially when she went back to her room after breakfast to find her bed made, her dirty clothes carried away (only to be returned, cleaned and, if needed, pressed) and quite often fresh towels in her bathroom.

She had thought of talking to Jack about it.

Then she thought better of it and kept her peace.

They all dug into the food and drank their beverages and things calmed down considerably as partaking of food and beverages was wont to achieve.

Once Joy's plate was clean, Jack ordered, "Mum, tell the story." He paused, Joy opened her mouth to speak and Jack went on, "No embellishments."

"The embellishments are the best part!" Yasmin protested.

"No embellishments," Jack asserted.

"I don't think I can do it without the embellishments," Joy told Jack.

"Yes you can," Jack told Joy.

"It'll be boring," Yasmin told Jack.

"Precisely," Jack told Yasmin.

"Will someone please tell us something?" Lila demanded. "The weather is turning and I want to get to the hayloft to take some snapshots of The Point during a thunderstorm, if we get one, which it looks like we will."

Everyone looked to the windows and saw that the sun was struggling against the thickening cloud cover. The clouds were no longer white but a threatening dark gray.

Belle loved sun and she loved snow and she loved rain, but she especially loved thunderstorms.

She always had.

Belle so loved them, Lila always did one landscape in each series she painted during a thunderstorm or a fierce downpour. These she never sold but gave to Belle and most of them hung at the cottage while some of them Gram and Mom carted around from place to place because Belle's cottage wasn't that big.

They were even more famous than her other works because their existence was known but they weren't sold, never viewed and, therefore, had acquired a mystique.

No one knew she painted them for Belle and no one knew Belle had most of them. Therefore no one knew they were, by far and away (in Belle's mind), her grandmother's best work.

Something emanating from Jack captured Belle's attention and her eyes moved to him.

She saw he was studying her grandmother contemplatively. Belle remembered that he owned one of her pieces and he likely was interested in her grandmother's remark.

It was then Belle decided she'd show him the pictures. She never showed them to anyone, unless her friends came to the cottage, and most of her friends had no idea they were in the presence of famous but secret masterpieces and Belle didn't tell them.

Jack, Belle guessed, would know.

And Jack, Belle guessed again, would appreciate the opportunity of a viewing.

"All right then, I'll try to tell it with no embellishment," Joy said, not sounding at all happy and pulling at Belle's attention.

Belle looked from Jack to Jack's mother as she began.

"Over two hundred years ago, I think it was 1798, or something like that, the master of this castle was named Joshua Bennett," Joy started.

"He was known to be very clever, somewhat forbidding, quite accomplished, shockingly handsome and a complete womanizer."

"Is this necessary to the story?" Jack asked, though it wasn't a question, as such, more a demand for his mother to move along to the important stuff.

"I have to give the back story," Joy protested.

"No you don't," Jack retorted.

"The back story is the best part!" Yasmin repeated (almost) her words of minutes before.

Jack's gaze swung to her and she clamped her mouth shut under the heat of it.

"I'm giving the back story," Joy declared mutinously. Jack shook his head with frustration and Joy carried on, "Meanwhile, living in the village, was a woman named Brenna Addison. Brenna was known to be very sweet and very pretty but also quite quiet. Brenna had made a bad marriage. Not that her husband wasn't well-to-do, he was a wealthy merchant, but that he didn't treat her very well."

"What do you mean, he didn't treat her very well?" Rachel asked.

"He beat her, and you have to know it had to be bad because that was likely very hush-hush at the time and probably not entirely frowned upon but everyone knows it happened. It's an integral part of the story," Joy answered, throwing an obstinate glare at Jack as if daring him to challenge this fact.

Jack stayed silent and Mom and Gram's eyes moved to Belle.

She didn't see them. She felt them but she ignored them and kept her own gaze glued to Joy who continued telling the story.

"Brenna and Joshua didn't meet until after Brenna's husband had taken some voyage and his ship had wrecked. Everyone assumed he was dead. The story goes that no one was sad to hear it because Brenna was a lovely girl and everyone in the village liked her," Joy recounted. "Joshua and Brenna *did* meet, however, at a ball in the drawing room of this very castle. They say they fell in love the minute their eyes met and they were virtually inseparable from that moment on. Within mere months of meeting, they were married and quickly thereafter had two children, Lewis first, then Myrtle. Lewis was the vision of Joshua, Myrtle the exact same of Brenna. They were all very happy, Joshua settled down, Brenna blossomed under his devotion and the children grew up in a house of love."

Yasmin moved, lifting her feet up to the edge of the chair, wrapping her arms around her calves and resting her chin on her knees, obviously settling in for the good part.

Belle felt a tiny shiver slide through her because she suspected, since the child ghosts were, firstly children and secondly, ghosts, the good part was really the *bad part*.

Joy went on with the story.

"The problem was, Caleb Caldwell, Brenna's first husband, had *not* died in the shipwreck. He survived. Without his health then, after he recovered, without any money or papers and being a long, long way away, it took him years to get home, but he finally did. Needless to say, he was *not* happy to find that his wife had married another in his absence and bore him two children. They say what made him even more incensed was that Brenna was happy, delightfully happy with her new family, far happier than she ever was with him."

Joy drew in a breath and continued.

"He didn't look himself, older, thinner and with significant scars, no one recognized him. He came back to the village and learned what he learned but he never shared who he was. Instead, he plotted against Joshua, Brenna and their children."

"I don't think I like this," Belle whispered and realized she was pressing herself into Jack's side and his arm was tighter around her shoulders.

Even though she realized this and normally she would move away, she absolutely *did not* even *consider* such an action.

Instead, she too, lifted her feet so her heels were in the couch and dropped her knees so her legs were resting on Jack's thigh. She turned into him and put one arm around his stomach, the other one she burrowed so it could wrap around his back. Then she put her cheek on his shoulder and held on.

As she was doing this, Jack gave her a squeeze and said softly, "Poppet, it's just a story. It's a sad one but it happened a long time ago."

Belle nodded against his shoulder even though she didn't feel the least bit better at what he said.

"I'll hurry through the sad part, darling," Joy assured her and then, as promised, swiftly went on, "Obviously, he killed them. He waited until Joshua was away on some business trip, he snuck into the castle, suffocated the children in their beds, dragged Brenna to the cliffs and threw her into the sea."

"Oh my God," Rachel breathed.

At the same time Belle whispered, "Oh my goodness gracious."

At the same time Lila murmured, "That jackass."

Joy continued.

"Joshua returned, learned his family was dead and he went mad, as anyone would. He stopped at nothing until he hunted down Caldwell. He brought him back, Caldwell was tried, found guilty and they strung him up," Joy told them then looked at Belle. "It doesn't have a happy ending for Brenna, Lewis and Myrtle but Joshua did find love again. He remarried and had three more children. Though," her eyes moved away from Belle, "they say he was never again as happy as he was with Brenna."

"You skipped over the part where Joshua found Caleb, played with him a little while, until Caleb was mad as a hatter then Joshua got sick of the game, ended up beating the crap out of Caleb and then brought him back barely alive," Yasmin informed Joy and looked at Mom. "That's one of my favorite parts."

"I can see why," Mom muttered.

Belle ignored this exchange and asked Joy, "The children have been haunting the castle ever since?"

Joy gave Belle a small smile. "Yes, my dear, ever since. But, most important for you to know, until they were murdered, they lived here happily. And they live here happily now. They spend their days playing, probably just like they did when they were alive. They've never done anything mean or that first thing to harm anyone. They've even had some mortal friends along the way who they've talked to a little bit."

"This is where the story gets good," Yasmin told them happily, apparently unaware that she'd given away the fact that she thought *every* bit of the story was good.

"They talked to people?" Belle asked.

"Oh yes, not many, but they did it," Joy answered.

"What did they say?" Lila inquired.

Belle felt Jack's body still against hers and Joy's eyes moved to her son.

She bit her lip nervously, Belle did not read this as a good sign and then Joy's gaze swung to Gram. "They'd just tell stories of the masters and the mistresses of the castle."

"They'd do more than that," Yasmin put in. "They explained what had to happen to release them."

"Really?" Mom asked, leaning forward.

"I think that's enough," Jack interrupted. He gave Belle another squeeze and she looked up at him. "As you can see, even if they do exist, they're nothing to worry about."

Belle nodded, thinking of those children stuck for hundreds of years in this house without their mom or dad, and she felt that fact was even sadder than the fact that they'd been murdered.

She looked to Joy and asked, "What will release them?"

Joy's eyes flashed to Jack before they went to Belle. "Well, they don't exactly know."

"But they *think* that their mum has to come back," Yasmin explained. "They think that the master of this house, not any master, but one that's *exactly* like their father, has to fall in love with another woman, who's *exactly* like their mother. Once that happens, something else has to happen, they aren't sure what, and their mum will come back and sweep them away to heaven."

As Yasmin spoke, the air in the room took a funny turn.

And not, Belle knew, a good funny.

And Belle also knew exactly why.

It was not lost on her that she shared the same initials as Brenna Addison, Jack shared the same initials as Joshua Bennett, and Calvin shared the same initials as Caleb Caldwell.

It was also not lost on her that the back story (not including the shipwreck, but instead a divorce, and not including the ball, but instead a birthday party) sounded more than a little bit familiar.

"Holy crap," Mom breathed, her wide eyes locked on Jack and Belle.

"Rachel," Gram said with soft warning.

"Holy crap," Mom repeated.

"Rachel!" Gram snapped and Mom jumped.

"What?" Yasmin asked, looking between the two.

"Oh, nothing," Lila explained. "Rachel always gets a little freaked out about ghost stories. We lived in a haunted mansion once and both Belle and Rachel were a total mess."

"That wasn't a haunted mansion," Belle said, desperately latching on to something that had nothing to do with the fact that her and Jack's story so closely resembled Brenna and Joshua's. "You'd angered the neighbors, Gram." Belle twisted around to look at Jack and added, "They were not very nice, by the way, wild parties at all hours and they let their dogs do not good things in our front yard and never cleaned it up. They definitely deserved Gram having a word with them." Belle looked back to the room and carried on, "She just didn't stop at a word and painted about twelve of them, none of them nice, on the side of their house." She turned back to Jack. "After that, they kept playing tricks on us, nasty tricks that made Mom and I think the place was haunted." Belle twisted back to the room and finished, "We left shortly after that."

"You painted words on their house?" Yasmin asked Gram, grinning.

"Yep," Gram answered.

"She not only painted them, she stayed up all night. It was practically a mural," Mom put in. "It was awesome. Too bad they painted over it."

"What were they?" Yasmin queried further.

Gram opened her mouth to answer but Belle got there before her and suggested, "Why don't you share that later?"

Belle's words said later. Belle's face said *never*.

Gram threw Belle a smile and closed her mouth.

"Now *that* I find sad. A Cavendish mural painted over. Tragic," Jack stated dryly and everyone burst out laughing.

Except Belle, who turned to him and smiled.

Jack smiled back.

Belle felt his smile in lots of places, the best being her heart.

"Feel better about Myrtle and Lewis, poppet?" he asked softly.

Belle nodded.

"You'll feel safe in the castle now?" he pressed.

Belle nodded again.

He bent his head and brushed his lips against hers before he murmured, "Good."

Then Jack's arm wrapped around her back and he pulled her close right before Belle thought of the little ghost girl waving at her from the window.

And Belle wondered if she was the one that would help release those children and send them to heaven.

She also wondered if she'd have the courage to do whatever it was that might be required of her.

She decided that she probably wouldn't even as she vowed to find a way.

On that thought, they heard the first roar of thunder.

❧ ❧ ❧

It was hours later, when they were all in the dining room, the pudding dishes had been cleared away and everyone but Belle was enjoying coffee, that Belle turned her head to Jack.

"Jack," she called softly, intending to ask if he would mind if she accompanied him on his nightly after-dinner walk with the dogs.

Jack looked at her, his beautiful green eyes gentle with inquiry.

Belle wondered if she'd ever get used to how handsome he was (especially his eyes) and she opened her mouth to speak only to be cut off by her mom.

"Bellerina, after dinner, can I have a word?"

Belle looked to her mother and saw her face was earnest. A look Belle knew she couldn't deny no matter how much she wanted to walk with Jack and his dogs, and, she was forced to admit, she very, *very* much wanted to walk with Jack and his dogs.

"Of course," Belle said to her mom and turned back to Jack to finish what she'd started but instead asking him to delay his walk a bit but Jack spoke first.

"I enjoy your company when we're out with the dogs but I don't want you in that weather, poppet. The path gets slippery in the rain," Jack told her.

Belle looked to the windows. It was late evening but the day was not done as it stayed light until very late during summers in England. However, it was dark as night outside. The lightning and thunder had ceased but the rain was falling hard, heavy and steady and had been since that afternoon.

Belle's eyes went back to Jack and she nodded.

"I won't be long, love," he finished on a small smile.

Belle nodded again and returned his small smile.

"Well, I'm going in search of Myrtle and Lewis. If there's any time they'll show themselves, it'll be during a spooky, dark storm," Yasmin declared, throwing down her napkin and standing.

"It was a bright, sunshiny day when I saw them," Belle informed Yasmin.

"Same here," Mom added.

Yasmin waved her hand in front of her face. "Matters not, everyone knows ghosts like a good storm," she said with authority then continued. "I'm off, anyone want to join me?"

"You go on, darling, I'll find you in a bit," Joy said.

"You got it," Yasmin replied and left the room.

The minute she did, Joy turned to Jack and noted quietly, "I'm concerned about her."

Belle's eyes slid to Jack and she saw he was watching the door Yasmin just used, his jaw was tense and his chin lifted in acknowledgement of his mother's words.

"Why are you concerned?" Lila asked.

"She's trying to hide it but I can tell, this latest divorce is taking its toll," Joy answered. "Quincy is a good man and he adores her. At first I think he was confused and thought he could talk her round. That didn't work and now he's very angry that she's doing this."

Belle was surprised at this news, thus she shared, "Yasmin told me about him when she was in my shop. She didn't make him sound like a good man."

"Most of what she told you is likely untrue," Jack explained and Belle's startled eyes went to his. "Not that she's lying but exaggerating or telling tales, not to convince you but to convince herself. Yasmin has a habit of sabotaging her happiness."

Before Belle could respond, Joy continued, "Her first husband was a bit wild, just like Yasmin, but he loved her too. They burnt bright. Therefore, eventually they burnt out. It was probably for the best, though he too was a good man and would have done anything for her." Joy's eyes moved to Jack. "Yasmin has always had good taste in men. She's just constantly throwing them away."

Belle felt a funny, very unpleasant feeling steal through her at this reminder that Jack and Yasmin used to be an item. She'd been informed of that upon meeting them but it hadn't crossed her mind since. Mainly because Yasmin didn't act like an ex-girlfriend but like an adopted sister-daughter.

Her mind moved to Yasmin opening the hidden bar cabinet and how Yasmin knew exactly where to go and what to do.

Then her mind, which often liked to torture her, moved to the couch where Jack held her, kissed her and touched her and she wondered if he'd done the same to Yasmin there.

She licked her lips and her eyes caught on her grandmother's face.

Gram was smiling at her. It was a small smile and meant to be a reassuring one and Belle knew Gram knew her thoughts.

This small smile normally would work on Belle and had many, many times in the past.

But, at that moment, for some reason, it didn't.

"Have you talked to her?" Mom asked, breaking Belle out of her tortured thoughts.

"She won't listen," Joy answered.

"Maybe you should try," Lila suggested gently.

Joy looked to Jack. "Maybe Jack should try." She turned fully to her son. "She'll listen to you, darling, you know she will."

Jack nodded and replied, "I'll have a word."

Joy smiled at her son and murmured, "I better go find her."

She left the table and this heralded a mass exit, Jack stopping Belle on her way up the stairs to her mother's room.

When she'd tipped her head to look at him, he told her, "If you want to join me in the study later, you don't have to knock."

With that he leaned in, brushed his lips against hers and he was gone.

She stood where he left her for a moment, still feeling his mouth against hers and wondering if his open invitation to his study meant as much to him as it did to her.

Then she turned and climbed the stairs.

Gram was in her mother's room when she arrived and Belle knew immediately her mother didn't want "a word." Instead, Belle was going to get what they both referred to as a "talking to."

She walked across the room to the windows, saying, "I'm not sure I'm up to this, guys."

"Probably not but then again, when would you be up to finding out you were likely the conduit to release the spirits of two children bound to earth for hundreds of years, sending them straight to heaven?" Gram remarked.

Belle ignored her grandmother's remark, looked out the window and saw the rain had stopped. She also saw Jack, Baron and Gretl heading up the cliff path. Jack was wearing a dark rain slicker, his head bare, the wind blowing his thick hair.

Jack, Belle noted, looked good from behind in his rain slicker with the wind blowing his hair. She liked the way he walked, even on the slick path, with long, confident strides, his body at his command.

"Earth to Belle, come in Belle," Mom called, and Belle turned to see Gram at her side peering out the window.

"She's mooning over Jack," Gram informed Mom.

"Lots to moon over," Mom commented. "The man's got a fantastic behind."

Gram turned from the window, looked at Mom and shared, "I like his hands."

Mom grinned. "Yeah, he's got great hands. And, from Belle's look this afternoon, I'm guessing he knows how to use them."

"Mom!" Belle snapped as she walked from the window and threw herself on the bed in front of her mother.

She rolled to her back and her mother leaned over her. "It's just my way of saying I'm happy for you, honeypot."

Belle sighed and asked, "Can we not talk about Jack's hands?"

"Okay," Mom agreed happily. "Let's talk about his behind. That's a *much* better subject."

Belle rolled her eyes.

"Or his eyes. That man has unbelievable eyes," Gram noted as she joined them on the bed. "I was convinced they were contacts when I first met him but I don't think they are."

"They're not," Belle informed her, Gram smiled and Mom giggled.

Then Gram said gently, "I think you found yourself a good one this time, my sweet."

Belle was beginning to think her grandmother wasn't wrong.

And this budding knowledge scared the dickens out of her.

Therefore, she broadened her limits on the evening's subject matter. "Can we not talk about Jack, at all?"

"Sorry, baby, can't do that. That's why we called you in here," Mom told her.

Belle rolled to her side and crooked her elbow, putting her head in her hand and looking at her mom who was lounged the same way as Belle. Then she looked at her Gram who was leaning back against the pillows.

"Does he know about Calvin?" Gram inquired and Belle closed her eyes, hating the idea of thinking of Calvin and Jack in the same thought.

When she opened her eyes again, she answered, "No."

"You can't tell him," Mom said.

"You must tell him," Gram said at the same time.

Mom turned to Gram and asked, "What?"

At the same time Gram turned to Mom and asked, "What are you thinking?"

"She can't tell him," Mom reiterated.

"Why on earth not?" Gram queried.

"Cast your mind back to this afternoon, Mom, when Jack put us both in our place," Mom demanded. "In case you didn't get it from *that*, not to mention about half a dozen other examples I could give you, Jack's a *wee bit* protective of Belle. If he learns what Calvin did to her, he'll go ballistic. He might even spontaneously combust!"

Belle winced at the idea of Jack spontaneously combusting, however, she had to admit the very idea of Jack finding out about Calvin made her heart hurt.

Not only his reaction to this knowledge but what he might think of

Belle knowing she'd made the choice of Calvin in the first place and let his abuse carry on for as long as it did.

He'd think she was an idiot and worse, a coward for not putting an end to it the minute it started.

"That may be so, Rachel, but it's clear things are moving full steam ahead with Jack and Belle, and he's got the right to know," Gram returned.

"Okay, I agree, just not now. We need to wait until after Belle releases the ghost children," Mom replied.

"What?" Belle asked.

At the same time, Gram asked, "Why?"

Mom turned to Belle and declared, "Obviously, you have to release those children."

Belle felt her lungs expand and it wasn't a good feeling.

"Yes, that *is* obvious but I don't understand why Jack needs to be kept in the dark about Calvin for her to do it," Gram retorted before Belle had the chance to speak.

"First, if Jack knows Belle's history, he's going to cotton on to the fact that he shares Joshua Bennett's characteristics just as Belle shares Brenna's, both of them *exactly*. Once he understands this, do you think Jack, for one instant would allow Belle to lift even a finger to help those children?" Mom asked.

This was, unfortunately, true.

Who knew what Belle had to do to release Myrtle and Lewis?

It might be dangerous.

Jack would *never* agree to her doing anything dangerous.

He wouldn't even let her take a walk on a rain slick coastal path, something she'd done hundreds of times. It *was* England. It *was* Cornwall. Rain slick coastal paths were the norm and Belle walked *a lot*.

"Hmm," Gram muttered, which was her way of agreeing without actually having to agree.

Mom pressed her advantage and looked at Belle. "You can't tell him."

"I think," Belle said softly. "That something is happening between Jack and me."

Mom grinned and teased, "You think?"

Belle shook her head but went on to say, "Yes, Mom, I do. I also think it might not be a good idea to keep Jack in the dark about *anything*. He won't like it."

"Hmm," Gram muttered again, this time more firmly non-stating her agreement.

"Not mentioning it is the same as lying to him. I kept the pregnancy from him and he wasn't happy about it," Belle reminded them.

"You can say that again," Gram mumbled.

Rachel, however, was not deterred. "I saw those children today, and okay, they freaked me out. But once I knew their story, I thought about what I saw. The little girl gave me a wave and the boy was grinning at me. They seem sweet but it's too sad for words that they're stuck here. Something has to be done and we all know Jack will never agree to you doing it."

This, too, was true.

"Let me think about it," Belle suggested. "Maybe there'll be a time when I can explain things to Jack and get him involved. Maybe I can talk him around. Maybe he'll feel better about it if he has some control over the situation."

"What if that time doesn't come?" Gram asked.

Belle licked her lips and thought about the children she saw in the window.

Then she thought about the fact that they likely spent years in the castle with their still alive father. Watching him with his new family. Watching him grow old. Watching his new children thrive under his love and care. And watching him die.

And after that they were stuck here and alone with only themselves for company (and a few mortal friends along the way).

Belle looked at her Gram then her mom. "If that time doesn't come then we go it alone."

Gram looked uncharacteristically uncertain.

Mom smiled.

"That's decided, we'll get started," Mom announced and Belle felt a feeling of foreboding.

She had no idea *how* to get started but she knew without a doubt that her mother had a great number of ideas.

She also knew without a doubt that Jack wouldn't like a single one of them.

"We need to go back to Calvin," Gram said, and both Belle and her mother looked at her.

"Why?" Mom asked, her tone sharp, something which happened quite frequently during the rare times anyone mentioned Belle's ex-husband's name.

Gram's eyes went to Belle. "You've been getting a lot of media coverage. Now you and Jack are getting a lot. Soon, people are going to understand this is not only serious, there's a baby on the way. They're going to go nuts. Calvin has had to have seen this, but even if by some miracle he hasn't, he will."

Belle rolled to her back and pressed her fingers into her forehead.

Belle had been trying, and succeeding, in not thinking about this very thing.

She'd lived for months worried that Calvin would approach her after the news hit about what she'd done when that school bus went over the bridge.

At the time they'd been divorced for four years. She'd heard through friends he'd remarried. She hoped that he'd moved on.

But he'd been outrageously possessive when they were married. If Belle even glanced at another man, Calvin would lose it and Belle would pay the price.

Belle had fretted that the media would find out about Calvin and Belle and feed on it like everything else.

This, fortunately and miraculously, did not happen.

Then Belle had fretted that her appearance in the news would remind Calvin of her existence and he'd re-enter her life. He'd done it before, trying to win her back until he eventually gave up.

This, fortunately and also miraculously, didn't happen either.

However, pictures of Belle and Jack kissing, Jack holding her close to his side, Jack pressing his forehead to hers, would wind Calvin up until he was out of control.

And, since it was Jack, it would be worse.

Jack was a better man than Calvin in a lot of ways (heck, in *every* way), many which Calvin would never know.

But the ones he would know, that Jack was richer than him, famous, more accomplished and far more handsome, would drive Calvin up the wall.

Calvin had spent years convincing Belle that she was lucky to have him, that she couldn't dream of ever finding another man, that he'd gone slumming when he chose her.

The fact that Belle could catch the eye of a man far better than Calvin *and* the media rubbing his nose in it on a near day to day basis would drive Calvin over the brink.

He'd lose it and take it out on her.

Gram spoke again and Belle took her hands away from her face when she did. "You need to be careful, my sweet."

Belle turned her head to look at her grandmother and nodded.

"It's a good thing you're living here and Jack's taking you to work," Gram stated. "Just keep your eyes peeled, and in the meantime your mother and I'll frequent the shop. But, until you tell Jack what happened with Calvin, I don't want you to go anywhere alone, okay?"

"Okay," Belle whispered.

"He won't hurt you again, honeypot," Mom reassured. "We wouldn't let him and now, Jack won't."

In her heart, Belle knew this was true.

And her heart spoke to her soul and they both came to an agreement.

It was just her mind that worked against her.

"I think Joy would tackle him and beat him senseless," Gram commented.

"I'd hate to think what Yasmin would do," Mom added.

"I don't hate to think of it," Gram grinned.

"Can we not talk about Calvin anymore?" Belle asked quietly.

Both her mother and grandmother looked at her and a miracle occurred.

For, at the same time, they agreed.

❧ ❧ ❧

Belle sat in the window seat of her bedroom wearing a cotton nightgown in a pretty pastel plaid, a drawstring tie at the bodice forming a ruffle along the neckline and wide, ruffle-edged straps. It came down to mid-thigh, and to ward off the cold brought on by the change of weather, she'd put on a pair of thick, pink socks and pulled on a short, pink, jersey dressing gown with a wide hood.

She'd designed the nightgown and robe, a new line of clothing that she'd added to her inventory last summer that had taken off like a shot.

She had not, of course, designed the socks.

The storm had come anew, bringing with it flashes of lightning and rolls of thunder.

Belle watched it and let it clear her mind, which fortunately worked.

After her discussion with her mom and Gram, instead of going to Jack, which had been his unspoken but understood wish, she'd stayed in her mom's room. They'd lain in bed and chatted like they'd done thousands of times before, never lacking for conversation.

She was enjoying some time alone with her mother.

But she was also avoiding Jack.

No longer because she was scared of him, it was now because she was scared of her feelings for him.

Therefore, sitting in her window in her room non-thinking, she was also avoiding her thoughts.

And thus she was startled when the door opened and she heard the jangle of dog tags.

She looked that way to see Jack's form silhouetted in the light from the hall, Baron and Gretl forging straight toward Belle.

The light was extinguished when Jack closed the door and Belle's mind was gripped with fear, wondering at his mood, wondering how he'd feel that she didn't accept his invitation, wondering if he was angry with her.

Absently, she scratched both dogs' heads while she watched Jack walk toward her.

She could barely see him, the moon was shadowed by clouds and there was no light on in her room. But she could see that he was fully clothed, though she couldn't see what he was wearing, it looked like a long-sleeved tee and a pair of pajama pants.

Instead of shifting her and settling behind her (which she kind of hoped he'd do), she watched in frozen silence as he sat on the window seat by her bent legs.

The dogs moved to accommodate him and she heard them settle not far away.

Then his shadowed hand came out and the backs of his fingers ran the length of the side of her thigh from knee to hip, pushing her nightgown along as his fingers met it.

This made her tremble but she trembled in a different way than he normally made her tremble because this was not a sexual touch but a tender one.

"What's on your mind, poppet?" he asked and she noted immediately he didn't sound angry or even put out.

He sounded gentle and curious.

"Nothing," she told him.

"Nothing?" he asked, now sounding slightly disbelieving but mostly teasing.

"The storm has cleared my head," she explained, and she saw Jack's head turn to look out the window. When he didn't reply, she added, "I love thunderstorms."

She saw him face her again and he remarked softly, "I see." She didn't know what he saw but he told her, "This is why Lila paints thunderstorms."

She'd been right. He knew about the Storm Series.

Belle nodded but worried he couldn't see her nod so she said, "Yes."

"She loves you a great deal," Jack remarked. "Though, I've noticed she hasn't offered *me* any lemon drops."

Belle felt a soft giggle float up her throat and instead of pushing it back, she let it go.

When she did, Jack moved.

But he didn't settle in behind her.

He settled opposite her, positioning his long legs so they were cocked on either side of her, his feet against her hips.

She found something about this profound.

It was as if he sensed she needed space, and although he wasn't willing to give it to her, he *was* willing to give it to her in a way that was a compromise that worked for both of them.

This settled in her heart, it settled in her soul and, finally, it settled in her mind and Belle relaxed.

She relaxed so much she shared, "She likes your hands."

"Pardon?" Jack asked.

"Gram. She likes your hands."

Belle could swear she saw the white of his teeth through the shadows before he muttered. "Well, that's something."

"Mom likes your behind," Belle blurted.

Caught up in a moment of relaxed sharing, she didn't think to censor her words and she felt the heat hit her cheeks, glad, for once, that Jack couldn't see it.

"I think I could have died without learning that information," Jack returned, and Belle instantly wished for magical powers to turn back time, but Jack's legs pressed against hers for a moment before they relaxed. He carried on in his low and rumbly tone, "Even so, my love, there's never anything you can't share with me, no matter if I don't want to hear it."

Belle swallowed and looked out the window.

"Belle," he called. "Did you hear me?"

"Yes," she told the window.

If this was true (and, considering he'd used his low and rumbly voice, it had to be), she could tell him about Calvin and she could tell him about her desire to help Myrtle and Lewis.

It would be a risk but she had to learn to take them no matter how much they frightened her.

Not only for herself but also for their child and finally, she suspected, for Jack.

She turned to face him and announced, "I'm worried about Myrtle and Lewis."

She felt his eyes on her, the trill went up her spine straight to her scalp but he didn't speak for a moment.

Finally, he did.

"I guessed that would happen."

"You did?"

"Poppet, you dove into the freezing sea to save a busload of school children. It isn't a fantastic leap to guess you'd want to release two child ghosts to heaven," he replied.

"It's not the same," she returned.

"It's not?" he asked.

"No," Belle answered.

"How is it not the same?"

She shook her head and looked back to the storm. "It's just not. That day, with the school bus, I didn't think. It wasn't like I watched it happen and I thought, 'Here I come to save the day.' I didn't think at all. If I did, I would never have done it." Her voice dropped to a whisper and for some reason she kept sharing, "I don't even remember most of it."

She hadn't spoken of this to anyone save her mom and Gram, of course, and the counsellor she had to see when she'd stopped sleeping.

Other than that, she hadn't spoken of it.

Not once.

Even though lots of people had asked, she'd never uttered a word.

His voice had gentled considerably when he asked, "You don't remember it?"

Belle shook her head again and kept her gaze at the window.

"I remember stopping, getting out of the car and climbing over the railing, standing at the side of the bridge, staring into the sea, watching the bus sink."

She felt his body go still and the air in the room went instantly thick but she just kept talking.

"Then I remember diving in like it was a swimming pool, not the November sea. It was freezing cold, instantly chilled to the bone cold and I felt bits in the sea hitting my body as I swam down. I don't even know what those bits were but I do know they scared the heck out of me."

She gave a shudder, his legs pressed hers again, and still she kept going, thinking bizarrely that Jack needed to know this. In fact, for some reason, she thought he *deserved* to know it.

"I had to open my eyes and it was dark, murky. I could see the bus. The water was somewhat shallow so it wasn't that far. Far enough to submerge the bus, though, and fast, weirdly fast. It had fallen on its side, the wrong side. The door was against the sea floor, the back doors wedged against a rock. There was air in the bus, I saw the kids banging on the windows, the bus driver frantically trying to open them." Her voice dropped to a horrified whisper, "It was hideous, the sea felt like it was saturated with their fear."

At this, Jack apparently had enough of giving her space.

He leaned forward, put his hands to her waist and pulled her to him, twisting her and dropping his knees so she was cradled in his lap, his arms tight around her.

When he'd settled her, she felt his heat warm her and looked up at him.

"I don't remember anything else, Jack. Not one second of it. The kids come and see me at the shop, sometimes at my cottage. Their parents bring them. They act like I'm some kind of superhero. They bring me gifts, some of it silly stuff, like stickers. Sometimes it's cakes their moms make. In the beginning, I didn't remember a single face. It was like someone else had done it and I was impersonating her."

Belle stopped talking and when Jack didn't reply, she continued.

"Now, of course, I know them, all of them."

"Post-traumatic stress, poppet," he murmured, giving her a squeeze.

Belle tucked her forehead into his neck. "That's what the counsellor said." She moved so she could wrap her arms around his middle and whispered, "The bus driver told me," she stopped and added, "his name is Bob, by the way, and he comes to visit me too."

"I bet he does," Jack muttered, and Belle kept talking as if he didn't speak.

"Bob told me that the bus was filled with water at the end. He was the last live person I pulled out. The window he'd opened to get the kids out had filled the bus with water. He knew I was getting tired. I was too cold. I was slowing down. He was injured in the crash, dislocated his shoulder. So were some of the kids, bouncing around in that bus. Two of them were trapped. He couldn't get them loose before I got him out. Though he tried. Nearly drowned doing it. He didn't want me to keep going back knowing the bus had been filled, knowing those kids were trapped." She stopped and swallowed. "But I did. I don't remember it. I don't know how I did it but I pulled out the dead kids." Belle took in a shattered breath and said in a trembling voice, "Davey and Penny, they were called."

Jack's arms got so tight, they took her breath and he ordered, "Stop talking, Belle. Just stop."

She squeezed her eyes tight, pushed closer to Jack's warmth and breathed, "I don't want to remember, Jack. Never. I *never ever* want to remember."

"No one's making you remember, poppet," Jack said softly.

"I know," she whispered.

"What you did was extraordinary. You couldn't have done any more," Jack told her.

"I know," Belle repeated.

"Clear your mind, love," Jack advised.

She nodded against his neck and pressed even tighter to him, feeling his arms do the same.

She took in a ragged breath and asked, "Do you think we could do anything for Myrtle and Lewis?"

She felt Jack's body go solid under hers then it started shaking.

Her head lifted and she looked at his shadowy face.

"Jack?" she called then heard his chuckle and it was her turn to go solid. "What's funny now?"

"Poppet, you just shared an inspirational but unbelievably terrifying story considering it was *you* who did what you said you did. I love that you're the kind of person who would do something like that. What I *don't* love is the thought of you giving yourself hypothermia and likely nearly drowning while saving a busload of kids, no matter how heroic. I also don't like the trauma you have to endure when you think of it. Therefore, after witnessing that trauma less than a minute ago, I'm not overly enthusiastic that you're willing to throw yourself into another heroic endeavor to save the souls of two nonexistent ghosts."

She pulled away slightly and looked in the direction of his face. "I doubt it would be dangerous."

"Belle, *they don't exist*," Jack retorted with what she could tell was waning, if amused, patience.

"I saw them. Mom saw them. Joy's been seeing them for years!" Belle reminded him kind of loudly.

"No offense, love, but you're a little emotional at the moment and our mothers aren't exactly the kind of women who live lives ruled by logic and reason."

Belle's eyes narrowed. "Are you saying I saw two ghosts, ghosts many others have seen before me, because of *hormones*?"

She heard his chuckle again and stiffened at it again before he said, "No, I'm saying a lot has happened to you, some of it you just shared with me and that you're willing to believe in something in order to keep your mind off something else that distresses you."

"So, you're saying I'm seeing ghosts because of post-traumatic stress?"

"Perhaps."

"So what about everyone else who has seen them?"

"Poppet, the story of the murders of Joshua Bennett's family is famous. The resultant whisperings of the ghosts of his children haunting this castle is just as well-known. You might not remember having heard them but you likely have. Myrtle and Lewis are lore in this area of Cornwall. Your mother, likely the same. My mother, definitely the same. She knew of them before she moved into the castle after she married Dad."

Belle found she was aggravated, not shy, not retiring, not meek, nor mild but straight-out annoyed.

At Jack, who, she noted with irritation, was stubborn.

And a bit of a know-it-all.

Therefore, she asked tartly, "Okay, since they don't exist then you won't mind me doing...whatever...to help them on their way."

Jack was silent a moment before he replied, "Knock yourself out, love."

Belle smiled but Jack's arms gave her a small shake.

"Just as long as you or your mother, who I'm assuming gave you this idea and is in on it with you, or your grandmother, who also disappeared after dinner, or Mum and Yasmin, who, if they get wind of this will want to join in, don't put yourselves in danger."

"We won't put ourselves in danger," Belle assured him, still smiling.

"I want you leading the pack," Jack demanded. "I shudder to think what your mother would have up her sleeve."

"Don't worry, Jack. Mom will listen to me," Belle kind of lied.

She *might* get her mother to listen to her.

She also might *not*.

Jack was silent another moment before he muttered, "I get the feeling I'm going to regret this."

"Everything will be just fine," Belle promised cheerfully.

Jack's hand lifted and his fingers tangled in her hair.

"Can we go to bed now?" he asked, his voice dipped low and sexy and Belle's belly did a flip.

Bed, with Jack, would be good.

Although bed, with Jack, could also be a place where things could get even more complicated.

Belle's heart and soul were already ready for that.

Belle's mind, however, wasn't quite there yet.

Therefore she requested, "Can we watch the storm awhile?"

Without hesitation, something else that helped convince her mind, just not entirely, Jack shifted her so her back was no longer to the window but she was facing it.

Then he lifted his knees and she fell between them.

His arms resumed their place around her, her torso twisted, she wound her arms around Jack, placed her cheek to his chest, her lower body curled between his legs and Belle lay in the protective shell of his large frame.

Thus, they watched the storm.

The thunder had long since died, as had the lightning, but the rain slammed against the panes.

Belle relaxed in Jack's arms, and there she fell asleep.

Lewis and Myrtle

Myrtle stood invisible in the corner of the room as her beloved Jack lifted her newly beloved Belle and carried her to bed, Jack's dogs jumping up to follow close at his heels.

Jack rested her in bed, carefully took off her dressing gown then pulled off his shirt and Myrtle blushed but she didn't move.

She watched Jack join Belle in bed as Gretl settled on her side, but Baron, although he lay down on his belly, watched Myrtle.

Myrtle gave the dog a friendly wave and Baron let out a gentle woof.

"Quiet, Baron," Jack ordered softly, and instantly Baron put his jaws on his front paws but he didn't take his blinking eyes from the girl-child ghost.

Myrtle walked backwards, melting through the wall and once through, she zoomed to where Lewis was hovering at the window in the eastern turret, watching the storm.

"Lewis, Lewis, Lewis! Belle's going to help us!" Myrtle cried upon reaching him, grabbing his arm to give it a good shake.

Lewis turned to look at his sister.

"She can't help us, Myrtie Mine," he replied, using the nickname their mother had given Myrtle so many years ago. "She has to be—"

"She saved a *bunch* of children from *drowning*. I heard it. She told Jack the *whole story*," Myrtle explained excitedly.

Lewis's ghost form went still at this news.

"She's a real-life *hero*," Myrtle announced. "She's going to find a way. I *know* she is. I could tell by her voice. *Everyone* is going to help her. Everyone but Jack, that is," Myrtle told him then suggested brightly, "I think we should appear in front of Jack!"

Lewis rolled his ghost eyes to the ceiling then back to his sister.

"I keep telling you, no. You're always wanting to appear in front of Jack. You wanted to appear in front of Gareth too."

"I liked Jack's father," Myrtle sulked. "I don't know why you won't ever let us—"

"I don't either," Lewis explained for the millionth time. "We just can't. I don't know why, I just feel it. We can't. Something will happen, something *bad*." He floated closer to his sister. "Please, Myrtle, just listen to me and don't do anything silly. If Belle wants to try, we can help *her*. But you have to promise me you won't appear in front of Jack."

Myrtle looked sullen a moment but eventually she nodded jerkily.

"Promise me, Myrtle," Lewis pressed.

"Lewis—"

"Say it out loud."

She crossed her arms on her chest then said waspishly, "I promise."

If Lewis could breathe, he'd have let out a breath.

The rules were, if you promised out loud, you couldn't break the promise, both of them knew that *by heart*.

Myrtle floated away in full pout.

Lewis looked out the window and decided, not for the first time and he reckoned not for the last, that he *hated* storms.

Especially thunderstorms.

He looked at the spot where his then new ghost self had watched through the pouring rain and booming thunder, the bad man throw his struggling, screaming, crying mother over the cliff.

His thoughts were not on his mother but the woman who reminded Lewis of her.

Belle was a real-life hero.

This was good news, for Lewis knew (though Myrtle didn't and he hadn't told her in all their hundreds of years together, though he didn't know why, just like he didn't know why they couldn't appear in front of the masters, he just knew) that his mother, too, had saved a child from drowning in the sea.

It was one of the reasons why she was much loved in the village.

Therefore, Lewis had real hope.

And so he hoped like nothing else he'd ever hoped in his life (or his death), that the sweet, quiet, beautiful Belle could actually, truly, really help them finally go home.

13

DINNER AT THE COTTAGE

Belle

The next morning, Belle watched Jack close her shop door behind them before she hurried to the alarm panel and put in the code.

After she was done, she turned and jumped when she saw he was close.

He didn't put his hands to her jaw this time. Instead, he took her hand and led her to the stairway at the back of her tiny store, which led up to her workroom and away from the prying eyes of the media people peering through her window.

He didn't lead her all the way up, just halfway so only their legs were visible. There, he stopped, turning her to face him on the stairs.

"I have to go to work, love," he told her when he'd tilted his head down to look at her.

Belle nodded.

She was beginning to read the signs. He put on a suit when he "went to work." He wore jeans when he worked from the castle.

"Are you going to London?" she asked stupidly, because to ask was to get an answer and she didn't want an answer.

"No, I'm flying to—"

He didn't finish.

Of its own accord, her hand shot up and covered his mouth, and before she even thought to stop herself, she blurted, "Nope, no, I don't want to know."

She saw his eyes smiling at her though she didn't know if his mouth was and his fingers wrapped around her wrist and pulled her hand away.

"All right, we won't talk about my work. We'll talk about yours," he started, eyes still smiling. "Is Belinda coming in today?"

Belle nodded.

"Don't open the shop until she gets here. Send Nola or Carol down to help her. You stay up in the workshop," he commanded and continued issuing orders. "I'll phone or text you to let you know when to expect your new assistant, but I don't want you coming down until she gets here."

She found herself half pleased, half annoyed that he was telling her what to do in a way that said, quite clearly, he expected her to do it.

"You're very dictatorial, did anyone ever tell you that?" she asked, letting the half annoyed part take control.

"Occupational hazard," he replied, eyes back to smiling.

Belle looked down at the steps and muttered, "I bet you were a bossy kid, too."

Her head came up when she heard him roar with laughter and she couldn't be angry at him anymore because he looked way too darned handsome when he laughed.

Which, incidentally and contradictorily, she also found annoying.

His face had gentled after he laughed and she screwed up the courage to ask, "Are you going to be home for dinner?"

She watched his face shift from gentle to tender at her question and her heart started beating faster.

"Yes, poppet, though not early enough to come and collect you."

Belle looked to his ear, to the knot in his tie then with a great deal of effort, she forced her eyes to his and said, "No, um..." She hesitated then rushed on, "I was wondering if we could have dinner together."

"Of course," he replied.

"No," she said quickly before she lost her nerve. "What I mean is, can I make dinner for you? Just you and me at my cottage."

Something changed about him. She couldn't put her finger on it but whatever it was filled the very air. It made it smooth, silky, thick, like velvet trailing across her skin.

"I'd like that," he said softly.

Belle nodded again and swallowed before she went on, "My cottage is a short walk from here. You just—"

"I know where you live, Belle," he cut in, surprising her with this news. "Do you have enough to do here to wait for me to come and collect you?"

She nodded yet again. "I always have enough to do."

He moved into her space and said, "I'll let you know when I'm close."

"Okay," she whispered, liking the idea of knowing when Jack was close but not as much as liking it when he *was* close.

"I've got to go," he told her but he sounded like he didn't want to. In fact, he sounded like he *really* didn't want to and Belle felt that trill shoot up her spine.

She nodded once again but he didn't move.

She waited.

He still didn't move.

This went on for a while.

Finally, she asked, "I thought you said you had to go?"

"I'm waiting for my kiss."

A dozen trills shot up her spine and her scalp tingled so much she thought her hair would stand on end.

She was getting there. She'd even met his eyes and asked him to dinner.

She couldn't *kiss him*.

The last time she'd kissed him, it led to an orgasm on his couch.

Then she thought about him flying to God knew where. No copilot. Maybe ending his flight in a fiery crash somewhere remote where it would take days of concentrated search efforts (with dogs) to reach his beautiful but broken body.

She hated to admit it, even though she just took one, it was time again to take another risk.

So that's why she leaned into him, put her hands to his chest, slid them up so they were around his neck and she went up on tiptoe as she pressed her chest to his.

He helped, his hands coming to rest lightly on her waist and tilting his head down so she could put her mouth on his.

And Belle kissed him, softly at first, pressing further and opening her lips just a little bit.

He helped again, opening his mouth over hers.

So, timidly, she slid her tongue inside his mouth and touched it to his.

The second she tasted him, his arms wrapped tightly around her, hauling her against his body and up, taking her to the very tips of her toes (and beyond).

His head slanted and Jack took control of the kiss.

From there, it went wild and hot and nearly out of control.

It was *fantastic*.

Before it could careen entirely out of control, his mouth tore from hers but he held her close, his lips sliding to her ear.

"I like the way you kiss, poppet," he murmured there.

"That's good," she whispered back inanely, not completely in control of all her faculties and she heard him chuckle.

He set her on her feet but touched his lips to hers one last time.

"Have a good day," he said.

With that he turned and she watched him leave.

She stood on the stairs, back pressed against the wall, until her legs stopped shaking, her heart quit beating so fast and her scalp halted its tingling.

This took a while too.

Then she went to her workroom and got to work.

❦ ❦ ❦

Late morning when Nola, one of her seamstresses, was downstairs with Belinda, and Carol, her other seamstress, was upstairs with Belle, both Carol and Belle working at her two sewing machines, Belle's purse rang.

She ran to it, grabbed her phone, looked at the screen and saw it was Jack.

She pressed the screen to take the call and put it to her ear.

"Hi," she said and then gave herself a tiny shake because her voice, even on that one word, sounded breathy.

She mentally kicked herself for saying "hi." She should have said "hello" or a casual "hey, Jack" or a formal "Belle's phone."

"Hello, poppet." His deep, rumbly voice cut off her rampaging thoughts and slid through the phone into her ear giving her a long distance trill and tingle. "Olive is in transit. She and your new assistant should be with you this afternoon."

Belle's body went stiff. "Olive is coming?"

"She's decided to escort your new girl. I'm guessing she wants to meet you."

"Oh my goodness gracious," Belle breathed in horror only to hear Jack chuckle.

"She's a PA, love, not the Wicked Witch of London."

"Yes, right. Of course," Belle replied softly, feeling like an idiot.

"She'll like you," he assured.

Belle doubted that. She had a lot of people who liked her but she wasn't a master of the best first impression.

"Of course," she repeated not because she agreed. Because she thought she should say something.

"There's a lot to like, Belle," he continued, his voice getting low and very rumbly and it hit her that he was taking time out of his likely very busy day to reassure her.

Her mind got one step closer to going the way of her heart and soul.

"I'll be okay, Jack," she told him.

He was silent a moment then said, "You'll know her anywhere. She has peach hair."

Belle forgot about her mind, heart and soul, let out a startled giggle and asked, "Peach?"

"Don't ask me," Jack replied, amusement in his voice. "I'll see you later, my love."

He rang off and Belle heard his last two words over and over in her head until Carol called her name.

She focused on her colleague who was watching her closely.

"He's fit, *way* fit, but girl, you're a mess," Carol remarked.

Belle walked over and sat down next to Carol at her sewing machine. "I know. I'm *such* an idiot."

Carol grinned at her. "He doesn't think so and that's *all* that matters."

This was simple but it was absolutely true.

"He's coming to the cottage for dinner tonight," Belle shared, and Carol's brows drew together in confusion.

"I thought you were living with him."

"I am and so is his mother, my mother, my grandmother and, a lot of the time, his ex-girlfriend now adopted daughter slash sister," Belle revealed.

"One word for that and that word is '*eek*,'" Carol noted with a smile on her lips. "I'm guessing you want some alone time."

"I want to show him my grandmother's landscapes," Belle replied honestly and Carol burst out laughing.

When she quit laughing, she teased, "That's what they all say, dear."

Belle saw the humor and grinned before she asked, "So what do you reckon I should make for a fabulously wealthy man who orders breakfast from his housekeeper every morning, has his bed made for him every day and flies to work in a plane?"

"Meat and potatoes," Carol answered instantly. "Unless they're poofs or celebrity chefs, which are just other words meaning poof, men like meat and potatoes. All men. Even fabulously wealthy ones." She got up and walked to her purse. "Leave it to me. I'll go to the store. I'll stock you up. He probably eats so much fancy food, a little home cooking, he won't know what hit him." She moved back to Belle and held out her hand. "Keys to the cottage."

Belle walked to her purse, dug in and gave Carol her keys and some money.

A little wiggle of fear spiraled in her belly, she looked at Carol and opened her mouth.

Before she could utter a word, Carol said gently, "I've had dinner at your house, Belle, three times. You're a great cook. Americans usually are. I'm not kidding, love, he won't know what hit him."

Belle nodded, watched Carol leave, and wiggle of fear gone, she went back to work.

❧ ❧ ❧

Mid-afternoon, Belinda's head popped up at the landing to the stairs and Carol and Belle looked at her.

Her eyes were bright and her face was flushed.

"You have got to see *this*," she breathed in apparent rapture before her head disappeared.

Belle and Carol looked at each other, got up and headed down the stairs.

In her shop, as well as three customers, was a peach-haired woman wearing, bizarrely, a full-on, boxy tweed suit with a light wool turtleneck under it and thick tights even though it was twenty-nine degrees Celsius outside.

There was also a light-skinned, black man with close-cropped hair, dark-brown eyes, a strong, square jaw and the body of a defensive lineman including broad shoulders and massive height that Belle guessed was at least two inches taller than Jack, and Jack was *tall*. He was wearing an impeccably cut suit and he could easily be scouted as a leading man in a variety of Hollywood movies including romantic comedies but *especially* action films.

In other words, he was gorgeous.

Not James Bennett gorgeous but as close as Belle ever got.

Eyes to the black man, Belle walked to the peach-haired lady.

"Belle Abbot." She heard and she tore her attention from the man and looked at Olive who was speaking.

"You're Olive," Belle said idiotically.

"That I am," Olive replied and stuck her hand out.

Belle took it and Olive's fingers closed around hers. Olive's grip was so firm it was a little scary and she shook Belle's hand so stoutly, Belle's entire frame shook with it and the whole time her hazel eyes never left Belle's face.

Belle returned her look as best she could and the woman dropped her hand.

"This is Dirk," Olive said, motioning to the black man. "He's your new shop assistant."

Belle's mouth dropped open as Belinda cried, "Isn't that *great?*"

"Oh my goodness gracious," Belle whispered, her eyes glued to Dirk. "You're a man," she told him.

He grinned and his white teeth flashed so brightly Belle was temporarily blinded.

"Last time I checked," he answered, his voice so deep it hit the room like a thunderclap.

"Oh my goodness gracious," Belle repeated.

"Until this morning, he worked on Sloane Street. Now he works for you," Olive announced.

Belle looked back to Olive and asked hesitantly, "Um, can I talk to you a second?"

Before Olive could answer, Belle grabbed her hand and dragged her to the back of the store, up the stairs and into the workshop.

There, she whirled on her and got close. "Does Jack know that's my new shop assistant?"

Olive's eyebrows went up. "Not exactly. He told me to get you an assistant. He usually doesn't follow up once he gives a directive. He just expects it to get done. Which it always does. Hence Dirk," she finished, throwing a hand casually toward the stairs.

"I think," Belle said in a voice filled with portent, "he's expecting it to be a girl."

"He said 'get the best.' I got the best," Olive declared. "The best just happens to be a man."

"I'm not sure he's going to like this," Belle informed her.

"Why not?" Olive asked.

"Because, well..." She paused, not certain how to point out the obvious because it should *be* obvious. She went with, "He's a *man*."

"So?"

"It's not just any man, he looks like a superhero," Belle shared. "Or, at least, he looks like he could play one on TV."

Olive leaned back, crossed her arms on her ample chest and grinned. "I see. You think Jack'll be jealous."

"Um..." Belle began but her mind screamed, *yes!*

"Let me tell you something, Belle Abbot. Jack Bennett doesn't get jealous. A woman's stupid enough to look another way, which by the by has never happened, as in *never*, he'd let her. He doesn't have a lot of patience for idiots," Olive informed her.

"I act like an idiot all the time," Belle shared.

Olive's grin turned into a smile. "Well, that may be so but you're also darned pretty, you smell good and you have more dignity in your little finger than every woman Jack's ever dated while I've been working for him all combined. So I'm guessing you get a free pass on being a pretty, dignified idiot who smells good."

Belle stared at her, dumbstruck then asked on a whisper, "You think I have dignity?"

"I think anyone who can ignore those vultures outside for a year and who turns down offers to cash in on a tragedy has dignity. Yes. And lots of it," Olive answered but wasn't quite done. "You've got so much dignity I'm soaking some up just standing next to you."

It was such an outrageous thing to say, Belle let out a surprised giggle.

"I'm thinking you have dignity too," Belle told her.

"Yes, of course I do," she replied breezily. "Though, I lose some of it when Jack calls me on a Sunday afternoon and tells me to find a shop assistant by the next day."

Belle's heart dropped. "I told him he should leave you alone on a Sunday."

She leaned in conspiratorially. "My dear, what on earth would I do if Jack didn't shake up my life every once in a while? I'd be bored silly. Anyway, as a reward, I got to sit next to Dirk in a limousine for the last five hours." She leaned closer. "You should get a whiff. He smells good too."

Belle couldn't help it. She let out another giggle. This one was louder, longer and not self-conscious in the slightest.

After a few seconds, Belle realized that Olive had joined her in giggling.

❦ ❦ ❦

"I like Olive," Belle told Jack as they walked along the narrow cobbled street, Jack's arm around Belle's shoulders, only a few, straggling photographers keeping their distance and taking photos.

It was evening, the sun still in the sky, the heat staying on the day but a gentle breeze was blowing off the sea.

Olive had long since gone to the castle to settle in as she was staying for a few days as well as to find accommodation for Dirk as he was moving for the time being to St. Ives.

Belle had spent the afternoon attempting to stop Belinda from declaring her undying love for Dirk and explaining her minimal operation to him.

She found he knew his stuff, he had several suggestions, not just about how she ran her store but how she produced her line, all of them excellent, and she'd told him to do whatever he wanted and keep the ideas coming.

Then she, Belinda, Carol and Nola spent a goodly amount of time explaining how fantastic St. Ives was, where to shop, where to eat and how to get along with the tourists.

Dirk didn't seem at all fazed with his rapid change of scenery.

In fact Dirk was entirely laidback.

Except when an obvious journalist walked in, his beady eyes on Belle.

Dirk got in his way, looked down at him from his colossal height and demanded to know. "Are you buying something for your wife?"

With more audacity then sense, the reporter replied, "I'd like to talk to Belle a second."

"Ms. Abbot is available only to customers," Dirk returned.

"It's just a few questions," the man said.

"You've got two seconds to leave before you're ejected," Dirk retorted.

The man smiled. "You put your hands on me, I'll—"

Then Dirk put his hands on him and deftly and efficiently ejected him from the shop.

"I'm calling the police!" the journalist shouted from the street.

"I'll look forward to speaking with them," Dirk replied calmly and closed the door.

It was then Belle lost her battle to stop Belinda who, eyes on Dirk, breathed, "I think I love you."

Dirk grinned a blinding grin. "That should make our working relationship interesting."

Belinda fluttered her eyes and smiled.

Things returned to normal after that.

As normal as they could be with the media at the door and a movie-star gorgeous new shop assistant working with the boy-crazy one she already had.

On their walk, Jack squeezed her shoulder. "That's good. Olive called me, she likes you too." He paused then said, "She also told me about Dirk."

Belle read between the lines, mainly because his voice was filled with humor, that Olive had told Jack about Belle's reaction to Dirk.

She decided her best course was to ignore this and said, "He ejected a reporter today."

Jack's arm tensed spasmodically on her shoulders before he muttered, "I haven't met him and I already like him."

"Though, the bad news is, you've lost Belinda's blind devotion. She's now in love with Dirk."

Jack looked down at her. "I didn't know I had it."

She stared up at him in astonishment.

Was he blind?

Then again, women probably fell in love with him when he walked down the street. Like at that very moment, women were probably looking out the windows of restaurants as Belle and Jack walked by, all of them falling madly in love with him.

"You had it," she told him instead of sharing her thoughts.

"My heart bleeds," he remarked dryly and pulled her closer, curling her so her torso was twisted to his even as she was walking forward. Her arm had to wrap around his stomach for balance and she had to tip her head way back to look up at him before he murmured, "Maybe you can fill the void."

"I'll try," she breathed, he grinned and leaned down to touch his mouth to hers.

He straightened and uncurled his arm so she was walking plastered close to his side, not half plastered to his front.

He did all of his without breaking stride.

If she tried something like that she'd fall flat on her face.

He could, she thought, do anything.

Anything.

They walked silently the rest of the way to her cottage.

She shared her cottage with a neighbor. They owned the garden level. Belle owned the elevated ground floor.

Therefore they walked up a short flight of steps to get to her door, each step held a pot of burgeoning flowers. Her cottage was painted white. The front door was a brilliant, Prussian blue. She opened the door and led them into the mud room, her many jackets hanging on hooks, ready for her walks.

She closed the door behind Jack but grabbed his hand when he ducked his head to avoid the low ceiling at the foot of the stairs in preparation for climbing them.

He turned to her in inquiry.

"I didn't ask you here just to make you dinner," she told him and she watched as his body braced. "I asked you here to show you something."

He didn't speak so she moved around him but kept her hand in his. He ducked again as she guided him up the stairs to the landing, which led to her back hall as well as to her kitchen, her bath and her second bedroom. Then she took him up two more steps to the back hall and turned left into the living room.

She knew when he saw it because she felt his body jerk through his hand.

He stopped dead in front of her couch.

Belle stood beside him and looked at the massive canvas hanging over her couch.

It depicted a graceful, Savannah mansion (the "haunted" one where they'd once lived) with lushly blooming garden, an oak tree in front, moss hanging from its branches. Its colors were muted, beautiful blues and grays mostly, and lightning split the sky behind the watery portrayal of the house.

"The Storm Series," Belle whispered and felt his hand squeeze hers before, slowly, his head turned and tilted down to look at her.

She caught her breath at the raw look in his eyes, a look she couldn't read but it felt as velvet as the air from that morning.

"I have most of them here at the cottage," she went on nervously when he didn't say a word. "I thought you'd appreciate seeing them." He still didn't speak and she began to feel funny. "You can, um…" She hesitated then surged on, "Take your time. Wander the house. I'll start dinner."

With that she dropped his hand and escaped to the kitchen.

Carol had told her the menu. Fillet steaks that Belle was to grill then sprinkle with Stilton to melt onto the meat. Baby new potatoes, carrots and fresh *petit pois* for the boil. Fresh baked rolls from the bakery down the street to complete the main meal. Pudding was a tarte Tatin, also from the bakery down the street, for Belle to heat and serve with famous Cornish clotted cream.

Belle would have preferred to make everything herself, including the rolls and the tarte, but she didn't have time. Instead, she did the limited prep work, put the water on to boil, the oven on to heat the grill and was setting the table when Jack arrived in the kitchen.

She looked up from the table, still placing a knife in its spot.

"Did you see them all?" she asked and his eyes moved around the walls in the kitchen. "I don't keep any in here. Too much moisture," Belle informed him.

"Of course," he muttered.

"Did you see them?" she asked, straightening.

His eyes came to her. "I saw them."

"Aren't they beautiful?" Belle queried softly.

He watched her a moment then he replied, "I was wrong yesterday. Your grandmother doesn't love you." Belle felt her brows draw together in confusion before he explained, "Those pictures, pictures she painted for you, there aren't words to describe that kind of love."

Belle stared at his beautiful face as her mind finally caught on.

She knew.

She *knew*.

She knew anyone who would understand the hidden meaning

behind her grandmother's paintings was someone who would never hurt her.

Someone she could trust.

Someone who would keep her safe.

And she also knew what she had to do.

That didn't mean she wasn't terrified out of her skull.

But that didn't stop her from walking to the oven, turning off the stove, flipping off the grill and then walking to Jack.

She again took his hand and guided him down the two steps to the landing then up the two steps to the hall.

"Belle," he said behind her but she turned right to her bedroom.

She dropped his hand just inside the door but walked in further and turned.

Looking in his eyes, she flipped off her shoes and crossed her trembling hands in front of her, grabbing her dress.

"Belle," he said her name again. It was deeper this time, husky and rough but she didn't see him because she was pulling her dress up over her head and then off.

She'd barely got her arms free, she definitely didn't get a chance to focus on him but he was right there, she felt his hands at her bottom and she was going up.

She dropped her dress, wrapped her arms around his neck, her legs around his hips and she was turned, moved and then falling backward to the bed.

It started wild and out of control, and neither Belle nor Jack did anything to stop it.

He had her out of her underwear and him out of his clothes before she could whisper, "oh" (which she did).

Then she pushed him to his back, her mouth on him, lips brushing, tongue tasting, her body igniting as she worked her way down his broad chest, over the planes and angles of his belly and lower, her hand moving to wrap around his hardness, her thumb lightly rolling over the tip.

That was all she got.

He flipped her to the back and did the same thing down her chest and rounded belly, until his mouth was between her legs.

At the feel of him there, she arched her back and neck as he lifted her calves over his shoulders.

Calvin *never* did this to her. He hated it. He expected her to put her mouth on him but he didn't return the favor.

Jack was good at it. So good she was writhing under his mouth, noises escaping her lips, her hands deep in his hair holding him to her and she felt it coming and it was going to be beautiful.

Suddenly his mouth disappeared, Belle gave a soft cry of protest but his body came over her. He didn't rest his weight on her but rolled them, her on top. Without delay, he jerked her knees to straddling him. He shifted his hand quickly between them and sat up, taking Belle with him, filling her as they went.

Her head dropped back with the delicious feel of him deep inside and her arms wrapped around his shoulders and held on tight.

His hands went to her hips and she tipped her head to look at him.

"I thought I remembered," she whispered, her mouth against his. "How good you felt."

"Belle," he murmured, his voice hoarse, a hand sliding into her hair and fisting in it with gentle force.

"I thought I remembered," she repeated, beginning to glide up. "But I didn't remember you feeling half this good."

She didn't get the chance to slide back down.

She found herself on her back, Jack up on his forearms, his hips pounding into hers.

She loved it, every nanosecond of it.

Of which there weren't many.

It built and exploded with raw, exquisite intensity.

So much, she almost missed his thrusts deepening and his breath catching against her neck before he sighed.

She took his weight for only a moment before he pulled her legs up his sides, hands behind her knees and, keeping them connected, he rolled to his back.

She rested her forehead against his jaw, trying to get her breathing back to normal. Jack stroked her spine as she felt his erratic breaths with the rise and fall of his chest.

Okay, so, she'd just taken a risk, she'd jumped in with both feet and found something hugely rich and rewarding.

Then her mind, never her best friend, took her back to the morning after their first night together, reminding her of what she said.

It reminded her how Jack responded. How he'd been stunned and insulted when he realized she actually believed he'd used her as a prize in a competition with his brother.

And she *had* believed that.

Thus she'd walked away and not looked back.

Then she'd gotten pregnant and didn't intend to tell him.

And she *again* threw his supposed behavior with his brother in his face in the bathroom after she'd had All Freaking Day Long Sickness and *again* in the stables.

She'd done all this when (not including the time he was angry at her when she first came back into his life), he'd never been *anything* but that Jack of the first night.

Okay, maybe he had been something else but that something was his being *much more* of the Jack of that first night.

She was the idiot to end all idiots.

And she'd been right when she wasn't able to non-think that evening on the cliffs.

What she'd done wasn't rude.

It was unforgiveable.

"Oh my God," she whispered right before her body froze solid.

Instantly, he stopped stroking her spine and his arms wrapped tight around her.

"Belle," he called.

"Oh my God," she repeated, pushing away from him, causing their bodies to disconnect but he held even tighter.

"Belle," he called again, one arm moving up so he could wrap a hand in her hair.

"Let me go, Jack," she whispered, her voice sounding ugly with fear.

He tugged gently at her hair but she resisted, keeping her forehead pressed against his jaw and pushing at his chest.

"Belle, damn it, look at me," he bit out, and when she didn't he rolled again so he was on top.

She took a goodly amount of his weight at her hips, his legs tangled with hers but he twisted his torso away and rested his weight into his forearm in the mattress at her side.

His other hand came to her jaw and he turned her to face him.

When her eyes met his, he looked a mixture of concerned and irritated and asked in a curt voice, "What's in that head of yours, poppet?"

She studied him for a moment then two. All she could think was that he was criminally handsome even looking concerned and irritated.

Then she burst into tears.

She covered her face with her hands and tried to roll in the opposite direction but he caught her and pulled her to him, positioning them both on their sides, his legs still tangled heavily with hers, his arms tight around her.

"Jesus, Belle, what is it?"

She shook her head and his fingers wrapped around her wrist and pulled one of her hands from her face.

"Belle, talk to me," he demanded.

She moved her other hand and looked at him, tears still streaming from her eyes.

"That morning after I met you, I walked down the hall to my room thanking my lucky stars that I met you," she announced, her voice quiet and trembling and she felt his body go still but she ignored it. "Then I... then things..." she hesitated, "then everything happened. And I said the most *awful* things to you." A sob surged up and tore free and she shoved her face in his chest. "And I just realized I was wrong. I was wrong!" she cried and pressed her hand into his chest, not to get away but to let go some of the feeling she felt.

She tilted her head back and shouted, "I spit on my stars!"

These words brought on another wave of tears and Belle shoved her face in his chest again, the sobs rocking her body.

Jack let her cry, stroking her back with one hand, the other one gliding through her hair then up, his fingers sifting in only to glide back through.

She got control of her tears (not much, but some) and tilted her head back again. "I'm not crazy and this *isn't* hormones," she declared hotly.

"All right, love," he replied in a gentle voice.

"I'm just not good at being rude," she explained. "Rude is *the worst*. And what I did was *beyond* rude. It was *unforgiveable*!" she ended on a near shout.

Jack stopped stroking her back and hair and leaned into her so she was on her back again and he was looming over her, legs still tangled with hers.

"I think that's for me to decide, don't you?" he asked and her body jerked.

She stopped crying and stammered, "Wh-what?"

"It's for me to decide if what you did was unforgiveable," he repeated, his hand coming to her face and gently wiping away her tears.

He was right.

"You're right," she whispered and held her breath.

He must have noticed it because his eyes dropped to her mouth and they were smiling. "Poppet, I forgave you a long time ago. Around the time I saw you resting your forehead against a toilet seat, talking to our child."

"That's not very romantic," she blurted then her eyes grew wide at yet *another* display of her rampant rudeness and he burst out laughing.

He shoved his face in her neck and his arms went around her before he rolled them to their sides again and looked at her.

"Okay, how about when I caught you pushing Baron out of your room one of the first nights after you moved into The Point?" he suggested then carried on. "Or when I saw you sleeping in the hayloft. Or when I kissed you later. Or when you tried to stop me from fighting Miles. Or when you kissed me in bed the next morning. Or, just after, when you got out of bed and tried to make rules. Do you want me to go on?" he asked.

Belle shook her head, though she kind of did but her heart had stopped beating on his first suggestion and she was having severe diffi-culty breathing. If he went on she might accidentally suffocate herself and then where would they be?

His face got closer. "Even if I hadn't forgiven you, time and again, I would have done it when you told me you thanked your lucky stars when you met me."

"Jack—" she began, but he cut her off and he was using his low and rumbly voice when he did it.

"We're not speaking of this again. It happened. It's over. This is us moving on."

That was nice, *really* nice, but Belle felt the need to apologize.

So she said again, "Jack—"

He interrupted again, "Am I understood?"

"Jack—" she tried again.

His face got even closer. "Belle, tell me I'm understood."

"You're understood," she whispered but stubbornly she went on. "But I want to say I'm sorry."

She caught his smile right before his hand cupped the back of her head and pressed her face to his throat, his other arm holding her tight.

"My love, you already said it when you guided me into this room," he told the top of her head and then he kissed her there.

Finally her body relaxed into his and she wrapped her arms around him.

"I need to tell you something else," she said to his throat and she felt Jack's large frame get tight.

"Belle, I'm feeling pretty fucking good right now, don't piss me off."

She thought about his warning then took another risk.

"It's just that, I think you should know...I feel safe with you."

His tight frame grew statue still.

Then it relaxed.

Then he murmured, nearly inaudibly, "It's the gift that keeps giving."

She thought she heard what he said but to be certain, she tilted her head back to look at him and asked, "What?"

He looked down at her. "Nothing, poppet."

She decided to let it go, got up on an elbow and looked down at him. She tilted her head in inquiry and watched his face grow soft when she did it.

"Do you want dinner?" she queried.

"Not right now," he replied, rolling to his back and taking her with him, his hands going into the hair on either side of her head and holding it back. "Right now," he started, bringing her face closer, and when her lips were against his, he stated, "we're going to work up an appetite."

And they did.

By the time they ate, they were *ravenous*.

And it was safe to say even *well* before he ate the delicious steak Belle cooked for him, Jack Bennett didn't know what hit him.

But he liked it.

❧ 14 ❧
BREAKFAST AT THE COTTAGE

Calvin

Calvin Cole looked at the picture of his ex-wife and James Bennett in the paper, and not for the first time in the past week he clenched his teeth.

They were casually strolling, his arm curling her upper body to his, her arm wrapped around his stomach. She had her head tipped back and his head was bent. Calvin could see a grin on Bennett's lips even as their mouths were touching.

They were kissing for all the fucking world to see.

And Calvin knew that James Bennett was fucking Belle.

The bastard was fucking *his wife*.

His eyes dropped to the caption and he read it for the twentieth time, *James and Belle, still loved up in St. Ives*.

"That fucking *bitch*," he snapped and threw the paper on the table.

His new wife walked in and he looked at her.

She was blonde, it was a brassier blonde than Belle's but it would do. She was also thinner than Belle which irked him. And she had faded-blue eyes, not at all the arresting gray of his first wife's.

She didn't dress as well as Belle either.

Nowhere near as well.

She put a plate of scrambled eggs, bacon and toast in front of him.

"I hope that's okay," she said quietly, like a fucking mouse, placing her own plate on her mat and sitting beside him.

Calvin didn't answer. His mind was occupied with that picture, burnt on his brain. Like the one of them fucking *kissing* in Bennett's fucking Jag, of all fucking cars. Calvin had always wanted to own a Jag but never had the money. Or the one where Bennett was holding Belle's face and fucking *kissing* Belle's forehead.

Angrily, he forked up some scrambled eggs and put them in his mouth.

He nearly spat them out.

His eyes moved to his wife as he chewed and swallowed.

"There's no garlic in these," he said with soft menace and watched her shoulders curl toward to her ears.

He fucking *hated* it when she did that.

"Yesterday, you told me you wanted pancakes, Calvin. I made sure we had what we needed for pancakes. You changed your mind this morning and we didn't have garlic," she whispered.

"Did you at least put cheese in the goddamn eggs?" he went on and she swallowed.

"We only had parmesan but it was fresh parmesan," she whispered again and his hand flashed out, quick as lightning, the backs of his knuckles striking with perfect, practiced aim on her cheekbone.

She cried out and put her hand to her cheek as he leaned threateningly toward her.

"Go to the fucking store and get some *fucking* fresh garlic and some *fucking* cheddar cheese and make the *fucking* eggs properly," he clipped right before he picked up his plate and threw it across the room where it, and all the food on it, exploded against the wall.

She got up, mumbling, "I'll be right back."

She tried to escape but he caught her hand and snapped, "Belle made my eggs *perfectly*. I didn't even know good eggs until *Belle* fucking made them."

His wife had heard this before.

Often.

Especially in the last several months when Calvin's precious Belle had become The Tiny Dynamo.

He threw her hand away from him and she ran from the room.

Calvin picked up the paper and opened it to the picture of Belle and Bennett.

And he sat and waited for his eggs.

Belle

Belle woke in the warm curve of Jack's body.

He was in her bed with her in her cottage.

Other than the fact that she missed the dogs, she liked this.

She liked it a lot.

Maybe she could lure Jack to her cottage for dinner again.

Maybe that night.

She lay there waiting for him to wake and when he didn't she carefully slid out from under his arm and went to her dresser. She put on a pair of undies and slid on a pair of black yoga pants and a white, shelf-bra camisole.

She went to her linen closet and grabbed her extra supplies. Belle always worried about running out of *anything* just in case of freak blizzards and the like. Not that this had ever happened, but it *could*. So she always kept extra stocks of *everything*.

She got two new toothbrushes, her extra cleanser and moisturizer and a new box of toothpaste.

Then she went to the bathroom, did her morning business, pulling her hair away from her face with a wide, black band.

That done, she went to the kitchen.

As she normally did for the last however many months, Belle walked to the kitchen window situated at the front of the house and saw the photographers.

When she did, she sighed.

Then she turned to the coffeepot.

Carol, what she told Belle yesterday was "forward-thinking," had also purchased eggs, bacon, cheese and bread. "And other bits and bobs," Carol said.

Belle got to work making the coffee, setting the table, mincing the garlic, grating the cheese, slicing the bread and was whisking the eggs when Jack walked in.

He was barefoot, wearing only his trousers, his glorious chest on display, his hair tousled in a way that was too sexy for words.

She went into an instant trance at the sight of Jack looking like *that* while walking into her kitchen. She decided somewhere in the back of her mind that was still functioning that he *definitely* should be locked up for the betterment of womankind.

And Belle's druthers would be that he was locked up in her cottage.

She was so in a trance, she barely moved when he hooked her with his arm around her waist, hauling her to his body and his mouth crushed down on hers in a kiss so mind-boggling, it was a wonder her trance didn't turn into a coma.

When his head came up, he demanded, "Fucking wake me before you get out of bed."

He sounded not loving morning fresh but irritated.

"What?" she breathed, still not over his kiss.

"Wake me before you get out of bed," he repeated.

"But," she whispered idiotically, "that's rude."

His face got close. "It isn't rude if I ask you to do it."

"But," she went on, still idiotically, "what if you need your sleep?"

His other arm circled her. "After last night, Belle, I need my sleep. I still want you to wake me up."

"Why?" she asked.

"It doesn't matter why," he returned and his hand came up, tangling in her hair then he commanded, "Just wake me, kiss me, tell me good fucking morning and then you can get out of bed."

"Oh...kay," she replied hesitantly but not happily.

Most of his demands were bossy, definitely, but also somehow sweet.

This one was just weird and very concerning.

She dropped her eyes to his shoulder and felt her stomach clench.

His hand tugged gently at her hair, her gaze went back to his and she saw his face had gone soft.

"I'll get used to it, having you," he explained and his voice had gone soft too. "Right now, I'm not used to it."

It dawned on her that she'd run away from him the first morning after they'd been together. Since then she had been either avoiding him or escaping him on a regular basis, including crawling out of bed in the mornings before he woke.

Therefore this particular beast was a beast of her own making.

She pressed closer and wrapped her arms loosely around his waist.

"I'll wake you," she promised.

He gave her a squeeze and warned, "You should probably know, even when I'm used to it I'll still want a kiss before you leave our bed."

"That won't be hard to do," she assured him.

That's when he grinned.

That was it then. He was done. No yelling, threatening, throwing things or hitting her.

She felt secret relief.

This made her grin back.

"Do you want eggs?" she asked.

He looked to the counter saying, "I'm starved."

She gave him a squeeze and when his eyes came back to her, she smiled at him with genuine, unabashed excitement and cried, "Great!"

She exuberantly tried to pull away but got about an inch before he hauled her back against his body.

When she looked at him, he called, "Belle?"

She tilted her head in inquiry, still smiling happily and returned, "Yes?"

His eyes shifted to her mouth for a moment before going back to hers.

"*My* Belle?" he asked.

The question made her breath catch, and she didn't know the answer but she knew what she *hoped* it was.

He also had a strange look on his face, warm, even tender, but also like he too was in some sort of trance (but apparently, during his trances, he could actually talk, he just couldn't say much).

"Are you okay?" Belle queried.

"Are *you* okay?" Jack queried back.

She smiled again and answered, "Yes."

"You seem pretty excited about eggs," he remarked cautiously.

She tilted her head again and leaned into him. "You haven't had *my* eggs."

Then she gently pulled out of his arms, got him a cup of coffee, pulled out two skillets, the butter, put the toast in the toaster all the while babbling.

"My dad taught my mom how to make eggs. Then they got in a competition about who could make them best. When I was old enough, they *both* taught *me* how to make them. Everyone agrees mine are the best of them all. Even me and I try to be humble but I can't be about my eggs, they're that good. And anyway, I get to cook for you. Elaine, or whoever, cooks for you and I don't get to do anything. Boiling some veg and grilling some steaks isn't the same as really *cooking*. So, yay!"

She threw butter in one skillet, slices of bacon in the other, turned on the burner under the bacon, so busy she hadn't felt the air turn velvet all around them.

When he didn't speak, never looking at him, she kept babbling.

"You should know, by the way, if Dad should show up, which he might considering the pictures in the paper, that Mom and Dad didn't have a nasty divorce. They still love each other. They hook up every time they get together. They just got a divorce because Dad's kind of wild and Mom knew it would drive her bonkers so she let him go rather than let it get ugly."

"Your dad is wilder than your mother?" Jack asked in a voice that said he found that hard to believe.

She threw a grin at him over her shoulder. "Yes. *Definitely*. He's nuts." The toast popped up, she whirled around, snatched it from the toaster, began slathering it with butter and asked, "Would you get the jam out of the fridge, please?" she paused and added, "And the grape jelly."

"Grape jelly?" he inquired and she threw him another grin.

"It's an American thing. Mom sends it to me." She looked back at the toast and kept talking. "We have grape jelly. We have grape candies too. We don't do blackcurrant." Belle gave a shiver at the very thought of blackcurrant.

She heard the fridge open and Jack said, "I'm guessing you don't like blackcurrant."

"No," Belle replied in a way that left nothing to the imagination about how much she detested blackcurrant and she heard him chuckle.

"You eat jelly for breakfast?" he asked.

She finished buttering the toast, put more bread in the toaster, picked up a wooden spatula and turned to him.

"It isn't English jelly, we call that Jell-*O*." Belle put great emphasis on the "O." "It's jelly-jelly, like jam, without the bits in."

Her kitchen was small, Jack's big frame made it smaller but it became tiny when he suddenly closed the fridge door, took a wide step toward her and got right in her space.

She leaned back as he leaned in and his arms slid around her.

She looked up at him and saw the warmth was definitely in his face as was the tenderness, also definitely, but there was something else there. She couldn't put her finger on it. It was partially amusement but the rest of it she didn't know.

But it made him look...happy.

It was, incidentally, his best look *ever*.

Even so, breathless and feeling a trill up her spine even as a strange spiral of fear curled in her belly, Belle said softly, "Jack, I'm making eggs."

"I switched her on," Jack replied bizarrely.

"What?"

His face dipped closer and he repeated, "Somehow, I switched her on."

It was then Belle realized what she was doing, how she was behaving and just how much she was *talking*.

Her eyes slid to his ear and his arms grew tight as he gave her a firm but gentle shake.

"No, love, stick with me," he said.

"I need to make the eggs," she muttered to his ear.

"Look at me," he demanded, her eyes slid back to his and his head bent so his forehead could rest on hers. "I'm looking forward to your eggs. I'm also enjoying learning about your father and grape jelly." Somehow, even though he was as close as you could get, he managed to get closer when he kept talking. "You can be this woman with me. You don't have to switch off, poppet."

Belle didn't speak.

Jack didn't either.

Finally, Jack moved, touched his mouth to hers and then his lips drew away an inch. "Or you can be whoever you want to be."

At his words, Belle's soul sighed.

He let her go, went back to the fridge, bent into it and she watched him pull out the grape jelly.

He put it on the table, walked to her, put his hand to her jaw, slid his thumb across her cheekbone, dropped his hand and walked out of the room.

Belle dazedly turned back to the eggs.

Slowly, she smiled a small smile at them.

By the time Jack returned, the eggs, bacon and toast were done and she was serving them onto warmed plates. He'd put on his shirt, partially buttoned up the front but his feet were still bare.

Silently, she set the plates on the table.

Jack sat, as did she.

They started eating.

After about a minute, Jack called her name and she lifted her eyes to his.

His hand came back to her jaw and he said solemnly, "These are the best eggs I've ever tasted."

"Really?" she asked softly.

"Really," he answered just as softly.

He took his hand from her jaw and continued eating.

Belle took in a breath for courage and queried, "Are you going to try the grape jelly?"

"No," he answered immediately, taking a bite of bacon.

"Why not?"

His gaze came to her and he said in all seriousness, even though his eyes were dancing, "I have a rule. I don't eat purple food."

She felt a giggle bubble up inside her and she let a little of it escape.

"Grapes are purple," she informed him.

"Grapes are naturally purple. That," he indicated the grape jelly with a jerk of his head, "is *not* a color nature intended. Therefore, I amend my rule. I don't eat chemically-induced purple food."

Another giggle bubbled up inside her, it was softer, quieter and she let it free.

After she was done giggling but before she'd resumed eating, Jack's hand came toward her again. This time it didn't go to her jaw but around her neck. He pulled her forward, leaned forward himself and he kissed her.

It wasn't long and it wasn't hard.

It was soft, sweet and thorough.

When he was done, he let her go, sat back and resumed eating.

Belle studied him a moment before she asked shyly. "Do you want to know more about my dad?"

"Is it going to frighten me?" Jack asked back.

"Probably," Belle answered honestly.

He looked at her and smiled. "Tell me about your dad."

So, she did.

🦋 🦋 🦋

Belle sat in the Jag as Jack drove them to The Point.

They'd showered at her place (as in, *together*, which she'd never done with a man and it was *nice*). But she didn't have extra supplies of makeup and stuff for her hair (and he didn't have anything), so he had to take her to The Point then back into town once she'd gotten ready for her day's work.

Alone he'd walked across St. Ives to collect his car, leaving Belle at the cottage with orders not to leave the house even if she saw his car in front of it. He would, he informed her, escort her through the cameramen.

He drove back, parked in front of her house and collected her at the door.

Even though the street was narrow, her steps were right on it and it was about a ten foot walk, as he said he'd do, Jack escorted her to the passenger side, closing the door after she'd settled in.

Then he drove them out of St. Ives.

Belle watched the scenery and wondered what life had in store for her now that she'd taken this, what she considered the ultimate risk.

Practically before she began to ponder it, she decided not to wonder about it.

Whatever would happen, would happen.

This was so *not* Belle Abbot, it wasn't funny.

But she had enough to worry about, what with a baby on the way and ghosts to send to heaven.

She'd worry about it later.

"Can we do that again?" she asked Jack.

"What, my love?"

"Stay at the cottage, just you and me?"

His reply was instantaneous. "Absolutely."

"You'll need to bring some clothes," she told him and when he didn't reply, she added, "and the dogs."

She heard his chuckle and looked out the window toward the sea.

And Belle Abbot, worrier extraordinaire, felt at peace.

15

ALL RIGHT

Jack

Later that evening, Jack drove Belle back to The Point.

She'd called him that afternoon to inform him that they could not, again, spend another highly enjoyable evening alone together in her quiet cottage. A cottage that was simple, inviting and subtly feminine all of which, Jack thought, was very Belle. A cottage where he found almost instantly he was completely at ease.

Instead, Belle was under strict orders from Lila to come home that evening.

They had, in the overwhelming fullness of their reconciliation, forgotten to call home, not that it even once crossed Jack's mind. He was not used to being accountable to anyone for his whereabouts.

Also, as said reconciliation had been intense and thoroughly engrossing, they hadn't heard Belle's phone ringing in her bag, or Jack's, which was muted by his clothing.

Therefore Lila and Rachel had spent the evening wondering where they were and not liking being engaged in this activity.

This was what they learned upon arrival at The Point that morning.

Lila, followed by Rachel then, far more slowly (because she was likely only lending moral support or being polite) followed by his mother, confronted them in the hallway when they walked through the front doors.

It had been short and to the point.

"Belle Ursula Abbot," Lila said in a severe voice, addressing her like she was ten years old and Belle's hand went to her mouth.

"Holy heck," Belle muttered under her hand, her eyes adorably huge with guilt. She took her hand away and breathed, "I forgot to call."

"*That* you did," Lila declared and stomped away.

"We've been worried *sick*," Rachel added then *she* stomped away.

Belle and Jack looked to Joy.

"I told them not to worry," Joy said casually.

Jack and Belle made no reply.

When they didn't, Joy smiled and asked, "Did you two have a nice evening?"

"We were also having a nice morning," Jack returned.

"That's lovely," Joy's smile deepened, "Have you eaten? Do I need to call Elaine?"

Jack assured his mother they'd eaten and she'd given them another smile and wandered away.

Now they were on their way to The Point at Lila's command.

In other words, they were in trouble and being punished.

Jack found it entirely unacceptable that he was a thirty-eight-year-old man escorting his thirty-five-year-old pregnant girlfriend home because they'd spent the night having unbelievably great sex and forgot to call, thus they'd pissed off her grandmother.

He was not used to doing anything other than what he damn well pleased.

He'd been doing exactly what he damn well pleased for over twenty years.

And what would have pleased him was to pack a bag, load up his dogs and spend the fucking night at the cottage with Belle who he'd make absolutely certain was naked the vast majority of the time.

However Belle felt it necessary to perform this act of contrition.

He found this odd, he didn't like it but he'd speak to her about it later.

At that moment, he had another mountain to climb.

"Belle," he called, and he felt rather than saw her eyes turn to him from their study of the landscape.

"Yes?"

"I spoke to Elaine today," he told her.

There was silence then a hesitant and somewhat confused, "That's good."

"About your things," Jack went on.

"My things?"

"She's moved them into my room."

He heard her sharp intake of breath.

"Jack—" she began.

Jack cut her off. "There's no longer any reason why you or I have to roam the halls in our pajamas every night."

"But..." she started and trailed off.

He glanced at her to see she was staring at him. He saw she looked that annoyed confused or a confused annoyed, he again didn't know which.

He still thought it was adorable and wanted to grin but he bit it back, looked at the road and asked, "Can you give me a reason?"

"A reason for what?"

"A reason why you or I need to be roaming the halls at night."

There was more silence then a quiet, "No."

"Good. That's settled then," Jack declared decisively.

"Jack!"

"Belle," Jack said to the windshield.

"What will Elaine think?" she asked and Jack couldn't help it, he burst out laughing.

When he glanced at her swiftly again, the confusion was gone. She was still staring at him, definitely now just cross, before turning his eyes to the road.

"Poppet, you're pregnant. I think Elaine has guessed by now we've been sexually active."

There was another moment of silence, she sighed and asked, "Don't you think it's too soon?"

"What's too soon?"

"Any of it. *All* of it," she replied.

He knew what she was asking.

Jack looked to her lap, reached out and took her hand then his eyes turned back to the road. He brought the back of her hand to his mouth and brushed his lips against her knuckles.

He dropped their hands to his thigh and kept hold of hers.

"No," he stated simply.

"You're sure?" she whispered.

At her question, a number of memories rapidly tore through his head. They included that tendril of hair against her neck the first night they met. The way she responded to his first kiss and every one since. Last night, the third time he'd had her, after they ate, when she was on top, moving on him but bent forward, her face in his neck, the sexy noises she made sounding direct in his ear while he felt her sleek, tight wetness sliding against him. And that morning, her excitement about eggs and her resulting, adorable chatter.

"More than I've been of anything in my fucking life," he replied firmly.

He felt her hand convulse in his.

Finally, she said softly, "Okay."

The Point came into view, and Belle, clearly ready for a subject change asked, "How did The Point get its name?"

"It's a house on a cliff," Jack replied.

"I know but how did it get its name?" Belle repeated.

He gave her hand a squeeze, "Chy An Als, in Cornish, means 'house on a cliff.'"

She let out a surprised giggle, something she'd been doing a lot lately, the sound of it something he enjoyed immensely and said, "That's it? Your ancestors named their formidable castle the House on the Cliff?"

"Apparently they weren't very creative," Jack remarked dryly.

She emitted another giggle.

Jack squeezed her hand.

She squeezed his back and said in an amused whisper, "I love it."

"The name or the house?" Jack asked.

"Both," Belle gave her answer, an answer which Jack thought earned her another brush of his lips on her hand and that was exactly what he did.

He'd parked in front of the house and they were halfway up the steps when she stopped and turned to him.

Jack looked down at her.

She met his eyes instantly which made Jack smile.

"I have a feeling," she started softly, "at some point you should explain *exactly* what I agreed to in the car."

There was no anxiety in her voice or self-consciousness in her posture.

She knew it was important, Jack moving her things to his room.

But she wasn't frightened of it.

This indicated to Jack that she trusted him.

He had the intense desire to snatch her into his arms and carry him to their room and, in celebration, christen it exhaustively.

He controlled that desire and instead told Belle, "We'll talk soon, poppet."

She looked away and kept walking up the stairs saying only, "Okay."

They'd stepped a few feet into the entry hall when Rachel, wearing another of her strange T-shirts, this one green with yellow writing that declared I SAID...I WANT *COFFEE!* came flying down the stairs.

"I found them," she shouted, skidding to a halt in front of Belle and Jack before she continued excitedly, "And they sound *perfect.*"

"Who sounds perfect?" Belle asked.

"The Ghost Helpers!" Rachel cried with enthusiasm and Jack tensed.

"The Ghost Helpers?" Belle asked Jack's question and she asked it in an alarmed tone that reflected Jack's feelings precisely.

"Yes." Rachel got closer. "They don't work together all the time but Cassandra thinks this might be a case where they need to team up."

"Cassandra?" Belle queried.

"Cassandra McNabb. She's a clairvoyant white witch," Rachel answered.

"Fucking hell," Jack muttered and Rachel's eyes went to him.

"No, she's good. I called her references," she informed him.

"Fucking hell," Jack repeated at the thought of a witch having references and Rachel's eyes narrowed ominously.

"You said she's working with someone?" Belle put in quickly, seeing, and probably knowing far better than Jack, the level of portent behind Rachel's narrowed eyes.

They cleared when she looked back at her daughter.

"She works with The McPherson!" Rachel announced grandly as if this meant anything at all.

"The McPherson?" Belle inquired.

Rachel came forward and wrapped her arm around Belle's waist, moving them deeper into the hall.

"I called a friend of mine in Tucson who knew some Native Americans who had healers amongst them who bought rare herbs from some women who they said were in a coven. These women knew another coven on the East Coast who knew Cassandra who knew The McPherson," she rambled her explanation. "And Cassandra says he's *the best*. They just helped to dispatch a particularly nasty ghost witch up in Devon."

"Dispatch?" Belle asked with concern.

"Well, they sent *her* to hell," Rachel replied and Belle pulled out of her mother's arm.

"We don't want Myrtle and Lewis to go to hell!" she exclaimed.

"No, of course not!" Rachel exclaimed back, "I told Cassandra the story and she knows they're supposed to go to heaven. She was happy to accept the gig."

It was at this announcement Jack decided it was time to enter the conversation.

"The gig?" Jack asked and Rachel looked at him.

"Yes, the gig. She does this kind of thing for a living. Not just ghosts, other stuff. Talking to family members beyond the veil. Whipping up potions. Things like that."

Jack ignored the ludicrous notion that anyone would have such employment and focused on the more important issue at hand.

"You're saying you've hired her," Jack stated. When Rachel nodded, Jack asked, "How much?"

"Thirty pounds an hour, plus expenses," Rachel answered.

"Fucking hell," Jack muttered yet again.

At the same time, Belle cried, "Mom!"

Rachel looked at her daughter, "What? She's highly specialized. I thought that was a bargain."

"Who's going to pay her?" Belle snapped.

"Your grandmother, for one, me for another. I'm not destitute you know," she hesitated, "Though I should look into getting a job. Do you think I could help at your shop?"

Before Jack could speak, Belle said briskly, "Of course you can work at my shop. That isn't the point. The point is this could take *hours*. What does this McPherson person charge?"

"I haven't chatted with him yet. I'll talk to him when he and Cassandra get here tomorrow," Rachel answered.

Belle opened her mouth but Jack got there before her.

And when he did, he simply said, "Belle."

She closed her mouth and turned to him.

When her eyes met his, Jack went on, "I thought I explained you were leading the pack."

He watched Belle wet her lips but she didn't reply.

Therefore he repeated yet again, "Fucking hell."

"It'll be just fine," Rachel reiterated nearly the same exact words her daughter said to him the other night while they were sitting in the window of her room.

"Do I need to get involved in this?" Jack asked.

At the same time, both Belle and Rachel exclaimed, "No!"

Jack approached their huddle, got very close to Belle and put his hand to her jaw.

When she'd tipped her head back to look at him, he demanded, "You be safe." Not taking his hand from Belle, he turned his head to look at Rachel and warned, "You keep her safe."

"Of course!" Rachel snapped, "You don't have to tell me that."

"I feel better doing it," Jack replied.

"Why?" Belle asked and Jack looked back to her.

"Because when you two make the mess I've the feeling you're going to make and I'm forced to extricate you from that mess, I'll be able to feel superior and say, 'I told you so,'" Jack answered, feeling his lips twitch.

Belle's eyes dropped to his mouth and he saw her lips form a small smile.

Before any more could be said, Joy rushed into the hall.

Her eyes were glued on Jack, they looked worried and her face was pale.

Jack's body tensed, he dropped his hand from Belle's jaw and turned to his mother.

"What is it?" he asked.

She stopped close but looked to Belle swiftly before her eyes flew back to Jack.

"Miles just pulled up," she answered.

The air in the hall changed. Jack felt fear coming from Belle and his mother, undoubtedly for different reasons, and anger coming from Rachel.

To make matters worse, Lila chose that moment to descend the staircase and she did this quickly.

Her eyes were on Jack and for once they didn't look filled with dislike or rebuke. He didn't spend much time assessing her look but the time he did it looked like she was silently offering him moral support.

Therefore, he knew that she also knew Miles was there.

He also knew that somewhere along the line he'd earned Lila Cavendish's acceptance and, possibly, her regard.

Jack didn't have time to consider Lila's acceptance or regard nor did he have time to make it to the doors and intercept his brother.

One was already opening so Jack moved to Belle and got close, curving an arm around her shoulders and tucking her front to his side. She immediately wrapped her arms around his middle.

Miles barely got the door closed before Jack said, "I thought we had an understanding."

Miles turned from the doors and walked to them, stopping well away. The bruising and cuts on his face that Jack had given him hadn't entirely healed but they were far less noticeable. He carried a magazine rolled in his hand.

Jack couldn't read his expression.

Miles's gaze went to their mother.

"Mum," he said.

"Miles," she whispered.

His eyes moved to Belle, and Jack watched them change.

He did not like the way they changed, not in the slightest.

"Belle," Miles said softly.

Belle pressed closer into Jack's side and breathed, "Miles."

"Miles—" Jack began but Miles looked at him and started speaking.

"I'd like a word."

"You've had your words. Too many of them as I recall and none of them good," Jack returned.

Miles looked from Jack, to Rachel, to Lila.

"You're Belle's family," he said, a polite smile forming on his lips.

Rachel and Lila were cautiously silent for once and Jack spoke again.

"Miles, we had our conversation. I thought I made my feelings clear."

"A word, Jack. Five minutes of your time," Miles requested.

"Jack," Joy urged softly.

He knew his mother wanted him to concede and Jack's mouth went tight.

"In the study," Jack clipped.

Miles nodded and moved toward the study.

Jack let go of Belle but Belle didn't let go of Jack so he looked down at her.

"Are you going to be okay?" she whispered her sweet question and the even sweeter way she uttered it cut through him sharply but pleasantly.

He nodded.

Then he bent his head to brush his lips against hers, gently disentangled himself from her arms and followed his brother to the study.

Once there, he closed the door behind him and walked into the room.

Miles was at the window staring out to sea.

Jack moved to the side of his desk, stopped and crossed his arms on his chest.

"Miles, say what you have to say and then I want you gone," Jack demanded and his brother turned to him.

He didn't waste time, unrolled the magazine, opened it and held it out to Jack.

Jack took it and saw it was a celebrity rag. The pages Miles showed him were a spread of "the history" of Jack, Belle and Miles.

The title of the article pronounced, *To the Victor Go the Spoils*.

Jack's mouth tightened with irritation at the title and he flipped to the next page, then the next. The article was six pages long but barely had any text.

However, there were a goodly number of photos.

All the ones of Miles had been chosen to make him look the fool. Shots captured when he'd looked angry or impatient, either emotion contorting his face in an unpleasant manner. They'd also managed to get a photo of him, what Jack guessed was several days ago, his face battered, his eye blackened.

On the other hand, the photos of Jack and Belle were chosen for different reasons.

There were pictures of Belle before she met Jack, head bowed, looking stylish and regal, ignoring the cameras.

There were pictures of Jack, head up, strides wide, also ignoring the cameras.

There were also pictures of Belle and Jack recently, kissing in his car, walking close together, clearly an item. They looked intimate, they looked smitten and it appeared they were lovers even before that was again true.

Jack looked from the magazine to Miles and asked shortly, "Your point?"

"I can't bear it any longer, Jack. I look like a fucking fool."

Jack thought, rather unkindly and not for the first time, that his brother was, indeed, a fool. He'd had Belle for a month and he hadn't done everything in his power to keep her. Instead, he'd mistreated her, actively and with mal-intent.

Jack didn't share this, instead he repeated, "Again, your point?"

"I'm asking you to do something," Miles told him.

Jack leaned a hip on his desk, threw the magazine on it and put his hand to it, saying, "I have no control over the media, Miles."

"No, I know you don't, but..." he stopped, looked away then continued in a voice where Jack knew what he said next cost him. "This can't go on with you and me. It hurts Mum and if Belle is going to be in your life for any amount of time, which it appears she is—"

"She is," Jack cut in firmly and watched Miles's body jerk.

His face grew hard and he said, "You're my fucking brother."

Jack's patience slipped a sizeable notch. "You didn't think of that when you were insulting the mother of my fucking child direct to her face."

"I'm sorry about that," Miles gritted through his teeth.

"I'm not the one you need to apologize to," Jack returned.

"Like you'll let me speak to Belle," Miles snapped.

"No, I won't," Jack agreed, remembering his brother's taunting vows, during and after their fight, to make Jack pay.

Vows that stated he'd do it through Belle.

Miles straightened and Jack watched him clench his teeth before he remarked, "It took a lot for me to come here."

"Explain why I should care about that," Jack suggested.

"What I'm saying is, I've made the first step. You should meet me halfway."

"As I recall, you used the woman who would become important to me as a prize in a competition." When Miles opened his mouth, Jack kept going. "I don't give a fuck if you were dating her at the time. You had to know Belle. You'd been dating her for a fucking month. Therefore you had to know she wasn't the type of person to jump into someone's bed if that someone didn't matter to her. And matter to her a great, fucking deal."

Jack watched Miles's mouth clamp shut, knew he scored his point and he continued.

"Then you told her *I* wanted a crack at her, knowing Belle had made her choice and what that might mean to her and knowing how she would react to something like that. You didn't take your loss like a man. You did what you did out of spite."

Miles's brows snapped together in confusion. "I didn't tell her that. Where she heard that, I've no idea."

Jack studied his brother and saw, to his surprise, he wasn't lying.

Still, he carried on, "Regardless, when I caught you with her, you were physically abusing her. Then, months later, when you knew she was pregnant and I'd moved her into my home, which is something that should have given you a clue as to what she meant to me, another clue was the fact you walked in on us kissing, you didn't duck out quietly. Instead you abused her verbally." Jack watched his brother's face go tight but he didn't let up. "Therefore, Miles, I don't think I need to meet you halfway."

"We should have talked about this four months ago when it happened," Miles told him, "I was angry. You must understand I was angry."

"Anger doesn't excuse physically abusing a woman. Nor verbally doing it," Jack retorted.

"She fucked my brother while she was dating me!" Miles clipped.

"No, *I* fucked *her*. There's a subtle difference, Miles. You know me. You knew her. You had to know the way it happened. You can't think I believe for one second you didn't. You took your anger *at me* out on *Belle*. As a result, I nearly lost her and I'm finding it hard to forgive you for that."

"And *you* can't believe for one second that, if the same thing happened to you, and a woman you cared about spent the night with me, that you wouldn't be livid," Miles shot back, and Jack's patience slipped another considerable notch at his brother's very selective memory.

"If a woman I cared about spent the night in your bed, my first thought would be that you could have her," Jack returned with complete honesty and the look on Miles's face showed he knew it.

As he would.

As it had happened before and, even though Jack didn't need to remind him, he did.

"For instance, when you fucked Yasmin."

Miles looked away and muttered, "That was a long time ago and you two weren't exactly together."

"It was a long time ago. That doesn't change the fact that, years ago, you discovered Yasmin and I were having difficulties because of a ridiculous argument she blew out of proportion. We'd grown up with her. You knew the way Yasmin behaved. How she'd take any opportunity to screw up her life. You also knew how I felt about her. You purposefully got her pissed out of her skull and took her to your bed. When she admitted it to me, she was a fucking mess because she knew it was over. And it was, irrevocably. I shouldn't have forgiven you, or Yasmin for that matter, but I did. That's *two* women in my life you've toyed with because of this ridiculous compulsion to best me, and if I didn't make it clear in the stables I will now. I'm done, Miles. This is finished."

Miles stared at Jack and Jack returned his stare.

This went on for quite some time.

Finally, and quietly, Miles said, "I'm done too, Jack."

"I'm supposed to believe that?"

Miles nodded and repeated, "I'm done."

Jack shook his head but Miles took a step forward, Jack pushed away from the desk and Miles stopped.

"This is my family we're talking about," Miles kept at him, still quietly, and when Jack didn't speak Miles continued, "Not just you, but Mum, even Yasmin isn't talking to me and now Belle's expecting. That's my niece or nephew she's carrying, Jack. And I'm banished from my own fucking house."

"You brought it on yourself," Jack retorted ruthlessly.

"I know!" Miles shouted, "God damn it, I know." Jack watched his brother swallow and then he said, "Dad would be so pissed off, Jack, if he saw us now. He'd be furious."

"He'd be furious at you," Jack returned.

"I know," Miles whispered, shut his eyes, opened them and focused on Jack. "Okay, not halfway, Jack. You win, I apologize. I'll apologize to Belle."

"That's not going to happen," Jack cut in.

"You can be there," Miles put in quickly and repeated, "You can be there, Jack. And I'll try to..." He hesitated then carried on, "Figure out why I do the things I do and I'll control it."

Jack's eyes narrowed and he remarked, "Yes, I guess you will. A nice reunion of the Bennett brothers to show the press that you aren't a sore loser and we're one big happy family."

"That's not what this is," Miles informed him.

"That's what you led with the minute I entered this room," Jack retorted.

"It's eating me. I've admitted that but it's more and you know it." He paused then reminded Jack, "We used to be close."

"We haven't been close since Yasmin," Jack reminded Miles.

"We can get that back, if you'll let it happen. Mum would be thrilled and you know Dad would have been."

Jack's body went solid, his patience vanished and his voice went low when he warned, "Don't use Dad in your games, Miles. Don't you fucking dare use Dad in your games."

"It isn't a game," Miles asserted.

"I'm afraid you're going to have to prove that to me," Jack replied.

Miles leaned forward in supplication and vowed, "I will. I promise I will."

"Good luck with that," Jack returned, disbelief evident in his tone.

"You'll see," Miles stated.

Jack leaned against his desk again, his posture back to casual, his voice anything but when he spoke again.

"This turns out to be a game, Miles, that's it. We're through. You'll never return to The Point and I won't want to see your face again. If I do, you won't like what happens."

"It isn't a game," Miles declared fiercely.

Jack took in a breath, and upon letting it out he said softly, but his voice was vibrating with meaning, "It better not be."

❧ ❧ ❧

Jack watched the bathroom door open, Belle took two steps out, looked at him where he was lying on his side and up on an elbow in bed and she stopped dead.

"Poppet, come here," Jack said quietly.

When he spoke, she jerked out of her freeze and walked to him, looking nervous.

He knew this was difficult for her. Everything was happening quickly even if some of it was by her own design.

If he had been in the same situation with any other woman, Jack would give her some space. He would give her an opportunity to get her thoughts together, get used to her changed living arrangements, the changes in her body, the media intrusion, a new employee, him.

With Belle, he was absolutely not going to do any of that.

Instinctively he knew space and Belle was not a good thing.

Firstly, and most importantly, because it was likely she'd use it to question his commitment to her, her trust in him and, in the end, to retreat.

Secondly, she'd been dealing with a great deal for some months on her own, traumatic memories and misguided guilt, all with the media breathing down her neck. She had, to appearances, handled it beautifully on her own.

However, she was not on her own anymore.

There was only so much one person could take and Jack decided she'd had enough.

Therefore, she had, indeed, had enough.

Belle going it alone was a memory.

Although it started well, it had not turned out to be a good day.

After Jack's discussion with Miles, Jack had gone to talk privately to Belle to ascertain if she was willing to listen to an apology from his brother.

After he told her he would be with her, Belle had agreed.

It all fell apart when they were waylaid on the way back to the study by the other three women living in his house.

This meant that his mother and her mother and grandmother were all in attendance when Miles apologized to Belle.

Jack didn't mind this but Miles did. He tried to hide it but he failed.

Therefore, Miles's apology came out stilted and sounded unconvincing.

This did not go over well.

Although Belle accepted his apology, Rachel and Lila clearly didn't, and Joy was looking less than impressed with her son.

Regardless, Miles, as usual, pushed his advantage and stayed for dinner. Jack did not want this neither did Belle nor, by appearances, did Rachel and Lila. They all acquiesced to Miles's request mainly because everyone was attempting to accommodate Joy, who it was not hard to read wanted reconciliation between her sons.

Dinner, also, didn't go well.

Belle retreated completely. Jack didn't know why but it was likely due to acute embarrassment because of her past relationship with Miles, her current one with Jack mingled with Miles's past treatment of her. Through dinner, she barely even glanced at Miles much less anyone else at the table.

Lila and Rachel, in an obvious attempt to behave themselves and not cause Joy distress, were practically silent.

Jack's mother was nervous and therefore chattered uncontrollably.

Luckily, Olive had come back to the castle after successfully browbeating some innocent cottage owner who wanted to charge summer rates for Dirk's extended residence in his property (she convinced him to charge winter rates regardless of the fact that Jack could afford double the summer fees until Dirk found more permanent accommodation in St. Ives).

Olive joined them for dinner and would intervene, often hilariously, when Joy's chattering started to become frantic. Although Belle never laughed, Rachel and Lila did.

Miles had switched from being wooden to being overtly charming which was, unfortunately for him, just as unconvincing as his apology had been.

Jack noticed all this vaguely. His attention was devoted to alleviating Belle's obvious discomfort. This he did by holding her hand on the table between courses and engaging her in quiet, private but short conversations.

He also touched her face once, when, even at his request, she didn't meet his eyes. Gently, he put his fingers to her jaw and turned her to face him as she continued to speak to his shoulder.

When he did this last, Jack caught Miles looking at them. He clearly saw Miles's irate glare before his brother gained control of his expression.

At any other time, seeing that, Jack would have thrown him out.

With everyone on edge and his mother desperate for a brotherly reunion, Jack did not.

However, he did escort Miles to the door directly after coffee.

"I hardly need to be shown the door as I've been using it since I could walk," Miles informed him as Jack pulled open the door.

Jack, having already lost his patience, ignored his comment and replied, "It's only fair to warn you, Miles, you aren't doing very well proving your wish to change."

At Jack's words, Miles's mouth went tight. Without speaking, Miles lifted his chin to Jack and walked out the door.

Jack immediately put his brother out of his mind and went in search of Belle so they could walk the dogs.

Belle's attitude altered the minute she knew Miles was gone. Their walk was long and for the most part comfortably silent. They held hands the entirety of it, and Jack found it an immensely pleasant excursion.

Upon their return, however, Joy informed Jack that Yasmin was on the phone saying she urgently needed to speak to him.

Jack left Belle with Joy and spent the next half hour listening to Yasmin, who had apparently been informed of the evening's activities by Rachel, unnecessarily warning him that Miles couldn't be trusted.

He knew that. He knew his brother was planning something.

And he hated it.

He hated it that their relationship had deteriorated to this point, and he hated knowing Miles intended to use Belle to destroy it beyond repair.

He hated that his hands were tied for, with Miles's current submissive behavior, Jack had no choice but to let it play out or he ran the risk of upsetting his mother. Thus, considering how Joy was accepting Belle and her family into the fold, this meant that eventually, when Miles made his play, Miles and his mother's relationship would also be destroyed beyond repair.

Jack was making quick and immensely satisfying progress in winning Belle but he knew he had to take care not to do anything to damage her fragile trust.

Further, she was pregnant with his child but hell bent on helping Myrtle and Lewis all the while coping with significant life changes.

Therefore, with recent events, he hated it that he also had to protect her from his fucking brother.

Jack watched as she stopped beside the bed. He leaned forward and took her hand, gently pulling her into their bed and his arms. He rolled to his back, taking her with him so that her torso was resting mostly on top of his.

When she lifted up on an elbow and looked down at him, his hand came up and he tucked her hair behind her ear.

When he did this, her eyes slid to the pillow beside his head and she asked, "What did Yasmin have to say?"

Jack ignored the direction of her gaze and answered honestly, his words bringing Belle's eyes quickly back to his and they'd grown wide.

"She told me not to trust Miles."

"She did?"

"She did," Jack replied and he saw her head tilt in confused inquiry.

"I thought you were all close," Belle said.

"We were, once," Jack answered. "Yasmin's mother was a good friend of Mum's. They were here often. When Yasmin's mum divorced her dad, Yasmin was still very young. Her mum moved them from London down here, a few miles away. We grew up together."

"What happened to make you not close?" Belle asked.

Jack didn't want to talk about what happened. Not at that moment. Not when Belle's clothes were hanging in his wardrobe, her tubes and bottles were in his bathroom and her warm, soft body was in his bed.

Instead, he slid a hand up her spine and into her hair. He cupped the back of her head and put pressure there until her lips where on his. Softly, he touched her mouth with his own then rolled so she was on the bottom and his torso was mostly on hers.

He lifted his head and told her, "It's a long story, poppet, but it's not for tonight. I'll tell you some other time."

"Why don't you tell me now?" she queried, and he smiled before he dipped his face closer to hers.

"Because, now, I'd rather welcome you to your new room." He gave her another brief kiss before continuing, "We started the day well and it went to hell. I intend to salvage the night."

He watched her eyes grow warm and felt her hands glide along his skin as she wrapped her arms around him.

Then she whispered shyly and very sweetly, "Okay."

Jack smiled again before he kissed her, not briefly this time and, after that, together, delightfully, they salvaged the night.

❦ ❦ ❦

Jack was dead asleep when he felt Belle's body jerk violently against his.

Seconds later, he was wide awake when he felt her jerk again then again.

In between these jolts, she was shivering uncontrollably in his arms even though her skin felt unnaturally hot.

Quickly, Jack moved away, rolling her to her back while he called her name.

She didn't wake and instead he heard her make a disturbing whimpering sound deep in the back of her throat.

Jack rolled to his back taking Belle with him and reached a hand out to turn on the light. Then he circled her with his arms and gave her a mild shake.

"Poppet, wake up."

She jolted again even as her head came up, her face pale, eyes sleepy but cloudy, the look in their unfocused depths lost and frightened.

"Belle," Jack called softly, his hand coming up to pull the hair away from her face, "look at me, love."

She blinked and her gaze came to his.

"You're awake," he told her. "You're safe."

Rather than be assured by his words, he felt her body trembling and watched her eyes fill with tears.

"Jack," she whispered, her voice husky with sleep but the sweetness was gone.

She sounded frightened and defeated.

At her tone, Jack's arms tightened reflexively around her and he rolled them to their sides.

"Poppet, put your arms around me and hold tight," he ordered, and without delay she did, even as she tucked her face in his throat, her body still shaking. He kissed the top of her head before asking, "Did you have a nightmare?"

She didn't hesitate with her reply.

"I remembered," she whispered, her voice hitched on a sob and brokenly she carried on, "Jack, I remembered the bus. I dreamed the whole thing. The whole thing. Penny, Davey, *everything*." The shaking became intense and uncontrolled, wracking her body against his and she kept speaking in a voice filled with horror, "Oh my God, Jack, I remembered everything. Every second."

Jack pulled her deeper into him. Keeping one arm tight around her waist, he let his other hand drift up and into her hair, his fingers sliding through it and then back again.

"You just had a nightmare. Talking about it the other night made you—" Jack started but Belle's head snapped back and she looked at him through tear-filled eyes.

"It *wasn't* a nightmare," she spoke fiercely through her crying. "It all came back to me. It was *awful*. I knew I didn't want to remember it, Jack. *I knew it.*"

"Poppet—" he began again but she jerked her head in the negative and clenched her arms tight around him.

"Now it's there. I'll never get it out of my head. Never. Never, never, *never*," she declared.

A fresh wave of tears overcame her and she pressed her face into his throat again.

"Hold tight to me, love," Jack urged and when she did he continued, "It's over. It's done. You're here and safe. It's finished."

"Their eyes were open, Jack," she choked, and he felt his own body jerk at her hideous words, but she either didn't feel it or ignored it and went on, "They were staring at me but not seeing me. Their hair floating. Their arms adrift. Oh my God, Jack. It was so terrible. It was unspeakable. Oh my God. Oh my God."

She began chanting these three words and rocking in his arms and Jack repeated, "Hold tight, love."

She shook her head but held on to him.

"Take deep breaths," he demanded but she shook her head again, forcefully this time, and then tilted it back with a sudden snap.

"What if that happens to Nathan?" she asked hysterically, eyes round with fear and horror. "Oh my God, Jack, what if—?"

Jack cut her off by saying firmly, "That's not going to happen to our child."

Panic undeterred, her hands moved to his chest and pushed but he held her close as she exclaimed, "Jack, what if he's smothered in his bed like Myrtle and Lewis?"

Jack gave her a gentle shake in an effort to break through her irrational fear. "Belle, he's not going to be smothered in his bed."

This effort as well was unsuccessful.

"We shouldn't have a baby. Anything could happen," she declared and suggested wildly, "You're rich! Too rich! You own a castle, for goodness sakes! No one owns a *castle*. What if he's kidnapped? Held for ransom!"

Still attempting to control her rampaging hysterics, Jack rolled into her and covered her body with the warmth of his. "Belle, calm down. He's not going to be kidnapped."

"It could happen!" she asserted, voice rising. "It happens all the time!"

"It doesn't happen all the time," Jack returned. "In fact, it rarely happens."

"It *could* happen." she pushed.

"It isn't going to happen."

"But it *could*," she stressed.

"It isn't going to," he repeated.

"But it *could*!" she declared on a near shout.

"So you're saying we shouldn't have a child because there's an absurdly remote possibility that he might get kidnapped?" Jack asked.

She nodded instantly and added, "Or smothered in his bed. Or drowned in a freak bus accident."

It was then Jack realized she was no longer trembling, crying or pushing at him. Her hands were resting lightly on his chest and she was gazing up at him defiantly.

Because of this, the humor of her words suddenly hit Jack and he couldn't stop himself from chuckling.

"What's funny now?" she yelled, again pressing against his chest, now angrily, at the same time declaring, "This is *not* funny, James Bennett. If anything is not funny, this...is...*not...funny!*"

He dipped his head and gave her angry mouth a soft kiss before pulling a scant inch away. "Poppet, our child is not going to get kidnapped, smothered or drowned in a freak bus accident."

"You can't promise that," she snapped.

All humor vanished from his voice and he watched the anger fade from her face and fear replace it when he replied, "No, you're right. I can't." He lifted a hand to cup her jaw, his thumb moved to stroke her cheekbone and he kept talking before she could say a word. "I can't promise he won't sprain his ankle or burn his fingers or fall off his horse either."

"Jack—" she started, her voice trembling but he didn't stop.

"I can't promise he'll mind us when we tell him what to do or that he'll get good marks in school or that he'll bring home only girls we like or that he'll listen to music that doesn't drive us mad."

As he spoke, he watched her face begin to grow soft and the storm started to shift out of her eyes.

After a moment, she whispered, "But I like all kinds of music."

At her words, Jack grinned. "Odds are, he'll find some you hate."

She regarded him a moment and her gaze finally cleared.

"This is true," she told him, the sweetness back in her voice and he saw her mouth form a small smile.

Jack rolled again to his side, moving her to hers and he held her close as his face got closer.

"What I can promise is we'll do the best we can and we'll keep him as safe as we can." His hand tangled in her hair and he pulled her head gently back so he could get even closer before he finished, "And even when he's pissing us off or we're worried about him, I can promise you that we'll be happy we took this risk."

He felt a shudder move through her body and she pressed tighter to him before she asked softly, "Do you think Davey and Penny's mum and dad were happy they took the risk?"

Jack's reply was immediate, "Yes."

She wet her lips before her eyes dropped to his throat and she whispered, "I suspect you're right."

He gave her hair a soft tug and her gaze came back to him.

"Are you all right now?" he asked, and he watched her blink, her expression turning oddly startled before it cleared.

"I think I am," she answered, sounding surprised by her own words.

He brushed her mouth with his and said, "Good."

Then he moved to turn off the light but she moved with him, her hand coming up to grab his forearm and he turned back to her in inquiry.

"I think I am," she repeated. "I think I'm all right."

Jack stared at her a moment before he said, "I got that, poppet."

She shook her head and came up on a forearm to look down at him. "You don't get it, Jack. I said, I think I'm all right."

Jack rose to his own forearm to look her in the eyes. "I'm sorry, love, but you're going to have to explain to me what I don't get."

"I'm all right," she repeated, and when she did Jack smiled instead of laughing, which he preferred to do but it would likely have annoyed her.

He wrapped his fingers around the back of her neck, pulling her closer.

"Repeating it isn't going to help me understand, Belle," he explained.

"I remembered," she whispered, her voice solemn. "I remembered something horrific, something I didn't think I could handle." She leaned closer, put her hand on his chest and looked directly into his eyes. "And I'm all right."

His fingers at her neck gave her a squeeze. "I'm glad, my love."

He started to move to switch off the light again but turned back when she said, "Jack, no."

His eyes caught hers and he waited.

"I'm not strong," she admitted softly. "You know that. I've never been strong. Never in my whole life. If I'd been alone, I wouldn't have been able to handle that." Her hand went to her belly as did her gaze before returning to him. "Or this," she threw her arm out, "or anything."

"Belle—" he started to disagree, but she finished what she intended to say using words that tore through his system, searing a direct path straight to his soul.

"But I'm all right because I'm not alone. I'm all right because I'm with you. Tonight, *you* made me all right."

Jack's body went still, his eyes held hers for a long moment and he forgot about the light. He forgot about going back to sleep. He forgot about everything.

He forgot that he graduated top of his class.

He forgot that he'd been made captain of the rugby team not because of his name but because of his abilities.

He forgot that he'd turned his back on the family business and built his own company from nothing.

He forgot the thrill he felt when he'd earned his first million pounds through his own hard work.

He forgot when he earned his second.

He forgot all the times he'd bested his brother.

And he forgot the last words his father said to him, telling Jack that he made him proud.

He forgot about everything he'd ever achieved, everything that ever mattered to him, and in that instant he thought that if he'd never succeeded in anything again, that would be perfectly fine.

Because he'd made Belle feel all right.

When he came unstuck, he didn't turn to the light.

He shifted into Belle's soft body and she readily accepted his weight, his mouth on hers and his hands trailing along her skin.

And although they'd made love in his room four times before. Although he remembered every second of every time, all of them magnificent and one of them life-altering in a way Jack would be grateful for until the end of his days. None of them were as beautiful as that night when he slid inside her as her fingers glided into his hair, her calves wrapped around his thighs, his tongue tangled with hers and that sexy noise slid from her throat into the depths of his.

She was not filled with fear, with panic, with anxiety.

She was filled with him and his child, moaning her desire into his mouth.

And Jack was making her more than all right.

16

THE THIRD GHOST

Belle

Belle drove her own car back to The Point, her mother beside her.

Mom had wanted to drive but Belle pitched a rude, un-Belle-like fit.

She hadn't driven a car in weeks, hadn't made but the meals she prepared for Jack, hadn't done a load of laundry, hadn't even made her own bed.

It was driving her up the wall.

She was pregnant, not invalid!

Therefore, she was going to drive herself and her mother home and no one was going to stop her.

Even though she was annoyed that everyone was treating her like she was a fragile piece of glass, it had been a good day.

The first *really* good day in a very long time.

She'd woken in Jack's arms. Then she took a shower in Jack's bathroom (with Jack). She'd put on her makeup at his bathroom mirror while she listened to him talk on his phone in the bedroom. He'd even zipped the zipper at the side of her dress (which was, she saw, getting tight).

And they'd walked down to breakfast together holding hands.

Belle Abbot holding hands with James Bennett while they walked through his huge, imposing castle on their way to breakfast like it was the most natural thing in the world.

She thought she might have a major panic attack at the very thought of settling into life by Jack's side. She thought she'd spend all her time questioning his attraction to her and also questioning her trust in him. She thought she would make excuses to run away, to protect herself, it was too soon, there were too many ifs, she wasn't good enough for him, she couldn't feel safe with him.

She thought her mind, as it always had done, would work against her.

But none of that happened.

It was, for some reason, easy.

It seemed to come naturally.

And this, Belle was certain, was all because of Jack.

He was good with her and her crazy behavior. He was also good with her crazy mother and grandmother. Further, he was good with his own crazy mother. And lastly, he was good with the equally crazy Yasmin.

He'd been overrun by women—*crazy* women—and he didn't seem to care.

Not even a little bit.

What he seemed, and what Belle was taking a risk to believe, was a man who had a lot of patience, a bizarre (to Belle's way of thinking) but ever present sense of humor, more than a little bit of tenderness and what appeared to be a lot of love.

Belle was betting everything important in her life (her sanity, her faith in her fellow man, things like that) that she was right.

That morning after breakfast, Jack had driven her to work while Olive went straight to the airport where he was going to fly them both to London. The gods were definitely smiling on them because the day before, after Jack had publicly spent the night in Belle's cottage, the media were in a frenzy.

That morning, however, something else must have been happening in the world. There were half as many photographers and they hung back, none of them shouting questions.

Apparently, Jack and Belle were still news, just old news.

There were, she guessed, only so many pictures worth taking of Jack walking Belle to her store.

And for that, as she had done a half a dozen times that morning, she thanked her lucky stars.

Jack had left her at the store. After, of course, on the stairs, he'd given her a long, sweet, thorough kiss and told her to have a good day.

Belle's mother had come later in the morning to be Belle's newest shop assistant. Dirk had taken Mom under his wing, and even though the media seemed to be losing interest, the customers definitely weren't. It was high season in St. Ives and Belle's store was a crush. This happened during high season, but because of her recent spate of popularity in the papers it had shot straight to ridiculous.

Belle was happy to leave Dirk and Mom in the shop while she, Nola and Carol saw to their business upstairs with Nola or Carol wandering down when things got too mad, which wasn't often. Dirk was Super Shop Assistant. He was the only man Belle knew who could multitask and do it while charming every customer into buying that one do-I-really-need-that item which he did by giving them a blinding grin. That was it. He said nothing, just grinned at them.

It made for a brilliant day.

It also helped knowing she'd be going home to the criminally handsome Jack Bennett, the father of her child and, apparently, the real-life, walking, talking, breathing, kissing, making love, showering together and holding hands man of her dreams.

She only had two moments that caused blips in her day and they came back to back.

The first was when she was alone in the workroom, Nola off to get sandwiches, Carol downstairs to help with the crush.

Belle was drawing a pattern for a new blouse she was going to introduce when the vision of Davey and Penny, sightless and lifeless, their limbs floating eerily in the water, seared through her brain.

At the memory, she pulled in a deep, horrified breath at the same exact moment her mobile rang.

The display said, JACK CALLING.

Belle stared at the phone, stunned for a second.

She picked it up and hit the green button on the screen answering it in a quiet voice by asking, "How did you know?"

There was silence then Jack queried, "Belle?"

She didn't respond to his call, instead she repeated, "How did you know I needed you to call?"

Jack's voice no longer sounded questioning. It sounded alert when he inquired, "What's happened?"

She shook her head, realized he couldn't see her and answered, "Nothing. I just, two seconds ago, remembered Davey and Penny. Then you called as if you knew I needed you to call. How did you know?"

"Poppet," he replied, his voice soft and warm, "I wish I could tell you I knew you needed me but I didn't. I was calling to tell you I wouldn't be home for dinner."

"Oh," Belle murmured.

"Are you okay?" he asked.

"Yes."

More silence then, "Belle."

"Really, Jack, I'm fine," she assured him, though she wasn't.

She couldn't shake the feeling that it was uncanny the minute her mind had filled with terrible, frightening images, and even though she didn't consciously think it, unconsciously she needed him and all of a sudden he called.

There was something weird about that.

Wonderful but weird.

"Poppet—" She heard him call softly in her ear.

"Jack, I'm fine," she repeated, stronger this time.

There was silence a moment before he asked, "Will you walk the dogs?"

Belle didn't like the sound of that and inquired, "How late are you going to be?"

"You'll wake up next to me."

Holy heck.

"That sounds like it means you'll be really late," she whispered tentatively.

"Yes, my love," he replied cautiously.

"Does that mean you'll be…" she paused, her heart clenching, she swallowed and asked in a rush, "flying in the dark?"

He didn't answer her question.

Instead he declared, "I'll be safe."

"Will you be flying in the dark?" she asked again.

"Maybe," he answered, his tone still cautious.

"Oh my goodness gracious," she breathed.

"Poppet, I've flown in the dark before."

"Okay," she replied swiftly, thinking it best that she didn't think *at all* about him flying in the dark. It was hard enough *driving* in the dark when you had headlights and even high beams.

But dark sky was just *dark*.

Did they have lights on planes?

And, if they didn't (and even if they did!) how would he know his way? How would he see if something was flying at him, a bird, *another plane*?

Belle knew there were instruments and all that kind of stuff, still her heart skipped a beat.

"Lots of times, my love," he continued to try and reassure her.

"Okay," she lied.

"I'll be fine."

Belle could take no more and therefore, as ridiculous as it sounded and as crazy as she knew he'd think she was, to protect her fragile sanity she started chanting, "La la la, I'm not involved in this conversation, la la la."

She heard him chuckle before he changed the subject and prompted, "Baron and Gretl?"

Happy to be on a much safer topic, she replied, "Of course I'll walk them."

"If it rains, ask Lila to do it," he ordered.

Belle walked from her drafting board to the window and looked out, unseeing.

"Oh, so it's okay if Gram slips on the wet, treacherous cliff path but not me?" Belle tried to tease, slightly embarrassed about her chanting and wondering vaguely how long it would take for him to grow tired of her neuroses.

It took Calvin, if memory served (and it did), two weeks and three days after their honeymoon to grow tired of it.

"She's lived a full life," Jack teased back audaciously, pulling her from her thoughts and startling a giggle from Belle, but she stopped laughing when she heard him murmur in his low and rumbly voice, "Jesus, I love that sound."

"What sound?" Belle whispered, caught up in his voice.

"The sound of you," he replied and finished, "happy."

That trill went up her spine straight into her scalp and she felt her belly dip, and he wasn't even looking at her. He wasn't even in the same *town* as her.

"Jack—" she replied softly, warmth in her voice.

He cut her off but there was warmth in his voice too, "Don't wait up for me, love. I'll see you in the morning."

"Okay."

"Good-bye, poppet."

"'Bye, Jack."

Then he rang off.

And she stared out the window, smiling to herself before her eyes caught on something and focused.

It was that man she'd seen days earlier, the ruggedly handsome one with the dark-brown hair. He was standing in the same spot as he was before, his head tipped back and he was looking at her through the window.

She took three hasty steps back and just stopped herself from falling into a crouch.

"Holy heck," she breathed, thinking that was not a matter of coincidental eye contact.

He was there for a reason and he was watching her.

Her heart was beating a mile a minute and she retreated three more steps and considered calling Jack back. Then she considered screaming for Dirk.

Instead, with effort, she pulled herself together.

He was standing outside looking in her window. The first time she saw him, he was gazing at her, a kind and benign expression on his face. This time was just the same.

He wasn't charging her store and kidnapping her.

He didn't flash her or even look weird.

Belle took a shaky, calming breath.

She was pregnant. She was hormonal. She was living in a haunted house. She wasn't making her own bed or her own food. She was falling in love with the criminally attractive James Bennett if she wasn't *already* in love with him, head over heels in love which, she had to admit, she pretty much was (who was she kidding, she *totally* was).

And, if she wasn't mistaken, he was falling in love with her too.

She didn't have a weird, kind-looking, handsome stalker.

He was probably a local she hadn't yet seen. Someone new to town, waiting for his wife to finish in some shop. Maybe *her* shop.

Men stood outside waiting for their women all the time not wanting to be shopping at all but definitely not wanting to be drawn into a clothing shop where they would invariably be asked, "Does my butt look big in this?"

In fact, Belle had considered putting a bench outside for these gentleman so they could have a rest, it happened so often.

Cautiously, she approached the window, and when she did, he was gone.

She took a huge breath and forced herself to relax.

So, she'd taken a big risk, jumped into shark-infested waters and found herself something so rich and rewarding it was impossible to believe her good fortune or the strength of the lucky stars that shone down on her, recently, both day and night.

She wouldn't allow her mind, which consistently played nasty tricks on her, to create problems that weren't even real.

So she set it aside and went back to work.

Now she was driving home with her mother and she knew her evening would be full.

Not with Jack, having dinner, walking the dogs then spending the evening with him in his study, eventually going to bed together and making love.

No, with Cassandra McNabb, the clairvoyant white witch with

good references and The McPherson, an unknown entity, both who dispatched ghosts to hell.

"Are you sure about this Cassandra person and The McPherson?" Belle asked her mother as The Point came into view.

"I've got a feeling in my bones," her mother replied calmly.

Belle nodded and smiled.

It might be crazy but that was good enough for her.

Yasmin's sporty Audi was in the forecourt and Belle parked her not-so-sporty Peugeot next to it.

Rachel eyed the Audi and remarked, "I love Yasmin's car. She let me drive it the other day." Belle switched off the ignition and looked at her mother as she continued, "Maybe you should ask Jack to buy you one of those."

Belle stared at Rachel in disgusted shock before she hissed, "Mom, I can't believe you just said that."

Her mother's eyebrows went up. "What? He's stinking rich. He lives in a castle for goodness sakes and you're carrying his child. The least he could do is buy you a cute car."

"He's already housing me, feeding me *and* you *and* Gram, *by the way*. Not to mention, he's paying for Dirk," Belle reminded her.

"So?" her mom replied.

"So, I think that's enough, don't you?"

"No," Rachel returned. "Like I said, he's stinking rich and you're carrying his child which, *by the way*," she mimicked the same tone Belle had used on her, "he seems delighted about." She turned to her door, muttering, "Tomorrow, I'll have a word."

Belle hastily exited her side and shouted after her mother, "Don't you dare ask Jack to buy me a car!"

"Oh! Brilliant!" Yasmin called from the steps. "What kind of car are you going to get?"

Belle closed her eyes.

"One like yours," Rachel called back.

Belle opened her eyes and glared at her mother.

"Brilliant!" Yasmin repeated, her happy gaze on Belle. "We can be car twins." Belle was trying to wrap her mind around the concept of "car twins" while she walked forward and witnessed Yasmin's face falling.

"Though, Jack's a Jag man. He's always owned Jaguars." Her expression brightened. "If he gets you one of those, you should get green. I love green Jags. British racing green. Lush."

Belle walked up the steps announcing, "Jack is not buying me a car. My car is perfectly fine."

"No...it...is...*not*," Yasmin decreed, sliding her arm through Belle's elbow and walking her through the open door. "You're a national treasure, a *stylish* national treasure. Your boyfriend is hot and he's rich and he's famous *and* you're having his baby. This all means you need a *great* car."

Yasmin, Belle decided instantly, not only liked to spend her trust fund money, she liked to spend *any* money, no matter whose it was.

"Can we stop talking about the car?" Belle asked when they hit the entry, and Rachel, with effort, pushed the heavy door closed behind them.

"Oh yes!" Yasmin whispered with excitement. "Let's talk about The McPherson." Yasmin's gaze moved to Rachel and it was dancing. "He's here and he's *hilarious*. I came out to tell you. Wait until you meet him."

She linked her other arm through Rachel's elbow and propelled them all to the library.

Belle liked the library almost as much as she liked the drawing room, the morning room and Jack's study. It was also lined with books and somehow managed to be both austere and welcoming.

It was austere because it too was huge with a massive fireplace. But the musty scent, the many books (which everyone knew equaled "relax and stay awhile"), the worn leather couches and comfortable armchairs with ottomans made it welcoming.

Yasmin let them go so they could walk into the library single file and Belle halted at what she saw.

A big man with lots of white, disheveled hair and ruddy, pink cheeks was standing, arms crossed on his chest, legs planted wide, wearing full Scottish gear.

That was *full Scottish gear*—kilt, hose, sporran, garter flashes, knife in his sock, ghillie brogues, top to toe Scottish gear.

Belle had been to Scotland. She'd seen men casually wearing kilts but this was something else.

But it wasn't just him.

The woman with him was gorgeous with a mess of rich, dark brown hair which Belle could see only because there was a lot of it. Mostly the crown of her head was covered as it was wrapped tightly in a big scarf that had moons and stars printed on it and long, ragged edges that tangled in her hair.

She also had long, thin scarves, three of them that Belle could count, their ends dangling and tangled with a variety of long and short silver necklaces around her neck. She further had silver bangles on both wrists, silver earrings at her ears and silver rings on all her fingers. She was wearing a belt made out of big silver disks threaded through the belt loops of her jeans not to mention another scarf wrapped lower on her hips.

She wore so much silver, it made her mother's copious silver self-ornamentation seem tame.

Belle stared at them, stunned.

They looked *exactly* like two, crazy "Ghost Helpers" would look.

If Jack met these two, he'd have a fit.

Then he'd eject them.

After that he'd demand that Belle give up her quest to send Myrtle and Lewis to heaven.

"Holy heck," she whispered.

"Aren't they *great*?" Yasmin asked.

"Holy heck," Belle repeated.

"I *love* your scarves!" Rachel shouted, moving forward and greeting them both.

Belle hung back.

Gram and Joy were there as well, and as Belle continued to stand frozen to the spot, her mind consumed with all the ways Jack would lose his mind when he met Cassandra McNabb and The McPherson, Gram spoke.

"My granddaughter is a little shy."

The McPherson regarded Belle a moment, his eyes narrowed.

Then his face cleared and he grinned a crooked, mad grin.

"Get over here, lass!" he boomed. "Let The McPherson get a good look at you."

"Um…" Belle muttered.

"Come on, come on…" he urged, moving toward her and Belle wanted to retreat, she *really, really* did, but she thought it might appear rude.

The McPherson got close and put a big, gentle hand between her shoulder blades and propelled her forward all the while looking down at her.

"I'm Angus McPherson of The McPhersons, at your service," he announced.

"I'm Belle Abbot," she whispered timidly.

He stopped her close to the huddle of women that had formed in front of the fireplace.

When he spoke again, he was no longer booming. It was quiet and as gentle as the hand he'd put at her back.

"I know, lass. Know you, know what you did. Never met a hero. Been one, a number of times, never met one. Least, not a wee slip of a girl like you."

She'd tilted her head to watch him speak, and as he did, she pulled in a breath.

"No, lass," his voice was still quiet when he talked on, "we won't talk about it. I know it makes you uncomfortable."

She didn't know how he knew that unless Cassandra, the clairvoyant white witch soaked up her vibes somehow and told him but Belle didn't say anything. She just nodded.

"Now!" Angus McPherson was back to booming. "Let's get this ghost business sorted!"

"I'm Cassandra," the witch came forward, a smile on her face, her hand extended.

"Belle," Belle replied and took her hand.

When Belle's fingers closed around Cassandra's, through her hand she felt Cassandra's body jerk. Then the woman went still, her smile died and her eyes grew hazy.

Belle grew concerned when she didn't come out of her sudden, weird trance and Belle's hand gripped Cassandra's more firmly as she lost her shyness and moved closer.

"Are you all right?" Belle asked but Cassandra didn't answer. She just kept staring at nothing, vacant, looking lost.

Angus got close and whispered, "Cass?"

"What's happening?" Joy asked, her tone concerned.

"Cassandra," Belle called when Cassandra still didn't focus. She got closer, her hand squeezing and Cassandra's hand squeezed back, so hard it caused pain. "Cassandra!" Belle called again, sharply. Now she was worried. "Are you okay?"

"Cass!" Angus bellowed, putting a meaty hand on Cassandra's shoulder and shaking her.

All of a sudden Cassandra's eyes widened and she yanked her hand from Belle's like Belle's hand burned.

She stared at Belle, her eyes full of something Belle couldn't read but whatever it was, it made Belle's worry intensify.

Significantly.

"Bloody hell, mate," Cassandra whispered.

"What?" Belle asked in a breathy voice.

Cassandra opened her mouth, her eyes dropped to Belle's stomach and she closed it. Her gaze swung to Angus and Belle could tell she was trying to communicate something but Belle didn't know what.

"Is something wrong?" Lila was now close and watching Cassandra.

"Nothing, just that, I think there's a complication," Cassandra answered, backing up and away from Belle.

Angus, however, stayed close.

"What complication?" Yasmin asked.

She, as well as Belle's mom and Joy had also closed ranks.

"I can't say for certain, right now. I need to..." she stopped abruptly, her head jerked then her face went pale.

Belle felt the blood run from her own face and she glanced at her mom when Rachel snapped, "What is it now?"

Cassandra came back into the room swiftly and announced, "I need to stay here. In the castle. So does Angus."

Belle felt Angus grow still beside her but it was Joy who spoke. "Why? Is something—?"

Cassandra cut her off, "I need to do some readings."

"What kind of readings?" Joy asked hesitantly.

Cassandra started moving toward the door. "I'll explain later. I need to get set up now." She stopped at the door, turned and asked suddenly and bizarrely, "Do you have a cat?"

Joy shook her head but said, "We have dogs. German shepherds, two of them."

Cassandra wrinkled her nose in disgust and dropped her eyes to the floor mumbling, "Dogs. Bloody useless." Her gaze went to The McPherson and she declared, "Angus, we need to chat."

Angus ambled to the door saying, "You got it, lass."

Lila followed them, determinedly insisting, "Wait just one damned minute."

Both Cassandra and Angus halted their exit and looked at Belle's grandmother.

"What, exactly, is going on?" Lila demanded to know.

As Belle, with her mother on one side, Jack's mother on her other side and Yasmin close, stared at the three at the door, Cassandra's gaze leveled on Gram.

"I can't be certain and I don't want to alarm you but I think there aren't two ghosts in this house."

"There are," Joy blurted. "I've been seeing them for forty years!"

"I saw them too!" Rachel added. "And so did Belle."

Cassandra shook her head but stated, "There aren't two ghosts." Her gaze took in everyone in the room. "I think there might be *three*."

Joy gasped.

Lila's head whipped around to look at Belle.

"Bloody hell," Yasmin whispered.

"Oh lordy," Rachel breathed.

Belle talked around her heart which was lodged squarely in her throat.

"*Three?*" she asked.

Cassandra's eyes settled on Belle. "I don't know, mate. I'm sensing something." She turned her gaze to Lila. "Let me do some readings. I'll let you know the minute I know."

"How long will that take?" Lila inquired.

"I don't know. It could take an hour. It could take five days. He might not want to be sensed, might go into hiding," Cassandra answered.

"He?" Joy asked.

"He," Cassandra replied and then took in a breath. On her exhale, she tried to calm them all. "There's nothing to panic about, not yet anyway. Just let me get to work."

"Go! Work!" Rachel demanded sharply.

Cassandra gave Angus a look, Angus nodded and they both left the room.

Everyone in the room was silent.

Suddenly Joy's body jerked and she rushed forward, muttering, "I need to get some rooms ready." And with that she left the room.

At her words, Belle's terror intensified and she looked at her mother. "Mom—"

Rachel took her hand and gave it a reassuring squeeze. "Nothing to worry about, honeypot. We've got the Ghost Helpers on the case. Everything will be fine."

Belle turned to her mother. "*That's* what I'm worried about. They're going to be *staying* here."

"I think that's good," Yasmin put in. "A timesaver. They don't have to drive to work. They can just get up, have breakfast and then," she clapped her hands, "get right to it."

Belle looked at Yasmin and asked, "Did you *see* them?"

"Sure," Yasmin replied casually.

"Did you get a good *look* at them?" Belle went on.

"Sure," Yasmin repeated. "Seriously, Belle, they're cool. Before you got home, we told them the whole Myrtle and Lewis story and they sounded like they knew exactly—"

"Yasmin," Belle interrupted her, being uncharacteristically rude but she thought the situation warranted it, "you've known Jack longer than all of us. What do you think *he'll* do when he sees those two and finds out they're staying under his roof doing *readings* and going into weird *trances* and, I don't know," she paused as her hysteria escalated and finished with, "being outrageously Scottish?"

Light dawned and Yasmin whispered, "I see what you mean."

"I think—" Belle started but her grandmother interrupted her.

"I think that we should let the witch do her work. I think, if Belle has a word, Jack will come around. And I think we all need to be vigilant. Whatever that was wasn't good and the best thing we can do is let the experts go about their business."

"Gram—" Belle began but was interrupted again.

"You'll have a word," Gram demanded.

"But—" Belle tried yet again but was interrupted yet again.

"Bellerina, have a word."

Belle sighed then whispered, "I think you might be overestimating my influence over Jack."

At that, Lila laughed.

As did Yasmin and Rachel.

And they all laughed like what Belle said was hysterically funny.

Which it was *not*.

"I'm not being funny!" she snapped.

Gram came forward and pulled Belle loosely into her arms.

Putting her cheek against her granddaughter's, she said softly in Belle's ear, "I think you're underestimating your influence over Jack." She pulled away and looked in Belle's eyes and when Belle opened her mouth to speak, hurried on, "We'll see who's right, hmm, my sweet?" Belle closed her mouth and stared stubbornly at her grandmother when Lila repeated firmly, "Have a word."

Belle stepped out of Lila's arms and crossed her own over her baby bump.

On a sigh, she gave in, "All right, I'll have a word."

"Just," Rachel added, getting close and putting her hand on Belle's upper arm, "give me a chance to ask about the car first."

"Mom!" Belle cried.

"No. Seriously. I don't want him in a foul mood when I ask him. He might say no," Rachel said.

Belle decided to let it go.

She was, as she reminded herself hourly, pregnant, hormonal, living in a haunted castle (now with *three* ghosts) and falling in love with Jack Bennett.

She had to pick her battles and while doing so guard her reserves.

And she needed her reserves in order to have her "word" with Jack.

"I'm going to take a nap before dinner," she announced, deciding that would do wonders for her reserves.

"Good idea, honeypot. I'll wake you in an hour, okay?"

Belle nodded and she left.

She only felt better when she found the dogs, guided them to her and Jack's room and lay down on their bed.

And she only felt better because Baron and Gretl were with her and she was in a room that was now her and Jack's and lying on a bed that could be described using the word "their."

But she couldn't help but wonder about the possible third ghost, who "he" might be and what Jack was going to think when she had her "word."

❦ ❦ ❦

Belle woke before Rachel came to her room.

She lay in the bed still a bit sleepy but feeling rested.

Her hand went to her stomach and she felt the hardness there.

"Well, sweets," she whispered to her belly, "I promised life would eventually go back to normal and boring but your daddy knew better, didn't he?"

She splayed her fingers wider and smiled at the thought of Jack as "Daddy."

Her mobile, sitting on the nightstand, sounded.

She picked it up and it said, JACK CALLING.

There it was again.

He was on her mind and then he called.

She couldn't shake how weird that was.

Or how wonderful.

She slid her finger across the screen and put the phone to her ear.

"Hi," she said softly.

She could hear the smile in his voice when he replied, "Belle."

"You okay?" she asked, swinging her legs over the side of the bed.

She heard dog tags jangling as both Baron and Gretl moved forward for pets.

Belle didn't disappoint, holding the phone to her ear with her shoulder, she pet them both at the same time which was how they preferred it.

"Yes, poppet. I called to let you know I'm taking off in fifteen minutes. I finished earlier than I thought."

Belle felt a rush of happiness.

Which was quickly followed by a rush of anxiety.

"Um..." she paused before saying weakly, "Jack."

He was silent then his tone was cautious when he asked, "What is it?"

"Well..." she began, not knowing how to have her "word" but kind of happy that she was having it on the phone where she didn't have to watch him blow his stack in person (and *before* her mother could ask about the car).

"Belle." His voice was no longer cautious, it held a warning.

"We met Cassandra and Angus today."

There was more silence, a sigh then, "Angus?"

"The McPherson."

Jack's tone was now filled with humor when he asked, "His name is Angus McPherson?"

Belle again thought Jack found the weirdest things funny.

"Yes. Why?"

Jack replied through chuckling, "That's very Scottish."

"You don't know the half of it," Belle muttered.

"Pardon?"

"Nothing," Belle said quickly, "Um...I have to tell you something."

Again with the silence before he said softly, "Anything, my love."

She felt her belly melt, her heart melt and her mind registered that head over heels love business when she heard his tone and his words.

Both of which made her anxiety fade clean away.

Therefore she told him, "Angus and Cassandra are staying at the castle."

"That's fine," he replied immediately.

Belle blinked before she parroted, "That's fine?"

"Yes, Belle. We've plenty of room. Not to mention if they stay, it'll save on their expenses."

Belle was surprised at how easy that was.

She, however, thought it best to forewarn him, "They're a little bit strange."

His voice was back to sounding amused. "She's a clairvoyant witch and he's a Scottish ghost hunter. I figured they'd be strange, poppet."

"No, I mean," Belle took in a breath and said, "they're *really* strange."

"She's a clairvoyant witch and he's a very Scottish ghost hunter," Jack repeated. "I figured they'd be *really* strange."

Belle couldn't help it, she giggled.

Then she gave him the full story. "Cassandra's doing readings. She thinks there's a third ghost."

There was more silence, this longer and far, far heavier.

Finally, he said, "A third ghost."

"She isn't sure. She's doing readings."

"Readings," Jack replied.

"I don't know what that means," Belle told him. "I've been napping but I do know she seemed very keen. Cassandra, I mean. She started straight away."

Belle decided not to tell Jack that Cassandra was keen in a weird, scary way that made Belle's heart lodge in her throat. Jack, she figured, probably wouldn't like that.

"Readings," Jack muttered again, sounding at a loss.

"Jack?"

She heard him sigh another sigh and he assured her, "It's fine, Belle."

"Yasmin thinks they know what they're doing."

"It's fine."

"Yasmin seems pretty certain."

"Poppet, I said, it's fine."

"Okay," she whispered.

"I'll be home soon."

"Um..." she muttered again and Jack was silent so Belle forged on, "Angus wears a kilt." This was met with more silence so she continued, "And hose, ghillie brogues, a sporran, the whole lot."

She heard him burst into laughter.

It was, she thought, very funny. So, softly, she laughed with him.

"I'll be home soon," he repeated when she'd stopped laughing.

"Okay, see you."

"Good-bye, poppet."

"'Bye, Jack."

He disconnected, Belle took the phone from her ear and put it on the nightstand.

She stared at it realizing she forgot to tell him about Cassandra and her scarves.

She licked her lips and took in a breath through her nose.

Oh well, he didn't seem overly upset about the rest so Cassandra and her abundant use of accessories probably wouldn't faze him.

She leaned forward and gave each dog a thorough head rub, saying, "I'm hungry. Let's see about dinner."

Baron woofed and Gretl got to her feet and did an excited circle.

Belle got up and walked from the room.

The dogs were at her heels as she made her way down the hall, her mind on her now grumbling belly and wondering how long it would take Jack to fly home.

Therefore, as she reached the top of the stairs, it took her by surprise when both Baron and Gretl closed in and started growling.

She stopped and looked at one dog then the other.

Both were pressing close to her legs, both looking back down their bodies, both had teeth bared.

"What on—?" Belle started to say but stopped when movement caught her eye and she looked down the steps.

A young, black-headed boy was racing up them.

Not racing, as in *treading*, but drifting, swiftly, like a shot.

He was see-through.

Belle's mouth dropped open.

The boy's pale, ghostly face suddenly filled with terror and he halted.

"*Belle! Watch out!*" She heard his eerie, disembodied shout right before the dogs started barking and snapping and she felt what seemed like a hand at her back, shoving.

She lost balance, automatically reaching into the air but there was nothing to grab on to.

Therefore she tumbled down the stairs.

She tried to stop her fall but her head cracked against the fifth step with such force she was unconscious by the time her body rolled to a rest at the foot of the stairs.

Lewis and Myrtle

Myrtle zoomed directly to Belle but Lewis floated in suspended animation in the middle of the stairs and, head tipped back, he stared in horror.

The bad man stood at the top of the steps, grinning.

He could see him, see him for the first time ever.

See him shimmering through.

"You," Lewis whispered, shocked, scared and angry.

The bad man lifted his ghostly hand and touched his index finger to his forehead in a mocking salute before he glittered and disappeared.

"Help! Help! Help!" Myrtle shouted, her unearthly voice echoing through the stone hall, mingled with Jack's dogs' frantic barking.

Lewis heard footsteps as he floated down.

Myrtle was drifting in a crouch over Belle's motionless body as the dogs circled, sniffed and kept howling.

"Oh my God." They heard breathed and they looked at who they knew was Yasmin, a family friend both of them liked a lot, mostly because she was funny.

She was staring at them in dazed disbelief.

"Go! Get help!" Lewis shouted, his strange, ghostly voice now echoing with the dogs' frenzied woofs.

Yasmin ran forward toward Belle and Myrtle drifted away.

She dropped to her knees beside Belle then her head snapped up and she looked at Lewis, demanding, "What happened?"

"Get help!" Lewis replied.

More steps, more people and Yasmin's head jerked around to look over her shoulder.

"Call nine nine nine!" she cried.

"She fell down the stairs," Myrtle informed the pretty witch who was dialing on her phone.

The Scottish man crouched beside Belle, ignoring Myrtle and Lewis, intent on his effort of feeling for a pulse.

"Belle!" They heard shouted as Rachel arrived, her face white. "Oh Belle! Oh my God! What happened?"

Rachel was shoving in as Lila and Joy made it to the scene.

"Yes, there's been an accident. Chy An Als Point. Belle Abbot has fallen down the stairs," the witch said. "She's unconscious."

"Belle, honeypot. Belle?" Rachel's hands were on her and Lewis went to Myrtle, pulling her back.

"She's got a pulse. It's strong," the Scotsman told the witch then he moved to pull Rachel away as he soothed. "Don't move her. We need to let her lay, lass, wait for the paramedics."

"I can't let her lay!" Rachel shouted, her eyes wide, tearful and full of fear as she began to struggle against the Scot.

"Her pulse is strong," the witch said into the phone.

"Keep holding her hand, Yasmin," Lila said softly, getting close, and dropping down, she gently pulled Belle's hair away from her neck.

After she did this, she continued to stroke her granddaughter's hair even after she sucked in breath when she saw the blood at Belle's temple.

"She's bleeding!" Rachel wailed, her struggles turning frantic.

"It's a head wound, love. We've got to let her lay or we might do her more harm," the Scotsman tried to calm Rachel while gently pushing her back.

"She's bleeding," Joy whispered in a voice so horrible, everyone knew she was referring to something else.

They stilled and looked down at Belle, even Myrtle and Lewis.

There was, they saw, blood pooling between her legs.

"She's pregnant," the witch said urgently into the phone. "And she's bleeding between her legs."

Lewis turned and pushed his sister through the wall.

"Lewis!" Myrtle shouted, fighting his push but he was determined and he kept hold of her, darting through the ceiling to their turret.

He still held her when they arrived at their window.

"Lewis! I want to be sure Belle is all right!"

"Myrtle, we can't be there," Lewis said softly.

"But—"

"We're *ghosts* Myrtle. Don't you think they have enough to worry about without two *ghosts* hanging around?"

She snapped her mouth shut right before she burst into tears.

Lewis pulled her deeper into his arms.

"I want her to be all right, Lewis! She has to be all right! She's sweet! She's Belle!" Myrtle cried into his boyish chest.

He stroked her hair.

"She'll be all right," he lied.

It was a lie because he feared she wouldn't.

The bad man was there.

How he was there, Lewis didn't know.

He hadn't been there for over two hundred years.

Or, at least, Lewis had never seen him, never sensed him.

But he'd pushed Belle down the stairs. Lewis saw him do it.

Myrtle's head tilted back, non-existent tears the color of pearls still sliding down her cheeks.

Her voice was quivering when she asked, "You promise she'll be all right?"

He nodded solemnly, and even though it was against the rules, Lewis lied yet again, "I promise, Myrtie Mine."

Myrtle pressed her cheek against her brother's chest.

And Lewis closed his eyes tight, trying to shut out his fear for Belle and his terror of the bad man so he could think about what he needed to do to keep himself, his sister, and Belle (if she was all right) safe.

He held Myrtle a long time.

But he didn't come up with any answers.

Belle

Belle opened her eyes and she knew immediately she was in a hospital room.

She didn't hurt.

She didn't feel anything.

But groggy.

Her eyes focused and she saw Jack sitting by her hospital bed illuminated by the soft glow from the lamp on the nightstand.

His mouth was tight, his face was hard but his eyes were gentle.

She remembered what happened and whispered, "The baby?"

He leaned forward instantly and in that instant, his expression changed and she saw the pain slash through his features.

And she knew.

She closed her eyes.

"Poppet," he called and she felt him take her hand.

She turned her head and pulled her hand away.

"Belle, love."

"Go away," she whispered, still groggy but now feeling something.

And that something Belle felt was empty.

His hand came to her jaw but he didn't force her to look at him.

She felt his thumb drift over her cheekbone, slowly, softly.

Then his hand disappeared, and from behind her closed eyelids she saw the light go out.

She thought he'd leave.

She *wanted* him to leave.

But instead, she felt her hand taken in his again and his grip went firm when she tried to pull away.

She didn't have the energy to fight it.

So she kept her face averted and her eyes closed as he held her hand.

Later, she felt his forehead come to rest on their joined hands.

That was when the tears seeped out from between her closed eyes.

17

JACK'S SUNDAY

Jack

Jack woke, and the minute he did he knew Belle, who was tucked in the curve of his body, was also awake.

She was always awake before him. And always, for some reason only known to Belle, she lay in bed until he woke.

His arm resting at her waist got tight and her body went stiff in response.

He always pulled her closer when he woke.

And always, for some reason only known to Belle, she grew stiff when he did.

He closed his eyes with frustration.

He knew what the morning would bring and what the day would bring. It had been three and a half weeks since the accident and every day was the same.

Belle had had a concussion, a sprained wrist, some intense bruising and she'd lost their child.

Considering the staircase was made of stone and it was a long drop, the doctor told them they'd been "lucky."

And Jack felt lucky.

She could have broken her neck, broken her back or her head injury could have caused brain damage.

None of this happened.

She was alive and breathing and was released from hospital within a few days.

For this, regardless of the crushing loss they'd endured, Jack felt lucky.

Belle, on the other hand, it was overwhelmingly safe to say, did *not* feel lucky.

During her short hospital stay, she had been far more quiet than normal, her moments of silent contemplation far more frequent and far longer, and for the first time Jack did not enjoy them.

Indeed, these moments were so frequent and so long, if she wasn't having one, she was sleeping.

Jack allowed this. She had told him when she did this she was trying *not* to think and he hoped, in this instance, she was successful.

When Jack, in his Jag, and Rachel and Lila, in Belle's car, went to collect her when she was released, Belle's game began.

There were no photographers mainly because the first night Jack was there, after sitting with Belle until she woke and remaining with her until her quiet tears subsided and she'd again fallen asleep, he'd demanded a first thing in the morning meeting with the hospital CEO. When he had that meeting, he told the CEO if that first word was breathed about Belle being an inpatient, why she was and what she'd lost, Jack would stop at nothing until he'd closed the hospital down and the CEO, personally, would never work again.

The CEO believed him but he wasn't hard to believe. Jack meant what he said and everything about the way he said it screamed it.

Therefore, they had thankfully not had that additional worry.

After she was released, when they were at the back doors where the cars were parked, Belle started toward the Peugeot.

"Belle, honeypot, you're riding with Jack," Rachel had said gently.

Without looking at her mother or Jack or anything but the pavement, Belle replied softly, "I want to go to the cottage."

Lila got close to her granddaughter. "Belle, my sweet—" but Jack interrupted her.

"Take her to the cottage."

Both Lila and Rachel's eyes flashed to him and he saw Belle's body grow tight. He nodded to her mother and grandmother, they both gave him intense looks but they didn't demur and helped Belle into the car.

He watched them drive away then he got into his Jag and drove to The Point.

Once there, he found his mother, told her to pack whatever Belle needed and then he went to the kitchen and told Elaine to pack what the dogs would need for an extended stay at the cottage.

Then, in his and Belle's room, beside his mother, he packed what he would need for an extended stay.

All of this he put in the boot of his Jag, he called the dogs and loaded them up and he drove into town.

He had a suitcase in each hand and a dog at each heel when he opened the door to Belle's cottage.

Lila stood at the head of the stairs as he walked up.

He dropped the suitcases on the landing as the dogs nosed around the small house.

Without first offering her a greeting, Jack said, "I'll need keys and someone should go to the grocery store."

"I'll go to the store," Rachel, who had appeared in the back hall, offered immediately and bustled into the kitchen.

"I'll find keys," Lila murmured and she bustled into the kitchen too.

Jack went to Belle's bedroom.

She was lying on her side on top of the covers, her hands in prayer position under her cheek, her right wrist wrapped in a bandage, her eyes were open.

She lifted her head when he entered then, without any further reaction, her head dropped back down on her hands.

This didn't faze him. After being treated to days of this kind of behavior while she was in hospital, Jack was used to it.

However, this time, as she was not in a narrow hospital bed having just fallen down the stairs, he took off his shoes. At the same time Gretl and Baron came in and started nosing at the side of the bed for Belle's attention.

She reached her left hand out and stroked each dog alternately.

Jack joined her in bed, being careful as he knew she was stiff and sore, he settled behind her.

She stopped stroking and went still.

"Jack—" she whispered.

He cut her off as his arm slid around her waist, "Quiet, love."

"I think—"

"Quiet."

"We shouldn't—"

He carefully pulled her into his body. "Belle, I said quiet."

She kept her body stiff but whispered, "Okay."

She resumed stroking his dogs' heads until they settled in, lying by the bed.

And Jack held her until she fell asleep.

Only then did he cautiously leave the bed. He went back out to the car to collect the things he hadn't been able to carry when he arrived.

As he filled the dogs' bowls with water and food and set them in the kitchen, Lila came in.

"She's still asleep," Lila whispered. "I've closed the door."

Jack nodded.

Lila studied him, her eyes soft. "Are you okay?"

His reply was instant and honest. "No."

He watched as she closed her eyes and he felt his gut get tight at witnessing the pain in stark relief as it settled on her features.

"Lila, are you all right?" he asked in return.

Her eyes opened and she gave him a sad smile as she shook her head.

"Whatever your child feels, and that extends to whatever your grandchild feels, you feel it too. Happiness or despair, you feel it right along with them." Jack's jaw got hard and Lila came forward, put her hand to his arm and continued in a quiet voice, "I know that's difficult for you to hear right now but I've every faith you'll learn this yourself, my man, I know you will…" she paused and whispered, "someday."

Jack nodded again. He didn't have it in him to answer mainly because his chest had tightened along with his gut and he was finding it more important at that juncture to focus on breathing.

Lila got closer and her voice dipped quieter when she advised, "Don't let her pull away."

"I won't," Jack vowed and it was, indeed, a vow. His words were low and they vibrated.

Upon hearing them, he saw Lila's eyes register surprise before they warmed. The sad smile disappeared, a hopeful one took its place and she squeezed his arm.

Later, Rachel came in carrying groceries and Jack went out to retrieve the rest.

Later still, Belle woke and sat in the kitchen with Jack while Rachel and Lila made dinner and even helped do the dishes when they were finished eating.

Shortly after, Lila and Rachel made their way to the door.

Belle followed them to the landing, her expression confused.

"Where are you going?" she asked her mother.

"Home, to The Point," Rachel answered, giving Belle a kiss on the cheek.

"But, I thought—" Belle started.

"I've got painting to do and we've got guests, Cassandra and Angus," Lila reminded Belle, moving in for her own kiss.

"But, they aren't guests. You hired—" Belle began again after she received her kiss.

"We'll come and visit tomorrow," Rachel assured her daughter.

"No, tomorrow's Sunday. Sundays are Jack's days," Lila, to Jack's surprise (and satisfaction) told Rachel.

Belle's body jerked but Rachel said, "Oh, right." She looked at her. "We'll be back on Monday."

"But, my car," Belle said. "I'll need—"

Jack slid his hand along her waist, pulling her to his side and interrupted her, "If you need to go anywhere, love, I'll take you."

She looked up at him, her face wan, the bandage still at her temple, dark circles under her eyes even though she'd slept a good deal the past few days, and she mumbled, "But—"

His fingers gave her a squeeze at her waist and he promised softly, "Whatever you need, poppet, I'll get it for you."

He saw tears fill her eyes, she swallowed, looked to his shoulder, his ear and away.

Then she said, "Okay," but she didn't mean it.

They spent a quiet night in front of the television until she fell asleep, her head against his bicep, which she was using for a pillow.

He took her to bed and woke with her already awake in front of him.

His arm got tight and her body grew solid.

"Belle," he whispered into her bent neck.

"You should go," she said back.

It was then his body grew solid.

"Why?" he asked.

"I don't want you here," she told him, her voice quiet and remote, her words felt like acid injected straight into a vein.

He ignored the pain and replied, "Sorry, my love, I'm willing to give you just about anything you want but I'm afraid that's something I can't give you."

"There's no reason anymore for you to *be* here," she explained, her voice still quiet, her head tipped down, her body remained tight.

Her words slashed through his gut and he pulled her vaguely resisting body closer before he asked, "Why would you say that?"

"Because you were with me for the baby and now there's no baby, so—"

She stopped speaking when his arm clenched even tighter.

"I wasn't with you for the baby," he told her, his voice as tight as his arm, his temper rising but he controlled it, barely.

"It's okay, Jack. I'll be okay eventually. You can just—"

"Belle—" His voice was a warning.

"Seriously," she said firmly.

"Seriously," his reply was even more firm, "I wasn't with you for the baby. I was with you for *you*."

"I can't believe—"

He cut her off even *more* firmly, demanding, "Believe."

"Jack—"

He interrupted her again, "This is the first and last time we're having this ludicrous discussion."

"Jack—"

"Belle, don't say another word."

"But Jack—"

His arm shook her body gently. "Belle, not another fucking word."

She grew silent, her body stayed taut.

For his part, Jack used those moments to control his anger and seek patience which he had the feeling (and he was right) he would need a lot of in the coming weeks.

Finally, she said quietly, "The dogs need to be walked."

Thinking that walking the dogs would be a good opportunity to control his temper and find his patience, he agreed, "I'll see to it."

He then kissed her shoulder and left her in bed.

They spent a tense Sunday together.

Then they spent a tense Monday together, Jack waking after Belle, holding her tight body close for long moments before she told him the dogs needed to be walked. He kissed her shoulder, left her in bed and walked the dogs. After that was achieved, he worked in her living room while she puttered around her house.

This went on.

Eventually he had to go to London and she had to go back to the shop.

As the days slid by, she remained distant and on edge, and Jack resolutely remained close, calling her during the day, the conversations short, one-sided (his side) and stilted, and coming home to her cottage at night. She'd make him dinner then he'd work, she'd listen to music on her MP3 or they'd watch television. All of this done in silence.

They rarely talked, but as he was allowing her emotional distance, he refused to allow her physical distance.

He nestled her close when they were both on her couch. He held her when they were in bed. He took her hand in his when he walked her to her store in the morning or when he was able to collect her in the evenings. And he took every opportunity he could to pull her into his arms and brush his lips against hers.

Often, when this happened, he'd see her wet her lips anxiously or tears would fill her eyes but she said nothing and didn't avoid his touch nor did she respond to it.

Rachel, Lila, Joy and Yasmin were never far but they also gave Jack and Belle the space they needed to move forward and heal.

Unfortunately, neither of those things was happening.

Jack had decided early after the accident he would wait for his chance to break through.

She'd lost a child and he had no idea, not carrying it, how that felt.

Jack, too, lamented the loss of their child. He was looking forward to sharing that with Belle, looking forward to every aspect of it with great anticipation. Anytime he thought of their loss, remembered his mother's voice on the phone when she called to tell him what had happened, Lila greeting him at the entrance to the hospital, whispering to him that Nathan was gone, seeing Belle lying bandaged and asleep in her hospital bed, his chest would get tight.

But whatever he felt was simply emotional. It had not been tied to the physical. He'd not had a child in distress die inside him.

And he couldn't imagine her pain.

Therefore he was willing to let her have her head.

However, he thought Belle would give him an opening, something, anything.

She was not doing that.

And, even though it had been only three and a half weeks (albeit a very *long* three and a half weeks), Jack was losing patience.

It was Sunday, *their* day, and it was bloody well time for him to break through.

His face nuzzled the hair at the back of her neck and he whispered, "Belle."

"You need to walk the dogs," was her reply.

"In a minute."

Her stiff body got tighter at his unprecedented response.

Every day for three weeks when she'd said that, Jack had left her and walked the dogs.

She hesitated a moment before she told him, "It's not nice to make them wait."

"We'll walk them in a minute."

Her tight body grew rock solid.

Then she whispered, "We?"

Now was the time for him to begin to break through.

Therefore, Jack informed her, "You need to start taking your walks again."

"I—"

Jack interrupted her, "You also need to start eating more."

"But I'm not hun—"

"You also need to start designing," Jack cut her off again. "Dirk tells me that you haven't begun producing the winter collection. It's September, you need winter stock."

"But, I—"

"And we need to go back to The Point." When her body grew so solid it felt like she'd shatter if she moved, Jack shifted and buried his face in her neck. "I love your cottage, poppet, and I understand why you needed to be here but it's not our home."

"Home?" she breathed.

"Home," he replied and his mouth moved to her ear. "It's time to go home, my love."

"But, Jack," she whispered, "*this* is my home."

He kissed the skin behind her ear and her solid body gave a delicate shiver.

His frame absorbed it gladly and he felt like shouting in triumph.

Finally, for the first time in weeks, she gave him something.

Instead of shouting his triumph, he murmured, "Your home became The Point when Elaine moved your things into our room."

She started to shift but he held her firm and moved over her to kiss the hinge of her jaw.

"But—" she began.

"You told me I'd have to explain what it meant when you agreed to moving your things to my room. Now, I'm explaining."

"But—"

"It's time to go home."

"But—"

Jack was unrelenting. "This evening, we're moving home."

He shifted away, let her drop to her back, but when she did, her eyes went to his shoulder, his throat, his ear.

Then she said, "Jack—"

He cut her off again by brushing his lips against her own before he whispered, "Now, poppet, we can make love or we can walk the dogs. Your choice."

He watched close up as her eyes finally met his and she blinked.

"Make love?" she breathed.

Jack grinned and teased, "Is that your choice?"

Her eyes grew wide and her body, which had relaxed, went stiff again before she retorted sharply, "No!"

Undeterred, he nevertheless relented and, still grinning, he announced, "Then we'll walk the dogs and *then* come back and make love."

Her hands came to his chest and she gave a useless shove for Jack wasn't going *anywhere*.

"We can't make love," she snapped.

"All right," he replied and bent his head to nuzzle her neck. "If you're not ready for that then I'll make you come with my mouth and, after, if you feel up to it, you can do the same for me."

She gave him another ineffective shove and demanded, "Get off!"

He ignored her and mused against her neck, nudging her earlobe with his nose, "Or maybe we can do it at the same time."

Her hands stilled and she whispered, "Oh my goodness gracious."

There it was. Another something.

Her words made him smile. His hand drifted from her waist upward and stopped by her breast, his thumb stroking the side.

She liked that. She'd always liked that. Very much. From their first night together he discovered how much she liked it.

She liked it no less now because her body melted under his and her hands slid up his chest so her fingers could curl on his shoulders.

Thank God, he was getting somewhere.

Not about to lose his advantage, his mouth slid over her jaw to touch hers.

Speaking against her lips, he stated his preference, "As much as I like the idea of having the taste of you in my mouth while your mouth is wrapped around my cock, I might get distracted and not hear those sweet, sexy noises you make. So, if you don't mind, I'd rather make you come when I can concentrate and listen to you and you can return the favor later."

Her eyes grew wide before they went languid.

Watching it, Jack realized that yes, thank God, he was definitely getting somewhere.

"You've never spoken to me like that," she murmured, the fingers of one hand curling around his neck, her body had grown soft but it was moving restlessly under his.

Oh yes, definitely getting somewhere.

"No," he replied and touched her mouth in a brief kiss. "I haven't."

He didn't have to ask if she liked it, he knew from her response she did.

"Jack—" she whispered, the hand at his neck moved, her fingers gliding in his hair, her actions belying her next words. "I'm not ready for this."

He touched her lips in another brief kiss before he said, "All right, my love, I'll be sure to spend a lot of time *getting* you ready."

"Holy heck," she breathed but her fingers put pressure against his head, her head lifted and she touched her mouth against his.

When she did, he growled his triumph into her already opened mouth, slanted his head and slid his tongue inside.

She immediately emitted one of her sexy, little noises and his already hard cock jerked at the sound.

Baron and Gretl moved, their tags jangling and they both barked.

This was right before they heard a banging at the door.

Jack's head came up and twisted as the banging continued, loud and unabated.

"What the fuck?" he muttered.

Belle had grown tense underneath him, and feeling it, Jack decided he was going to wring the neck of whoever was at the door.

"Would a reporter bang on the door like that?" Belle whispered, her voice filled with anxiety.

"No," Jack answered as the banging stopped but, within seconds, it continued and he stifled a frustrated growl.

"Mom and Gram wouldn't bang like that," Belle told him as, with regret, he moved away from her warm body and their warm bed.

"No, they wouldn't," Jack replied though he figured they would but not on Sunday.

He exited the bed and Baron and Gretl started circling to the bedroom door and back to Jack.

He heard Belle's movement, looked back and saw her sitting up and throwing the covers back.

Jack stopped in his progress to the door and ordered, "Don't move."

Belle halted her legs in mid-swing and asked, "What?"

"Don't leave that bed."

"But—"

"Belle."

She stared at him a moment before her legs settled and she whispered, "Okay."

"I won't be a minute," Jack told her and watched her nod.

Then Jack, barefoot, bare-chested and wearing only pajama bottoms, stalked through the house, down the steps to the front door and threw it open.

A tall, sandy-blond-haired man with intensely blue eyes stood outside wearing a beat-up leather bomber jacket, a pair of faded jeans and a T-shirt stating his fondness for The Rolling Stones.

He had an even more beat-up leather satchel over his shoulder and, alarmingly, a large, even *more* beat-up leather bag sitting on the stoop by his foot.

His eyes bugged out when they fell on Jack's face.

"Jesus, you're the famous, rich dude," he declared.

Jack scowled at him. "I am indeed. And you are?"

The man's face split into an easy, wide, white smile and his hand shot forward toward Jack before he said, "Jensen Abbot, Belle's daddy."

Jack stared at his hand, vaguely disappointed that he couldn't commit homicide against Belle's father and then he took his hand, introducing himself by saying, "Jack Bennett."

"Dude, I *know*," Jensen Abbot replied. "Christ, photos of you and Belle are *everywhere*." He dropped Jack's hand. "You two look sweet together. Sah...*weet*. Never thought my precious girl would find someone to complement her, because, hey man, I don't have to tell you, she's *beautiful*, but, seriously, dude, you...are...*it*."

Jack had no reply to that, however, he did get the impression that perhaps Belle hadn't been entirely forthcoming with how wild her father was and she had painted a verbal picture of Jensen Abbot that was rather wild.

"I came to surprise my baby girl and see how she's gettin' on with all this shit so, um, you think you could let me in because I kinda wanna see my daughter and I seriously need a caffeine fix. You know what I'm saying?"

"Of course," Jack murmured, stepped back and motioned to Baron and Gretl to go up the stairs which they did.

Jensen didn't delay. He picked up his bag and barreled up the steps after the dogs.

While he did so, he shouted, "Bellerina, get your ass out here and give your ol' dad a hug!"

Jack had made it to the landing in time to see Belle come running out of the bedroom wearing her nightgown. Then he watched as she threw herself in her father's arms.

"Dad!" she shouted happily as Jensen swung her around. Jack thought there was one thing good about Jensen interrupting Jack's determination to break through during his Sunday, and that was hearing Belle sounding happy for the first time in weeks.

Jack watched as Jensen hugged his daughter while the dogs danced around them and Gretl gave an excited woof.

Jensen pushed Belle a bit away and his gaze went immediately to the significantly faded bruise and stitched cut at her temple.

Then he exploded.

"Holy *shit*! What the *fuck*!"

For some strange reason, his eyes slashed to Jack and, Jack noted, they did this accusingly.

Jack was taken off-guard. He thought Jensen was there because of the accident but apparently he didn't know. Jack also couldn't imagine why Jensen was glaring at him with murder in his eyes as if Jack himself had shoved Belle down the stairs.

He had no time to come to terms with either of these thoughts.

Belle's face had grown pale and Jack bit back a curse before suggesting to Jensen, "Perhaps you and I can have word in the living room."

"Yeah, we'll have a fuckin' word. We might have two," Jensen ground out and his gaze swung back to his daughter as his hand curled around the side of her head, his thumb under the cut. "I mean, what the *fuck*?"

"Dad—" Belle whispered, her body swaying toward her father and her hand came up to his, her fingers wrapping around his wrist. "I'm okay."

"Girl, you've got a head wound," Jensen returned.

"I'm okay," she repeated softly.

But Jensen was not appeased. His hand dropped but twisted and Jack watched him catch Belle's hand and give it a squeeze. All the while his eyes were on Jack, and Jack noted he didn't look happy.

"Get your dad a cup of joe, girl. Your man and I are gonna have words," Jensen said without taking his gaze from Jack.

"I think—" Belle started, but Jack moved to Belle's side and curved his arm around her waist, bringing her close and kissing her temple above the cut.

His mouth moved to her ear and he said gently, "Belle, love, show your father the living room and then, please, make some coffee."

"But—"

Jack gave her waist a squeeze. "Please."

Her eyes searching his, she took in a breath, wet her lips and finally nodded.

She turned to her father and invited, "Come on, Daddy."

As Belle took her father to the living room, Jack went to the bedroom, dressed in jeans and a T-shirt and then walked into the living room where Jensen Abbot was staring out the window.

Belle's father's attention came to Jack the minute he entered the room and he watched Jack close the door.

The door barely clicked in its frame when Jensen demanded, "Don't make me wait, man."

Jack turned and crossed his arms on his chest.

"Three and a half weeks ago, at my home, Belle fell down the stairs."

"Jesus Christ," Jensen bit out then his eyes narrowed. "How?"

"Pardon?" Jack asked.

"My girl ain't clumsy. How'd she fall down the fuckin' stairs?"

This was, Jack thought, a fucking good question.

One he had not thought to ask as he'd been preoccupied with seeing to Belle and dealing with losing his child.

"I don't know. We haven't spoken of it," Jack answered.

"Well, when she gets in with the coffee, we'll be fuckin' speakin' of it," Jensen threatened and Jack walked toward him.

The way Jack did it, Jensen rightly pulled himself up to his full height.

"You won't mention it," Jack declared.

"What the—?"

"I wasn't there," Jack explained away what he had the uncomfortable feeling was Jensen's implication that Belle didn't fall down the stairs but that Jack had some hand in her injury. "I was flying from London to Cornwall at the time. No one witnessed it. She was found unconscious at the foot of the stairs."

Jensen relaxed a bit and asked in a less hostile tone, "Did she trip?"

"I don't know but you won't mention it," Jack stated inflexibly.

The hostility was back when Jensen asked, "Why the fuck not?"

"Because she was pregnant when she fell and she's not pregnant now." Jack watched the blood drain from Belle's father's face and he softened his tone when he went on, "She's not handling the loss of our child well, Jensen, and I need you to handle her with care."

Jensen's eyes grew wide. "*Your* child?"

"Our child, yes," Jack replied.

He looked away and pulled a hand through his hair.

Jack thought upon meeting him that he, like Rachel, looked years younger than he must be.

At that moment, he looked old enough to be Belle's grandfather.

"Bellerina," he whispered to the floor, and Jack thought even his voice sounded old when he looked at Jack and said bizarrely, "I really need to get me one of them cell phones. Rachel's probably been frantic tryin' to get a hold of me."

Knowing, from what Belle told him, that Jensen Abbot was an American nomad, no home, traveling from city to city taking on whatever "gig" (Belle's word) he could find, as a musician (he played piano) or a dealer (he dealt blackjack) or anything else that came up, Jack reckoned that Jensen was not wrong. It was likely Rachel had been frantically trying to reach him.

"You're here now," Jack replied and the man nodded.

Suddenly Jensen went still and inquired, "Handle her with care?"

Jack felt his jaw grow hard but he tried to keep his voice soft when he replied, "I meant no disrespect. What I meant—"

Jensen visibly relaxed and his grin spread right before he cut in and assured, "I know what you meant, man, and I know it wasn't disrespect." He clapped Jack on the shoulder stoutly and his grin widened into a smile. "Glad to see my girl's got herself a good man. 'Handle her with care,'" he muttered. "I like that, I should write a song about that." He looked around Jack toward the door and shouted, "Girl, where's my coffee!"

Jack had no chance to say another word as Jensen rounded him and marched to the door.

However he had a feeling his Sunday with Belle was no longer just his.

And he was right.

❧ ❧ ❧

"Jenny!" Rachel shouted as she flew through the enormous entrance hall of The Point and threw herself in Jensen's arms.

Belle and Jack followed Jensen inside, Gretl and Baron trotting in with them heading straight toward the kitchen and food.

Jack watched as his mother, Lila, Yasmin and a big, strange, white-haired man wearing a kilt and a dark-haired woman wearing an effusive number of scarves and silver jewelry wandered in behind Rachel.

Then his eyes swung to Jensen and Rachel and he saw, to his shock, they were shamelessly necking in the entrance hall.

Shamelessly and *passionately*.

And, after this went on for a while, Jack realized they were necking shamelessly, passionately and, apparently, tirelessly.

For the first time in three and a half weeks, Jack found himself chuckling.

When he did, Belle's head twisted sharply to face him, her eyes narrowed and his chuckle became laughter.

She looked back to her mother and cried, "Mom!"

Rachel, slowly (very slowly), realized she had an audience and she broke from her lip lock with Jensen but she didn't move away.

Cuddling her ex-husband, her fingers playing with the collar of his jacket, her head resting on his shoulder, she looked at her daughter, a smile on her face, and muttered, "Sorry honeypot."

"I'm not sorry." Jensen grinned unrepentant at his daughter, his arm around Rachel. "It's been too long, little girl."

Belle made a frustrated noise and Jack's arm, already around her shoulders, curled and he pulled her into his side.

"Oops!" Rachel all of a sudden uttered and looked up at Jensen. "Jenny, we're not allowed to embarrass Bellerina."

Jensen looked down at Rachel but his eyebrows went up. "Says who?"

"Says Jack," Rachel replied. "He's kind of protective of Belle and he's forbidden it."

"Yeah," Jensen was still grinning. "I got that impression right off."

"Really?" Rachel asked curiously, twisting so her front was plastered against Jensen's and her arms went around his waist. "What happened?"

"I'm sure we'd all like to know but perhaps you two can cotton on to the fact that there are other beings in the universe so that everyone can meet Jensen," Lila broke in and Jack chuckled again.

"This isn't funny," Belle whispered at his side and he looked down at her.

"Poppet, you're wrong," Jack whispered back, a grin on his face and it didn't leave even when he bent his head to touch his grinning lips to her pursed ones.

Introductions were made including Jack meeting Angus and Cassandra. Then they moved, everyone settled in the morning room and Joy ran out to see to refreshments.

"How you getting on, lass?" Angus boomed gently when they were all seated.

His question was for Belle but strangely his eyes were on Jack.

As were Cassandra's.

"I'm okay, Angus," Belle answered, busy with pressing the hem of her skirt over her knees, her head bent, and she didn't notice Angus wasn't looking at her.

"You?" Angus barked at Jack, and Jack tipped up his chin.

Angus was studying him intently and Jack didn't like it.

Jack had no way of saying anything, not in company, so he held the Scotsman's stare and he didn't laugh when Jensen declared, "It's all going to be okay now 'cause *I'm* here."

Belle's head came up and she smiled at her father.

"Oh lordy," Rachel muttered. She was cuddling so closely with Jensen in the corner of the couch opposite Jack and Belle that she was nearly in his lap. Her eyes came to Jack and she said, "I hope this place is fortified. Jensen can be a bit wild."

Jack opened his mouth to speak but Jensen beat him to it.

"That gives me an idea! Let's have a party!"

"Jenny, we're not having a party," Lila decreed.

"Woman, we're havin' a party." His gaze swung to Jack and he attempted to enlist reinforcements. "Jack, my man, you agree we could use a party, doncha?"

"I'm not sure we're ready for a party," Jack replied and Jensen's brows drew together.

Then he informed Jack, "Dude, when things get heavy, a party's the only way to go."

"Daddy," Belle said quietly, "I'm not really in the mood for a party."

Jensen's gaze went to his daughter, his brow unfurrowed, his eyes went soft and he gave in immediately, "All right, baby. No party."

At that moment, Jack decided he liked Jensen Abbot.

Rachel popped out of her chair and pulled Jensen up with her.

She wrapped her arms around his waist and suggested, "How about a one on one party, you and me, right now?"

"Oh my goodness gracious," Belle whispered.

"Now you're *talkin'!*" Jensen shouted.

"Holy heck," Belle breathed.

"We'll be back in an hour," Rachel told the congregation with no embarrassment whatsoever, and she led Jensen out of the room.

"More like twelve," Lila muttered under her breath and called after the departing pair, "See you at breakfast!"

They heard Rachel's giggle and Jensen's laugh as Joy rushed back in.

"What'd I miss?" Jack's mother asked excitedly.

"Well, we're *not* having a party and, apparently, Jensen and Rachel are off for a twelve hour sex-a-thon," Yasmin answered. "Other than that, you didn't miss much."

"Ah," Joy sat in the corner of the couch Jensen and Rachel just vacated and went on dreamily, "Young love."

"Joy, they're both fifty-five years old," Lila told her.

Joy looked at Belle, winked and amended, "Ah, young-at-heart love."

Belle smiled at his mother and Jack realized as his chest squeezed in a mixture of pain and pleasure, he hadn't seen her smile at all since the accident, but today, with her father's unexpected appearance, she'd smiled several times.

It was then Jack thought that perhaps he should have let Jensen have his party.

Suddenly Angus stood up and demanded, "Bennett, a word."

Belle went tight at his side and Jack tipped his head back to look at the Scot.

"Is it necessary you have your word now?" Jack asked calmly.

"It was necessary I have it three weeks ago. But now's going to have to do," Angus shot back.

Belle's tight body got tighter and Jack felt his jaw follow suit.

"Is something wrong?" Belle asked.

Angus's face softened when he looked down at Belle. "Nothing's wrong, lass."

"But—"

"Just want a word with your man," Angus went on.

Jack felt her body get as tight as it was that morning when it felt like it would shatter at the slightest movement before she asked, "Is it about the third ghost?"

"Let's not worry about ghosts for now, shall we?" Joy said hurriedly and Jack's gaze cut to his mother.

She knew something, something that concerned her greatly, a reaction she was trying to hide.

Jack instantly made his decision.

He gave Belle a squeeze and a kiss on the side of her head before he said, "I'll be back in a minute."

Belle's eyes never left him as he stood, her expression was anxious and her cheeks had lost the healthy glow her father's visit had returned there and were again pale.

He leaned over her, taking her chin between his thumb and forefinger and he pressed a kiss against her lips before whispered, "I'll only be a minute, poppet."

"Okay," she whispered back.

His eyes sliced to Angus and he led the way to his study.

He closed the door and saw Angus standing, legs planted wide, arms crossed on his barrel chest when Jack turned to the room.

"You got whisky?" Angus asked.

"It's ten thirty," Jack replied. "Can you wait until an appropriate hour to have a drink?"

"It's not for me, lad, it's for *you*."

Jack did not think that boded well.

"Speak fast, McPherson, I need to get back to Belle."

"What you need to do, Bennett, is to quit mollycoddling her. She'll find her way."

Jack's patience, not exactly in a healthy state, instantly frayed at this man he did not know in the slightest having the gall to tell him what to do.

Therefore his voice was low and obviously angry when he replied, "I met you fifteen minutes ago and you barely know Belle. Don't think—"

Angus cut him off by saying, "My wife was with child when she was knocked over by a car."

Jack felt as if he'd been punched in the gut, hard, thus he made no reply.

Angus continued, "My wife survived. My child did no'."

Jack clenched his teeth and he still made no reply.

Angus kept speaking.

"I mollycoddled her, like you're doing. I did it for months. I lost her those months and I feared she'd no' come back to me. I eventually had to take a job and when I did, she had to be responsible for herself. When I got back, she was better. I took the hint and tried to be normal." Angus strode forward, stopped two feet away and put his big hand on Jack's shoulder. "The grieving process is the same for everyone, lad. You're doing Belle no favors by no' helping her move to the next stage. The time has come and gone for mollycoddling. It's time now for normal."

For some reason, Jack found himself sharing, "We're moving back to The Point today."

Angus smiled a crooked, highly demented smile that made Jack question his sanity even after Angus just displayed he had a grip on it. "That's good news, lad. Good news."

Jack was finished and therefore asked, "Are we done?"

Angus dropped his hand. "'Fraid no'."

"Finish it," Jack demanded.

Angus took a step back and asked, "You sure you don't want that whisky?" When he caught Jack's hard look he hurried on, "Cass and I been working while all this was going on."

Jack stared at the man before informing him, "You should know I've never seen Myrtle and Lewis and I don't believe they exist. I'm humoring Belle, my mother and Belle's family. I have little interest in this."

"You might change your mind when you learn Belle is Brenna Addison Bennett reincarnated," Angus replied.

Yes, Jack decided, Angus McPherson was definitely mad.

And Jack didn't relish the idea of a madman living in his home with his family.

Therefore, Jack's voice was ominously quiet when he asked, "Pardon?"

"Belle's Brenna reincarnated. Cass hasn't had a chance to confirm if you're Joshua but we're guessing you are."

"That's absurd," Jack bit out.

"It's the truth," Angus shot back.

Jack crossed his arms on his chest and he scowled at the Scot.

"Cass felt it the minute she touched Belle," Angus stated. "Seeing as so much was going on, you didn't shake her hand when you met her. To confirm it, she needs to touch you."

"Perhaps I should be more clear," Jack replied. "When I said I had little interest, I meant I'm not participating in this farce."

Angus leaned forward. "Think about it, lad. We know your story with Belle, the women have shared it. And we know *you*. A body can't escape *you*. You're all over the papers, all over the magazines. We know your history, most especially with women. Then, one night, you meet this girl and within hours you know you want to spend the rest of your life with her? Doesn't that strike you as odd?"

Deciding he was done and it was time to get back to Belle, Jack shook his head and started toward the door saying, "This is none of your fucking business."

"You and Belle are connected," Angus called after him.

Jack stopped, hand to the doorknob, and turned back, "Yes, we are. But there's nothing odd about it."

Angus hadn't moved from his spot. "No, you're right, it isn't odd. It's beautiful. But when I say you're connected, I mean in more ways than you can imagine. It's rare and it's exquisite when it happens and it's happened to *you*. You and Belle are connected supernaturally. You belong together. You're destined for one another. You felt it immediately and don't stand there and tell me or yourself you didn't."

Suddenly, Jack remembered the first time Belle's eyes fell on him. He remembered it felt like a sledgehammer had hit him in the gut.

And he remembered being extremely irritated that, when she was introduced to him, she hadn't offered him her cheek to kiss and this made him so annoyed, he'd forced that on her.

He also remembered, practically the moment he met her, he'd maneuvered her into his arms and, only moments later, he'd had the irrational desire to kiss her.

Lastly, he remembered, in the dead of night, only hours after meeting her, when she was standing at his side in his shirt next to his dogs that he already considered her *his* woman, and he remembered he felt a possessiveness unparalleled in his entire history with the opposite sex.

Therefore, bearing in mind that his history with the opposite sex was considerable, he had to admit that all of this was more than odd. He'd never thought about it, never questioned it, it was simply the way it was.

However, now, he was forced to think of it and his eyes narrowed on the Scot.

"I see it's coming to you," Angus muttered.

Jack moved back into the room.

He hated doing it but he had no choice but to prompt Angus, "Go on."

Angus only nodded once then said, "When I say reincarnated, I'm not talking about what people think I'm talking about. What I mean is, Brenna Addison and Joshua Bennett's souls carried the spirits your and Belle's souls carry. It isn't that you're Joshua and she's Brenna. You're you and she's Belle. But you both carry this spirit, a trace of life on this earth that never dies even when its host does. It lives on with one purpose. It's always seeking its mate, yearning for it and is only at peace when it finds it."

The idea was ludicrous.

Jack didn't share this thought but he knew his face showed it because Angus sighed and suggested, "How about we give that time to sink in?"

Jack wanted to advise him not to hold his breath but Angus wasn't done.

"The thing with this is, these spirits, these traces, these bits of life, they seem to be anchored to The Point in some way. Not anchored here for good and ever because, if they were, Belle wouldn't have Brenna's trace. But the action is anchored here. What needs to happen is anchored here. Cass and I don't think it's been that way through eternity. We think something has anchored those traces here, brought you both here. We think they're here because they have to be for Myrtle and Lewis."

"So, what you're saying is, Belle, being at least a trace of their mother come back to The Point, can set them free."

Angus nodded but said, "Problem is, Myrtle and Lewis have disappeared."

Jack stared and asked, "Pardon?"

"We've done reading after reading. There are no ghosts in this house."

This, at least, was good news.

Jack crossed his arms on his chest and replied, "So your work is done."

Angus took in a deep breath before he said, "No' likely, lad. The children were there when Belle fell down the stairs."

At this unexpected news, Jack felt his entire frame grow tight.

"What?" he asked on a menacing whisper.

"We all saw them. Yasmin got to Belle first. She said they were hovering over her when she arrived."

"They hurt Belle?" Jack ground out, knowing his words were insane and not giving a fuck.

"No, they were upset, shouting for help. I wasn't paying much attention but, looking back, they seemed scared. Or at least the boy did. Problem is, since they've disappeared, we can't ask them what they saw."

"What the fuck does that mean?"

"It means something happened that night. They saw something, something that frightened them and they've disappeared. Probably for their own protection. We can't find them. But they're not *gone* because they can't go. They can't leave this place unless they're released. They just don't want to be found. It isn't unusual. What's unusual is that neither Cass nor I can sense them and none of our readings are finding them, and we're both pretty good at this kind of thing."

"Now what?" Jack asked.

"We've got to talk to them. Cass felt another entity when we first came to this house. That entity has disappeared too. No traces of him, no signs, like he wasn't even here, like he's never been here. The children, there are traces of them everywhere. I can feel they've been in this room as I'm standing here with you right now. The third entity, we've got nothing."

"And, this third entity—" Jack started.

"Is what I think frightened the boy."

Jack's chest grew tight as his mouth murmured, "Caleb Caldwell."

"That's my guess," Angus agreed on a nod.

Jack's chest grew tighter and his voice sounded hoarse when he said, "Belle."

"That was my guess too," Angus replied. "It would be strange, him being here. A ghost has to have some connection with the place it haunts. It has to be a place they spent a lot of time in or the place they died in. But it isn't unheard of for a ghost to find a connection to someplace integral to something that happened in their life. Even so, we did readings on the top of the stairs, the bottom of the stairs and every step besides. We gave it everything we got. There's nothing there. No ghost leaves *no* trace. It's impossible."

Jack, to his sheer disbelief, found himself stating, "We need the children."

"Aye, lad, we need the children." Angus shifted uncomfortably and asked, "Has Belle said—?"

Jack cut him off. "We haven't spoken of it. I assumed she tripped."

Angus nodded again. "Aye, and she might think she did even if Caldwell was present. He'd have to trick her into the fall or, say, appear before her and make her lose her balance, something like that. Ghosts can't touch humans unless they have a spell to give them powers. We've got the diary of a local girl. Cass found it in the library in town. I'll share that with you later. But, as far as we can tell, Caldwell had no dealings with a witch who could give him that power and, even though this diary mentioned a good deal about him, the local girl doesn't note that he dabbled in the dark arts. To be able to touch Belle, he'd have to have a spell. To be able to banish all trace of himself, he'd have to be very powerful. Although Cass is sure she felt something else, we've yet to discover what that was." He leaned forward. "But, Jack, something scared that wee ghosty lad. Something that made him disappear when he's had full run of this house for centuries without any indication he feared anything here. We need to call him out."

Jack shook his head. "Do whatever you do but Belle and I aren't moving back to The Point today."

Angus threw his head back and hooted before looking at Jack. "Lad, you think we've been sitting back drinking whisky and chasing ghosty vibes? Belle's protected. Cass has got her covered. Cass has got *everyone* covered. The whole house has so much protection it'd take a powerful coven to break through and, even for them, it'd take *days*."

Jack was far from convinced but before he could share this with Angus, Angus spoke again.

"I know you don't believe all I'm saying but believe this, I take my work seriously. My family, for generations, has been doing this work and we *all* take it seriously. We live it. We breathe it. It's our legacy. In all my time doing this work I've no' let anyone down and I'll no' start with you, and I sure as hell will *no'* let The Tiny Dynamo down." He leaned in before he finished, "Do you get me?"

He certainly sounded serious but Jack didn't reply. He just held his stare.

Angus let it go and urged, "Talk to Belle about that night, Jack. We need to know what she saw and what she *felt*."

"And, if there was some other..." he paused and then clipped out the word, "*entity*, what would you be looking for?"

"A cold draught is usually the way," Angus answered. "It could feel like a slight breeze. It could be she saw her breath, like she was out in the chill air. Sometimes the ghosties appear full on, like Myrtle and Lewis like to do. Sometimes it's just a feeling. Even if she just had a feeling she wasn't alone, Cass and I need to know."

Jack took a breath in through his nostrils and then he said what he couldn't believe he had to say.

"I'll talk to Belle."

Angus smiled his demented smile. "Good lad."

Jack continued to say what he couldn't believe he had to say, "I need to get back to Belle but I'll want a full briefing."

Angus didn't give the slightest indication of smugness.

He just nodded and agreed, "Absolutely."

Jack nodded back and then he and Angus started back to the morning room.

They didn't make it.

They didn't because they ran into Miles going the same direction.

"Miles," Jack called, his voice curt, and he watched his brother turn.

When Jack saw him, he noted there was something about Miles's face, something Jack couldn't quite read, but whatever it was it put Jack on edge and this only intensified when he heard Angus suck in breath behind him.

Miles rearranged his features and changed directions. Meeting Jack, Miles embraced his brother's stiff frame.

"Jack, I'm so sorry," Miles murmured, clapping him on the back while still embracing then releasing him and stepping away. "Elaine told me you and Belle were here. I thought I'd go—"

Jack cut him off. "Now's not the time, Miles."

Miles's face grew tight then his eyes moved to Angus and they grew wide. "And who might you be?"

"The McPherson," Angus announced, his booming voice, which Jack had noted in his short time with the Scot always had a warmth underlying it no matter if he was booming, hooting or telling you ridiculous facts about his job.

Now, Angus's voice was stone cold.

"I'll bet you are," Miles muttered, humor in his tone and not nice humor.

"Miles—" Jack started and his brother's eyes cut to him.

"I just want to see if Belle's all right," Miles stated.

"I'll save you the trouble," Jack told him bluntly. "She's not. She fell down the stairs, sprained her wrist, gave herself a concussion, split open her temple which called for five stitches and she lost our child. One isn't 'all right' when that happens."

"Jack—" Miles began.

"Time, Miles," Jack interrupted. "We need time."

Miles's face turned obstinate. "I'm trying to do the right thing here."

Jack lost his patience, leaned toward his brother and clipped, "And I'm telling you the right thing is to give us...some fucking...*time*."

Miles glared at Jack, shifted his glare to Angus then back to Jack and he said tersely, "Tell Belle she's in my thoughts."

"I'll be certain to do that," Jack lied.

Without another word, Miles walked away.

"Who, on the good God almighty's earth, was that?" Angus asked, watching as Miles disappeared.

"My brother," Jack replied.

"You're not close?" Angus asked.

"Not even a little," Jack answered.

Angus pursed his lips as if he was trying to stop himself from talking then he said softly, "Bad seed, lad."

"You can say that again," Jack muttered under his breath and then turned and led the way back to the morning room.

※ ※ ※

After Jack and Belle had coffee with the assemblage, Jack escorted Belle and Lila to the stables. As Lila forged ahead, Jack and Belle walked silently, hand in hand.

It wasn't, Jack was relieved to note, one of their recent tense silences.

Instead, Belle seemed more at ease. He knew this because, instead of holding her body stiffly away from his, she walked close, her fingers curved around his palm, her shoulder brushing his arm.

He helped her up to the loft the way he'd done it the first time they were in the stables together, coming up directly after her, his hands under hers on the rails, his frame protectively close to her body.

Once in the loft, Jack realized that Belle hadn't protested their ascent. In fact, at the base of the ladder, she'd simply glanced at him, waiting for him to come to her, expecting him to take care of her.

Instead of celebrating this crowning achievement in one of the myriad ways he would have preferred, he controlled his urge and looked around the loft.

Jack saw that, since the last time he'd been there, Lila had been busy. She'd taken over the space, swept it clean, there was another table filled with paint tubes and brushes, a bean bag and some rugs and there were half a dozen canvasses tilted against the wall, all of them covered. An unfinished one sat on one of now three easels set up by the sliding doors. And there were snapshots of the view taken at different times of the day and through different weather tacked to the walls.

The unfinished painting was, Jack was fascinated to see, going to be part of her storm series and even unfinished it was already spectacular.

After giving Belle a kiss, which was more than a brush on the lips, deeper, longer, making a statement but not something that would cause her embarrassment in front of her grandmother, Jack left and went back to the house.

He found Angus and Cassandra and, in his study, he allowed Cassandra to take his hand.

The moment she did, Jack watched as she went into a trance for long moments, her eyes unfocused, her face growing pale.

Jack's gaze slid questioningly to Angus, but Angus just gave him a nod and Jack waited, although he did so impatiently.

Finally, Cassandra came back to herself and pulled away.

Taking a step back, she said decisively, "Yep, mate, you're Joshua."

Jack again looked at Angus then back to Cassandra and found himself saying "So, my soul holds his trace."

This, for some bizarre reason, made her laugh.

When she got control of her hilarity, she shook her head. "No, Jack, you *are* Joshua."

Jack's eyes sliced back to Angus.

Angus caught Jack's look and muttered, "We've a professional difference of opinion about what reincarnation means."

"I see you gave him that trace business," Cassandra said to Angus, her voice amused.

"It's the way it is, lass," Angus shot back.

"It *isn't*, Angus. I mean, whoever heard of *traces* of souls drifting through eternity? That's rubbish!" Cassandra retorted.

"And whole beings reincarnated again and again throughout time isn't rubbish?" Angus returned hotly.

"Nope," she replied calmly.

Angus's face got redder than its normal red and Jack astutely surmised the Scot was about to blow.

Jack, thinking *both* theories were rubbish and also thinking that them having a passionate argument about it was preposterous, was quickly coming to the end of his patience.

Therefore he cut in, "Are you done with me?"

Both their eyes came to him and Cassandra said, "For now."

Jack nodded, left the room, found Yasmin and asked her a favor to which she agreed. Then he and Yasmin drove to Belle's cottage and Yasmin packed Belle's belongings while Jack collected his own and the dogs'. They took them to the car then they took them to The Point.

Jack collected Belle from the stables, they had a late lunch and, after lunch, she wandered away and disappeared.

He found her in the library seated in a chair she'd pulled to the window. Her legs were tucked underneath her, a sketchbook was in her hands, a box of colored pencils on the armrest, the page was blank and she was staring out the window.

He walked to her, pulled the sketchbook out of her hand, tucked it under his arm then took her hand and pulled her out of the chair.

She watched him do this as if she was in a trance herself before her body jolted and she started, "Jack—"

He ignored her, leaned down, grabbed the box of pencils and, his hand still in hers, he guided her to his study.

There, he dropped her hand and positioned a chair at the window behind his desk. He went back to her, led her to the chair and, with a gentle shove, he pushed her into the seat. He gave her back her sketchbook and pencils and turned to sit behind his desk.

As he opened a file, he felt her eyes on him.

"Jack," she called softly.

"Yes, love?" He kept his eyes on the papers in front of him and forced himself not to look at her.

He was attempting to establish normal.

Before the baby died, they hadn't had time to create a "normal," but when they did he had decided this would be it.

"Nothing," she whispered.

Minutes later, when he allowed himself to glance at her because he heard her pencils scratching on her pad, he saw her head was bent and she was drawing.

He pulled in breath slowly and, just as slowly, he released it.

And when he did, some of the tightness he'd been carrying in his chest for three and a half weeks released as well.

They all had dinner together, Jack made certain Belle came with him when he walked the dogs and when they returned, they sat talking with Lila, Joy, Yasmin, Cassandra and Angus.

When it was clear Belle was ready for bed, most of the others having already left one by one, Jack, his arm around her waist, guided her up the stairs.

She was Belle and therefore unable to hide her reaction to the stairs, which he knew throughout the day she'd avoided. He stayed close, his arm firm around her, his tread steady, and they made it to the top after which he heard her let out a little sigh.

He wanted to give her a squeeze or a kiss, some reward for facing that fear but he didn't call attention to it and simply led her to their room.

Now he was lying in their bed on his side, waiting for Belle to finish in the bathroom.

His eyes were on the door when it opened and she came out, wearing a simple pale-green nightgown with thin, satin, pastel-blue straps and a matching sheer pastel-blue ruffle at the hem, which came to mid-thigh. Her hair was down, her cheeks were pink and she was rubbing lotion in her hands. But her eyes, which skittered around the room looking anyplace but the bed, betrayed her nerves.

And, Jack thought, she'd never looked more beautiful.

"Come to bed, poppet," he called softly when she hesitated.

She wet her lips and walked to the bed.

Gretl and Baron had greeted her at the bathroom and they followed her. She paused to rub their heads and then commanded quietly, "Down," and they both settled at her side of the bed.

She turned to him and hesitated, so Jack leaned forward, took her hand and gave her a gentle tug. She came toward him, he caught her at the waist and pulled her over his body as he yanked the covers up to her waist.

She lifted up with a forearm in his chest and looked down at him.

"Jack." Her sweet, musical voice was tentative, her glorious gray eyes were stormy and she announced, "We need to talk."

"We do, poppet," Jack agreed and he watched her face register surprise.

For the purposes of containment, as well as other reasons, Jack's arm tightened at her waist and his other hand slid up her back to capture her hair in a loose fist.

"Belle, I need you to tell me about that night."

Her body jerked before it grew tense and her eyes, stormy before with whatever thoughts she carried, were tempestuous now.

"Why?" she asked, the thread of fear starkly evident in her tone.

He used her hair to pull her face to his and he touched his lips to hers before letting her draw back and answered, "Because I need to know and because you need to share so you can let it go."

"Jack, I don't think—"

"Belle, love, we need to talk about this."

"But, you—"

"Tell me, poppet, say it fast then it'll be over," he encouraged.

"But—"

His arm tensed and she stopped speaking, "Belle, tell me, I need to know."

She gazed at him a minute, her cloudy eyes dark.

She closed them tight, opened them and whispered, "I don't want to tell you because you aren't going to believe me."

It was then his body tensed.

He forced himself to relax and asked, "Why wouldn't I?"

She shook her head and in return Jack gently shook her.

"Belle, whatever happened, I'll believe you."

She wet her lips nervously before she asked, "You will?"

"Yes, I will," he replied firmly.

He watched her swallow then she said, "It's going to sound daft."

"It won't sound daft."

Her eyes moved from his to his shoulder then his ear and he watched as she came to a decision before she nodded. Her gaze finally came to rest on his and she spoke.

"Okay, you need to know." He nodded in encouragement and she continued, "I'd just got off the phone with you. I was hungry and I told the dogs we were going to see about dinner." She stopped talking and Jack's fingers released her hair but slid through its length, coming back to slide through again and he felt her relax against him as she went on, "I was walking down the hall. I was preoccupied, the dogs were with me and then, all of a sudden..." she paused again and took in a breath but didn't continue.

"Go on, poppet," Jack urged, still stroking her hair as his other hand started to draw circles on the small of her back.

She nodded again and whispered, "I was at the top of the stairs. The dogs, they had pressed close to my legs and for some reason, they started to growl." Jack stopped his hands stroking and circling and he wrapped his arms around her as she carried on in a barely there whisper, "It was strange. I started to ask them what was wrong but I saw…"

When she seemed to falter, Jack pressed gently, "Keep going, love."

She shook her head but, her eyes locked on his, she said in a rush, "I saw movement on the stairs. It was Lewis. He was drifting up the stairs toward me. He was going so fast, Jack, so very fast. I could tell right away something was wrong."

Jack's arms convulsed but she kept talking.

"He stopped and shouted at me. I don't remember what he said but I remember that he knew my name. He shouted my name and then…" Jack felt her body begin to tremble and her hand moved up, her fingers curled around his shoulder, digging in, holding on. "Jack, I swear, I felt a hand in my back and it pushed." Tears came to her eyes and she whispered, "It pushed me down the stairs."

Jack's arms spasmodically tightened and it took effort to loosen his hold.

"Do you believe me?" she asked softly, the tears still shimmering in her eyes.

"Of course I do, love," he replied absently, his thoughts on Angus's words, that a ghost couldn't touch a human which meant, if Belle had been pushed, someone had pushed her. "Did you see someone there?" Jack asked.

She shook her head. "I didn't get the chance to look."

"The dogs, you said they were growling. Do you think they saw Lewis?"

Belle kept shaking her head. "Lewis was in front of me but when I glanced down at the dogs, they were looking behind us."

"Did you feel anything?" Jack inquired.

Her face turned from fearful to confused and her head tilted to the side before she asked, "Feel anything? You mean the hand in my back?"

"No. Anything else. Did you feel anything?" Jack repeated. "Hear anything? A presence. Did you sense someone there?"

She shook her head. "No, nothing. But the dogs did and I think Lewis saw something."

"You didn't hear footsteps, sense someone moving behind you?"

She kept shaking her head. "Nothing. But my mind was somewhere else. I just woke up from a nap and had talked to you and..." She stopped and her eyes slid to his ear.

"Belle, love, look at me," Jack commanded gently and after a long moment, when her gaze finally moved to his, he urged, "And what?"

"And the baby," she whispered and his chest, which had relaxed, got tight again at her mentioning their child. "I was talking to the baby about you, before you called. And, when I was walking down the hall, I was thinking about dinner and you and wondering how long it would take for you to get home..."

At those words, instantly, the tightness in his chest released and he cupped the back of Belle's head and pulled her face close to his throat.

She resisted but only a little before her body relaxed into his.

When it did, Jack asked, "What were you saying to the baby about me?"

He was gratified to feel her nuzzle closer, pressing her forehead against his jaw as her fingers clenched his shoulder. "Just telling him that you were right. I'd met Cassandra and Angus that evening and they were so strange. I was telling the baby you were right about it not going back to normal and boring."

"I *was* right, my love, things are definitely still not normal and boring, and with those two and your father in the house I fear things will not be normal and boring for some time."

Her body tensed but almost immediately eased and he couldn't believe his ears when she let out a short, strangled giggle.

His arms clutched her even closer and he was beyond thrilled when she didn't resist but instead melted.

After several long, satisfying moments, Belle shared on a whisper, "I know you're going to think I'm even crazier, but, Jack, I'm scared of the stairs."

"That isn't crazy, Belle, not after what happened."

Her fingers pressed into his shoulder and she cuddled even closer. "Okay, but, this is even crazier." She pressed ever closer and admitted, "Jack, I think there might be something in this house that wants to hurt me."

He rolled to his side, taking her with him and he placed his fist under her chin and tipped it up so he could look in her eyes. They were still stormy with worry but the tempest had subsided.

"Tomorrow, we'll talk to Angus and Cassandra."

She tilted her head into the pillow, and seeing it and loving it when she did that, Jack couldn't stop his smile.

"We will?" she asked.

He nodded. "We will, poppet. They've been working while we've been away and they assure me you're protected."

Regardless of the fact that there was evidence to suggest that there was something amiss in his house and something mysterious about his connection with Belle, Jack still thought Angus and Cassandra's assertions were rubbish.

But he knew Belle didn't.

And he was willing to use whatever he could to calm that storm in her eyes.

His tactic succeeded.

She took a shuddering breath and gave him a tentative smile.

Jack allowed himself a moment to let her smile settle in his chest and his gut before he gave Belle a squeeze, rolled and turned out the light.

When he had them settled, the front of Belle's body cocooned to his, she spoke softly, "Jack, we need to talk about something else."

"What, love?"

She hesitated and said, "This."

"This?"

"This. Here. Now. You. Me."

He gave her a squeeze and whispered, "No, poppet. The one thing that we don't need to talk about is this. Here. Now. You or me."

"But—"

"All of that is the only thing that's good and right in this fucking crazy mess."

She was quiet then she asked, "It is?"

"Don't you feel it?" Jack asked in return.

Her reply was breathy and hesitant, "I want to."

He gave her another squeeze. "Then do it."

"But, the baby...it's what drew us—"

Jack gave her another, tighter squeeze, halting her words. "I thought I said we weren't going to have this discussion."

"But we have to!" she cried, her voice beginning to rise.

His hand came up to fist again in her hair and he used it to pull her head back gently.

His lips sought hers in the dark and he reminded her, "Belle, if you remember, there was no baby when I made you mine."

"Jack—"

He cut her off. "It's a sad fact that there's no baby now. It hurts to think about it. It makes my chest tight and my gut ache. But it doesn't change the fact that you're still mine."

"It makes your chest tight?" she whispered.

"And my gut ache."

"Really?" she breathed.

"Yes, my love." He tucked her face in his throat and went on, "But even with our loss, after your accident, I still felt lucky because I didn't lose you." He spoke cautiously, not wishing to feed into her fears but needing her to understand. "You could have been hurt in a much worse way, poppet, and, you being here, in our bed, in my arms, for that, I feel lucky."

He could barely hear her when she asked, "You, James Bennett, feel *lucky*?"

"Yes, poppet," he tipped his head so his lips moved against her hair. "I couldn't lose you and, I promise you, my love, we'll make another baby when the time is right. For now, we need to just be. You and me, we need to just be."

"You and me," she whispered.

"You and me," he repeated.

"You..." she hesitated then said her next words in a way that made them sound impossible, "like me."

He smiled into her hair. "Yes, Belle," he gathered her closer before finishing, "I definitely *like you*."

And, after saying those ridiculous words that in no way defined how he felt about her, he couldn't stop his chuckle.

She stiffened in his arms and asked, "Why is that funny?"

"I'll explain some other time."

"Explain now," she demanded.

"Some other time."

"Jack—"

"Poppet," he interrupted her and ordered, "Sleep."

"But—"

"Sleep."

"I think—"

He gave her a gentle shake and demanded, "Belle, sleep."

She held herself stiff and muttered, "Bossy."

Jack smiled into the dark and advised, "I'm afraid you're going to have to get used to that, love."

It took her a while but, finally, she relaxed and said on a sigh, "I guess I'll try."

And, again, he couldn't stop his chuckle.

☙ ☙ ☙

Jack's Sunday was not quite complete.

Because in the middle of the night, the dogs started barking loudly.

He jerked awake and felt Belle do the same in his arms.

"What the fuck?" he muttered, but before he could ascertain what was wrong, the door to the bedroom flew open.

Jack came up and twisted in bed as the room suddenly flooded with light and Jack stared in stunned disbelief as Angus and Cassandra charged in, Angus, wielding a whip and Cassandra brandishing what looked to be...

He stared incredulously...

A *twig*.

"We'll not harm ye, wee ghosty!" Angus boomed, his eyes across the room.

"She's vaporizing!" Cassandra shouted.

The dogs barked.

Jack threw the covers back and knifed out of bed.

His body went rock solid when he heard an ethereal, boy's voice shout, "*Myrtle!*"

At the sound, Jack's body stayed still but his head whipped around and he saw Angus circle the whip over his head but when he flicked it out, it fell to the ground.

"The turret!" Cassandra yelled and ran from the room.

Angus, his kilt awhirl, followed her.

"Don't hurt them!" Belle shouted.

She was out of bed and running after Angus and Cassandra, the dogs, still barking, at her heels.

Jack ran after her and caught her at the waist in the hall.

"Don't hurt them!" Belle screamed after the departing Angus and Cassandra, her body straining against Jack's hold and Angus whirled back.

"We won't hurt them, lass."

Then he was gone.

Belle turned urgently to Jack. "Jack, don't let them hurt the children."

Jack grasped her hand and tugged her swiftly down the hall to Lila's room. Turning the handle, he shoved open the door, switched on the light and Lila came immediately up in bed and stared at them.

Before she could say a word or even blink the sleep from her eyes, Jack ordered, "Do not let Belle leave this room and keep the dogs close."

Without waiting for a response, he left.

He went back to Belle and his room, pulled on jeans, a T-shirt and trainers and ran to the eastern turret where he knew most sightings of the child ghosts took place.

He was climbing the spiral, stone stairwell at a run, taking the steps two at a time, when he saw Angus and Cassandra descending.

"We lost them," Cassandra informed him, sounding disgusted.

Jack planted himself on the stairs and glowered up at the witch and the Scot.

"What. The. *Fuck*?" he demanded to know, enunciating his words perfectly clearly.

"We'll talk downstairs, lad," Angus said in a soft boom.

"What the fuck?" Jack repeated.

"Downstairs."

"Here," Jack clipped, "now."

Angus and Cassandra shared a glance then they looked back at Jack.

"We figured something like this would happen. Belle and you coming back, the children would make an appearance to be sure you were okay," Cassandra explained. "We gave ourselves a glamor so they wouldn't sense us and hung out. We both felt her when she arrived in your room."

Jack ignored the absurd notion that they'd given themselves "a glamor," whatever the fuck that was, and bit out, "Who?"

"Myrtle," Cassandra answered.

"We wanted to catch her before she could disappear again so we could ask her some questions," Angus added.

"So you came charging into our room, likely scaring the hell out of her, and her brother by the sounds of it, which means they'll disappear again," Jack snapped.

"We didn't think she'd get *away*," Angus replied.

"Well she fucking well did," Jack returned.

"That was unexpected," Cassandra muttered.

Jack's eyes sliced to the witch. "Unexpected? You're supposed to be clairvoyant, for fuck's sake."

She pressed her lips together and had the grace to look embarrassed.

"After this debacle, I'm supposed to trust that you two can keep my family safe, *Belle* safe, while ridding this castle of ghosts?" Jack asked and his voice was dangerous.

"So you believe in them now." Angus grinned his demented grin.

Jack felt his jaw grow hard before he said, "I didn't see them but I heard the boy and you didn't answer my question."

"Well, that's something, it'll be better if you believe," Cassandra put in.

Jack's angry gaze swung to her, he ignored her comment and commanded, "Perhaps one of you will answer my *fucking* question."

"Calm down, mate. It isn't like this gig is easy. It's not like it's a love potion. Ghosts can be unpredictable," Cassandra told him.

"Especially child ghosts. They're always the toughest to deal with," Angus grumbled.

"One of you, I don't care who," Jack cut in, "have two seconds to give me *one good reason* not to toss you out on your asses *right fucking now*."

"Cassandra leaves, half of her protection goes with her," Angus replied swiftly. "It's connected to her essence. There will be some protection but we're guessing, considering the unusualness of this job, that you need all you can get, lad."

Jack glared at the Scot.

"And, regardless of this, Angus is the best in the business. You couldn't get better," Cassandra put in.

"Thanks, Cass." Angus grinned at her.

"Well, it's the truth," Cassandra said to Angus.

"I know *that*. Still, nice to hear," Angus returned.

"Fucking hell," Jack muttered.

Angus looked at Jack and his face grew serious. "I promised you, I'd no' let you down. This is a setback but, Bennett, that promise holds true. I'll no' let you down."

"You need to be patient," Cassandra added.

"And *you* need to understand that Belle and my room is off limits," Jack returned.

"We can't—" Cassandra started.

"Off limits," Jack repeated firmly.

Cassandra opened her mouth to speak but Angus got there first.

"Cass, let it go," Angus muttered out the side of his mouth. "If he's declaring limits, that means he's no' kicking us out on our arses."

"Oh yeah," Cassandra muttered back.

"Fucking hell," Jack muttered in return.

Cassandra's face grew soft and she murmured, "Patience, mate, seriously, you have to trust us."

Jack was unaffected by her soft look. "I'll trust you when you give me reason to do so. Until then, you need to know, another stunt like this, you're gone."

"Understood," Cassandra said immediately.

Jack scowled at them both trying to ascertain if they did, indeed, understand. When he could tell by their faces they did, he turned his back on them, stalked down the stairs and to Lila's room.

The minute he entered, Belle flew to him.

His arms closed around her as her hands settled on his chest and her head tipped back.

"The children?" she asked.

Jack's gaze slid to Lila then back to Belle. "They've disappeared again."

"Damn it to hell," Lila muttered.

"Gram's been telling me that Cassandra and Angus can't find them," Belle told him.

Jack put his arm around her shoulders and moved her to the door. "We'll have a full briefing tomorrow."

"Do you think they're okay?" Belle asked as Jack whistled for the dogs and nodded his goodnight to Lila.

He had no idea how to answer her.

Firstly, he now did, indeed, believe there were ghosts, as outrageous as that concept was. He couldn't believe his ears but he also couldn't deny he'd heard, distinctly, a young, disembodied voice shouting the name Myrtle.

Secondly, given the fact that they *were* ghosts, he doubted they were okay.

Lastly, they were being pursued by the Laurel and Hardy of ghost hunters and therefore felt the need to flee then disappear, which meant they were seriously not okay.

"I'm sure they're fine, love," Jack murmured his lie.

"I hope so," Belle whispered and before he closed the door behind them, Jack locked eyes with Lila who was biting her lip.

"It'll be fine," Jack assured Belle but his words were also meant for her grandmother.

As he closed the door, he saw Lila pull herself up and nod.

Jack waited for Belle to say her goodnights to her grandmother before he guided her and their dogs to their bedroom.

And, approximately fifteen minutes later, dogs settled, Belle's weight heavy in his arms, Jack looked at the clock and saw that it was twelve o three.

Finally, he thought, *this fucking Sunday is over.*

18

HAPPY

Belle

Belle woke up, hearing her own low, deep-throated moan.

This, she realized immediately, was because Jack's hand was cupped on her breast, his thumb doing lazy circles around her nipple which did delicious things to her state of being, and his tongue was gliding along the skin behind her ear which made those delicious things *delectable*.

"Jack?" she whispered, her brain not yet connected to her body and her body not under her control.

This point was further proved when, the instant Jack heard his name, he shifted her to her back and covered her with his long, hard frame, his lips taking hers in a deep, open-mouth, tongues-tangling, mind-boggling, upon-waking kiss.

It had only been weeks since he'd kissed her like this but Belle had forgotten how good it felt. She'd forgotten how much she loved Jack's kisses. She'd forgotten how lost she could get, forgetting to be meek and mild, becoming the Belle she wanted to be.

Therefore, she kissed him back.

He growled in her mouth.

His growl shot straight between her legs and those legs became restless.

Jack rolled to the side, his mouth never disengaging, his kisses long and sweet, his hand drifted down her belly, over her hip then, against her mouth he demanded in a deep, hoarse voice that sent shivers through her, "Open your legs for me, poppet."

Belle didn't hesitate. Her legs parted for him and as his tongue danced with hers, his fingers trailed down the insides of her thighs then up, along the edges of her panties then down again, feather-soft on her sensitive skin.

She wrapped her arms around him, mindlessly sliding her fingers along the muscled skin of his back, his sides, his waist, anywhere she could reach.

Somewhere from far away, she heard Jack murmur, "Further, Belle."

"What?" she breathed, confused, her mind disengaged, her entire being centered on her thighs, his fingers and all the beauty she was feeling.

"Spread your legs further, love," Jack whispered and she felt another rush of heat and wetness between those legs, and because of that she did as he demanded and felt her reward, his smile against her lips. "That's it, poppet, open for me." At his encouragement, she spread her legs even wider.

His mouth took hers in another hot, demanding kiss as his fingers continued their beautiful torture, whisper-light touches, so close but not close enough. She'd tense, preparing for his touch, needing his invasion, certain it was coming but then they'd glide away.

When she thought she could take no more, suddenly they were there, lightly dancing across her panties in a sensuous tease.

She moaned deep in her throat and felt his groan against her tongue.

He pulled away, muttered, "So fucking wet," and then he was gone.

"Jack?" she breathed in sudden confusion but she needn't have worried. She felt his hands strong on her hips, pushing up her night-gown then pulling down her panties then his mouth was *right there*.

She arched her back right before she lifted her hips, seeking maximum contact with his mouth, his tongue and all the glorious things they were doing to her.

"Oh *God*," she moaned, rocking her hips against his mouth.

She'd forgotten how good he was at this.

How could she forget?

She was close, so close, her hands in his hair, demanding more.

Suddenly, she lifted her torso up, scooted away and Jack's mouth disengaged.

Desperate for something else, she pulled at his shoulders and he came over her, rolling to his back, taking her with him, muttering, "Belle—"

She lifted, sitting astride him, pulling his upper body to hers and her mouth went to his.

"Teach me," she begged against his mouth, rubbing herself against his groin.

"Belle, love, I don't under—"

"I've never done it. Teach me how to do it at the same time," she pleaded and she saw his eyes flash hot before his hand fisted in her hair, crushing her mouth to his as his other hand came between their bodies.

She felt him guide himself inside.

Her crazy, spinning-out-of-control world, all of a sudden righted the minute he slid inside.

Instantly she started moving up and down, riding him, frantic as he kissed her and his thumb pressed between her legs, its strong, determined circling sending shudders down her thighs.

"I felt so empty," she muttered against his mouth. "Jack, so empty." Her voice was husky, her words not coming from her brain but somewhere else. "It's so good to be full of you again."

"Belle," he murmured, her name coming at her as deep and throaty as her words had been and his mouth captured hers again. He sat up, her head tipping down to keep contact with his mouth, her movements became frenzied, his thumb more determined and he tore his lips from hers and ordered, "Finish, my love."

She shook her head, holding back, wanting to wait, wanting to feel more of this, more of him, wanting to be full of him forever.

His hand in her hair tilted her face to his and he demanded, "Finish, love, right now."

And she did as she was told, still rearing uncontrollably against his hardness, seeking, demanding, impaling him deep inside her even as her climax scored straight through to her soul.

It was so intense, so thorough, Belle was, many heady moments later, disappointed to see that she'd missed his.

Before she could form a thought, Jack fell to his back, taking her with him, pulling the covers over their bodies without losing their intimate connection.

She tucked her face in his neck, her thoughts scattered. She tried to catch even one and found the only thing she could focus on was his warmth, his body hard and strong under hers, their connection making her feel complete.

One of his hands traveled up and down her back as the other slid through her hair and after a while, he murmured, "I missed you, poppet."

She felt the tears well, and without her faculties engaging, she couldn't stop them from sliding from her eyes.

"Belle?"

"You don't think I'm wanton?" she blurted, her embarrassed mind swiftly filled with recent memories of her begging, her desperation, her frantic movements.

She felt his body shake under hers and her head lifted so she could look at him.

He was laughing.

"What's funny now?" she wailed, and both his hands came to her face, his fingers gliding into her hair but his thumbs moved along the tears on her cheeks.

He didn't answer her.

Instead, still chuckling, he asked, "Why on earth are you crying?"

Her eyes moved to his ear, which she found now with lots of practice was the safest place to look, *especially* if he was naked.

She considered his question.

Then she answered his ear with, "I don't..." her voice hitched and she finished on a stammer, "don't know."

His hands on her face tensed and he ordered gently, "Look at me."

She licked her lips and her eyes met his.

His eyes were warm, they were tender, they were amused and...

She stared at him, her heart leaping.

She hadn't seen it in weeks but she saw it then, right in his eyes.

He looked happy.

Her tears instantly stopped and, out of the blue, she asked, "Jack, are you happy?"

The warmth in his gaze intensified mere moments before he burst out laughing and his arms wrapped around her so tight she was forced to collapse against him and tuck her face into his neck again.

"What's funny now?" she demanded over his laughter.

His voice was still vibrating with amusement when he answered, "You're here. I'm here. You're in my arms and I'm still inside you. I just watched you come so hard I thought for a second you were going to pass out and, I have to admit, love, my orgasm was nearly as fucking good as yours and you're asking me if I'm *happy*?"

There was a lot there but Belle's mind immediately honed in on the part she thought she needed to get straight.

"I didn't, um," she hesitated then skipped over the embarrassing bit, deciding he'd figure it out, "so hard that I nearly passed out."

"Poppet, your eyes rolled back in your head and I could swear for a moment you were in a trance," he replied.

She pulled against his arms so she could glare down at him.

Seriously!

How smug could he be?

"Hardly," she snapped.

He grinned.

It was then she realized he was teasing.

"Stop teasing me, Jack," she demanded.

"Stop being so easy to tease, Belle," he returned, still grinning.

She slapped his arm and demanded, "Stop it!"

Jack rolled her to her back, their bodies disconnected but he tangled his legs with hers and let a goodly amount of his warm weight rest on her, which was *almost* as nice as feeling him inside so she didn't protest.

He was still smiling when he looked down at her. "All right Belle. No more teasing." He touched his lips to hers and when he pulled away, his expression was still tender and amused but his words were serious. She knew this because they were low and rumbly. "To answer your question, yes, Belle, for the first time in what feels like a long time, I'm happy."

She felt her belly melt and so did her body.

Because she believed him.

And she knew it was her that was making him happy.

Not the thought of her having his baby. Not temporary insanity. Not the heretofore unknown prospect that they were living in an alternate universe.

All of these (and then some) were possibilities her mind came up with in the last three and a half weeks as to why he didn't, without delay, leave her when he found out she'd lost their baby.

No, she made him happy in the real, the here, the now.

She, Meek and Mild Belle Abbot was making him, criminally handsome James Bennett, happy.

She let that thought settle in her heart, her soul and, finally, her mind, and surprisingly even her mind let that thought be.

His hand sifted into her hair at the side of her head and his eyes stayed tender but lost their humor when he asked, "Now, poppet, what I'd like to know is, are you?"

She sensed this question meant a great deal to him so she answered honestly.

"No." When she watched his jaw get hard she lifted her hand, rested it against that hard, handsome, morning stubbled jaw and continued on a whisper, "But, with all your help, I'm getting there."

His forehead dropped to hers and he murmured with feeling, "Thank God."

Afraid but feeling ready, Belle admitted softly, "I'm sorry I went away. I missed you too, Jack."

She felt the air turn velvet all around them as his face went soft.

Then she felt nothing at all but his lips on hers and his arms crushing her tight.

☙ ☙ ☙

Belle and Jack walked hand in hand into the dining room.

They were late for breakfast.

Everyone was there, including, surprisingly, Olive.

"Hi, Olive," Belle smiled at the woman as Olive's gaze came to her.

"Belle, you look beautiful, as ever," Olive replied, her attention sharp, and Belle had the weird impression Olive not only could read her thoughts but was doing so.

Then Olive looked to Jack and she gave him the same assessing stare.

Jack pulled out Belle's chair, she sat and he helped her scoot it to the table before his hand cupped her jaw, his thumb slid along her cheekbone and she saw that tender look in his eyes as the sweet feel of velvet hit the air.

His hand dropped, he moved around her and sat at the head of the table.

Belle, temporarily in Jack and Belle Land where no one else existed, came back into the room and glanced at her audience.

Joy, Yasmin, Gram and Mom were engaged in sipping coffee, slathering toast with butter and forking eggs into their mouths. They were veterans of Jack's loving demonstrations and didn't notice a thing.

Olive was glancing between the two of them and seemed to find her readings of Jack and Belle post-accident, heartbreaking loss of unborn child were acceptable *but* she was keeping an eye out. And yes, Belle barely knew Olive but she could still read that with a look.

Cassandra was looking amused but this look was directed at Angus.

Then she said (bizarrely), "*So* Joshua."

"Lass, *no' even*," Angus (bizarrely) flashed back.

Belle's dad was staring at Jack.

Then he said, "*Dude,*" as if this one word spoke volumes.

Jack's eyes went to Belle's father and he asked, "Jensen, to which 'dude' at this table are you referring?"

"You," Dad replied.

"And?" Jack prompted.

"Seriously," Dad answered on a grin though that wasn't really an answer, it was clear her father thought it was.

Jack's brows went up then his gaze came to Belle as if she could interpret.

"Don't ask me," Belle murmured and Jack looked back at her father.

"Jensen, would you care to elaborate?"

But her father apparently did not care to elaborate because he looked at Mom and remarked, "Is it me or do English dudes speak funny?"

"'Elaborate' is hardly a funny word, Jenny," Lila spoke up.

"Do *you* say 'elaborate?'" Dad asked Gram but before Gram could respond, Dad went on, "*I* don't say 'elaborate.' Jesus, I don't know anyone who says 'elaborate.' I don't even know what 'elaborate' means."

"I say elaborate," Olive put in.

"You don't count, you're English," Dad retorted.

"Jack means explain, Dad," Belle decided, unusually unwisely, to wade in.

"Well, why doesn't he just say 'explain?'" Dad demanded to know.

"Jack's sitting right there, Jenny, don't talk about him like he isn't even here," Mom scolded. "It's rude."

At her mother's words and the look on her father's face when he heard them, with lots of experience with this type of situation, Belle's stomach plummeted and she muttered, "Oh dear."

At the same time Gram mumbled, "Uh-oh."

And Jensen Abbot didn't contradict Gram and Belle's years of experience.

Therefore, as if he didn't have an audience, most of whom he'd known less than twenty-four hours...

And as if he wasn't the guest at the rather opulent dining-room table in an imposing castle owned by his daughter's criminally handsome, unbelievably rich, unmistakably famous boyfriend who he *also* had known for just a hint more than twenty-four hours...

Jensen's voice rose.

"Woman, tell me you didn't just call me rude."

Mom as well (and as usual), instantly forgot her audience when she returned, "Jenny, I did because you *were*."

"Rachel—" Gram tried to intervene but Dad put his hand up, palm toward Gram, the whole time he did this his head was twisted to Mom.

"I'm not rude. I'm *never* rude," Dad told Mom. "That's the best thing I gave our daughter. *Consideration.*" Dad moved his glare to Belle. "Isn't that right, baby girl?"

Before Belle could speak, her mother did. "Jeez, Jenny, Jack's sitting right there and you went on and on about how he talks and then spoke about him like he wasn't in the room."

"Mom—" Belle decided to give it a go, knowing she'd fail but she tried anyway.

"Give your mom and me a second, girl," Dad said, as if he hadn't just, seconds earlier, tried to drag her into the discussion. He was again looking at Rachel when he demanded, "Take it back."

"Don't be childish, Jenny," Mom scoffed and Dad's face went red.

Gram looked at the ceiling and Belle bit her lip for they knew this heralded an escalation in hostilities.

"I'm thinking that sex-a-thon should have been longer," Yasmin muttered to Cassandra, and Cassandra laughed quietly.

Clearly not hearing the byplay, Dad shouted, "Don't call me childish!"

"I'll call you whatever I want!" Mom shouted back.

"Jensen, Rachel, look at me," Jack demanded in a way that both their eyes moved to him immediately.

Belle caught a look at her grandmother's face. Lila was gazing at Jack expectantly and her expression said, "This is going to be good."

Belle looked back at Jack when he ordered, "Take it somewhere else."

"But—" Dad started to protest.

"Now," Jack ordered.

Dad's eyes went wide before he recklessly commented, "You're young enough to be my son."

"True, but barely," Jack replied. "However, this is my table and you're sitting at it. Rachel was not kidding when she said you don't embarrass Belle. Since you didn't listen to her, I'll repeat it and you better listen to me. You don't embarrass Belle. If you do, you'll find yourself not welcome at this table. Understood?"

Instead of getting angry or embarrassed, Belle watched as her father's eyes lit.

They swung to Belle and he remarked, "I love it, little girl, you caught yourself a live one!"

Jack called Dad's attention back to him when he repeated, "Jensen, I asked if I was understood."

Dad grinned at Jack and said, "Dude. Sure. No embarrassing Belle. I'm not stupid. I got it." Then, like an adolescent with attention deficit disorder (in other words, per usual), his eyes focused on the pots of jam and he asked, "Can someone pass me that marmalade? It's *the shit*. Who said English food is crap? These sausages are fuckin' *great*!"

As Belle watched Jack's jaw get hard (again), Belle felt it welling up inside her, and even though she tried to hold it back, she couldn't. Therefore, she leaned forward and grabbed his fisted hand that was resting on the table right when he opened his mouth to speak or, possibly, explode.

His head turned to her and she was softly giggling when she squeezed his hand and shook her head.

Through her giggles, she said quietly for his ears only, "Let it go, honey. Trust me, it isn't worth it."

At her words, for some reason the air instantly went velvet, his eyes grew soft and tender and his hand unclenched, twisted, caught hers and gave a squeeze before he let her go, let his irritation go and calmly poured them coffee.

Yes, Belle thought, watching him pour his coffee after he'd poured hers, the feeling was back.

Head over heels in love.

And that empty feeling that settled inside her in a way she thought it would never leave after the baby died started, slowly, but surely, to fade away.

"Now that the entertainment portion of the morning is over," Gram announced. "Perhaps we can discuss more pertinent issues."

"Yeesh," Dad muttered. "How long ya'll been here? Lila's talking all English."

"'Pertinent,' Jenny, means 'important,'" Mom whispered back.

"Whatever," Dad mumbled.

Yasmin snorted.

Belle ignored this because she watched Jack's serious eyes lock on Angus before he announced, "Olive and I have work and so do you and Cassandra. Let's do this now."

"You got it, lad," Angus agreed.

Jack looked to Lila. "How much does Belle know?"

Belle stopped reaching for the toast when Gram answered, "She knows Myrtle and Lewis were there when she fell, she knows they've disappeared and she knows all the readings have come back negative."

Belle's eyes scanned the table and she asked, "Is there more to know?"

Everyone, including her father but not Jack, looked uncomfortable.

Jack looked annoyed.

His eyes caught hers and he explained, "Apparently, poppet, you and I are Joshua and Brenna reincarnated."

At his announcement and what it might mean that he knew, Belle felt her own eyes grow wide, her heart skipped a beat and her gaze flew to her grandmother.

Lila gave her a quick, negative shake of the head.

Belle swallowed and looked back to Jack, asking, "We are?"

"Not reincarnated *reincarnated*," Angus put in. "You see—"

"Give it up, Angus," Cassandra interrupted at the same time Jack clipped, "Not now."

"What not now?" Belle inquired.

"Nothing, love. The important thing is," Jack took her hand, "something or," his eyes cut to Angus when he said, "some*one*," he looked back at Belle, "was there the night of the accident."

Belle nodded. "The third ghost."

"Perhaps," Jack muttered.

"Perhaps?" Angus asked.

Jack's green eyes were intense when he studied Belle a moment before he asked, "Are you all right to talk about this?"

Knowing what he meant, Belle nodded.

Jack looked at Angus. "Belle and I talked about things last night. She says someone pushed her."

"Oh my God," Joy breathed.

"*What the fuck?*" Dad, clearly having been briefed at some point, exploded.

"*Pushed* her?" Lila whispered angrily.

Belle nodded at her grandmother then chanced a glance at her mother's pale face.

"She didn't hear anything, feel anything or sense anything," Jack stated, his eyes on Angus, obviously filling him in. "She just felt the hand in her back."

"Impossible," Angus muttered.

"I felt it," Belle whispered.

Jack didn't whisper when at the same time he said nearly the same words, "She felt it."

"This is not good," Cassandra declared.

"You think?" Dad snapped.

"Did anyone here that night see anything? Anyone?" Jack asked and Lila, Joy, Yasmin, Rachel, Cassandra and Angus all shook their heads but Jack pressed, "Hear a car? See headlights? Hear doors opening? Anyone moving around the house?"

"Nothing, Jack," Rachel said softly.

"We were working but we would have noticed something like that," Cassandra put in.

"We need to talk to those children," Angus added.

"Can you reach them?" Jack asked.

Angus and Cassandra exchanged a look then Cassandra nodded at Jack. "There are ways."

"I don't want them hurt," Belle said softly.

"Belle—" Jack started but she shook her head.

"Or afraid," Belle went on. "I don't want them hurt or afraid."

"Poppet, you said Lewis was there and he saw something. We need to know what he saw," Jack replied gently.

"I know, Jack, but I don't care. They're children," Belle said.

"They've been around for two hundred years," Yasmin put in.

Belle looked at Cassandra and Angus. "That's true. Do they age mentally?"

Angus looked like he was biting the inside of his lip. Cassandra took in a deep breath.

"Well?" Belle pushed.

"They're arrested," Cassandra answered. "They experience life on our plane and they learn, say, about cars and fashions and news. But, they don't *mature*. At least not in my experience. Angus?" She turned to the Scotsman.

"No, lass, they're still wee ones," Angus replied. "Like Cass said, arrested, psychologically and emotionally."

Belle looked back to Jack and repeated, "I don't want them hurt or afraid."

Jack studied her a moment before he looked at Angus. "Does that tie our hands?"

"A bit, lad," Angus replied. "We'll have to get creative."

"Then get creative," Jack demanded.

"What happens now?" Joy asked.

Everyone looked at Angus and Cassandra.

It was Cassandra who spoke.

"First, we have to know what we're dealing with. Is there another entity, or not? Second, if there's another entity, we need to know who he is and what his purpose is here. And, once we know that, we need to decide what to do with him."

She looked around the table and continued.

"Third, we need to understand what the children know about this other entity and their own situation. Our goal is to release them but we've no idea how to do that. There are ways to dispose of ghosts but that means *disposal*. We want these children to go to the next plane. To do that, we have to find out how to help them get there. It's different for every ghost, what will send them to the next plane, whichever one they're destined for. From local lore, the children seem to have some idea, which is good, most ghosts don't. We'll need to piece it all together and see what we can do."

She stopped talking but everyone kept looking at her.

"That's it?" Yasmin asked.

"It isn't an exact science," Cassandra answered.

"It isn't science at all," Dad muttered.

Angus ignored Dad and added, "I think we may need to bring in reinforcements."

"How much is that going to cost?" Gram asked, her voice rising.

Angus opened his mouth to speak but Jack got there first.

"Do it."

Angus closed his mouth and his eyes swung to Jack.

"Do it. I don't give a fuck who it is, how sane they are or how much they cost," Jack clipped. "Just do it. I want this done."

Angus nodded but he said stoutly, "Lad, The McPhersons charge by the job, not the hour. It's the same flat fee for everyone."

"And I'm knocking my rate down fifty percent, because, well," Cassandra stopped talking, her eyes hit Belle, Belle's cheeks became hot and Cassandra looked back at Jack, "just because."

"Dude and dudette, I don't know if you read the papers," Dad informed them, "but Jack's loaded. He drives *a Jag*. I know, I rode in it yesterday. It's sah...weet."

Before Belle could take exception to her father encouraging the Ghost Helpers to overcharge Jack, her mother perked up.

"Speaking of cars, Jack, I've been meaning—"

Belle's blood pressure soared and as it did so, her mouth said, "Mom—"

"In a minute, honeypot," Rachel didn't even look at Belle but kept talking to Jack, "See, her car—"

"Mom!" Belle snapped.

"What about her car?" Dad asked and then he looked at Belle. "Isn't it safe?"

"It's safe, Dad," Belle assured her father and looked at her mother. "And Mom, shut up."

"What's this about?" Jack asked, his eyes narrowed.

"Rachel wants you to buy Belle a Jag. British racing green." Yasmin explained helpfully and Belle's heart squeezed.

Belle clutched Jack's hand, which still held hers, and said urgently, "Jack, you don't have to buy me—"

But Jack was looking at Olive, "See to it."

Belle's mouth dropped open.

"Yee ha!" Rachel shouted.

Olive nodded and said firmly, "Done."

Lila grinned at Belle.

So did Joy.

"And Rachel and I want to be car twins," Yasmin added, pressing the advantage.

Belle heard the blood rushing to her ears and wondered if you could fight back a stroke.

"What kind of car do you drive?" Dad asked.

"Audi TT coupe," Yasmin answered.

"Sah...weet." Dad smiled.

"Lease an Audi for Rachel," Jack said to Olive, and Belle's hand jerked in his but he ignored it and turned to Lila. "Is there anything you want?"

"Oh my goodness gracious," Belle whispered.

"Nope," Lila grinned at him. "I'll just borrow the Jag or the Audi whenever I need to take a joyride."

"I'm thinking Corvette," Dad threw in.

Belle had had enough and therefore announced, "If you buy or lease my father a Corvette, Jack, I swear I'm going to jump into the Channel and not stop swimming until I hit France."

"Bellerina!" Dad shouted.

Jack studied Belle, his eyes lit with amusement, and he looked at Dad. "Sorry, Jensen. The Abbot luck just ran out."

"Always the fuckin' way," Dad muttered.

Belle decided to ignore it all and announced, "I need to go to work."

"You need to eat breakfast," Jack reminded her.

She looked down at her empty plate and mumbled, "Oh yeah, right."

"I'll find Elaine," Joy said, bustling out of the room.

Jack looked at Angus and Cassandra and stated firmly, "And you two need to go to work."

"Oh yeah," Cassandra replied, smiling, "right."

They both got up and moved from the room.

Belle picked up her coffee cup and took a sip of its now not-so-warm, but still thankfully, caffeinated contents.

"Can I ask at this juncture," Olive inquired sounding perplexed and not at all happy to be that way, "what on earth you're on about with ghosts, entities, reincarnation and Corvettes?"

Belle looked at her peeved face and couldn't hold back a little giggle.

"I'll explain it after I take Belle to work," Jack replied.

"If you're cracking up, Jack Bennett, I'll need to inform the Board," Olive said staunchly.

"If you inform the Board of one word uttered at this table I'll need to reconsider the glowing appraisal I wrote on Friday," Jack returned.

"Oh yeah," Olive's cheeks went pink, "right." She looked at Belle and whispered loudly, "I'll consider informing the Board *after* I get my rise and bonus."

That was when Belle's little giggle frothed forth as full-blown laughter.

And since her laughter was full blown she missed Jack's warm smile aimed at her.

But she didn't miss the velvet feel that hit the room.

❦ ❦ ❦

"Mate." Belle heard and she stopped on her way to Jack's study and turned to see Cassandra coming her way.

Jack was going to take her to work, it was well late and Belle was glad that Jack had hired Dirk for the past three and half weeks he'd been a godsend.

After breakfast, Belle had run to their room to do some finishing touches on getting ready and Jack had gone to his study to give Olive some instructions so she could start work while he was driving Belle into St. Ives.

"Hi, Cassandra," Belle greeted.

"You live in Crazy Land," Cassandra replied, a smile on her face as she arrived at Belle. "I mean, Angus and I just did a job up in Devon and those people were pretty nutty but your parents..."

Her dark-brown eyes were dancing and her words were borderline covetous.

"I know," Belle said quietly. "I'm pretty lucky."

"You are, mate," Cassandra replied and her face gentled. "But with the good comes the bad."

Belle looked into Cassandra's kind eyes, pulled in a breath through her nose and nodded.

"Let's be sure this ends good," Cassandra went on and then held up a necklace. It was a thin, long, silver chain on which hung a small glass amulet surrounded by pretty filigreed silver and it looked like it was filled with baby-pink powder. "I need you to wear this at all times," Cassandra instructed.

Belle caught the amulet in her palm and Cassandra draped the chain over Belle's hand.

"What is it?" Belle asked.

"Protection. An all-rounder. I don't know what we might be up against so this is pretty powerful stuff. Should keep you safe from just about anything."

Belle blinked at her. "Anything?"

Cassandra nodded. "Can't stop a bullet but there are things it *can* stop. The powder in that amulet is fifteen years old. It's *fermented*. In witchcraft, time is power, power is time. All the best spells, potions and protections have to agitate, the longer the better. Fifteen years, mate, means that powder's like gold dust."

Belle stared at the fragile glass ball anxiously. "What if it breaks?"

"Belle," Cassandra got close and grinned, "you think I'd put what amounts to protective gold dust in an unprotected vial? Nothing can break that amulet. Trust me."

"Okay," Belle whispered as she put the chain around her neck and the amulet came to rest just below her breasts. She looked up from what appeared, for all intents and purposes, to be a pretty, filigreed glass charm and smiled at Cassandra. "Thank you."

Cassandra's hand came up, gave Belle's upper arm a squeeze and she started, "You're—"

But she didn't finish because at that moment they heard a loud crash coming from the study.

Belle's heart dropped to her feet then those feet, frozen for a split second, ran toward the study.

Cassandra was at her heels.

When Belle hit the room, Jack was facing down Olive who looked pale.

Jack, on the other hand, looked furious.

No, Belle thought, shrinking back so much she bumped into Cassandra, he looked *murderous*.

And he was talking.

Or, more to the point, thundering.

"*...fucking report!*"

"I put it on your desk weeks ago," Olive replied.

Jack lifted a newspaper and threw it on his desk with such force it slid across, taking everything with it in its path.

"With that?" Jack roared.

"With that, yes, Jack," Olive sounded shocked and upset and maybe a little scared.

Belle was more than a little scared at Jack's fury, the intensity of which she would have never imagined he was capable.

And this made Belle want to run.

Unfortunately Cassandra was the strong sort of woman and she probably never ran from anything.

Therefore she called attention to their presence in the room by asking, "What's up?"

Jack turned to them, his eyes zeroed in on Belle and they narrowed ominously.

Thoughts of running a fleeting memory, Belle froze in terror under his heated stare.

"You were married?" he asked.

He was no longer roaring, his voice was low, menacing, showing his fury in a vastly more terrifying way.

His question made every cell in Belle's body petrify.

"What's going on?" Joy entered the room.

Jack ignored his mother and demanded, "Belle, I asked you a question."

With great effort, she cleared her throat but even doing so, her voice was breathy when she replied, "Yes."

She barely finished the sibilant ending of her word when Jack clipped, his tone no less infuriated, "He beat you."

Joy gasped and Cassandra made a strangled noise.

He'd found out.

Oh God, he'd found out!

Belle couldn't answer, she just nodded.

"For years, he beat you?" Jack pushed, his eyes spearing Belle, his words feeding his own rage.

"How..." Belle's voice hitched but she persevered, "How did you find out?"

"Well *you* sure as hell didn't tell me, poppet," he bit out.

"Jack!" Joy snapped.

Jack ignored his mother again and answered Belle, "The papers. Front page. With photos. Would you like to see?"

The newspapers. Of course, the stupid, *stupid* newspapers.

"N-no," Belle stammered, her eyes glued to Jack.

"No, I suggest you don't," Jack agreed immediately.

"Maybe you should calm down, mate," Cassandra advised softly but firmly.

Jack ignored her too, his eyes searing into Belle.

She felt their heat like laser beams and he repeated, "He beat you?"

"Jack—" Belle whispered.

"He raised his hand to you?" Jack didn't let it go.

"Jack, darling, don't—" Joy tried to soothe, moving forward.

Jack only had eyes for Belle, his questions stopped and this time he made a statement. "He hurt you."

Belle just stood frozen to the spot and stared at him.

"Again and again." Jack's voice was cutting and she knew it. She knew. If he found out he'd think she was weak and he'd judge her for it and she'd been right. "Come here, Belle," Jack suddenly ground out and when Belle stood unmoving, Jack shouted, *"Come fucking here!"*

"Jack, darling, calm down," Joy demanded, stepping in front of Belle.

"Get out of her way, Mum," Jack ordered, but Joy shook her head and Jack threatened, "I won't ask again."

"What's happening?" Rachel whispered as she walked in the room.

"Take Belle out of here," Cassandra said urgently.

"Belle, *get over here!*" Jack commanded, his voice close to being back to a roar.

"What on earth is happening?" Rachel whispered, this time fear threading her voice.

Cassandra moved behind Joy, shielding Belle, repeating, "Rachel, *get her out of here.*"

Something about Cassandra's words caused something in Belle's brain to fire. Finally the demand from her brain reached her feet, she turned and she ran.

She got ten feet down the hall before she was caught at the waist by a strong arm and then she was going back.

Fear sounded in a muffled way deep in her throat as Jack backed her against the wall and caged her with his body.

She winced and braced, waiting for it to happen, the blows, the slaps, the punches, the pain.

But instead, his hands came to her head, sliding down her hair to her neck, over her shoulders, down her back and he pulled her to his hard body, his arms wrapping around her tight.

"He hurt you." Jack's voice was no longer angry.

There wasn't a shred of fury in it.

Instead, it was tortured.

Slowly, Belle's head tilted back and she looked at his face.

It was ravaged.

"Again and again," Jack's voice throbbed.

Her heart clutched.

"Jack—" she whispered.

"Again and again."

"Jack, stop it."

His hands retraced their path up her back, her shoulders, her neck to frame her face.

"Again and again," he whispered.

Tears filled her eyes and spilled over. "Please, stop it."

"I'll kill him."

"Jack, stop."

"I'll fucking kill him."

"Jack, please."

Jack's neck bent, his forehead touched hers and Belle watched his eyes close as he murmured, "He hurt you."

"It's over," she whispered.

His eyes opened but he didn't lift his head even as both his thumbs slid along the wetness at her cheekbones.

"Your dad thought I hurt you," he said softly.

"He didn't mean anything by it," Belle assured him quietly. "They're protective of me now."

His head moved a scant inch away. "Why didn't you tell me, poppet?"

She swallowed and admitted, "I didn't want you to think badly of me."

He shook his head and a humorless smile touched his mouth before he said, "You should have told me."

"I'm sorry," she said in a barely there voice then, frightened out of her mind but needing to know more than needing to give into her fear, she asked, "Are you angry with me?"

Jack didn't answer.

His hands left her face and his arms closed around her so tight she lost her breath.

"Does that," she wheezed over his shoulder, "mean you're not angry?"

His mouth at her ear, he replied, "Yes, it fucking well does."

Her body relaxed into his and her arms slid around his waist.

"You seemed pretty angry when you were in the study," she reminded him.

His nose nudged her ear before he whispered, "You'll have to forgive me, poppet, I just found out the woman I love had been married before, not to mention beaten viciously by her first husband. I was a little out of sorts."

Belle's tears stopped as did her breathing.

Jack said, "The woman I love."

The woman he loved.

She was the woman he loved.

"You love me?" she breathed.

His head came up and his beautiful green eyes captured hers.

And he didn't have to answer.

Because she saw it, stark, right there in his beautiful green eyes.

For a second.

Then he pulled away from the wall, grabbed her hand and started stalking down the hall, dragging her behind him.

He looked over his shoulder and ordered, "Call Dirk. Tell him Belle isn't coming in today."

Belle looked over her shoulder too as she ran to keep up with his ground-eating strides, and she saw her mother, Olive, Joy, Rachel and Cassandra all gazing after them. Joy and Rachel were crying. Olive and Cassandra were smiling.

Jack continued, "Olive, you're on your own for the next few hours."

Then they were at the stairs, climbing up, and before Belle could wrap her mind around what was happening, he had her in their room.

"Jack—" she started but he stalked to the bed, turned, sat, pulled her right along with him and laid back.

She fell on top of him, he rolled, pinning her to the bed.

She blinked up at him.

"All right, Belle, starting with your first living memory, I want it," Jack demanded.

Belle blinked again then asked tentatively, "Want what?"

"All of it."

She blinked yet again and asked incredulously, "Are you...um, are you talking about my life's history?"

"Every minute you can remember."

Belle put her hand to his neck in an effort to check his temperature and not appear like she was checking his temperature (just in case he was, say, *delirious*) and breathed, "Seriously?"

"Every minute."

"That's going to take a while," she whispered. "I have a pretty good memory."

"We'll call up for lunch."

"But—"

"And dinner."

"Jack—"

His hand came to her face and his thumb slid across her cheekbone.

"Belle, talk."

"Most of it's boring," she warned him.

"Belle—" Jack warned back.

She snapped her mouth shut.

Then she said, "Okay."

Then she told her life story to criminally handsome James Bennett.

The man she loved.

The man who loved her back.

Jack

Jack stood in the bay window of his study, Baron and Gretl lying at his feet, his eyes trained to the view.

It was night, late, the sky midnight blue with fluffy dark-gray clouds breaking the ink, the sky seamless with the dark of the sea, the muted white caps of intermittent waves fracturing the pervasive shadowy hue.

It was extraordinary, calming, beautiful in its vast simplicity and, until just over five months ago, Jack had never really noticed it in his life.

He allowed it to move through him, lightening the tightness in his chest, the heavy feeling in his gut.

But it didn't halt the thoughts assailing his brain.

Joshua Bennett, James Bennett.

Brenna Addison, Belle Abbot.

Caleb Caldwell and Calvin fucking Cole.

Belle had been married. Married to a man that hurt her.

Again and again.

Just like Brenna.

He already understood the coincidences that bound him to Joshua and Brenna to Belle were more than coincidental. He'd heard Lewis's disembodied voice. He understood the impossible was happening.

Now he knew it deep in his soul.

And this meant Belle was not safe.

Brenna had been tossed over a cliff.

This was not going to happen to his Belle.

I love you, Jack Bennett.

The words Belle whispered to him twenty minutes ago after he'd made love to her, while he still held her in his arms, she held him back and just before she'd drifted off to sleep sifted through his head.

And as they did, they settled into his heart.

No, Jack thought, his jaw tightening, not one thing was going to happen to his Belle.

He heard the door open behind him but he didn't turn.

He still didn't turn when he heard Olive's voice.

"You called?"

The view stopped working, his chest got tight and that heavy weight settled in his gut.

"I want you to find someone to find Calvin Cole," Jack told the window. "And when he's found, I want him dealt with."

"Are you going to be specific about *how* you want him dealt with?" Olive asked.

Yes, he most certainly was.

"When it's done, he'll have absolutely no desire whatsoever to see Belle again."

"And do you have a limit as to how much you're willing to invest in this project?"

Jack's torso twisted so his eyes could fall on the shadow of Olive standing several feet in from the open door. As he did this, he heard dog tags jangling as Baron and Gretl's heads came up but they otherwise didn't move.

"As pertains to who you hire, your budget is unrestricted. But Calvin Cole will be convinced he has no desire, ever again, to see Belle and he'll be convinced of this without money changing hands."

There was a hesitation before, with a smile in her voice, Olive murmured, "I'll see to it."

She began to move to exit the room when Jack called, "I'm not done," and she stopped.

Jack took in a breath.

Then he ordered, "I want Mickey Dempsey brought to me."

There was another hesitation before, with uncertainty in her voice, Olive asked, "Jack, are you certain that's wise? He's a member of the media. You're used to it but Belle's plagued by it. She doesn't need any more attention. And if you anger this man, he might see she gets it."

"He had an agenda with that article and it wasn't to harm Belle. It was to expose Cole."

"I noticed that but I don't understand why you—"

Jack turned fully to her while cutting her off. "He's an investigative journalist. He uncovered something that the rest of the media, even after a year of her being under scrutiny, didn't find. He has skills. As I've explained it to you, you're aware that we're currently involved in an unusual situation where we have very little knowledge of what's going on considering what precipitated it happened over two hundred years ago. The story is old, the trail is cold and his skills might prove useful."

"I see," Olive muttered.

"Bring him to me," Jack ordered.

"Consider it done."

He always did after he gave Olive a directive.

Without another word, Olive left.

Jack turned back to the view and listened as his dogs again settled.

He studied it until it brought him peace.

Then he turned from the window, strode through his house with his dogs at his heels and he went to his and Belle's bedroom.

He disrobed and pulled on some pajama bottoms as he heard Baron and Gretl settle on Belle's side of the bed.

He then slid in beside his sleeping Belle, curled into her warm body and the peace he'd garnered from the view settled deep.

I love you, Jack Bennett.

Curled into Belle, Jack fell asleep.

❧   19   ☙

BEYOND BELIEF

Jack

"So, when will you be home?" Belle's honeyed voice asked in his ear.

It was afternoon the next day and Jack was sitting behind his desk in his London office. As he listened to Belle, his eyes went to the door, which had opened.

Olive stuck her head through.

Her lips moved, no sound came out but he saw them mouth, "Dempsey."

He lifted one finger to her. She nodded, ducked out and closed the door.

Jack went back to Belle.

"I have one more meeting and then I'll be on my way home."

"So, you'll be home for dinner," she murmured, sounding slightly uneasy and Jack's back went straight.

But his voice was gentle when he asked, "Is there a reason you sound concerned about my being home for dinner?"

"Just that, um, Dad has decided to commandeer the kitchen."

Jack closed his eyes.

"And," Belle went on, "he's done this because he's decided to intro-duce you all to American food."

Jack opened his eyes.

"He does know that I, and Mum, and Yasmin, have all been to America?" Jack asked.

"Um...I did inform him of that," Belle answered.

"Repeatedly," Jack added.

"Uh...yes. Actually, Joy shared that. He's still determined," she replied.

"And this dinner would entail?" he prompted.

Her voice was tight but not with anxiety, with suppressed laughter when she replied, "I don't know. It could mean his Texas chili, which is so hot it's inedible. Or it could mean his barbeque ribs, which are so messy we'll all have to wear bibs. Or it could mean his famous flame-grilled hamburgers, which would require, um..." she paused then stressed her final three words mock-ominously, "*an open flame.*"

The thought of Jensen Abbot anywhere near an open flame did not fill him with delight.

"Poppet," Jack said quietly, "The Point has withstood centuries of bad weather, wars, different political regimes, religious unrest and a triple murder. I like our home. You like our home. Please, for me, encourage your father to cook something that would not threaten its destruction."

He was pleased to hear her laughter wasn't suppressed when her sweet voice vibrated through her response. "I'll see what I can do, honey."

"I'd appreciate that," Jack muttered.

The humor was sadly gone and her voice was soft and strangely wistful when she said, "I know you're busy, Jack, but I need to share something with you."

His voice was also soft when he returned, "I am busy, love, but never too busy for you to share something with me."

She hesitated and whispered, "Thank you." Then she went on quietly, "I called Dr. Flanagan and made an appointment. As you know because of...well, everything...that I'm not and haven't been on birth control for a while. I think maybe we should, um...since we've started again, you know, yesterday and, um, last night and, uh…again this morning, maybe…we should see to that. I don't want to—"

"Excellent, my love," Jack whispered back. "When we're ready to try again, we'll plan it."

"Okay," she replied, her voice again soft and in it was also the wistful.

But a better kind.

"Do you want me to go with you to see Dr. Flanagan?" he offered.

"If you have time. If you don't, Mom or Gram will come with me."

"We'll talk about it tonight."

"Okay, Jack."

"In the meantime, we'll take other precautions."

"That sounds fun," she muttered and he grinned because she sounded like she didn't think it sounded fun at all.

"How about we make it fun, my love?" he suggested and his body reacted to her breathy one syllable response.

"Oh."

He took in a deep breath to control his reaction at the same time he struggled to control all his myriad thoughts as to how they would make it fun then unfortunately he had to change the subject.

"The man I'm meeting is here. I have to go."

"Okay," she repeated then whispered, "See you soon. Love you, Jack."

His body responded again to her last three words. Words she'd whispered to him for the first time last night. Words that affected him deeply then.

Words that affected him no less deeply now.

"And I you, poppet," his reply was low and vibrating. "See you soon."

"'Bye, Jack."

"Soon, Belle."

He heard her disconnect and he touched the screen on his mobile. He then dropped it to his desk, leaned forward and touched a button on the phone on his desk, which would buzz on Gillie's phone indicating that he was ready for his visitor.

Seconds later, the door opened and Olive walked in, escorting a rather good-looking man with dark-brown hair and the bulky, honed body of a prize fighter.

Jack had taken some time that day to do an Internet search on Mickey Dempsey. Without the time to give it the attention it needed, it was by no means thorough. Nevertheless, the articles Dempsey chose to write, most especially the exposés, painted a vivid picture of the man, his interests and his principles.

Jack held Dempsey's eyes as he walked in and without invitation sat in one of the two chairs angled opposite his desk. Only when Dempsey was seated in an insouciant lounge that was meant to communicate to Jack that Dempsey was not afraid of him, his money or his power, did Jack look to Olive.

"I'd like you to stay."

Olive nodded and sat in the chair next to Dempsey.

Dempsey watched her do it and cut his gaze back to Jack.

It was Dempsey who opened.

"As you can guess because I'm here at your unexpected request, I'm intrigued."

Jack wanted to be home with Belle, if not for whatever he faced being served at her father's hand for dinner. Therefore he did not delay.

"I require your services."

Dempsey's eyebrows shot up. "Now I'm more intrigued."

"Perhaps you expected something else?" Jack asked, knowing he did.

"My article came out yesterday and it has to be said, mate, you seem very protective of Belle Abbot," Dempsey remarked.

"You've been watching," Jack noted and Dempsey grinned.

"Avidly."

Jack lifted his chin. This didn't surprise him. He hadn't seen him but he already knew this to be true. It was another thing he'd learned in his brief research.

Mickey Dempsey was thorough.

Dempsey's gaze became intense. "I meant her no harm. I hope you understand that. And I assumed, considering the way you are with her, you would protect her from—"

Jack interrupted him, "Belle's fine. And your article yesterday is not why you're here."

"So maybe you'll get to explaining why I'm here?" Dempsey prompted.

Jack again lifted his chin. "First, I'll need your assurances that if you take the assignment I'm about to offer you, everything about it will be confidential."

Interest flashed in his eyes even as Dempsey straightened in his chair and shook his head. "Mate, I think you get what I do for a living."

"I do, indeed," Jack replied.

Dempsey held his gaze as he responded, "So it's not just what I do. It's who I am. And I can't turn it off because a billionaire asks me, threatens me or pays me."

Again, Jack did not delay.

"Belle's in danger," he shared, watched Dempsey's eyes flare with a different light and the man's head jerked.

Jack watched as he shifted slightly in his chair, his gaze never leaving Jack's when he came to the wrong conclusion. "You're you, mate. Cole is an ass but he would never be stupid enough to—"

Jack cut him off. "Cole is not my concern."

"Then what's your concern?" Dempsey inquired.

"Taking you back, I need your assurances that if you accept this assignment, everything about it will be confidential."

"And taking *you* back, I told you I don't work that way," Dempsey returned.

Jack took in a breath and nodded once. "Then I'm afraid I've wasted your time. But I thank you for it anyway."

Dempsey didn't move.

Jack reached for his mobile, and while tucking it into the inside pocket of his suit jacket, he looked to Olive and declared, "I'm off to the airstrip. Are you coming to The Point or staying in London?"

"I have a few things to do in London," Olive replied.

Jack stood, muttering to Olive, "Fine. I'll be working at The Point the rest of the week."

"Belle's in danger?"

This came from Dempsey and Jack, who had dismissed him, looked to him.

And when he did, Jack noted he didn't look intrigued. He looked concerned.

This also didn't surprise him. Indeed, he'd been counting on it.

"She is," he confirmed.

"What kind of danger?" Dempsey asked and Jack shook his head.

"I'm afraid I can't share that information unless I feel assured you'll protect the information I would share and thus Belle. As you've made it clear you won't, this meeting is over," Jack replied then moved to round his desk.

"Mortal danger?" Dempsey pressed as Jack moved, so Jack stopped at the side of his desk and trained his gaze on the man who also had risen from his chair.

"That's uncertain," he allowed then continued, "What *isn't* uncertain is that any danger that could confront Belle is intolerable."

"And you're implying I can help," Dempsey pushed.

Jack didn't give a straight answer.

Instead, he said, "When there's uncertain danger that could befall anyone, any and all help is welcomed."

"So you're implying I can help," Dempsey reiterated.

Jack said not a word and held his gaze. As he did, he watched Dempsey's internal struggle. Seeing as he did not know the man he had no idea which side was winning the conflict.

He'd know more when Dempsey noted quietly, "She's extraordinary."

"I'm aware of that," Jack agreed.

"I've not known a single soul like her," Dempsey carried on.

"As I have not," Jack agreed again.

"Dignity, a huge reserve of strength all framed in an immense vulnerability. It's quite remarkable," Dempsey carried on.

Jack didn't bother agreeing again.

He allowed Dempsey to study him before Dempsey whispered, "You love her."

Jack didn't reply.

Dempsey straightened his shoulders and demanded, "You're keeping Cole from her?"

Jack answered but he again didn't answer directly. "You have no reason to concern yourself with Cole's response to that article, Mr. Dempsey, and you knew that before you sold it or you wouldn't have sold it."

He couldn't be sure Dempsey played it that way until he watched the man's eyes flare in response to his assertion.

He'd been watching Jack and Belle together. If he didn't think Belle could withstand the article and Jack would protect her from whatever reaction it might cause in Calvin Cole, he wouldn't have sold it.

Yes, Mickey Dempsey had principles.

It was Dempsey's turn not to respond which, like Jack's, was his response.

Instead, he demanded, "You're keeping your brother from her."

Jack fought his body getting tight so he wouldn't show his response to the depths of Dempsey's understanding of his and Belle's circumstances.

And his voice was low with warning when he replied, "It would be a good idea, Mr. Dempsey, *if* we continue our relationship, that you let me concern myself with Belle. If your continued questions mean you're interested in the assignment I have for you, I'll inform you of what you should concern yourself with."

Jack watched Dempsey again struggle internally before he ground out, "I'm interested in the assignment."

Instantly, Jack pushed, "I have your word, everything, all of it, strictly confidential."

"You have my word."

"You won't expose me, you won't expose Belle, you won't share what you're told, what you find, what you see or who you meet," Jack pressed.

Dempsey's jaw got hard even as he failed to hide his increasing curiosity. "I won't."

"This will not find its way into a newspaper, magazine, book or any other form of the media, either factually or disguised in any manner."

"It won't," Dempsey bit off.

Jack went on, "Our agreement won't be put in writing until you come to terms with Olive after our meeting. But before that, I'll explain and in doing so before an agreement has been signed, I'll be relying on your word as a gentleman. Are you telling me I can do that?"

"You can rely on my word," Dempsey clipped and Jack saw in the man's eyes that he could. Therefore, he knew.

"Who was she?" he asked quietly and Dempsey's head jerked.

"What?"

"The woman you loved who was abused," Jack explained and watched Dempsey's body get tight.

But he surprised Jack by sharing, "My mum."

Jack held his gaze. Then he nodded.

With that he retraced his steps around the desk and sat down.

He only spoke again when Dempsey and Olive had both settled back in across from him but his eyes were on Dempsey when he did it.

"Prepare, Mr. Dempsey, for what I'm about to tell you will be beyond belief. Unfortunately, it's also true. And also, I wouldn't tell you if I didn't think you could help and I'll need you to do that without delay. You can discuss your fees with Olive later. Now, I need to know if you have anything else on your schedule that will prevent you from assisting us swiftly in this matter."

Dempsey shook his head. "I don't. Or at least nothing that can't wait."

Yes, Mickey Dempsey was curious.

And concerned.

Jack nodded, took in a breath, sat back in his chair, held the man's gaze and shared a story beyond belief.

Belle

Belle sat on her rug on her cliff by The Point, wearing faded jeans, a tight white tee and a warm, chunky oatmeal cardigan, all in order to ward off the chill in the strong wind that was blowing.

Baron and Gretl were nosing the grass and rock around her as the sea smashed against the cliff wall and the wind blew the hair she didn't bother to put in a ponytail before she came out.

It was after work, the shop closed. Her father was in the kitchen having promised no open flames or anything that might mean Jack would come home to a pile of rubble and not an imposing castle.

Rachel was with him having assured Belle she'd "keep an eye on your daddy, honeypot," which didn't assure Belle very much since her mom was almost as crazy as her dad, including in the kitchen. But at least it was something.

Gram was in the loft in the stables painting. Yasmin was on her way over for dinner. Jack was most likely on his way home. And Joy was assisting Cassandra and Angus with something.

And Belle was on her cliff *not* non-thinking.

Instead, unusually, she let her thoughts drift over her.

Over a year ago, her life turned on its head. Belle "Meek and Mild" Abbot who didn't take risks and lived cautiously in a cage controlled by her fears had done something crazy, but brave, and since then she'd become a national hero. She'd then been involved in a public love triangle with two of Europe's most eligible bachelors who happened to be brothers. She'd fallen in love with one of them and he with her. And now she was living in an imposing, haunted castle on a cliff.

Dipping her chin to her knees and wrapping her arms around her faded jeans clad legs, she smiled at the sea.

She didn't think of Nathan or his loss. Instead, she had decided, whenever Nathan came to her, she was going to beat back the pain by thinking of Jack's words of earlier that day.

When we're ready to try again, we'll plan it.

They'd try again and they'd plan it.

Three times in her life, only three, she'd taken a risk and jumped into cold, shark-infested waters, once literally (though those weren't shark-infested).

The first time she saved lives. Two were lost but she saved many others.

The other two times she'd done it for the same man.

The first time with Jack, she'd messed it up. The second time, she'd learned he'd forgiven her and he'd given her her reward.

And boy, what a reward it was.

When we're ready to try again, we'll plan it.

They had time, they were starting a life together in a hopefully soon-to-be not haunted but always would be imposing castle on a cliff, and when they were ready, they'd start a family.

Still smiling at the sea, Belle sighed.

Maybe, just maybe, Belle "Meek and Mild" Abbot might stop being so darned meek and mild.

She might, instead, take more risks.

She wasn't certain about this haunting business but the rest of it sure as heck paid off.

On this thought, Gretl, who was in front of her, twisted her neck to look down her body as Baron, behind Belle, gave a small, warning woof.

She'd just lifted her chin from her knees in order to look toward The Point to see what caught the dogs' attention when she heard, "Belle."

Her head turned, her eyes moved up and she saw Miles walking to her, the wind tousling his blond hair.

Holy heck.

She shifted her arms from around her legs, putting one hand in the rug to push herself up as the dogs roamed closer to her and she started, "Miles—"

He lifted a hand swiftly and interrupted her, "Please, Belle, don't get up. What I have to say won't take long."

She pulled in a breath and kept her head tipped back to study him. His handsome face seemed thoughtful but she could read nothing else.

To her disquiet, Miles finished his approach and dropped to the grass to sit a few feet away from her. As a response, Gretl settled on her belly at Belle's feet, her head up, eyes on Miles as Baron circled close.

"As you undoubtedly know, things have not been good, Miles, but I'm feeling better," She told him in hopes of heading off any nastiness. "I ask that you please don't mess that up."

He gave her a smile that didn't reach his eyes. "I'm pleased to hear that, gorgeous. That's why I'm here. To be sure you're okay. I came to The Point and tried to talk to you the other day but," he threw out a hand, "Jack wouldn't let me."

She still disliked that he called her gorgeous. It wasn't his place anymore as he well knew.

And she didn't like that smile. It did not say he wanted her to be okay. It said something else. She was sure of it.

"Well, I'm okay," she assured him anyway.

"Good," he muttered, his eyes moving to the sea, his body settling in like he did not, in fact, intend *not* to take long in what he had to say but as if he intended to stay awhile. "I assume, since you're still here, you're staying?" he asked the sea.

Belle didn't much like this lead in.

"Miles, perhaps you should—" she started to advise him to talk about his brother's future with his brother but he interrupted her again, his eyes cutting back to her.

"I promise, Belle, swear it's with your best interests at heart when I advise you, if you can, to curtail Jack spending time with Yasmin."

She felt her heart lurch and her shoulders get tight as his words hit her.

"I don't think—" she began again only to be cut off again.

"They were lovers," he informed her.

"I already know that." She couldn't quite keep the snap out of her voice though she also didn't quite try.

"And she's divorcing Quincy. She'll be free again soon."

Belle felt her eyebrows draw together at what he was implying.

"So you're telling me Yasmin will make a play for Jack?" she asked in disbelief.

"No," he answered. "I'm telling you that if Yasmin's free, Jack will make a play for her. And Yasmin won't make him work too hard. He's who she's always wanted, Belle, and I fear it's the other way around for Jack too."

She felt her blood begin to pound through her veins and for the first time in some time, the healing wound at her temple hurt.

Before she could say a word, Miles continued.

"They've known each other since we were very young. They have a connection that's grown throughout those years. What they had was passionate. And it never really ended. On some level, you must know that since she's still around and around *all the time*."

"You're beyond belief," Belle whispered, the wind carrying away her words.

"I'm sorry?"

She scrambled angrily to her feet, Gretl scrambling with her and Baron got close as she dashed her hair behind her ears in a (failed) effort to control it and repeated loudly this time, "You're beyond belief!"

Gretl woofed her agreement and Baron growled his warning as Miles got to his own feet.

"Belle, gorgeous, you know after what's happened to you I wouldn't tell you this unless I was looking out for you."

Belle just could *not* believe this!

She leaned into him and reminded him on an irate cry, "I just lost *a child*!" She threw her hand out to indicate The Point and reminded him, "And it was *your brother's child*. So, that means, *your brother* just lost *his child too*!"

"I know that," he clipped.

"And, a month after that crushing blow, you think it's in my best interests to deliver another one by coming to me and badmouthing your brother *and* our friend?" she queried heatedly.

He lifted a beseeching hand to her and urged, "Look around, Belle, it can't have escaped your—"

"What hasn't escaped me, *Miles*," she interrupted him on a hiss, "is that Yasmin has been nothing but kind and gracious to me and Jack has never been anything but loving and gentle. Except, of course, after I let my own anxieties and *your behavior* muddle my head then proceeded in making what could have been the biggest mistake *in my life*. In fact, the only person who has anything to do with *any* of this who has treated me unkindly is," she lifted a finger and pointed at him, "*you*."

His face went hard and he crossed his arms on his chest. "How did you know about our conversation?"

His question confusing her, she leaned back and crossed her own arms on her chest, asking back, "What conversation?"

"Jack and my conversation. At Mum's party. How did you know Jack said he wanted a crack at you?" Miles explained and Belle felt her own face get hard.

"He didn't say that," she returned.

"It doesn't matter who said what. It matters how you knew. Jack thinks I told you and we both know I didn't."

"None of this matters now *at all*, Miles."

"How did you know?" he pushed.

"It doesn't matter."

"Did Yasmin tell you?"

"It doesn't matter!" she cried and Gretl woofed again.

Miles stared at her then muttered, "She told you. And why do you think she told you, Belle?"

"She didn't tell me," Belle denied, shaking her head and in the heat of the moment admitted a moment of rudeness. "I overheard her and Joy talking."

"And you think that wasn't planned?" Miles sneered.

She felt her eyes grow round.

"You are," she whispered. "You *are* beyond belief."

Miles shook his own head. "Think about it, Belle. She was done with Quincy then and she wanted a free run at Jack. Or, more to the point, she wanted Jack to have a free run at her since she likes being chased. She saw how he reacted to you so she didn't delay in making that so."

Belle ignored the wind whipping her hair across her face and uncrossed her arms so she could plant her hands on her hips before she asked cuttingly, "You're telling me that Yasmin finagled Joy into a hallway she would have no idea I was walking down at the precise time she could have no idea I was walking down it to orchestrate a conversation that would put me off Jack. Is that what you're telling me, Miles?"

"You're getting to know her," Miles retorted. "She's very clever."

"Yes, she is. You know who isn't?" she queried but didn't pause for an answer although she did thrust a finger at him. "*You!*"

"Belle—"

Belle cut him off. "This is absurd, purposefully hurtful and I'm sorry to tell you, Miles, I'll not keep it from Jack. What you've said to one woman he cares about, about another woman he cares about cannot stand. You'll deal with him and, what's worse, *he'll* deal with *you.*"

On that, she bent, snatched up the rug and began to stomp past him but he caught her bicep, bringing her up short.

Goodness gracious, not *this* again.

She snapped her head back and hissed, "Take your hand off me."

"Don't be a fool, Belle. With the loss of that baby, your hold on him has slipped," he clipped back, not having convinced her to believe any of his venom, he went in for the kill.

And she could *not* believe he did it or the way he did.

Therefore, with a vicious twist, she pulled her arm free, shouting, "Take your hand off me!"

She took one step away, he began to lunge toward her but stopped and both their heads whipped around when Jack's voice cracked through the wind like a whip.

"Miles, right now, step *the fuck* back!"

Both Jack and Yasmin were coming their way, Jack's face thunderous, his strides wide and Yasmin was racing on high heels on the uneven path to keep up, her face pale.

Belle just stared at Jack who she hadn't expected to be home for at least another half an hour and who, as usual, was right there when she needed him.

She did this while her breath came fast and the rest of her attention focused on not screaming bloody murder.

"I arrived at the house ten minutes ago," Yasmin called. "I saw Miles going to you. I called Jack right away but he told me he was nearly here," she puffed. "Now, he's, well," she stopped next to Jack who stopped three feet away from Miles, eyes glued on his brother and she threw a hand out at Jack lamely before she finished, "here."

"Belle, you and Yasmin go to the house," Jack growled, his enraged eyes still on his brother.

Before either of them could move, Miles informed Jack, "Yasmin was the one to tell Belle that you wanted a crack at her," and after he spoke this semi-lie, Belle watched Jack's back shoot straight.

"I did not!" Yasmin cried.

Miles looked at Yasmin. "She overheard you talking to Mum in the hallway that morning."

When he imparted this information, Yasmin's eyes flew to Belle, light dawned, her face paled and she whispered, "Oh God, no."

"It's okay, Yasmin," Belle stated swiftly then added truthfully. "It was rude for me to eavesdrop."

Yasmin clearly wasn't thinking about Belle being rude.

She sounded horrified when she replied, "I'm so sorry, Belle." Her eyes moved to Jack. "And Jack, I had no idea—"

She didn't finish.

Miles had looked back to Jack who never tore his gaze from his brother and spoke over her. "You thought it was me. It was not me. It was Yasmin."

"And who told Yasmin it was me who wanted a crack at Belle when those words, Miles, came from *your* fucking mouth?" Jack asked, his voice low, rumbly and very, very angry.

Oh dear.

Belle needed to do something she just didn't know how.

Or, in fact, *what*.

"Miles did, of course," Yasmin whispered before Belle could figure it out.

"She misheard me," Miles stated quickly.

"She did not," Jack ground out. "You lied in an effort to cheat during a ridiculous, one-sided competition that I cannot fucking believe we're still discussing months after the drama was over and only fucking *weeks* after the woman I love was shoved down the goddamned stairs and lost our child as a result."

Miles's torso swayed back and he whispered, "You love her?"

"Jesus, Miles, what do you think this is all about?" Jack asked, planting his hands on his hips.

"You love her," Miles repeated in a whisper.

Jack didn't get a chance to respond.

Unfortunately at this juncture, Joy was racing up, calling out, "What's happening?"

"Belle, take Mum and Yasmin to the house," Jack ordered, his eyes still locked on his brother.

"Please, no fighting," Joy begged, arriving and immediately getting close to Jack so she could wrap her hands around his upper arm. "We were all getting along. Let's not go back to fighting." Her eyes moved to her younger son. "Please, Miles. Especially not now."

"I didn't come to fight," Miles told his mother. "Because Belle is sensitive, I took the chance to incur Jack's wrath in order to warn her, after what's happened, to tread cautiously."

Really, Belle thought in disgust, eyeing Miles, it *was* high time to stop being meek and mild if her sensitivity set her up for *this* type of kindness.

"We'll finish this, once and for all, between you and me," Jack clipped then again ordered, "Belle, take Mum and Yasmin back to the house."

Belle thought this was a capital idea and started to move but Joy asked, "Tread cautiously with what?"

"It doesn't matter," Miles answered. "She refuses to heed my warning."

"What warning?" Joy pushed as Belle got close and grabbed her elbow, trying and failing to pull her away.

"It doesn't matter," Miles repeated, his eyes on his brother.

Belle froze when Yasmin stated softly, "You took me away from him. I participated but you did it and you did it purposefully. Now, you're trying to take Belle from him too?"

"What's this? What are you talking about? *What's going on?*" Joy demanded, her hands giving Jack's arm a shake.

"Belle, get Mum and Yasmin back...to...*the house*," Jack growled.

Belle pulled gently at Joy's elbow, she resisted and Yasmin ignored all of this and asked Miles, "Why would you do that? What could possess you?"

At this, Miles's head turned slowly to Yasmin. "Possess me?"

"Yes," she answered quietly. "I've known you both what feels like my whole life and Jack has never done anything to deserve this. So yes, when you behave like this, Miles, what possesses you?"

"He sees something, he takes it," Miles replied and Yasmin shook her head.

"He didn't take me. I gave myself to him. The same with Belle."

"He sees something, he takes it, even if it doesn't belong to him," Miles went on stubbornly.

"This is fucking ridiculous. We're talking about *women*, human fucking *beings*," Jack muttered angrily and Miles's gaze sliced to him.

"Three times, with three women, they were mine and you took them."

At his words, Belle's body got tight, she felt Joy's get tight and she sensed Yasmin and Jack's getting tight.

"Miles, Yasmin—" Jack started.

"I loved her," Miles cut him off and Belle, Joy and Yasmin all gasped. "Before you took her, I loved her."

"Oh my God," Yasmin breathed.

"You should have—" Jack started again but Miles again didn't let him finish.

"I didn't have the time. You saw to that."

"She wasn't yours, Miles," Jack said, his voice less angry. "Neither was Belle and you know it."

"I don't know it," Miles replied.

"You know it, Miles, and there is no third," Jack returned.

"There's a third," Miles retorted.

"Who?" Jack asked.

"There's a third," Miles repeated.

"Who?" Jack pushed.

To which, Miles suddenly and frighteningly leaned in and roared, "*There's a third!*"

"Fucking hell, Miles, if I don't know—" Jack began to clip but Miles cut him off.

"You know, you bastard, dig deep down into your goddamned soul and you'll know *precisely* who she was and you'll know she was the worst of all," Miles bit out.

"Miles, darling, are you feeling quite all right?" Joy asked hesitantly and Miles looked to his mother, his eyes burning in a way that made Belle step back.

Joy saw it too. Belle knew this when she let Jack go and stepped back with Belle.

"No, Mum," he whispered, his voice strange, sinister, frightening. "I'm not all right. I've *never* been all right and you," he pulled in breath and seared her with the heat of his gaze, "you've *always* known it."

And with that bizarre, scary parting shot, he stalked between Jack and Yasmin and strode toward the castle.

"Jack, I think you should go after him," Joy whispered, her voice trembling and Jack stopped looking over his shoulder at his retreating brother and looked to his mother.

"I will." His eyes moved to Belle. "Please, love, get them inside."

Belle nodded.

Jack glanced briefly at Yasmin before he turned and strode after his brother. Baron went with Jack. Gretl stayed close to Belle.

"Let's do what Jack asks and get inside," Belle urged softly, hooking her arm through Joy's elbow and marching her to Yasmin while adjusting the rug under her arm so she could do the same with her friend. Then she led them firmly toward the castle.

"A third," Yasmin murmured as they walked, all their eyes on Jack and Miles who were now having what looked like a very unhappy conversation beside Miles's car.

"Do you know what that was all about?" Joy asked Yasmin.

"Some of it," Yasmin muttered in a way that said she wasn't feeling like sharing.

Therefore Belle quickly intervened by suggesting, "Why don't we go inside, open a nice bottle of wine and talk about it where we're comfortable?"

"Good idea," Yasmin agreed as they watched Miles jerk open his car door that Jack immediately slammed closed.

Oh dear.

Belle hastened their step. "And let's do that quickly," she murmured.

"Good idea," Yasmin agreed.

All three women raced up the steps where Belle, with effort, tugged open the heavy door and ushered them in.

"*Fuck you!*" She heard Miles shout, leaning in, his face an inch from Jack's granite one and she closed her eyes, sent him strength, and for him but also for Joy and Yasmin, with effort, she shoved the door closed.

❧ ❧ ❧

After a not-so-calming glass of wine and after Lila, who stood vigil at

387

the window, told Belle that Miles was gone and Jack had "prowled into the house" (her words), Belle gave him some time.

Now Belle stood outside Jack's study door and sought courage.

He loved her. He'd told her. He'd moved her into his home. He'd moved her into his room. He'd shared his dogs with her. And after she lost their baby, he didn't leave her side.

And she loved him.

She could do this.

She closed her eyes, opened them, lifted a hand and knocked on the door.

She got no answer and still got no answer after a repeated knock.

She stared at the closed door wondering what to do next.

And as she stared, it came to her.

Jack was beyond that door.

And he was hers.

For three and a half weeks after she lost their child, he didn't leave her side (well, most of the time, he *did* have to work).

Now he needed her at his.

Therefore she put her hand to the knob, turned it, opened the door and stuck her head through.

Jack was standing in the bay window looking out.

"Jack?" she called quietly and his torso twisted, his eyes coming to her.

"Belle, anyone else, they knock, I don't answer, they go away. You do not have to knock."

Belle wet her lips, buried a smile and walked in, closing the door behind her.

Yes, he was hers.

This unbelievably, *criminally* attractive man was...all...*hers*.

Jack watched her do this and when the door was closed he ordered her to do what she was going to do anyway.

"Come here."

She went there and when she arrived he turned fully to her, his hands coming to her waist then sliding around to hold her loosely. She lifted hers and rested them lightly on his chest, tipping her head back to look into his troubled, green eyes.

"Are you okay?" she asked softly even though she saw he was not.

"No," he answered harshly, giving her the answer she expected.

She moved an inch closer and his arms around her tightened.

"Are you going to *be* okay?" she asked.

"Are you okay?" Jack asked back and she nodded. He sighed before muttering, "Then I'll be okay."

That was *such* a Jack answer. So much so it made her heart *and* her belly warm.

So Belle moved closer and his arms got tighter, drawing her against him and her hands pressed into his chest.

"I'm sorry you had to endure another scene with Miles," she said gently.

"And I'm sorry he got to you which should not have happened," Jack returned again being *very* Jack, thinking of her and not himself.

"I promise, I'm okay. He just made me angry, that's all," she assured him. "And, um, now, what he's done is making me worry about you."

Jack took in her words and sighed again before saying, "Don't worry about me, poppet. You know this isn't the first time. I'm used to it."

That didn't make her feel much better.

"That was...it was...it seemed different." She hesitated then asked, "What exactly *was* that?"

Jack lifted a hand to cup her jaw, his thumb moving out to stroke her cheek and his voice was not harsh in the slightest when he replied, "You know, my love, that Yasmin and I were once together. What you don't know was, during a fight when Yasmin had broken it off with me in a way she did not intend to be permanent, Miles sought her out, got her drunk and had sex with her."

Belle gasped.

Jack nodded.

"I'm sorry to be blunt, poppet," he muttered. "But that's what happened. Yasmin admitted this to me, and not surprisingly we were then done in a way that was very much permanent."

She could not believe this and yet she could. Miles had a knack for being a very big jerk, and Yasmin had a knack for messing up her life.

Still, she hated it that Jack seemed always caught in the middle.

So Belle pressed even closer and she did the only thing she could think to do.

She whispered a heartfelt, "I'm sorry."

"I was then too," he replied, and his thumb stroked her cheek again before his hand slid down to curl around the side of her neck. "Now, I'm not."

Belle gave him a small smile and his eyes warmed when he saw it.

They grew intense and he continued, "I don't know what he said to you but I can well imagine. And I want you to know that not only are Yasmin and I done, we have been for a long time. Our relationship has changed to something we both enjoy that would never shift again. And, my love, that wouldn't have happened even before you. And although we have that history and it isn't pleasant, now, with you in my life, it doesn't matter anymore."

"I'm sorry to say you imagined well, honey, but I didn't believe him. Not even for a second. Not only because you're you but also because Yasmin's Yasmin," Belle assured him. "I knew all that before you told me."

"Good," he murmured and Belle gave him a squeeze. "What I did not know," Jack went on, his eyes losing focus and for the first time they drifted to *her* ear, "until today, was that he had feelings for her for some time prior to that."

Yes, she got that was a surprise not just to Jack but to Yasmin as well.

"And the third woman?" Belle asked, Jack's gaze came back to her and regained focus.

"I have no clue."

"He didn't share?"

"By the time we finished things, my brother was in no mood to share."

Belle definitely caught that.

"So are things...*finished*?" she inquired carefully.

"Absolutely," he stated firmly.

"Oh, Jack," she whispered, pushing her hands down so she could slide them around and hold him tightly too. "I don't have brothers or sisters so I don't know how this feels but it can't feel good."

"No, poppet," he muttered. "It doesn't feel good."

"I don't know what to do to help," she admitted and felt his arms give her a reflexive squeeze as his lips twitched.

"You're doing it."

Her head tilted to the side. "Just this?"

"Just this, Belle," he replied gently.

"This is easy," she told him. "I could do this for hours."

To that, his lips curled up but his head came down and he touched his mouth to hers before he moved back half an inch and suggested, "That's good then. So let's do this for hours."

Belle gave him another small smile but she shared, "I'm afraid we can't do that."

His head moved back another inch. "And why's that?"

"Well, first, Dad's done with dinner. You'll be pleased to know there was no open flame and he didn't have time to make homemade barbeque sauce. They also didn't have peppers that will burn out your throat, so chili was out. In the end he made meatloaf, which doesn't sound all that great but his is really delicious. And he also made apple pie which is definitely delicious."

"Right," Jack said. "That's first, what's next?"

Belle pressed even closer. "Well, yesterday, I told you all about my life. Tonight, you need to get started telling me all of yours. After dinner, of course."

Jack's arms gave her a squeeze and he reminded her, "I've lived longer than you, poppet. Yours took an entire day. I'll need more than an evening."

"It can be continued and you can tell me more tomorrow."

He grinned.

"And the next day," she went on.

His grin got bigger.

Belle pressed closer and got up on her toes. "And the next."

"That's a plan," Jack whispered.

"Good," Belle whispered back.

"Dude! Baby girl! What the fuck! You want it to get cold?" Belle's dad could be heard shouting. "Haul ass into the dining room. You got two minutes or we're starting without you."

To this, Jack asked bizarrely, "Is it Sunday yet?"

Belle's head tilted again and she told him what he had to know. "No, why?"

"Because Saturday night we're leaving all these mad people to their madness, we're taking the dogs, we're going to your cottage and we're not coming back until Monday."

"Now *that*," Belle breathed, "sounds like a plan."

"Count on it," Jack muttered, his eyes dropping to her mouth, his head descending toward hers.

She felt a trill race up to her scalp but still she whispered, "Jack, honey, the food will get cold."

"Let it," Jack murmured against her mouth before he took it in a sweet, deep, long, wet, delicious kiss.

They didn't get to the dinner table in two minutes. It was more like five.

But they walked in hand in hand and they did it after Belle had managed to make Jack feel better.

She sat down to dinner at Jack's side feeling like she'd just moved a mountain and she was proud of it.

And, even a little late, the food still tasted great.

Calvin

Calvin Cole aimed one, last, vicious kick into his prone wife's belly and watched her body jerk on the floor.

Then he bent over her and, ignoring her spitting blood into the carpet in front of her face and wheezing, he got close to her face and hissed, "Now get your ass up and *unpack*. You leave when *I* say I'm done with you. Not before."

Her eyes looking to the carpet that the side of her face was resting on, she slowly nodded, and he also ignored her wince of pain that this subtle movement caused.

He jerked upright and looked at the bags on the bed.

The bitch saw the article. The bitch heard shit at work. The bitch came home early and thought to leave him.

What the bitch didn't know was that he took shit at work that day too. Including his supervisor telling him they were going to have a meeting at the end of the week and that he felt it was best if Calvin didn't come into the office until the meeting.

Calvin knew what that meant.

Fuck.

He looked back down at his wife who hadn't moved and informed her casually, "You know, if I hadn't kicked Belle's ass out, I'd be married to a national fucking hero instead of fucking *you*."

After he delivered that, he heard the bell at the door go and he left her, stomping to the door.

Unable to move because every time she tried the pain wracked through her body so intensely she had to fight against going unconscious, his wife listened from her place on the floor to the murmuring of voices.

The murmurs went on for some time. Then her husband's voice got louder. Then angrier. Then louder and livid.

Finally she heard different noises, muffled grunts, muffled groans of extreme pain.

Calvin's groans.

She couldn't move to get to the phone to call 999 or go to her husband and help him.

She couldn't move but still…

Even if she could, she wouldn't.

20

CAN'T GET LOOSE

Jack

On his back, his hands wrapped around the sides of Belle's hips that were straddling his face, Jack pulled her deeper into his mouth and listened to and, better, *felt* her sweet, husky moan wrap around his cock.

This was because his cock was deep in her throat.

Feeling it, hearing it, her warm softness pressed the length of his torso, her taste on his tongue...fucking hell, he should have thought to teach her to do this a long, fucking time ago.

The first time she'd asked him to teach her would have been good.

Their first night they were together would have been better.

Digging his fingers in, he pulled her even deeper, working her harder and got another moan then he felt her mouth slide up and release him even as her hand wrapped around tight.

"*Oh my God.*" He heard her breathe.

She was close and losing focus.

He wanted back inside but he knew he was going to have to take her a different way.

Gently, he rolled her to her back and she moaned differently when he did. This moan was in protest.

He grinned to himself then moved her around in the bed. Once he had her head to the pillows, he reached to the nightstand and grabbed the packet.

"Come here, love," he ordered quietly, and her stormy-gray eyes moved from his hands to his face. She put one hand behind her in the bed, pushing herself up. Her other hand came to rest light on his stomach and her touch might have been light but it knifed through him. "Take this, poppet. Put it on."

She looked back at the packet then to him. His cock twitched as he watched the storm in her eyes grow stormier and she wet her lips as she took the packet from him. Then he watched her hands shake and fumble as she ripped it open and slid out the condom.

She was cute with her fumbling.

As cute as it was, no way in hell he was going to be able to wait or endure her fumbling as she rolled it on.

He took it from her and whispered, "Place your hand over mine."

Her head tipped back, her eyes caught his, she nodded again then he felt her hand move to round his as he rolled it on.

She wet her lips again, her head dipping to watch their hands move.

Jesus.

He was right, he couldn't wait.

"Lie back," he demanded, his voice thick and her head shot back again, she looked in his face, her pupils dilated then she did as she was told.

Finishing with the condom, he pulled her legs apart and settled between. She wrapped all of her limbs around him and he drove deep into her wet, hot silk.

Fucking bliss.

"Jack," she breathed into his ear, the fingers of one hand sifting into his hair, cupping his head and holding on.

Jack turned his head and took her mouth as he took her body. Her moans drove down his throat. His groans, then grunts drove down hers.

Finally she gasped against his tongue as every inch of her body, inside and out, tightened around him.

Yes. Fucking *bliss*.

Minutes later he growled against hers.

After he recovered he found she was giving him a sweet, deep kiss, her tongue dancing with his. Jack took over as he settled deep inside her, keeping one forearm in the bed to alleviate some of his weight while his other hand drifted over her soft skin to her waist then in, around her back and down where he cupped the ample cheek of her behind.

Finally, he released her mouth but only so he could slide his lips to her neck. He could still smell hints of her appealing perfume that she'd sprayed on the morning before.

It was Sunday morning. He'd awakened curled into her and his first thought was to give in to her request of several days before.

So he did to spectacular results.

"I like the way you smell, poppet," he murmured against her skin and felt her limbs convulse.

Then she whispered a sweet, "Thank you, honey."

He lifted his head and looked down at her to see the storm in her eyes had passed. They were now languid, content.

Happy.

He'd been wrong.

Being buried inside her was magnificent.

Seeing that in his Belle's eyes, *that* was bliss.

He grinned at the sight and continued speaking, "And the way you taste."

A flush of pink tinged her cheeks but she replied softly, "Thanks again. And, um...I like the way you taste too."

She didn't have to tell him that, he already knew but his grin got bigger as he muttered, "Good."

"And that was very nice," she went on and Jack couldn't help it.

His body collapsed on hers and he burst out laughing.

"What's funny?" she wheezed, he registered her breathlessness and carefully slid out then rolled them so she was full on top, straddling him.

"Very nice?" he teased when she lifted her head and looked down at him.

Her head tilted to the side and she stated, "Yes, and it was *so* nice maybe we should do it again."

"I'm thinking we'll do it again, poppet," he informed her, running his hands down her back to her bottom and up again. "It was so *very nice* we'll likely do it often."

When she told him the story of her life, considering her timidity, he was not surprised to learn she had very few lovers, in fact, only two before him. He was also not surprised to learn that Calvin Cole was a selfish one.

Although not delighted by the last, he was by the first. This meant he had the honor of initiating her to certain things. Things like they'd just done.

She'd also shared that he was the only man with whom she'd enjoyed sex at all. With her uninhibited response to him, this *was* a surprise. But she'd explained she'd only had what they had, what they'd just shared, what they would always share with him.

Only him.

And this didn't delight him, it thrilled him.

As he thought these thoughts, she studied his face and her hand slid up his chest to curl around the side of his neck before she suggested, "And maybe we can try some..." she hesitated then finished, "*other* things."

Jack's arms moved to close around her.

"What other things were you thinking, my love?" he asked gently.

"Well," she began, "I was thinking we could try other things *you* thought of."

He smiled up at her. "We can do that."

It was then she surprised him again, rather profoundly, by announcing, "And you can be adventurous. I've decided I'm not Belle 'Meek and Mild' Abbot anymore so I'm willing to experiment."

He was bloody ecstatic she was willing to experiment.

But something else she said caught his attention, his brows drew together and he asked, "You're not Belle 'Meek and Mild' Abbot anymore?"

She shook her head immediately as she awarded him one of her sweet, small smiles. "No. See, earlier this week, I thought about it and all my life I've been...well, I've let things hold me back. The three times I didn't, one, I saved some children and a bus driver from drowning and the other two, well," her eyes went soft and her hand slid from his neck up to his jaw as her face dipped closer and she finished, "the other two got me you."

Jack felt her words hit warm and heavy in his gut as his arms got tight around her and he rolled her to her back again, muttering, "Jesus, Belle." He settled partly on her, partly pressed to her side and tangled his legs with hers.

He was so moved by her words he was unable to say any more of his own.

Her hand didn't move from his jaw with his roll but she slid it to his cheek, cupping it and running her thumb along his cheekbone, her eyes holding his, no evasion, straight and true, and she whispered, "And you're gentle and loving and accepting, not only of me, my neuroses, my shyness and my silences but also all the craziness and the crazy people around you. So I figure this means I'm safe to jump in, feet first, to whatever's next for me," the fingertips of her hand against his cheek pressed in gently, "for *us*. So, like I said, I'm willing to experiment. Because, well," she grinned up at him and tilted her head on the pillow, "I just kind of did, and personally I think it went great."

One thing about that, it was a lot better than "very nice."

The other thing about it was *everything*.

Jack dropped his head, burying his face in her neck and yanking her body more fully under his before he muttered, "Jesus, Belle, I love you."

"I know, Jack," she whispered. "That's why I'm free not to be what I was before."

He lifted his head, locked his eyes with hers and reminded her, "Don't forget, poppet, I fell in love with that woman."

He watched her beautiful face get soft, her gray eyes grow warm, she lifted her other hand and both moved to curl around the sides of his neck as she replied quietly, "I'm still here, Jack. Just kind of improved."

"You don't need to improve," he told her, his voice vibrating. "I like you just the way you are."

Her face got softer, her eyes warmer and her fingers dug into his neck when she returned gently, "Well, with what we just did, I'm going to have to disagree. I think I could do with a little bit of adventure. Just as long as I do it with you."

That he couldn't argue with so Jack grinned.

Belle grinned back then continued, "Except, maybe next time, we should tear open the condom packet in preparation. I was a little impatient and in a bit of a state, I nearly dropped it."

Jack kept grinning. "I noticed that."

"If you're adventurous," she shared, "I might be *more* in a state."

God, he fucking hoped so.

On the thought, Jack's grin got bigger. "Then we should be prepared."

She nodded once in mock-seriousness, her hands sliding down to his chest and she agreed, "Definitely."

"It should be noted that I'm feeling in the mood to be adventurous about," he dropped his mouth to hers and finished on a whisper, "*now.*"

"Oh," she breathed against his lips, he felt that knife through him too and just as her hands slid around to hold on, his mouth took hers in a heated, wet kiss.

One of his arms sliced around her, the other one dove into her hair, he rolled them yet again so he was on his back and she was on top.

Then he heard dog tags as the dogs moved with agitation and Baron started barking. Seconds later, there was a loud knock on the front door.

Jack let Belle lift her head away from his as he growled, "This is not fucking happening."

And it shouldn't be. Yesterday evening, *early*, when he left The Point, he told everyone that he would be picking Belle up from her shop, taking her to her cottage and they wouldn't be seeing any of them until Monday.

Or hearing from them.

Any of them.

For *any* reason.

Therefore, there should not be a knock on the goddamned door.

He focused on Belle's face just as she noted distractedly and with disappointment, "But it's Sunday."

"Yes, love, it's Sunday, and unfortunately before we get adventurous, I'm going to need to commit homicide," he ground out and only felt slightly better when he heard her adorable, startled giggle.

He rolled her off him, flicked the covers over her, slid out of bed and snatched up his jeans. Stalking to the bathroom, he quickly dealt with the condom, something which he and Belle were successfully experimenting with in order to enjoy it as part of sex. Something which he'd be glad to dispense with once she was safely on the Pill.

He tugged his jeans on as he walked out onto the landing, both of his dogs circling to him and the top of the stairs and back again as he moved.

He prowled down the stairs, unlocked the door and pulled it open to scowl at Mickey Dempsey who was standing at the top of Belle's steps.

"I see Olive failed to inform you of this," he clipped instantly upon catching the man's eyes, "but Sundays Belle and I are not disturbed for *any* reason. I'll deal with this omission directly with Olive later. I'll deal with you now by telling you to hold whatever it is until tomorrow."

Without another word or allowing Dempsey to utter one, he stepped back and started to slam the door but Dempsey's hand shot out and caught it.

"You'll want to hear this," he stated.

"Is the world ending?" Jack asked and he could see Dempsey fighting a knowing smile.

Through it, he answered, "No."

"Then I don't want to hear it," Jack returned and put pressure on the door but Dempsey moved into the frame, blocking its closure with his shoulder.

"Not kidding, Bennett, you'll want to hear this," he said quietly and with not a small amount of gravity.

"Give me a hint," Jack bit off.

"The third soul is not reincarnated in Cole." He paused and held Jack's eyes as he finished, "Caleb Caldwell is reincarnated in your brother."

Jack felt his chest get tight just as he heard Belle say softly from the top of the stairs, "Oh my goodness gracious."

He looked to his feet, clenched his teeth, felt a muscle tick in his cheek then he looked to Dempsey and stepped back.

"Come in, stay down here, thirty seconds," he ordered. "Only then can you come up."

Without waiting to see if Dempsey agreed, he turned, ducked his head in order not to give himself a concussion on the low hanging ceiling and, once he'd cleared the ceiling, took the stairs two at a time.

Belle was at the top wearing a becoming nightgown (another one of her own, something he'd learned recently after asking was all she ever wore) and looking astonished.

"That man, Jack," she whispered as she lifted a hand and rested it on his chest. "I've seen that man."

"I'm not surprised," Jack replied. "That's Mickey Dempsey. I told you I recruited his assistance after he wrote the article about Calvin Cole. He watched us and thus, I would assume, you."

Her eyes grew unfocussed for a moment as she whispered, "Oh," then they focused on him and she stated, "Well, that explains that."

It was lucky she was so endearing or he'd be even more pissed at that moment than he was.

Instead, he was only mildly pissed and therefore he could gentle his voice when he asked her, "Now, I need you to get dressed and make coffee. Can you do that for me, poppet?"

She nodded. "Of course, Jack, I make coffee every day." She paused then finished, sounding somewhat disgruntled as if she missed having the chore of making coffee, "Or I used to before I moved in with you and started to get waited on hand and foot."

He was surprised at that juncture to find himself fighting back a smile.

She was blossoming and it wasn't happening slowly.

She trusted him. She trusted his love. She trusted in their future. And she knew he'd keep her safe. So he had the best of both because he had his cute, sweet, imperfectly perfect Belle and he had the Belle she gave him when he flipped on her switch.

Instead of smiling, he dipped his head, touched his mouth to hers, followed her to the bedroom, closed the door behind them, and as she moved around getting dressed, he pulled on a long-sleeved, black T-shirt.

Dressed, he walked out, closed the door again and saw Gretl sitting outside the door.

Baron was sitting in the living room where he found Dempsey.

"Beautiful dogs," Dempsey muttered.

Jack made no comment about his dogs.

Instead, he said, "Belle's going to make coffee in a minute. But you're going to explain now."

Dempsey grinned. "I could use some coffee."

Jack's head cocked to the side. "Did you miss the 'now' part?"

"Right," Dempsey muttered, moved to the window, glanced out over the rooftops to the obstructed but nonetheless lovely view Belle had of the sea then he turned back to Jack and crossed his arms on his chest. "This legend, Bennett, Addison, Caldwell, the children, the murders, it's very well-known."

"You disturbed my Sunday with Belle to tell me something I've known since I could process thought?" Jack asked, losing patience.

"What I mean is, it's known widely. St. Ives. Penzance. Land's End. Falmouth. Even as far as Newquay."

Dempsey had covered a great deal of ground in the last few days.

He still was not telling Jack something he didn't already know.

"It's legend," Jack agreed. "Legend with over two hundred years to travel widely. It's known beyond Newquay, Dempsey. It's written about in books. This doesn't explain why you think Miles is Caldwell reincarnated."

They heard the bedroom door open. Dempsey's torso shifted to the side to catch a look out the door of the living room to Belle moving through the landing, thus Jack's body shifted to block his view.

Dempsey's eyes shot to Jack and the grin came back.

"Protective," he muttered.

"You'll meet her soon enough," Jack returned. "And you've investigated her. If she was yours, you'd be the same bloody way. Now, focus. What did you find?"

"Ghost tale," Dempsey got to the matter at hand, "told around campfires. Kids telling it to scare the hell out of other kids."

"Dempsey," Jack warned low.

"For centuries, Bennett," Dempsey returned. "A shocking story, heartbreaking, brutal. So much so, there are not one but *three* local historians who've made it the focus of their field of study. And not only that, it was shocking, heartbreaking and brutal back in the day. It stunned local residents. Joshua and Brenna Bennett were popular, Brenna especially. She was adored. Her murder marked the locals. The fact that her children were taken made it worse. So there's a good deal these historians could study. And they shared it all with me."

"Explain," Jack demanded.

"Diaries of local residents, letters kept, archives of constabulary records. I haven't had time to go through it all thoroughly but the primary theme bled through almost immediately," Dempsey answered.

"And that theme would be?" Jack prompted when Dempsey didn't go on.

"Bennett and Caldwell had a lifelong feud," Dempsey replied and Jack felt his body get tight.

Dempsey continued.

"It was not private. It played out very publicly and started when they were young. It followed them into adulthood and business. Caldwell was not well liked, and the story goes this was because he was a cheat and a poor loser. Further, although Caldwell was not a peasant, not common, his family didn't have the kind of money the Bennett family had, still, he was ambitious. And most of that ambition was centered around besting Bennett. Unfortunately, Bennett was richer, smarter and better looking than him and always won. Caldwell didn't like this. From what I read, as boys even to young men, Bennett participated in these various contests, whatever they were, and in the end they included the pursuit of women. However, as Bennett matured and turned his mind to the family business, he lost interest in Caldwell and his competitions. In fact, Bennett was often in London and not in Cornwall at all. That said, it was widely believed that Caldwell still smarted that the games ended before he could best Bennett at least once."

As engrossed in the story as he was disturbed by it and its further similarities to his own life, Jack still heard Belle moving about the house so he lifted a hand. Dempsey fell silent and his attention cut to the door.

Jack turned to see Belle standing there, looking curious and tentative, her gaze on Dempsey. She was wearing jeans so faded they were nearly white and had a frayed split in one knee. She was also wearing a white slouchy sweater that was loose-woven and had a wide neck so he could see her white vest at her shoulders and through the weave. She'd pulled her hair back in a ponytail but tendrils had escaped and framed her face.

Even nearly first thing in the morning without makeup, she looked just as casually chic and adorably charming as she actually was.

She also, fortunately and unfortunately, looked like she'd just enjoyed a rather pleasurable orgasm.

Jack liked that the results of their lovemaking lasted some time for Belle.

No, he loved it.

Though, as usual, he wasn't keen on sharing it.

Without a choice, he extended an arm her way and called softly, "Come in, poppet, meet Mickey Dempsey."

Her eyes came to him, she gave him her small smile then she walked straight to him. She fitted herself tight to his side as his arm curled around her shoulders and hers around his waist but she leaned forward and extended her other hand to Dempsey who took it.

"It's nice to meet you, Mr. Dempsey," she said softly in her musical voice.

"Mickey," he corrected. "And nice to meet you too, Ms. Abbot."

She awarded Dempsey one of her small smiles. It was smaller than the ones she gave Jack but it was something and that something was something Dempsey liked. Jack saw it immediately as Dempsey's gaze grew captivated.

"And please," Belle continued, "call me Belle."

"Belle," Dempsey murmured, and he still hadn't let her hand go.

"Perhaps we can move forward with what you have to share so Belle and I can get on with our Sunday," Jack suggested pointedly. Belle pulled her hand from Dempsey's grip and Dempsey grinned at him. Jack looked down at her. "I explained I'd spoken with Mr. Dempsey and what I asked him to do," he reminded her of the conversation they'd had days before and he did this to share with Dempsey that Belle was aware of the situation.

She nodded up to Jack then to Dempsey and she informed them, "Coffee should be ready in a few minutes."

Jack had no intention of sharing coffee with Mickey Dempsey. He wasn't even going to ask him to sit down.

His blossoming Belle, however, had other ideas.

"Please, sit, Mickey," she offered, throwing her arm out to the couch.

There were times, Jack thought, when meek, mild and shy worked in his favor in regards to Belle.

This would have been one of them.

Dempsey smiled and sat on the couch. Again with no choice, Jack took an armchair and was slightly appeased when Belle perched on the arm in the perfect position for him to wrap an arm around her hips. Therefore he did this without delay.

"Sorry to say," Belle put in, "but I was eavesdropping. Small house, hard not to do," she told Dempsey.

"What he says does affect you, my love, and it is your house," Jack pointed out.

She looked down at him and whispered, "Right, of course."

Jack gave her hips a squeeze and looked back to Dempsey. "Why don't we continue?"

Dempsey nodded and did just that.

"As I was saying, although Bennett moved on, Caldwell did not. So, when Brenna Addison saved that child from drowning—"

Jack's arm got tight around Belle's hips even as he leaned slightly forward and whispered, "What?" at the same time Belle whispered, "Oh my goodness gracious."

Dempsey's brow furrowed. "Brenna saved a child from drowning. She nearly drowned herself doing it. It was one of the reasons she was so beloved. Didn't you know that?"

Jack shook his head. "I paid little attention to the legend."

"I hadn't heard that either," Belle said softly.

"I know you two are aware of the similarities in their story to yours, of course. But I thought you knew all of it. And all of it is near to identical to your own. Including Caldwell pursuing Brenna because of her beauty and popularity but also in order to win her in an effort to best Bennett. He made it clear after drinking heavily and bragging in pubs that he was keen to show Bennett his prize. That prize being Brenna."

Dempsey's eyes moved to Jack. "I'm relatively certain this sounds familiar."

"It does, indeed," Jack agreed, his voice low and annoyed but he wasn't annoyed.

He was uneasy.

"Although I can see why you'd think Caldwell is reincarnated in Cole," Dempsey carried on, his eyes moving to Belle and giving her a gentle look before they shifted back to Jack, "I hope you can see why I believe this isn't true. The initials are the same. The marital treatment is the same." He again looked to Belle and muttered, "Sorry."

"Please don't worry about it," Belle replied quietly.

Dempsey nodded then his gaze went again to Jack. "But the behavior, as I understand it, is your brother."

It was. Absolutely.

And this could mean that it was Miles who'd pushed Belle down the stairs. He'd lived at The Point all his life, grew up there. He knew every inch not only of the castle but of the land surrounding it. He could get to and in the house without being detected. He could get out the same way.

His brother.

His own *fucking* brother.

"We need to talk to Miles," Belle said, and Jack looked up at her to see her looking down at him as she continued, "We need to ask him to let Cassandra touch him." Her head tilted sharply to the side as her eyes moved over his face and she asked, "Jack, are you okay?"

Miles would not do that. There wasn't a chance in hell.

And he was most definitely not okay.

"We'll talk later, love," Jack muttered and looked back to Dempsey. "Is there more?"

Dempsey shook his head. "Not now. I thought it important to share my theory with you without delay so you could be aware your brother posed a possible threat. I've been loaned some papers, books, diaries, etcetera, and I have more reading to do, a few more people to talk to, and if I find anything, I'll contact you."

"Next time, call," Jack ordered and Dempsey's lips quirked.

"Did any of the stuff you've read talk about magic? Witchcraft? Anything like that?" Belle asked at this point.

"None at all," Dempsey answered but finished, "so far."

"So I wonder how that third ghost..." She didn't finish likely because she didn't want to cast her mind back to losing their child and how she did.

But at her words, Jack realized she hadn't put it together. She thought it was a ghost. She didn't think, possibly couldn't wrap her mind around the thought of Miles sneaking in and pushing her down the stairs, killing their child at the same time wounding her without thought that such a fall could kill her as well.

Miles had told him in the stables that Jack would pay. He'd vow to do it through Belle. And now, possibly twice, he'd tried. Once, he'd attempted to fill her mind with rubbish and prey on her fragility by planting ideas about Jack and Yasmin in her head.

Once, he might have attempted to take her away from Jack another way.

Lewis saw the "ghost."

They needed to find Lewis.

Now.

"I'm sure the coffee is ready now, Mickey. How do you take yours?" Belle asked, moving from the chair.

"He takes it by ordering it from the coffee house down the street," Jack replied for Dempsey, rising from his chair.

"Jack!" Belle snapped, her eyes moving swiftly to his and narrowing.

"We have to get to The Point as soon as possible," he told her. "We need to report this to Angus and Cassandra. They've been making little headway for weeks. This could be a breakthrough."

"Oh, right, that probably would be smart," she muttered.

Jack looked to Dempsey to see him gazing fondly at Belle. "You'll pardon our rudeness at not offering you refreshments." He spoke with politeness but it was a thinly veiled order.

"Right, mate," Dempsey replied.

Jack caught Belle's eyes. "I'll show Dempsey out. Then we'll have a quick breakfast and head to The Point."

She nodded, offered her hand to Dempsey who took it, to Jack's way of thinking, for several seconds too long, and finally Jack showed him out.

By the time he was back upstairs, Belle had his coffee ready for him and bread in the toaster.

They had toast, coffee and gave the dogs a quick walk. They then came back and had a shower together that Jack decided, even though it was imperative to get back to The Point, would be a long one.

A very long one.

And in the end, it was a very, *very* long one.

Then, on their Sunday alone together, Jack loaded Belle and his dogs in his Jag and headed to a castle full of people.

❧ ❧ ❧

As with every day since Jack broke through her grief, waking up with Belle meant the day started brilliantly.

As with everything happening in his home, the possibility of this continuing was unlikely.

And, upon arrival at The Point, their already ruined Sunday degenerated.

This was because Jack found he had more guests.

As they said they'd do, Angus and Cassandra had called in reinforcements. And after Jack explained he wished to speak with the not-so-dynamic duo in his study with Belle and no one else so as not to distress his mother with the news about Miles, he was introduced to them.

A brother and sister pair. Twins. They were Angus's niece and nephew, Lachlan and Lorna McPherson.

"Oh my," Belle breathed when the motley quartet sauntered into his study and he looked down at her to see she was gazing with shy interest at the twins.

Or, more accurately, the male one.

With narrowed eyes, Jack took them in.

They were in their late twenties. Both ginger. And both, Jack was mildly pleased to see, didn't appear in full Scottish regalia.

Lachlan wore jeans, boots and a sweater that fit close to his broad chest. Lorna wore a jean skirt, high-heeled boots, a form-fitting long-sleeved T-shirt and a long, colorful scarf wrapped around and around her neck.

And luckily, unlike Cassandra who was sporting what looked like six on three different places on her body including head, neck and hips, Lorna only had one scarf.

The female twin was more than slightly attractive. She was petite and rounded, much like Belle, but with masses of thick, curling red hair, delicate features and bright-blue eyes.

Her brother was surprisingly tall, towering at least six inches over his sister. His ginger hair was cropped short, the waves contained though longish and curling around his neck. He had a short clipped, red beard, craggy, dominant features with a high, strong brow all of this making him appear older than his twin.

But they shared the same startling blue eyes.

It took Lachlan McPherson approximately half a second to lock eyes on Belle and a half a second longer to grin a wolfish grin at her.

"Oh my," Belle repeated even more breathily.

"Jesus," Jack muttered and felt Belle start at his side.

Angus, not one to miss much, one of the few things Jack respected about him, didn't miss this.

Therefore, he clapped his nephew on the shoulder and boomed proudly, "He's a McPherson!"

This made Lorna roll her eyes and murmur, "Someone kill me."

Lachlan, his gaze still locked on Belle, noted, "You're prettier than your pictures."

"Thank you," Belle replied softly.

"By quite a bit," Lachlan carried on.

"Um...thank you," Belle repeated, dipping her chin and looking under her lashes at him.

Lachlan's wolfish grin turned predatory.

"Jesus," Jack repeated, again on a mutter.

"Uh, Lach, just to remind you, the man standing right there has a soul that's eternally bound to the woman at his side," Lorna informed her brother then finished bluntly, "There's no way in hell you're getting in there, mate."

Her brother swung his head her way and tipped it down to catch her eyes.

"I know that," he replied. "Doesn't make her any less pretty."

Lorna looked to Cassandra and shared, "He breathes therefore he flirts. This is my lot in life. Can you imagine being connected to him through blood *and* profession, and having to put up with this *constantly*?"

"I can imagine being connected to him but not through blood," Cassandra returned, eyeing Lachlan appreciatively, her words getting his attention and he turned his roguish grin her way.

Lorna sought another ally, found Jack and requested, "Please, kill me."

"I'd rather you tell me what your purpose is for being here," Jack retorted, not in a good mood and none of this making his mood any better.

"They've got the gift," Angus boomed, and Jack looked at the older Scot.

"Pardon?" he asked.

"The gift!" Angus boomed again without any further explanation.

"As I don't share Cassandra's reported powers of clairvoyance, you'll have to explain," Jack pushed with rapidly waning patience.

Lachlan threw himself in a chair and slouched back with his arms on the armrests. He then placed his ankle on opposite knee and reported, "We were on a job, it got hairy or we would have been here sooner."

"It was in France," Lorna added. "French ghosts..." she gave a delicate shiver, "not fun. Especially if they've been beheaded. That revolution of theirs left some seriously pissed-off phantoms and all of them are a pain in the arse."

"Holy heck," Belle breathed.

Jack crossed his arms on his chest. "This does not answer my question about why you're here now."

"They've got the gift," Angus repeated and Jack's eyes sliced to him so Angus quickly went on. "The gift. The feel. They can track ghosts."

"I thought that was your job," Jack remarked.

"Well, it is, lad," Angus returned. "Cassandra can sense them, so can I. If we can't, we can do readings. What I mean is, Lach and Lorna, they got the feel. That's how the McPhersons got started in this business in the first place. All of us got it, some of us stronger than others. Lach and Lorna, they got it the strongest of all. They can track them and they can *call them out.*"

"Oh my," Belle whispered.

Jack ignored Belle and looked between the twins. "And have you been doing that?"

"Aye," Lachlan muttered. "Got here about an hour ago but didn't even have to try. Minute we stepped over the threshold, we felt them. The wee ones, they're here. Hidden and scared out of their minds, but they're here. We haven't had time to pull them to us but they're here." His eyes shifted briefly to Belle exposing he knew the whole story before they came back to Jack, "The third ghost, nothing."

"Not one thing," Lorna put in. "Not even a little bit. No trace."

"This doesn't make sense," Belle noted quietly and Jack uncrossed his arms to wrap one around her and pull her to his side.

"Unfortunately, it does," Lachlan stated, coming out of his lounge. He sat forward and put his elbows on his knees, his gaze on Belle. "We got the briefing. Although Caldwell did his dirty deeds in this house and this could be a reason why his ghost would be tethered here, unlike Myrtle and Lewis, he isn't a ghost. He's like you with Brenna and Bennett here with Joshua." He tipped his head to Jack. "The triangle is not made of two reincarnated souls and a ghost. The triangle is complete only if the trace of the third soul finds its host."

Belle went still at his side, whispering, "Oh my God," and Jack pulled her closer as his own body got tight.

"So, we're dealing with a human," Jack surmised, this information uncomfortably and disturbingly matching Mickey Dempsey's theory.

"Absolutely," Lorna replied. "Cassandra nor Uncle Angus could feel him or read him anywhere. Except once. This means the night, erm..." she hesitated, her eyes also going to rest briefly on Belle before coming back to Jack when she continued, "the recent sad event occurred, whoever he is was in the house. And not only that, Cassandra sensed him here not only because his host was here but because Caldwell, active in the host, had taken it over."

This, Jack thought, was not getting any better.

"What on earth does that mean?" he asked aloud.

"It's likely," Cassandra entered the discussion, "and has happened before, that whoever pushed Belle didn't even know they were pushing her. They might not even have been aware they were here at all. If Caldwell's spirit is strong enough, he could take over his host's body and the host would have no memory of the acts he or she was perpetrating while Caldwell had control. It's almost as if they don't share a soul like, say, you and Joshua or Belle and Brenna. If it's like this then it's like a spirit inhabiting a body. It can lie dormant or it can take over. If it's strong enough and angry enough, it'll take over."

"That's bloody ridiculous," Jack growled.

"It may sound it, but it's true," Lachlan replied quietly, his eyes now on Jack, his elbows still to his knees but his body was alert in response to Jack's swiftly deteriorating mood and Jack made note not to underestimate him. A flirt with a ludicrous profession he might be, but by the look on his face and his posture it was clear he was not easily bested. "It would explain why there's no readings or traces of his ghost or presence in this house. If Caldwell had never taken over his host, even the children wouldn't sense his existence. He certainly would leave no trace, as you and Belle haven't of Brenna or Joshua."

"Does this mean Brenna or Joshua can take over Jack or me?" Belle asked and all members of the quartet nodded.

"Fucking hell," Jack clipped out.

"My guess, and Lewis might be able to confirm," Lorna stated, "is that's the way this has to go. Brenna, through you, has to do something. What, we don't know yet. Or, perhaps, both of you need to do something. That's what we've got to find out. All the players are here, we just don't know what they have to do to release the children."

"And how do you find that out?" Jack asked.

"We talk to the wee ghosties and hope they know," Angus answered.

"And if they don't?" Jack pushed.

The quartet looked amongst themselves then their gazes came to Jack. But it was only Angus that shrugged.

They had no idea.

"Bloody brilliant," Jack muttered.

"So you need to call them," Belle noted, her eyes going between Lachlan and Lorna.

"Aye," Lachlan answered.

"And if you do that, it'll be gently?" Belle asked.

"No harm will come to them, Belle," Lachlan replied softly.

Jack felt Belle straighten at his side and she declared, "Well then, let's do that now."

"Fucking hell," Jack repeated on a mutter.

"We have another problem," Cassandra remarked and Jack's eyes cut to her. "When we figure out how to send the children to the other plane, which we will do, Belle, I promise," she said to Belle. "We still have the reincarnated soul of Caleb Caldwell walking around. He intends harm. He's proved that and we need to neutralize him."

This was precisely what had been preying on Jack's mind since Dempsey shared his news on Belle's cottage steps that morning.

"Caldwell is reincarnated in my brother Miles," Jack told them what they needed to know but he didn't relish saying and felt all eyes on him.

"You sorted that, lad?" Angus asked quietly and Jack felt his eyes narrow.

"You knew already?" he shot back.

"Got the niggle when I first met him," Angus replied. "The diary I told you about, local lore we've been hearing, Cass and me pieced it together. We can't be sure, unless Cass touches him, but that's our guess."

Jack thought of Miles's visit earlier that week, targeting his Belle who was unprotected and he felt a burn start in his stomach as he asked bitingly, "Did you think maybe to *share* that niggle in an effort to protect the inhabitants of this house?"

"Laddie, you've made it clear you aren't thrilled about all the goings-on and Joy is a sweet lass. We're not sure of that kind of information, information about your brother, we share it with you without any proof to back it, do you think you'd pat us on the back and give us a medal?" Angus returned.

"Maybe not but I would have taken measures to protect the inhabitants of this house," Jack fired back.

Angus had the good grace to look uncomfortable as he muttered, "Point taken."

It was done, all was well so Jack decided to move the conversation forward.

"It's highly unlikely you can confirm this as it's highly unlikely that Miles will ever return to The Point. This I know since he's vowed not to do so again," Jack reported.

"He might not have a choice if Caldwell takes over his host. He won't even know he's doing it," Lorna put in. "Therefore, we need to seek him out and neutralize him."

"And uh, how would you go about doing that?" Belle asked cautiously.

"A spell, or, more accurately, a potion," Cassandra answered. "The good news is I have some. The other good news is, I've used it before and it works a charm. The bad news is, it's like medicine. You don't take it once and then, *poof*, entity gone. You have to take it once a month for the rest of your life in order to keep the spirit inside latent."

"Fucking hell," Jack muttered yet again.

"I think Miles is unlikely to do that," Belle remarked and Lachlan stood.

"Then he'll have to be convinced to do it," he stated firmly, and both Belle and Jack went still then Jack's body went solid when he saw Angus's demented smile.

"Lachlan has another gift. My laddie here has a way about him. He can convince folk to do a lot of things," Angus declared.

"Do you hypnotize them or something?" Belle asked curiously.

"Yeah, they go into a trance, a trance caused by his fists," Lorna muttered.

"Holy heck," Belle breathed.

"There's another option," Cassandra put in at this point and Jack, holding close to his dwindling patience and trying to ignore his increasing unease, looked to her. "We kill the soul he carries."

Belle gasped and Jack's body petrified but his mouth moved to say two words.

"Absolutely not."

"It won't kill him," Lorna added quickly.

"How could it not?" Belle asked, her voice rising with each word.

"He'll change, definitely," Cassandra explained. "From what we can tell, though, only some of his less appealing traits will be gone. Though, we can't know that, of course, since he was born with Caldwell in him. But it could be he is how he is because he carries Caldwell's soul. If we release that, he could just be...*him*. Whoever that is," she ended on a mumble.

"It's a ceremony," Lorna stated. "Mega power and mega cool. But, to be honest, the traces of a soul being torn from you isn't the most comfortable thing and, usually, you'd have to be captured because no one volunteers. And you'd also have to be bound to endure the ceremony because it can get a little intense. But the good news is, it holds no lasting effects. Except, of course, if the personality being torn away makes up most of your own. Then you can end up being a little, erm... *addled*."

Jack frowned at Lorna then transferred his frown to Cassandra.

"You are not performing this ceremony on my brother," he declared.

"Lad, we get you," Angus said quietly. "But what you need to get is that, even after those children are released, Miles carries the trace of Caldwell. If he doesn't agree to take Cass's potion for the rest of his life, Caldwell could conspire to do harm against you, Belle and your kin. Your brother wouldn't even know it." He saved his kill shot for last. "Your brother probably doesn't know what he's already done."

Likely because of all that was happening, and the entirety of it being beyond mad, Belle had not come to understand the fullness of the situation.

Until then.

And Jack knew she did when she whispered, "Oh my God, it was Miles who pushed me."

Jack curled her close, moving his other arm so he could hold her in both even as Angus said gently, "No, lass, no' Miles. Caldwell."

"I don't believe this." Belle continued whispering, and Jack lifted a fist to below her chin to tip her face to his.

"If this is true, my love, it's as Angus says. It wasn't Miles. It was Caldwell."

And he said that because he had to believe it. If he didn't, he, too, would go mad but it would be a far different madness than the benign lunacy sharing that room with him and Belle.

She pressed into him, sliding her arms around him. "We have to get him to take that potion, Jack."

"We do," he agreed though how they would manage that he had no fucking clue.

"Joy is going to need to talk to him, Jack," Cassandra stated quietly, and Jack's mouth got tight before his gaze moved to her.

"I don't want my mother involved in this," Jack returned. "Hell, I don't even want her *knowing* this."

"You're no' going to convince your brother to talk with us, lad," Angus replied cautiously. "And from what we know of the situation, Belle and Yasmin will have no better luck."

"It has to be Joy," Cassandra reiterated. "But I'll go with her. There's a few tricks I have up my sleeve."

"Lachlan has a way about him," Lorna put in, "and I've got a way about me." She grinned cheekily. "I've been known to be good at slipping in a potion here and there without detection. We make him docile, he'll be easier to talk to. We give him a talking potion, it'll all come out."

"See, laddie, we've got it covered," Angus announced, throwing his arms out and grinning his demented grin.

Jack wasn't certain he agreed.

However, he was certain he had no choice.

And he bloody detested it.

"Right," he said. "We'll talk to Mum. We'll call to Myrtle and Lewis and then we'll reconvene to decide what's next once we speak to the children."

"Uh...Jack, that we would be Lorna, Uncle Angus, Cassandra, Belle and me talking to the wee ones," Lachlan told him. "You can't be there."

"Pardon?" Jack asked low, his eyes narrowed on the younger Scot.

"As you know, we've been asking around, gathering intel," Angus cut in. "No master of this house has ever seen the children. They appear freely in front of others, members of the family, servants, guests. But no master. Not only no current master but also none of the sons. We think there's a reason for this. Though we canno' say for certain why, whether it's their wish or if seeing a master puts them in some danger. What we can say is that we need to abide by it if it's their wish, or, if it's the other way around no' forcing their appearance in front of a being that might place them in danger."

"Okay, I'll be there and I'll tell Jack all about it," Belle offered quickly.

"Aye, lassie," Angus grinned at her.

"No," Jack stated flatly and felt Belle's eyes move to him so he looked down at her.

"What?" she asked.

"No. You will absolutely not be in on this without me with you."

"But, they're children and they've never harmed anyone," she reminded him.

"This is true," he agreed. "But what they could say might be distressing and I'll not have that either. Let Cassandra and the McPhersons deal with this. They can brief us later."

"I want to be there," she pushed.

"And I'll not allow it," he returned and her brows drew together.

Then she whispered, "Allow?"

"Belle—"

She took a step back, out of his arms but she didn't go far and immediately dug in for a fight. He knew this when she planted her hands on her hips.

"Inside me is their mother," she announced.

"Belle—"

"And I'm here to release them," she went on.

"You're here because we're in love with each other and intend to spend the rest of our lives together," Jack reminded her.

"Well, that too," she muttered.

Jack pulled in a calming breath and repeated, "Belle—"

"I'm going to help those children, Jack. I'm going to be there when the McPhersons and Cassandra talk to them. I'm going to assure them we're going to do everything we can to get them where they need to go. And then I'm going to do everything I can in order to get them where they need to go!"

"Perhaps, poppet, we can talk about this without an audience," Jack suggested with strained patience.

"We could, I'm sure. Though it would be a waste of time because the result will be the same. I'm going to be there when they talk to the children. And there's a lot to do so we shouldn't dillydally," she declared.

She was lucky she used the word "dillydally" because Jack thought it was cute. If she hadn't, he'd have lost control of the shreds of patience he was clinging to.

Unfortunately, she used the word "dillydally" therefore Jack found himself biting off the word, "Fine."

"Fine," Belle replied, grinning at him, openly pleased she got her way.

"My love," Jack started to warn, "if you end up with nightmares or sitting in the window of our room attempting your non-thinking in order to get over unpleasant thoughts, don't come to me. I'll only tell you I told you so."

She moved into him, pressing her softness to his frame as she wound her arms around him, tipped her head back, kept grinning at him and whispered, "Balderdash."

It was. It was complete balderdash.

And he thought that word was cute too.

"Jesus," he muttered, winding his arms around her as well.

"Can we get to work or are you two going to continue your domestic through cuddling?" Lachlan asked, and Jack looked over Belle's head to pierce him with a scowl.

"Getting to work would be good," Jack told him.

"Excellent," he murmured, grinned at the floor and left the room.

Lorna followed her brother but she did it grinning at Cassandra who went with her.

Leaving them with Angus who announced, "Always the way."

"What's always the way?" Jack asked when he knew he shouldn't.

"The quiet ones," Angus replied.

"Pardon?" Jack queried.

"It's always the quiet ones who manage it. Before you know it even began to happen, you're already wrapped so tight around their finger, you can't get loose."

This was absolutely true.

"Good thing is, you don't want to," Angus finished softly, grinned his manic grin, turned on a whirl of his kilt and stomped out.

"Do I?" Belle asked softly and Jack looked from the door to her.

"Have me wrapped around your finger?" Jack asked back and she nodded. His arms got tighter as he answered, "Absolutely."

"How did I manage to wrap criminally handsome James Bennett around my finger?"

Criminally handsome James Bennett?

Jack smiled through his response. "If you don't know, poppet, it's not me who's going to tell you."

Her eyes drifted to his shoulder as she murmured, "I'll ask Mom."

Rachel wouldn't know.

Jensen would.

Jack didn't tell her that either.

He gathered her closer, dipped his head and at the tightening of his arms, hers tipped back.

When it did, he kissed her.

She kissed him back, she did it without delay, it got heated to the point she moaned sweetly into his mouth, and in so doing Belle Abbot wound Jack Bennett even tighter.

Lewis and Myrtle

"*Lewis! What's happening?*" Myrtle screeched as, powerless, they were pulled from their hiding place and they materialized in the eastern turret, Lewis standing strong, his arms wrapped tight around his quivering little sister.

She had her face tucked in his neck but Lewis looked around.

The witch was there. The Scot too, in his kilt. Two others were there, a brother and sister, like him and Myrtle, Lewis could tell.

And Belle.

They were all staring at Lewis and Myrtle, gentle looks on their faces.

But Lewis felt it coming from the red-headed siblings. The man was standing, feet planted apart, arms crossed on his broad chest. The woman had her hands on her hips. But Lewis felt their power.

They were holding him and Myrtle there.

When they arrived, though, it was only Belle who moved.

Coming toward them and crouching down, her pretty, soft-gray eyes on Lewis's, she whispered in her musical voice, "Hello, my darlings."

Lewis closed his eyes because her talking to him in that voice, that look on her face, it reminded him of...

"Belle."

That was Myrtle. Lewis felt her turn her head and rest her cheek against his collarbone. He opened his eyes and tipped his chin down to see his sister shyly looking at Belle.

"Yes, Myrtle. I'm Belle. I know who you are and I know who Lewis is. What I want you to know is, you're safe. All these people," she threw her arm out, "and I are here to help you."

"We know," Lewis told her.

She dropped to her knees then rested her bottom on her calves as she tipped her head to the side and asked, "You know?"

Lewis nodded.

"If you know we're here to help, why have you been hiding?" she went on gently and Lewis pulled his sister closer.

He looked to the red-headed woman before his eyes went to the man. "Let Myrtle go."

"Lewis, darling, we need to talk to you," Belle stated and he looked to her. "Don't be scared. We'd never, ever harm you. Not one of us."

"Please," he whispered, "let Myrtle go."

"I want to stay," Myrtle said quietly.

"She has to go," Lewis demanded, his back going straight, his gaze moving again to the red-headed man.

The man stared him straight in the eyes then looked to his sister and nodded.

Myrtle disintegrated in his arms.

Lewis drew in a ghostly breath.

"You're protecting her, right, laddie?" the older Scot asked and

Lewis nodded again. "She doesn't know you saw him," the Scot went on and Lewis nodded again.

"Who is he, sweetheart?" Belle asked and Lewis looked back at her.

"The bad man."

She scooted forward on her knees toward him, he held his place and she settled again. "Who's the bad man, Lewis?"

"You know," he replied.

He watched her pull in a soft breath before she queried, "Miles?" and Lewis's ghostly brows came together in confusion.

"Miles?"

"Is he the bad man?"

Lewis shook his head and Belle's eyes darted amongst the others in the turret before coming back to him. "Who's the bad man, then, darling?"

Lewis looked to the floor, shuffled his see-through toe through the floorboards and muttered, "Hurt Mum. On the cliff. Saw it. Watched it. But Myrtle and me were already dead."

"Oh, sweetheart," Belle whispered, her voice trembling with an ache that felt a lot like what Lewis felt deep inside whenever he thought of it the many, many, many, *many* times he remembered it over the years.

"Matey," he heard and his eyes went to the witch, "was Miles there the night the bad man hurt Belle?"

Lewis kept her gaze and nodded but replied, "Shimmered through."

"The bad man took control," the witch said. "He took control of Miles."

Lewis nodded yet again.

"You saw him, through Miles," she pressed and Lewis nodded again.

"Shimmered through," he repeated. "And he saw me."

"Oh God," Belle whispered and Lewis looked to her then leaned into her with ghostly, childish fervor.

"I wanted to help," he whispered back fiercely and her face melted in a way that both hurt to look at and made him feel really nice. "I wanted to help. I tried but there was nothing I could do."

"I know you did, sweetheart."

"He took your baby away." Lewis kept whispering and this time

Belle nodded. "I'm sorry," he finished so quiet, he could barely hear his ethereal words.

"Me too," she returned in a whisper just as quiet and he saw her eyes get wet. He watched her pull in another breath, this one trembling and she continued, "But we're not here about that. We're here to help you. We just don't know how and we need you to help us help you."

"You're here to send us home," Lewis stated and Belle nodded again.

"Yes, Lewis, we just need to know how. We're all ready. Jack and me with all this help from Angus, Cassandra, Lachlan and Lorna. Everyone's ready. You just need to tell us what we need to do."

"Don't know," Lewis told her and her head tilted again.

"You don't know?"

"Only know it's you."

Belle's eyes quickly darted to the others again before she looked back at Lewis. "Do you maybe have an idea?"

Lewis shook his head.

"Does Myrtle?" Belle asked.

Lewis shook his head again.

"Well, darn," Belle muttered, looking at the floor.

"You need to beware of the bad man," Lewis told her quickly and her eyes came back to him.

"I know, darling."

"He wants to hurt you."

"I know, Lewis. We're taking care of that."

"If something happens to you, Jack will never be happy. He'll never be happy again. And we'll never go home," Lewis kept going.

"Nothing's going to happen to me, Lewis," she said gently.

"Poppa was never happy. He smiled and he pretended. Sometimes, with the others, his other children, the ones he had with his new wife, it looked real. But when he was alone, we knew. Myrtle and me, we knew. He was always at the window, looking at her cliff. And when he did, his face was sad."

He watched the tears gather in her eyes as she scooted even closer and lifted her hand up, palm toward him and she whispered, "Stop, Lewis. Stop thinking about that, darling. Nothing is going to happen to me. I promise. Nothing. And we're going to get you home. I promise that too. Do you believe me?"

He held her eyes as he watched one tear fall and slide down her cheek.

Then he nodded again.

"Put your hand up, sweetheart, up against mine," she urged.

"You can't touch me," he informed her.

"Yes, I can. Put your hand up, Lewis, up against mine," she repeated and he did as he was told.

Just as he thought, his hand went through, melding partly with hers but when his eyes went from their hands to her face, he saw more tears, her lips quivering and a tenderness so deep, so familiar, so beloved, so longed for in her eyes, if he had breath, it would catch.

"I promise, darling," she whispered, her voice scratchy, "I'm going to get you and your sister home."

"I believe you, Belle," he whispered back and he did. He saw it.

He *felt* it.

"Think, Lewis, if you have any ideas, you let one of us know. You're safe with all of us. Anyone in this castle."

He nodded.

"You can't appear before Jack," she stated but it was a question.

He shook his head.

"Do you know why?" she asked.

He shook his head again. "Just that, something bad will happen."

She nodded. "Okay, Lewis. Jack understands. He'd like to talk to you, meet you, but he understands."

Lewis knew that. Jack was very understanding.

"Myrtle is going to be scared. Can I go to her now?" he requested.

"Of course, sweetheart," Belle replied.

He drifted back a few feet and she dropped her hand.

"I'll think, Belle, I promise," he told her. "And I'll tell you if I figure something out."

"Okay, sweetheart. Give Myrtle a hug for me."

Lewis screwed his face up and Belle smiled at him, dashing her hands on her cheeks to dry her tears.

"You were just holding her a few minutes ago," she reminded him.

"I just do that when she's scared," he informed her.

"Well, for me, give her a hug just because," Belle ordered gently.

"Oh, all right," Lewis gave in.

"Go to your sister, darling," she urged on another small, sweet smile.

He nodded and looked around at the gentle eyes on him.

Then he disappeared and went to his sister.

Belle

"I told you so," Jack's quiet voice that held a hint of humor rumbled through her and Belle, lying in the window seat between his bent legs, her upper body pressed to his, her cheek on his chest, lifted her head to look at him through the dark.

"Be quiet," she whispered.

She saw the white flash of his smile as his hand came up, his fingers sifting into her hair at the side, and he pulled it gently back.

"It's going to be okay," he assured her and she nodded.

"I felt it, Jack," she reminded him of what she'd told him earlier that evening. "When Lewis touched me, *I felt it*. I don't know what it was but *I felt it*."

"That just means you can help, poppet."

She drew in an unsteady breath.

Then she nodded again and rested her cheek back on his chest, giving him a squeeze with her arms that were wound around him.

Jack's hand left her hair so both his arms could close around her and he returned the squeeze.

She studied the inky night out the window.

After some time, Jack repeated on a murmur, "It's all going to be okay, my love."

"All right, Jack."

"Can we go to bed now?" he queried.

She nodded again, her cheek sliding on his chest.

Jack shifted, moving her with him. Picking her up in his arms, they exited the window seat and he carried her to bed.

The dogs settled on her side.

Jack settled curled into her.

"Sorry our Sunday was ruined, honey," she muttered into the night.

"It started brilliant and it's not ending all that badly. You're upset about Lewis and Myrtle but you're also right here," his arm around her tightened, "and that works for me."

She smiled into the pillow. That worked for her too.

Then she sighed.

After that, she whispered, "I love you, Jack Bennett."

"And I you, poppet," Jack replied.

Belle blinked into the dark room.

On the third blink, her eyes didn't reopen and she drifted into sleep in the protective embrace of James Bennett.

21

POSSESSED

Belle

Belle sat in the chair in the bay window in Jack's study as Jack sat behind his desk.

She had her sketch pad in front of her but her eyes were trained on the view.

She wasn't seeing the view though. She was thinking of the last four days, through all of which nothing had happened.

Not one thing.

Well, not exactly.

She woke up with Jack, she went to bed by Jack and she loved doing both. Jack also made love to her and, sometimes, he was adventurous in a gentle way and she loved that too (maybe even more). She always had breakfast with Jack, and usually, due to the hour, they were alone and she also loved that. If he was at home, she usually had dinner with him, though they were never alone but were surrounded by family so she loved that as well. And Jack always came home in time for both of them to take Baron and Gretl for a walk and she loved that too.

She also went to work but spent half her time working, half her time trying to convince Belinda that Dirk was not her prince charming come to St. Ives to sweep her off her feet except he didn't know it and had to be convinced. Belle was failing in this endeavor just as Dirk was failing in that same endeavor. This made work interesting and sometimes amusing if it didn't help to get it done.

Her father was still there, which meant anything could happen, but luckily he was behaving himself and mostly spending his time sightseeing, sometimes alone, sometimes with Rachel. This meant if he was (or they were) causing mayhem it was luckily somewhere else.

But although she'd seen and spoken to Myrtle and Lewis several times since Sunday, it was only to get to know them. And the more she got to know them, the more she liked them and the more determined she was to get them "home."

Other than that, nothing had happened. No great stroke of genius hit her as to how to release the children to the next plane. Lewis hadn't come up with anything. And neither did any of the Ghost Helpers.

"Calm before the storm, love, enjoy it," Jack had muttered when she'd shared her impatience with him.

And he was right. Something was coming.

She just wished it would *get there* so they could deal with it, she could take care of those children and everyone could move on.

But she currently had something else on her mind and that was the fact that Joy had finally talked Miles into having a chat. She, Cassandra and Lorna were with him at Yasmin's as Belle sat in Jack's study at The Point not seeing the view.

So she was also worried.

"Belle," Jack called.

"Yes?" Belle answered the view.

"Love, look at me," he ordered gently, her head turned to him and her eyes caught his green ones. "It will all be fine."

As ever, he knew her thoughts and he knew when she needed his reassurance.

That said, she wasn't exactly reassured.

"You keep saying that, Jack, but *nothing's happening*," she reminded him, not remembering you should be careful what you wish for because just as she said it, she heard the door fly open.

Jack's head whipped to it as he swiftly rose from his chair and Belle leaned and twisted to look around the back of her own.

Angus was advancing, looking agitated.

"Laddie, we got a—" he started to tell Jack but didn't finish.

This was because Miles stormed in after Angus, his face red and his expression murderous.

With just one look at his face, not even fully taking in his threatening gait, Belle's body froze solid.

"I cannot fucking *believe* you!" he shouted, stalking straight toward the desk and thus Jack.

Angus moved in front of him and Belle gasped and jumped from her chair, tossing down her sketch pad and pencil as Miles put his hands on Angus, threw him bodily to the side and Angus went flying, kilt awhirl, arms wheeling.

At that, the room became a bustle of action.

Jack quickly rounded his desk, growling, "Belle, do not move," just as Lachlan, Cassandra, Joy and Lorna came flying into the room, in that order.

"Miles, calm down," Jack ordered and Miles stopped in front of Jack, lifted a hand, planted it in Jack's chest and pushed off.

But Jack stood solid and didn't even sway. However, he did lift an arm to shove his brother's hand from his chest.

"Jesus, I cannot believe you. I cannot..." Miles leaned in, his face getting redder, "fucking...*believe you!*"

"Miles, I will repeat, calm down," Jack said in a low, even voice.

"Did you tell Belle that shit?" Miles bit out. "Did you tell Belle like you told *Mum* that I fucking *pushed your woman down the stairs?*" he bellowed the last words in fury.

Oh goodness *gracious!*

Suddenly the room again filled with action as Miles didn't pause for an answer but aimed a punch at Jack.

Belle gasped and took two steps forward but stopped when she saw Jack duck and Miles missed him. At the same time, Angus and Lachlan sprang forward and Lila, Rachel and Jensen raced into the room, Lila shouting, "What on earth is going on?"

Miles recovered, aimed another punch, Lila and Rachel gasped loudly and Dad ran toward the brothers as Lachlan latched on to both of Miles's arms and yanked them hard behind his back.

"Please, don't hurt him!" Joy cried, throwing a beseeching arm toward Lachlan and Miles while her other hand went to her chest.

Miles ignored his mother, struggled against Lachlan's hold, his eyes locked on Jack and he shouted, "*I did not push Belle down the fucking stairs!*"

Angus got close and said in his soft burr, "You didn't, laddie, the spirit inside you did."

Still jerking against his captor, Mile's enraged eyes sliced to Angus and he spat, "That's what that brunette bitch told me, old man, and that's *fucked up*." His eyes then cut to Belle. "I did not push you."

"Miles—" Belle whispered.

"Look at me," Jack ordered before Belle could say any more.

Miles ignored Jack too, his eyes riveted to Belle. "I swear to Christ, Belle, I did not fucking push you."

Jack got close. "Eyes to me, Miles."

Miles stopped struggling against Lachlan and glared at Jack. "I did not push her."

"You didn't," Jack said quietly. "I know that."

"Then why did you tell Mum I did?" Miles fired back. "She—"

"You didn't push Belle and I know it sounds insane, but although you didn't push her, you still did."

"I *did not!*"

"You were there, Miles," Jack told him. "You were seen."

"That isn't fucking *true*," Miles hissed, his eyes narrowing.

"You were seen," Jack repeated.

"Yes, by *a ghost*," Miles spat. "They told me. Jesus, Jack, seriously? You believe that shit? All these years, now you believe that shit? That is *fucked up!*"

"Okay, so where were you that night?" Jack asked.

"Not here," Miles immediately answered.

"Where were you?" Jack pressed.

Miles again jerked against Lachlan's hold but Lachlan held true.

He stopped just as suddenly and clipped loudly, "Tell the ginger to let me go!"

"I'll let you go, mate, you don't throw another punch," Lachlan said from behind him.

"I won't throw another punch," Miles bit out.

"Right, then I'll let you go you don't call me 'ginger' again," Lachlan went on.

"Lach, let the lad go," Angus said low.

Lachlan looked to his uncle then pushed Miles off and stepped back.

Miles immediately twisted around to glare at Lachlan then he turned back to Jack when Jack pressed on, "Miles, the night Belle was hurt, where were you?"

"I wasn't fucking here," he shot back.

"All right. Then where were you?" Jack kept at it.

"Not here."

"Then where?"

"Not...fucking...here!"

"Miles, if you weren't here, where were you?"

"*Not fucking here!*" Miles roared, stepped swiftly to a table that was close, grabbed a vase and threw it across the room.

It sailed safely between Jack and Lachlan but exploded against the wall.

Belle jumped as did others, and Joy cried, "Miles!"

The men closed in on Miles but he was now staring at the floor, body mostly motionless except he was breathing heavily. Jack correctly sensed he was no threat and lifted his hand to the other men to stop their advance, so they did.

He gave his brother a moment then, quietly, he said, "Miles, if you weren't here, tell us where you were so we can—"

Before he could finish, Miles's head snapped up and his eyes locked on Belle.

"I dream you."

The air in the room went still and Belle figured this was because everyone had stopped breathing. She figured this because she had.

Therefore, she had to force her question through stiff lips.

"What?"

"Since then. Since it happened. I wasn't there. But I dream it. I dream of pushing you."

"Oh my God," Joy whispered and Belle felt tears sting her nose.

"I didn't do it." Miles's voice was now raw. "In my dreams, I feel my hand on you, I see you going down the stairs. But I didn't do it. It's been torture but I swear to fucking Christ, Belle, I didn't do it."

"You dream it?" Angus asked quietly and Miles tore his eyes from Belle and looked to Angus.

"Yes," he bit off.

"Do you dream of anything else?" Angus questioned, and Belle watched in horror and distress as Miles's face became ravaged.

"I lose time," he whispered his admission.

"Bloody hell," Jack muttered.

Miles closed his eyes tight, opened them and looked at Jack. "Since I met her. Since I met Belle, I've lost time."

Jack held his brother's gaze even as he ordered, "Lila, Rachel, take Mum out."

"Jack, I—"

Miles and Jack both looked to Joy but it was Miles who spoke. "Mum, please."

Her teeth worried her lip as she studied her youngest son. Then she looked at her oldest but she nodded to the floor before she went out, Rachel and Lila following her.

Rachel closed the door.

Belle's attention went back to Miles to see he was addressing Angus when he said, "I dream of a woman. A woman and a man. I'm watching them. They're not from this time."

"Joshua and Brenna Bennett," Cassandra murmured and Miles looked to her.

"I don't know who the fuck they are but I wake up pissed off."

"He's got hold of you, laddie," Angus said gently and Miles's eyes swung to him.

"That's insane," he whispered.

Cassandra moved cautiously closer. "We can help."

Miles stared at her for long moments as everyone was silent.

His eyes moved slowly to Belle.

"I didn't push you, gorgeous," he whispered, his voice an ache, his eyes filled with pain and it was the first time she didn't mind Miles calling her "gorgeous."

"I know, Miles," Belle said softly and moved to the side of the desk but when she sensed Jack's eyes on her and glanced briefly at him to see his face hard and his head shake once, she stopped. She looked back to Miles. "Let them help."

She watched Miles pull in a ragged breath.

Cassandra sensed capitulation and pushed, "We have a potion."

Miles turned to her. "It'll stop this?"

She nodded.

"It's safe, mate," Lorna put in.

Miles moved his gaze to hers when she spoke before he lifted a hand and tore it through his hair with no small amount of agitation. When his hand dropped it seemed as if it took every effort for his eyes to move to his brother.

"I killed your child." The words were tortured.

"Miles," Jack murmured.

"Yasmin was right. It's like I'm possessed. All my life—"

"Don't," Jack interrupted, his voice a low rumble. "Just let them help."

For long, tense moments the two brothers held each other's eyes.

Then Miles nodded.

Jack looked to Belle. "Go to Mum, poppet. We need to talk with Miles."

She took one look at his beautiful, desolate face, nodded and moved swiftly to the door.

"Gorgeous."

She stopped at the door and turned at Miles's call. His eyes were wet with tears and she felt her stomach clutch.

"Like Jack said, Miles, don't. It'll all be all right," Belle whispered.

"I—" he started but Belle cut him off.

"Get help, Miles, and it'll all be all right."

He looked away, lifted a hand to the back of his neck and she saw him squeeze before he dropped it, again caught her eyes and nodded.

Belle nodded back.

Then her eyes swept through the occupants of the room and ended their journey resting on Jack.

She gave him a trembling smile, opened the door and ducked through, closing it behind her.

❧ ❧ ❧

The wind was high, there were clouds hiding the moon so the cliff path was dark before them. The dogs, usually happy to wander away and roam afield during their evening walks with Jack and Belle, sensed the mood and stayed close.

Jack held Belle's hand and Belle walked close beside him. So close their arms brushed as they moved and Jack held a torch to the path in front of them as they strode through the dark night.

"Talk to me," she whispered.

An hour after Belle left the room, Jack had come into the drawing room to guide Joy to Miles.

Five minutes after that, he came back to ask Belle to get her coat so they could walk the dogs.

Now they were on the path and it was Jack who had lapsed into a heavy silence.

"He's volunteered for the ceremony."

The words were harsh with concern and disquiet, as they should be.

Belle was instantly concerned and disquieted too. So much so, she stopped dead on the path.

Jack stopped with her, turned and looked down at her.

"I've advised against it," he shared. "He won't hear of it. He wants Caldwell out of him."

"So he believes that Caldwell is in him?"

"He admitted he's felt not himself often in his life. In fact, since he could remember. He also shared he often was driven to behavior that, later, he didn't understand but couldn't control. He never understood it. It even, at times, frightened him. He thought it was an unhealthy compulsion. Now he believes it's Caldwell. Because of this, it didn't take a lot of convincing."

433

"So he should take the potion. The potion works," Belle replied. "Cassandra promised."

"Yes, love, and he's already taken it as a preventative measure in the short run. But he's adamant. He wants Cassandra to perform the ceremony."

She moved into him, putting her hand on his chest even as her other hand still in his squeezed tight.

She leaned in and whispered, "Let me talk to him."

"You won't sway him," Jack stated.

"Let me try," Belle pushed.

"My love, he's wracked with guilt. He killed our child. He could have killed you. He's come to understand that and he can't live with it. Not like this. He's determined to pay a penance."

"He has to take that potion the rest of his life, Jack. That's penance enough."

"I've shared this with him. He disagrees."

"So let *me* share it with him."

"Belle," Jack whispered, letting her hand go but lifting his to cup her jaw as he dipped his face close to hers, "put yourself in his shoes. He pushed you down the stairs and took away our child. He didn't do it but he did. This knowledge is new and it's destroying him. I understand why he wants this. This..." he hesitated, clearly searching for a word before finding one, "*thing* inside him has controlled him. It's made him lose time where he has no idea what he's done. It's beleaguering his dreams and it caused him to commit a despicable act. He wants it gone. And I don't like it but, my love, I also don't blame him."

Belle hated to admit it but this made sense.

She leaned deeper into him and tried something else. "Okay then, when is this going to happen? Perhaps, given time, he can come to terms with it. He can see the potion is working. We can show him we're good with him and maybe he'll change his mind."

"Fortunately, he has no choice but to wait. The moon is waxing. Cassandra said it must wane before she can perform the ceremony."

Such was her relief, Belle relaxed all her weight into him and his arm stole around her as she did.

"Well, at least that's something."

"Indeed," Jack muttered his agreement.

Belle got up on her toes to kiss his jaw then she moved away. Jack caught her hand again, trained the torch to the path and they resumed their walk.

After several long moments of walking in silence, Belle remarked, "I should tell Lewis what happened. It may make him feel better about the bad man."

"Not necessary. After we were done speaking with Miles, Lorna and Lachlan left to call to him in order to share that information."

"Oh," Belle whispered then asked, "Does Joy know all that's happened and going to happen?"

"By the time we get back, she will. Miles, Angus and Cassandra are telling her."

"Oh," she repeated on a whisper, her worried thoughts turning to Joy and her reaction to all this and Jack's hand gave hers a squeeze.

They walked on for some time in silence.

Belle broke it, saying, "The bright side is, that's one thing down."

Through a low, soft chuckle Jack replied, "Yes, poppet, it's one thing down."

"Now we just have to free Myrtle and Lewis."

"Right," Jack's voice was still trembling with humor, "that's all we have to do."

"Someone will think of something," Belle declared with more hope than certainty.

"I bloody hope so," Jack muttered, the humor gone from his voice.

They walked on, neither speakin, the beam of the torch bouncing on the path in front of them, the dogs loping and circling the pair as they moved through the night.

Finally, Belle called, "Jack?"

"Yes, love."

"What are we going to do when there's no more drama?"

"Bloody enjoy it," he muttered but she stopped, tugging on his hand as she did so therefore he did too.

When he turned into her again, she looked up at him and asked, "Do you think it'll be boring?"

"Are you asking if I think life will be boring or if I'll become bored of you?"

When did he come to know her so well?

She didn't ask this out loud. She didn't have the chance.

This was because Jack ordered, "Wrap your arms around me, Belle."

She did as she was told and he returned the gesture.

She watched his shadowed face get close and only when it was an inch away did he speak.

"I thought we agreed you had me wrapped around your finger."

"Jack—"

"Belle, after a still-remains-to-be-seen clairvoyant white witch, a mad Scotsman and his twin niece and nephew who have supernatural gifts dispatch the spirit that is controlling my brother. And after we figure out whatever bloody thing we need to figure out to send two child ghosts, who have apparently been haunting my ancestral home for over two hundred years, to some other plane though we have no idea what that plane is nor how to do it *nor* did I even believe any of this existed mere weeks ago. And after your father, mother and grandmother drift to their next location where they can amuse and frustrate new people who are both lucky and unfortunate enough to be their next victims. And after I hopefully convince Yasmin not to break her husband's heart but also not her own...*again*. *Then* we can concentrate on three things. First, getting married. Second, being married. And, finally, third, creating a family."

Belle stopped breathing.

Jack did not. He kept talking.

"So, as you can see, I'll have no chance in the future to be bored, not, poppet, that you would *ever*," his arms gave her a fierce squeeze, "bore me because you won't. I can only imagine what Lila and Rachel have in their heads about their only grandchild and child's wedding, not to mention my mother. And then we might, *might* have a brief respite before I hope to God we fill that house with children. Then, we'll have decades of God knows what before we retire on an island, perhaps in Greece. By that time we'll be old and decrepit but, my guess is, you'll still be beautiful and definitely you'll be well dressed."

After his spectacular, amazing and beautiful speech, Belle blurted, "I love you, James Bennett," and his face dipped even closer.

"I know, Belle Abbot," he whispered.

"And, in future, when you ask me to marry you as in officially, just for your information, the answer is yes," she told him.

"Good to know," he muttered, his lips a breath from hers.

"And thank you," she whispered, and she felt his eyes look deep into hers through the dark.

"For what, poppet?"

"For being all that's you."

Belle barely finished the word "you" before her mouth was taken in a deep kiss while two strong arms closed tight around her.

She returned the kiss, her arms closing tight around Jack's shoulders.

And after Jack broke their kiss, he turned them toward home.

Their walk with the dogs was done.

And they walked back to The Point a lot faster.

22

THE OMEN

Jack

Jack walked into the austere room. A room in the old servants quarters that hadn't been used in decades. A room that had nothing but a table draped in scarves, cluttered with vials, scales, jars and bottles and holding burning incense and candles, more candles burned in all the corners and last, there was a bed on which his brother was tied with rope.

And when Jack walked into the room and took all this in, his throat closed.

He swallowed against it, locked eyes with Miles and strode directly to the bed.

"You don't have to do this," he told him quietly.

"I do," Miles returned firmly.

"Miles—"

"Jack, we've discussed this. Repeatedly. I need him *out*," Miles gritted then his eyes shot to Cassandra who had moved to stand on the other side of the bed.

If it was possible, which Jack wouldn't have thought it would be until he witnessed it, she was wearing *more* scarves and *more* silver.

Apparently, Wiccan ceremonial regalia included significantly over-accessorizing.

"The time is nigh," she said softly.

Jack's gaze sliced back to his brother. "Give it more time. You've said you've felt more yourself. You've lost no time. Give it until the next waning of the moon. We'll do it then if you're so fucking determined to do this."

"No," Miles stated curtly.

"Miles, you could end up not you," Jack reminded him, his voice harsh with concern.

"And how's it been, Jack, living with me being me?" Miles returned.

Jack closed his eyes and only opened them when Miles spoke again.

"I must do this and you know it."

Jack pulled in a sharp breath before he nodded. There was nothing more he could do. He'd talked himself sick, so had Joy as had Yasmin and, even once, Belle.

Miles was determined.

With nothing for it, he took a step away from the bed.

"You know the plan, mate?" Lachlan, who'd moved in silently beside Jack, asked and Jack jerked his chin up.

In the weeks between Miles's realization that he was possessed by the spirit of a murderer and his understanding of all that was happening at The Point, Miles had had an idea. An idea unfortunately or, perhaps, if it worked, fortunately he shared with Cassandra and Angus. An idea they thought was brilliant, but as usual with this group Jack was not entirely sure.

The plan was, once they tore the spirit of Caleb Caldwell free of Miles Bennett, they were going to capture it and tether it to this world for long enough to interrogate it before they dispelled it forever.

The entirety of the quartet assured him that Caldwell would not break free of these tethers to wreak havoc on his home and loved ones. Or, *more* havoc than he already had.

Nevertheless, Jack was taking no chances. This meant everyone, including his dogs, was somewhere else. Joy and Lila were at Yasmin's. Belle, Rachel, Jensen and the dogs were at Belle's cottage.

"Is everyone ready?" Cassandra asked.

"Aye, Cass," Angus answered, moving to the foot of the bed.

"Aye," Lachlan stated, putting a hand to Jack's back and they moved closer to the side.

"Aye," Lorna muttered, coming to stand a few feet away from Cassandra at the other side.

Cassandra looked down at Miles and whispered, "You are brave and I am sorry."

Jack didn't think that was a good start and he felt his body get tight.

Without delay, Cassandra lifted both her hands to the ceiling, arms out in a Y, one hand holding a twig. Her neck bent well back so her long hair and the ends of the scarf tied tight around her scalp fell down her back and she started murmuring.

Jack couldn't hear her until her voice grew stronger and the volume higher. It was mostly rhymes, not gibberish but mad all the same.

The entire thing was mad and he couldn't believe he was there at the same time he hoped to God this worked and his brother came out of it healthy and sane.

Jack watched as Cassandra spoke more, stronger and stronger, louder and louder.

And this went on for some time. So long, his eyes moved to Lorna who was listening, swaying to the rhyme and grinning like she was at some strange concert and enjoying the hell out of the vibe.

Entirely mad.

"Uh..." Miles muttered and Jack tore his attention from Lorna to look down at his brother and he saw Miles staring at Cassandra like he didn't know whether to swear or burst out laughing, "Seriously?"

Jack felt his lips twitch right before Cassandra cried, "*So mote it be!*" and her arms arced down.

She pointed the twig at Miles and Jack froze solid when a heavy, glittering stream of sparks shot right out of its tip and blasted Miles in the chest.

The instant it hit, Mile's body arched unnaturally from the bed, his back at such an angle Jack feared his spine would snap. His wrists and ankles were straining fiercely against their bounds. His neck was bowed back so far his head was well beyond his shoulders. And a painful, guttural, appalling, *loud* noise streamed constantly from his throat.

He did not look or sound in pain.

He looked and sounded like he was in agony.

"Stop!" Jack clipped as Cassandra kept the beam of sparks aimed at Miles's chest, her eyes riveted to him, her mouth moving now without sound but constantly. "*Stop!*" he shouted and began to move, but Lachlan clapped a hand strong and firm on Jack's shoulder and didn't let go.

"Hold steady, lad," Angus encouraged from his place at the foot of the bed, his gaze on Miles. He, like Lorna and Lachlan, all held a whip in their hands.

Jack looked back to Miles and Cassandra, the latter of which seemed to be trembling. She definitely was sweating even though she wasn't moving. And her concentration and the stream of magic hadn't wavered.

Miles was still making that hideous noise.

"God damn it! *Stop!*" Jack thundered, shirking off Lachlan's hand but Lachlan was moving, positioning one foot behind the other, raising the whip in his hand and Jack's eyes shot back to the bed just as the see-through human shape of a man tore violently free of Miles's body.

The noise died in Miles's throat and his body collapsed limply to the bed at the exact instant the three McPhersons moved, rounding their whips over their heads with swift, practiced movements and striking out. The tips of all three lashed out and whirled, catching the ethereal shape about the waist and holding him captive and floating above the bed. Every inch where the whips wound around the phantom, gold sparks crackled.

"Fucking hell," Jack whispered, staring at the man whose burning, incensed, frenzied eyes locked on Jack.

Then his mouth moved but the words that came out sounded hollow and sinister throughout the entire room.

"You will not win this time, Bennett."

"I didn't win last time, you bastard. You killed my fucking wife," Jack bit out.

"*You* got *my* wife *with child*..." Caldwell returned then screeched a demented, "*twice!*"

"She was bloody well Joshua's wife and you know it," Jack fired back.

"She was *mine!*" he roared.

"She was never yours," Jack retorted and tired of the conversation he was having with a fucking *ghost* so he moved it firmly on. "Now tell us about the children. How do we send them home?"

"I will not stop until I best you," Caldwell declared.

"Wrong, mate, you bought yourself a one-way ticket straight to hell by being a jealous, abusive, murderous arsehole," Lorna cut in and Caldwell's ghostly head turned her way. "Your ride on this plane is done. Your eternal ride isn't going to be too pleasant and you've got one chance to help yourself out. You can do that by telling us how we send those children to the next plane."

"I will best him," Caldwell reiterated, exposing his one-track mind.

"Laddie, you aren't getting this but you're stuck. You got these last minutes to do right before your judgement," Angus broke in. "Do right. Tell us what you know about sending those children where they can be at peace."

Jack watched Caldwell's burning gaze glare at Angus then he looked about the room.

"Fucking hell, that thing was in *me*?" Miles asked at this point, his voice barely above a whisper but it sounded healthy, strong and sane.

Jack relaxed (slightly) and pinned Caldwell with his gaze.

"Tell us about the children," he demanded and Caldwell held his stare silently. "Tell us about the children!" he repeated, his voice louder.

"The children do not matter," Caldwell whispered disturbingly.

"If you know something, tell us," Jack ordered.

Again with the disturbing whisper, "I will best you."

"You won't, I always win," Jack returned. "Now tell us...about...*the children.*"

And right then Jack felt ice fill his veins because Caldwell smiled an eerie, malicious smile.

"I already have," he kept whispering. "I've won. You don't know. You have no idea. But you'll never have her. *My* Brenna." His grin became more evil and he leaned toward Jack. "*My* Belle. If I can't have her, *you* never will. I've seen to that, James. It's already begun."

"He doesn't know anything, Cass, send him down," Angus ordered.

"What have you done?" Jack asked, not tearing his eyes from the spirit.

"Something I'll never tell. Something you can't stop," Caldwell answered. "Her body will again be broken by rock and sea."

Jack reached out, grasped Lachlan's whip and yanked hard, jerking Caldwell's ghostly frame his way as he roared, "*What have you done?*"

"Send him down, Cass! *Now!*" Angus boomed.

"*Smothered of air, broken by sea, pure souls taken by the hand of thee, dark spirit, attend your eternal sentence, as I will, so mote it be!*" Cassandra cried, a stream of sparks shot from her twig and it hit Caldwell in the gut.

His body jerked once, twice, three times then it exploded in white sparks that flew across the room, bouncing off the walls, floor, ceiling and all the inhabitants. The whip ends fell and he was gone.

Jack, breathing heavily, stared into the empty space where Caldwell disappeared until he heard Miles whisper, "Bloody hell, did that just happen?"

Turning swiftly and angling low, he put his face an inch from his brother's and demanded, "What did he do?"

Miles blinked, his head jerking and he said quietly, "Jack, I don't know."

"What was he talking about with Belle?" Jack clipped.

"Honest to God, Jack, I don't know."

Jack fisted his hand in Miles's shirt and got nose to nose with him. "He was in you. Search for it, Miles. *What did he mean?*"

He felt Angus's hand light on his back right before he heard him say, "Lad, step back. Let us see to your brother."

Jack ignored Angus. "Tell me, Miles."

Miles shook his head. "I don't know."

Jack pulled him up by his shirt and slammed him into the bed.

"*Think!*" he roared.

He vaguely sensed Cassandra working at the bounds at Miles's wrist then Miles, freed at his feet and one hand, pulled himself up the bed but he held Jack's eyes. Jack moved back half a foot and returned the gesture.

"I'll think, Jack, but honest to God, I swear, he didn't communicate with me but I'll try and I'll…" his eyes moved to Cassandra, "I'll work with her. With them. See if they can pull anything out."

Jack straightened and tried to control his thoughts, his breathing and the burn in his gut.

Angus moved in to release Miles from the last of his bonds.

"I know it doesn't seem good but we have a warning," Lachlan said low at his side. "It's always good to have a warning, mate. We'll be prepared."

Jack didn't feel good about this. Not any part of it.

In fact, he felt a burning in his gut that stated quite plainly that something was very wrong.

His eyes drifted to the space Caldwell's spirit inhabited moments before.

Then he took in a calming breath and looked to his brother who had shifted to sit on the side of the bed, leaned forward, elbows to his thighs.

"How do you feel?" he asked and Miles tilted his head back to look at his brother.

"Like I feel the morning after I've had way too much lager, about the same amount of vodka and washed that all down with a kebab that had a side order of grease," Miles answered.

"Far from pleasant," Jack told him. "But at least you're no longer harboring the spirit of a man who murdered women and children."

One side of Miles's lips moved up as he muttered, "Silver lining."

"What's one and one?" Cassandra asked.

Miles sat up and twisted to look over the bed at her.

"Two," he replied.

"Your name?" she asked.

"Miles Bennett," he answered.

"Is it wrong to eat babies?" she asked, and Miles muttered, "Jesus. Are you serious?"

Cassandra nodded, her face grave.

"Yes, bloody hell, yes, it's wrong to eat babies," Miles answered then twisted back and looked up at Jack before sharing, "This is fucking insane."

"And unfortunately it's not fucking over," Jack replied and took in another deep breath before he said Belle's words of weeks before. "But at least that's one thing down."

Miles grinned, pushed up from the bed and swayed until Jack's hand shot out and caught his. Palm to palm, his fingers tight around the side of his brother's hand, he held strong until Miles steadied.

And he still held strong when Miles again caught his eye.

"All right?" Jack asked quietly, looking deep into his brother's blue eyes.

Miles took in a breath, took a moment then he nodded. "All right."

"All right," Jack repeated and gave his brother's hand a jerk before letting it go.

"Jack?" Miles called and Jack looked at him again. "Nothing will happen to Belle. We'll all look after her. It'll be fine."

Jack kept hold of his brother's eyes a long moment before he nodded, hoping to God Miles was right.

He turned away and said to no one, "I'm getting a whisky. Then I'm getting in my car and getting Belle and my dogs. If you want a whisky, you better follow me because I won't be taking time over mine."

And on that, he walked out of the room with five people following him.

❧ ❧ ❧

"Good dogs," Jack murmured as both dogs came to him on the landing of Belle's cottage but neither woofed their greeting.

Jack gave them quick but loving scratches and walked directly to Belle's room. He moved to the side of the bed and saw her through the shadows sleeping in the middle. The moon was waning, the night dark, her wispy curtains closed. There was little light so all he could see was that she was on her side facing his side of the bed and she had her knees curled slightly toward her belly.

But seeing her peaceful, he decided he'd not wake her and take her home but instead join her in bed here.

Before he did that, he had three things to do.

"Stay with Belle," he whispered to his dogs and they settled on their bellies on Belle's side of the bed.

Moving back out, he carefully closed the door so as not to make any sound. Then he moved across the landing into the living room and closed that door.

Once in, he pulled out his phone and made his first call.

"All right, lad?" Angus answered after one ring.

"Go over everything, Angus, all of you. Every piece of information, go back to every person you talked to, bring in more witches, clairvoyants, soothsayers, I don't give a fuck what you have to do. Find out what he did. Find it out and find a way to stop it," Jack commanded.

"Already on it, Jack," Angus replied. "We got the whisky and we got our stuff spread out in your dining room. Miles feels crap but still, he's in with Cassandra now. She's going to hypnotize him. See if he can pull up any memories of his blank spots."

"Good," Jack returned, disconnected without a good-bye and made his next call.

On ring four he heard a sleepy, "Jesus, Bennett, it's after one in the morning."

Jack didn't delay.

"Tonight, Dempsey, I had a fucking conversation with the fucking ghost of fucking Caleb Caldwell."

Dempsey was silent for a moment before he replied, "I'm guessing with your ample usage of the word 'fucking' this conversation didn't go well."

"No, it did not."

"Do I want to know how you managed to have a conversation with a man who's been dead for two hundred years?" Dempsey asked.

"Considering your profession, I can only assume your level of curiosity is elevated beyond that of others so yes, you probably would like to know. You also probably wouldn't believe a bloody word I said."

"I'm hanging in there with this supernatural shit, mate," Dempsey reminded him.

"And you're getting paid to do just that," Jack's reminded Dempsey before he carried on, "Tonight, Caldwell shared he's put some plan into action and whatever it is has already begun. And whatever it is puts Belle in danger. And before you ask, that would be *mortal* danger considering he declared her body will be broken by rock and sea."

"Jesus," Dempsey muttered.

"Indeed," Jack clipped. "You told me there was nothing more to learn that would be of consequence, you've gone over it all. I want you to do it again and dig deeper."

"Bennett, firstly, crazy as your story is, half of me believes it. The coincidences are too stark for there not to be some truth in this."

"I'm obliged you think so, Dempsey, but, no offense, I also don't give a fuck if you believe. Right now—"

Dempsey cut him off, "I wasn't done. I just wanted you to know I don't think you're entirely mad."

"Brilliant," Jack muttered, for the first time after what he witnessed tonight wondering if Dempsey was right and he actually *was* mad.

Entirely.

Before Jack could fully assess his sanity, Dempsey continued.

"And I also have to remind you these murders happened two centuries ago. It was lucky I was able to find what I already found. You know I'm thorough and I promise you, I was no less thorough with this. There's nothing else to be found."

"Dig deeper," Jack ordered.

"Jack—" he used Jack's nickname for the first time and he did it sounding conciliatory.

Jack was in no mood to be pacified.

"Tonight, we tore Caleb Caldwell out of my brother," Jack shared and heard Dempsey's surprised grunt but kept talking. "When we did, we questioned him. We got nothing except for the fact that he was very certain he would best me. He was very certain because he told us he'd already set the plan into motion. Miles has told us that he's lost time. Caldwell has been able to take control of him and he has. Miles is going to work with the people I've hired to deal with the bloody supernatural part of this madness. *You* are going to see if there's some connection of the now to the then. Something he did back then, someone he worked with, something he used Miles in this time to do, something we missed, something that could harm Belle."

"All right, Jack, I'll dig deeper," Dempsey agreed quietly.

"Don't delay," Jack returned.

"Can I finish out the night sleeping?" Dempsey asked.

"Yes. It would be better that you were fresh when you get down to it," Jack allowed before concluding, "Goodnight, Dempsey."

"'Night, Jack."

Jack disconnected then made his final call.

"Mate, we're drinking whisky but we're still working," Lachlan said by way of greeting.

"Call Lewis," Jack ordered.

"Sorry?"

"Lewis. Call him. Speak to him. Find out everything he knows about that night. Anything he remembers about his mother, father and Caleb Caldwell. If he saw Caldwell in the village and who he might have seen him with. If he heard any talk. Anything."

There was a pause and Jack would understand he was seeking privacy when he spoke again in a low tone. "Uh, Jack, I get you're freaked but I also don't have to remind you that wee one was murdered."

"You don't," Jack agreed tersely.

"Belle wanted us to go gentle with the children," Lachlan reminded him of something else he hadn't forgotten.

"Then go gentle as you ask him all I've told you to ask him."

"Jack—"

"He'll tell you," Jack interrupted. "He'll want to help Belle. Be kind. Have a mind. But do it."

There was another pause before Lachlan agreed, "Right, mate. I'll get Lorna and we'll do it tonight."

"Excellent. We'll see you tomorrow."

"Right."

Jack disconnected again, pulled in a deep breath and on his second one, decided there was nothing more he could do.

This did not make him feel better.

He walked through the cottage, disrobed in Belle's bedroom and slid into bed beside her.

She wrapped herself around him immediately.

This made him feel better.

"Is Miles all right?" she whispered, and at the sound of her voice he knew she'd never been asleep but, as was her way, remained in bed to give him some time.

"He's fine."

"Did everything go okay?" she asked.

"It's fine," he lied.

"Jack, you got here ten minutes ago and came to bed just now. Are you sure everything is all right?"

"Everything's fine, Belle. I'm fine. Miles is fine. Everything is fine." He pulled her closer. "Now, I'm exhausted and I need to sleep."

Although it was wrapped warm around him, she held her body stiffly for long moments before she asked softly, "You wouldn't lie to me?"

In the more than three weeks since Jack broke through her grief, she'd been happy. There had been dramas. He'd seen a shadow pass over her eyes on occasion and he knew her thoughts were dark. Twice, he'd seen her run her hand over her belly, her face set in wistful nostalgia. And it was not pleasant nostalgia, it was melancholic. He gave her these times, times she needed to process the grief for their lost child. Times, unfortunately, she would likely always have if, eventually, less frequently.

But mostly, she'd been content, her giggles coming more often, her smiles regular.

And there was nothing Jack wouldn't do to make certain Belle remained happy.

Including lie.

"No, my love, I wouldn't lie to you," he whispered, gathered her closer in his arms and urged, "Now, sleep."

It took her another moment before her soft body yielded against his and she whispered, "Okay, honey."

She trusted him and he hoped to Christ nothing would happen to make her realize that this once, just this once, for her happiness, he didn't deserve it.

"Goodnight, poppet," he murmured.

"'Night, Jack."

Jack stared at the ceiling as he listened to Belle's breathing, so he heard when it deepened and evened and he felt it when her body melted in sleep into his.

And he kept staring at the ceiling for long hours after that.

So long, he was awake when she woke.

Exhausted, beyond concerned and feeling a feeling he didn't like that was worse than both—powerless—he still turned to her when he felt the sleep leave her. Then he put his hands and mouth on her, and as he did, he took off her nightgown and panties.

But without any sleep, exhausted, when she was ready, he made her do all the work. He shifted her over him, guided himself inside and sat up. Holding her moving body in his arms, his head tipped back, his hand cupping hers tipping it down so her mouth was on his as she rode him until she gave it to herself and kept riding him until she gave it to him.

And later, pretending all was well, he had breakfast in her small kitchen with her eccentric mother and father then he packed his Belle and his dogs in his car and he took them home.

23

LAST ONE DOWN

Lachlan

Lach had just rammed deep into her sweet, hot, very wet snatch when the thought assaulted him.

"Bloody hell," he whispered.

"Don't stop," the woman on her knees before him, her face in the bed, begged.

"Bad fucking timing," he muttered, pulled out and put his hands to her hips as he listened to her gasp in protest, the sound driving straight through his dick.

He whipped her to her back, spread her legs then jerked them up with his hands behind her knees and he positioned.

He drove inside.

Moving her calves to round him, he fell forward. He planted one hand in the bed at her side, arm straight, the other hand he moved between her legs.

"Hurry," he grunted as he thrust fast and deep and his thumb rolled.

"Oh God," she moaned.

Lach's eyes moved over her.

Her masses of hair were spread across the bed, her creamy skin was stark against the dark sheets and her beautiful face was extraordinary in its excitement.

Christ.

His need quickened exponentially and not just because he had things to do.

"*Hurry*," he ground out, grinding deep and circling tight and hard with his thumb.

Her neck arched back, her nails dragged down his chest and she repeated, "*Oh God.*"

Finally.

There it fucking was.

Lach moved his hand from between her legs, dropped to his forearm, let go of his control and kept thrusting deeper, faster and harder until he found it.

When he came down, her mouth was on his neck, he was breathing heavily into hers and her hands were roaming the skin of his back. He gave himself a second to recognize he liked the smell as well as the feel of her just as he liked the sweet, light way her hands roamed his skin before he pulled out and rolled off.

"Where are you going?" she asked.

"A minute, baby," he muttered, moved until he was sitting on the side of the bed, and he reached an arm out toward his jeans.

"Lachlan?" she called, and he felt the bed move as she did then he felt her hand slide up his spine right before her soft body pressed against his back.

Her scent came back to him.

Jesus, she really smelled great.

Unfortunately, as much as he wanted to, Lach couldn't allow himself to concentrate on her smell.

He had his jeans in his hand so he pulled his out phone, activated the screen, touched his thumb to it, slid it around, tapped it and put it to his ear.

It rang three times before his sister hissed in greeting, "This better be good."

Christ, he didn't want to know what he interrupted.

"Lewis was murdered first," he replied and at his words, the woman at his back gasped.

Shit, what was her name?

Emma. Right, Emma.

Emma was a pretty name but not right for her considering she was far beyond a pretty woman.

There was nothing on the phone for several seconds then Lorna asked in his ear, "What?"

"Lewis was murdered first. He told us he was murdered then he was suddenly in the eastern turret. Myrtle was murdered second."

"Lach, what are you on about?"

"Lorna, Lewis was murdered first. We know this because Myrtle's ghost joined him *after* he materialized in the turret. And the police records reported Myrtle's body was found in Lewis's room."

"So?"

"So, she could have heard something and gone to his room."

"Or she could have been dragged there," Lorna suggested.

"Either way, the wee boy was alone up in that turret when he saw his mother tossed from the cliff by Caldwell."

"Oh my God," Emma whispered and he felt her body leave his back.

He ignored this as Lorna repeated, "So?"

"So, wee Myrtle wasn't dead yet."

"Lach—"

"As far as we can tell from the timeline Lewis gave us, he materialized directly *after* he was murdered. Moments later, he reported he saw Caldwell and his mother outside in the storm. Caldwell was looking over the cliff and Brenna was gone when Myrtle's ghost joined her brother. If Caldwell was outside throwing Brenna off a cliff, who was inside smothering Myrtle?"

"Oh my God," Lorna breathed as it hit her.

"There were two of them. Caldwell had a partner. He killed Brenna while someone was inside smothering the children."

"Fucking hell," Lorna whispered.

"If Myrtle came into the room, she could have seen the assailant. And definitely she would have seen him if he dragged her there prior to killing her. And, Lor, we didn't question Myrtle."

"We need to get to The Point," Lorna decided.

"Yeah, we bloody do. Where are you?"

"Plymouth."

"I'm in Exeter. Get in your car. I'll meet you at The Point. You call Cassandra."

"You calling Uncle Angus?"

"He's already there. The party is tonight. I'll call him and get him to talk to Belle. Lewis is protective of his sister and Belle's protective of both of them. Uncle Angus is going to have to talk her into letting us talk to Myrtle."

"Is Cassandra there?" Lorna asked.

"I don't know. She was invited but she had a job and I don't know if it's done. Find out," he ordered. "Get her ass there. We have to talk to Myrtle then we have to figure out what's next."

"Right. On it and outta here. See you at The Point."

Lach touched his screen then he got up and swiftly moved, carrying his jeans across the room to the bathroom in order to deal with the condom.

When he came out, he had his jeans on and he moved directly to his jumper on the floor.

Emma was in bed, the covers tucked tight around her naked body. She was sitting on her ass, her legs curled into her chest, her arms wrapped around her calves, her eyes on him.

"What do you do for a living?" she asked quietly as he tagged his jumper from the floor, straightened and prepared to pull it on.

"You don't wanna know," he muttered and yanked it over his head.

"I'm thinking you're right," she whispered as he pulled the jumper down to his waist. "But you seem worried and, uh, we just had sex and it looks like you're leaving."

At her words, he focused on her.

She had great hair, dark, glossy and a lot of it.

And she had a fantastic ass.

He moved to the bed, put a fist into it, leaned toward her and touched his mouth to hers.

Then he moved back and caught her brown eyes.

Damn, but she also had great eyes.

"My job is strange and there's some danger," he told her, his burr soft and gentle, his mind processing the fact that her eyes getting wide was all kinds of cute. "To me but also to the people I do it for. A month ago, I left a job because there was nothing more I could do. No information to get, the trail was cold, the story dead and nothing was happening. It had been weeks and nothing. There were other jobs to do and we had to do them. So we made certain the protection was strong and we left. But I just figured out we missed something."

Her brows went up. "And you remembered that while you were inside me?"

He grinned and whispered, "Sorry, love. My job is intense and when I say that I mean sometimes lives are at stake."

She held his eyes a moment before she muttered, "At least whatever it is has to do with kids being murdered and lives being at stake. I suppose that's more important than um..." she threw out a hand to indicate her bed and finished, "whatever."

He liked that she understood. Not many women would and he knew this because the few he'd tried to explain it to didn't so he no longer bothered.

He liked it enough that his grin turned into a smile and he leaned in again, catching her at the back of her neck. He pulled her to him and kissed her, this time longer, deeper and wet.

She tasted great too and that night he discovered it wasn't just her mouth that tasted good.

She was blinking at him and looking dazed when he let her go.

It was a good look but, also unfortunately, at that moment it wasn't a look he could get lost in.

So Lach moved away, grabbed his socks and boots, sat on the bed and pulled them on.

He was swinging his leather jacket on and walking to the door when she called out, "Lachlan?"

He turned and looked at her.

"Aye?"

"Be careful," she whispered.

He didn't have time but the look on her face, the memory of her heart-shaped ass in his hands and tipped up for him to take, all that hair, her warm brown eyes soft on him and the sweet way she said that, he went back to the bed and kissed her again.

In the hall of her house, heading to her door, hearing the rain pouring down outside, he pulled out his phone to call Uncle Angus.

The Other

She stood beside the prone body of Angus McPherson on the floor in the corner of the room in the servants' quarters where she'd lured him.

The blood dribbled from his forehead into his eye and off his red nose.

His phone rang.

She reached down, pulled it out of his limp hand and looked at the display.

Then she put it to the floor, lifted her foot and smashed it with her heel.

The other ones, she hadn't smashed. In her time skulking about the house, she'd just collected them, turned them off and hidden them.

She didn't know why she smashed that one.

But it felt good.

She turned the lights out when she left and was certain to lock the door.

Mickey

Mickey was grinning at the female bartender and lifting his new pint of lager to his lips when his phone rang.

He pulled it out of his back pocket and looked at the display.

He felt his brows draw together, his eyes went back to the bartender and he muttered, "A minute."

She jerked up her chin and wandered down the bar.

Mickey took the call and put his phone to his ear.

"Dempsey," he answered.

"Mr. Dempsey?" a woman asked.

"Yes."

"I don't know. This is strange..." she trailed off.

When she didn't speak for some time but didn't disconnect, Mickey said into the phone, "Can I help you with something?"

"I, well, you're going to think I'm all kinds of barmy but, well, I've spoken with Dr. Holmes and he gave me your number to call you."

The minute she mentioned Holmes's name, Holmes being a historian with a doctorate, a specialty in Cornwall and a sub-specialty in famous local crimes including the Bennett murders, Mickey's back went straight and she had his complete attention.

"What's your name?" he asked.

"Mercy. Mercy Richardson."

"Ms. Richardson, why did Dr. Holmes tell you to speak with me?"

"He says the dreams I'm having are, well, he says you'd be interested in them."

Dreams.

Bloody hell.

"And what dreams are you having, Ms. Richardson?" Mickey inquired.

"They're very, erm, *strange*," she whispered but said no more.

"Please tell me about them," Mickey coaxed, not feeling good about this mostly because Bennett made it clear *he* didn't feel good about the fact that nothing came of all the work and research Mickey and Bennett's crew of whoever they were had done a month ago.

Mickey was convinced the spirit of Caleb Caldwell had been fucking with Bennett's head. One last shot before, if all this lunacy was true, Caldwell was sent straight to hell.

Bennett was not convinced of the same.

With absolutely nothing left to find and nothing left to do, Bennett's team had disbursed.

That didn't mean Bennett had to like it. He didn't and he made this clear.

He also had no choice and he made it even clearer he liked that even less.

"All right," she said in his ear, taking him from his thoughts. "Well, first, I've been having them for months. I tried to remember when they started, Dr. Holmes said that might be important, but I don't know exact. But I do remember they started a few weeks before all that news hit with James Bennett, The Tiny Dynamo and James's brother, Miles. I remember that."

Blood *hell*.

"Right, so you started having the dreams, then..." Mickey prompted.

"I know you probably think it's weird that I told you that about, well, Belle Abbot and James Bennett but, I don't know. I think it's important. Because, at the time, I thought I was dreaming about *them*. It felt weird because, you know, they were from another time and everything. Like, they didn't look like them, really, but still...they *were*. Then, *bang*! They're in the paper and they're together. It really freaked me out."

"As I suspect it would," Mickey muttered, seeking patience. "What else? Most important, what did you dream?"

"Okay, now, I know this all sounds bizarre—"

"How about this," he cut her off. "Just assume I won't think it's bizarre. All right? You don't know me but rest assured I've seen and heard a lot, Ms. Richardson, so just tell me your story and don't worry what I think about it. Yes?"

"Yes," she whispered. "Then, well, okay, so you won't think it's bizarre when I say it isn't like these dreams are *dreams*. It's like they're, well...*memories*."

Bloody fucking *hell*.

"Go on," he urged.

"The thing is, there's another man."

Good Christ.

"And..." Mickey prompted.

"And he's with a woman. And I see them. They don't see me. I think, well, it's crazy but I think I'm like a servant or something. And they don't see me or they don't care that I'm around. I exist but I'm not important. But, and Mr. Dempsey, this is disturbing as well as weird and it's the reason I went to Dr. Holmes. I asked around, who to talk to because I'm scared to go to sleep, it's *that* disturbing. And this is because, first, okay, I know you said don't say anything is crazy but this is. See, she's *a witch*. An...actual...hocus-pocus *witch*. And worse," she cried, warming to her theme, "they're plotting a murder. The murder of two children and a woman. And the woman's name is Brenna."

By the time she was finished, Mickey had thrown money on the bar and was on his way to the door.

"Ms. Richardson," he said into his phone as he made his way across the pub toward the door that would lead him to the driving rain outside, "start at the beginning, don't leave anything out, don't hesitate and tell me *everything*."

Twenty minutes later, Mercy Richardson had told Mickey Dempsey everything.

Five minutes after that, when Dempsey was unable to get Jack Bennett on the phone, he called a mate of his who was a pilot and he pulled in a favor.

Five minutes after that, he was headed to the airstrip.

Jack

"Poppet, have you seen my phone?" Jack called as he entered his and Belle's room at The Point.

"No," she called back through the closed door to the bathroom.

Jack stopped in the room and looked around.

Something was wrong and it was more than the something he'd felt was wrong the entirety of the six weeks since they dispelled Caldwell's spirit from Miles and even more than the something that had been nagging his gut all day.

As he took in their room, it hit him.

The dogs were not there.

This wasn't unusual but it was rare. If they weren't with him then they were with Belle. Or, oftentimes, Baron was with him and Gretl was with Belle.

But usually one or the other of them were close.

"If you need a phone, honey, mine's in my bag on the bed," Belle continued to talk through the door.

Jack moved to her bag on the bed, seeing some of the contents scattered over the duvet as he called out to Belle, "Do you know where the dogs are?"

"They're not with you?"

That nag in his gut clawed deeper as Jack sorted through her stuff on the bed and in her bag but found no phone.

"Fucking hell," he muttered, rounding the bed and pulling the house phone from its charger as he called back, "No, they're not with me."

He wasn't surprised when he hit the on button on the phone, put it to his ear and found it dead.

He wasn't surprised because five minutes before when he'd been unable to locate his mobile, he'd tried this in his study.

His eyes moved to the windows to see the rain driving against the panes.

And he wasn't surprised the house phone was dead because it happened often during storms.

They were due to meet the others in the drawing room shortly for pre-dinner drinks, so he gave up on making a call that could wait but was about to go in search of the dogs when the door to the bathroom opened and Belle walked out.

Jack stopped dead and stared.

She was wearing a flowing, full-length gown of smoky, dark gray, the color and fabric rich, striking and perfect for her.

One shoulder was bared, the dress held up over her other shoulder with a thick twist of the fabric that gathered the material tight across her chest and midriff, drawing attention to the sleek line of her neck, the elegant drape of her shoulders and the delicate length of her collarbone. The full, fluid fall of her skirt dropped to her feet, which were encased in spike-heeled, black satin sandals with fragile-looking straps, the ones over her red-painted toes embedded with rhinestones.

Her glorious hair was pulled up from her neck and away from her face but fat curls dangled from the arrangement and there were thick tendrils resting against the long line of her neck.

She was also wearing the diamonds he'd given her after she'd flown with him to London and spent the weekend with him there. An event that happened the weekend previous. It was his congratulations gift to her for not losing her mind during the flight. She didn't enjoy it with abandoned glee but she did control her fears and eventually relaxed and settled in.

The jewelry included a necklace that was one row ring of diamonds that sat at the base of her throat starting with a somewhat large but by no means ostentatious gem in the middle that became smaller as they rounded her neck. It had a matching bracelet, all the same size diamonds, and two-carat diamond studs for her ears.

Although not ostentatious, as would not befit Belle, there were enough of them and all of them were of the finest quality that the entirety cost a small fortune.

On his Belle wearing that gown, it was a dazzling display.

And last, on her left ring finger was the reason Joy insisted, regardless of Jack's continued concern about the fact they had not discovered Caldwell's plans or sent Myrtle and Lewis home, that they have the small, intimate dinner party they were having that night.

His engagement ring.

A Bennett heirloom cluster of diamonds surrounding a large cushion-cut diamond in the middle.

It was the reason for their trip to London the weekend before. It was the ring he slid on her finger when he'd officially asked her to marry him and she'd done exactly what she told him she'd do and immediately said yes. That was after she burst into tears but before she'd thrown herself in his arms and kissed him.

The dress she was wearing that she designed, the casual elegance with which she wore it and her unassuming beauty was what she gave him. The diamonds were what Jack could give her. The contentment registering in her eyes and her ease in her surroundings was what they could give each other.

All of it in one beautiful, shapely, petite woman. She embodied everything not only good and right between them but also, Jack thought uncharacteristically dramatically, in the entire fucking world.

"Weird, where *are* the dogs?" she asked, looking around and, for some adorable reason, twitching her wrist with the diamond bracelet on it.

"Belle, come here."

His voice was thick, deeper than normal, strange, and likely because of it her eyes shot to him. Then she stopped moving and studied him.

"Are you okay?" she asked, tipping her head to the side.

God, he fucking loved her. All she had to do was tip her head to the side and it hit him like a bullet.

That was how much he loved Belle Abbot.

"No," he answered and concern moved over her face so he finished, "But I will be when you come here."

The concern fled, her face grew soft and she moved directly to him, close, fitting herself right to his front, her arms sliding around his middle inside his dinner jacket, and as she did this his closed around her.

She tipped her head back and looked direct in his eyes.

"Okay, I'm here," she said softly. "Now are you okay?"

"Absolutely."

She smiled her sweet, small smile, the tips of her beautiful lips tilting up and she pressed closer.

"You know what I love?" she asked.

"What do you love?" Jack asked back.

"That Joy is doing this, celebrating us and it's just family and close friends. That she's happy with that. That you're happy with that. And that tonight I can wear a pretty dress and enjoy myself with the man I love who I'm going to marry with people who are important to me close and I don't have to mingle."

Jack grinned down at her, tightened his arms and dipped his head close. "If you like, our wedding can be the same."

Her brows drew together. "Are you sure?"

"I'd marry you in a Registry Office with only my family, your family and Yasmin there. I don't care."

She grinned back and agreed, "Then let's do that."

That was when Jack's brows drew together. "You don't want a big cake, a big dress, a big bouquet and a big day?"

"I didn't say I didn't want a big cake, a big dress and a big bouquet, and even if it was just you and me, it would still be a big day." She got up on her toes and finished on a whisper, "The biggest, *best* day ever, Jack Bennett."

Oh yes, he loved Belle Abbot.

"Excellent," he replied. "We'll do it next month."

With this he was awarded one of her lovely startled giggles but she said through it, "Fine by me."

"I'll get Olive on it," Jack remarked.

"Perfect," Belle whispered.

Yes, it would be perfect.

Unable to stop himself and not trying, he dipped his head even closer in order to kiss her.

Immediately, his Belle kissed him back. And Jack enjoyed it so much he decided to take his time and keep doing it.

So he did.

Therefore, when he finally stopped kissing his very soon-to-be wife and guided her to the drawing room, neither Jack Bennett nor Belle Abbot gave another thought to missing dogs or mobile phones.

They were both thinking more pleasant thoughts, such as their recent kisses and their bright future.

Lewis and Myrtle

"Lewis, Lewis, *Lewis*!" Myrtle cried, her ghostly body darting to her brother who, as usual during a storm, was floating at the window in the eastern turret, looking out and being moody.

"I told you," he said to the storm, "I don't want to go to the party, Myrtle. You go. Belle said she wants us there so go. But I'm going to stay here."

"Lewis, no! It isn't about the party," Myrtle exclaimed and something in her tone made her brother turn his eyes to her. "Something's wrong, Lewis. I *feel* it. We have to tell Belle."

"We can't tell Belle, Myrtle. Tonight she and Jack are celebrating their engagement. She'll be with him probably all night," Lewis reminded her. "And, by the way, if you go to the party, you can't let Jack see you. You have to be invisible unless he isn't looking."

She grabbed his vaporous hand and tugged. "All right, I'll be invisible if Jack's around but we have to go. We have to find someone. We have tell *someone* that *something* is *not right*."

She watched her brother's eyes narrow on her before he asked quietly, "What do you feel, Myrtie Mine?"

"I don't know," she shook her head, "I don't know. I just know it's *bad*."

Lewis studied his sister for only one second before he nodded.

"Right, then let's tell Angus."

Myrtle's phantom shoulders drooped with relief.

"Thank you, Lewis," Myrtle whispered and, holding hands, they floated swiftly to the stairwell and down but suddenly and inexplicably, something happened. It was as if their ghost forms hit a wall and they couldn't move.

"What on—?" Lewis muttered, looking down to his feet that strangely felt like they had bounds tied to his ankles and he saw the strange markings on the floor.

"*Lewis!*" Myrtle shrieked, his head snapped up and his eyes focused on the shadowy figure in the shadowed stairwell. "*Oh no, Lewis! It's her!*"

Her eyes were on them. They were gleaming through the dark with a preternatural light.

And she was smiling.

The children watched as she lifted her finger to her lips then she dropped her hand, leaned forward and touched the markings on the landing.

"That witch didn't think to protect *you*," she whispered through her manic smile.

Then she straightened, whirled and dashed away.

Cassandra and Yasmin

"I'm so sorry we're running late," Yasmin said words to the windscreen that were meant for Cassandra who was sitting to her left in the passenger seat of her Audi. "I know it's just family but it *is* formal and I couldn't decide what to wear. This is a hazard when you have three closets full of clothes."

"I'm sorry too, mate," Cassandra replied quietly, her eyes riveted to the road, her hand clenched around her mobile, which she'd tried and failed several times to use to phone Jack, Belle, Joy, The Point, Rachel, Lila, Jensen and Angus. "But we'll get there."

Before Cassandra left, Jack never believed she was clairvoyant.

Now, if he'd bloody answer his bloody phone, he'd find out she was.

And if he'd bloody answer his bloody, *bloody* phone, she could maybe save Belle's life.

And, bonus, free the children.

"You need to hurry, Yasmin," Cassandra said, still talking quietly.

She had not shared the vision she'd had while getting ready for the party at Yasmin's house. She didn't want to alarm Yasmin because the woman could be dramatic but mostly because she was driving.

"I know," Yasmin agreed. "But we're starting with drinks so we'll just miss a martini or two."

They'd miss a lot more if she didn't pull her finger out.

On this thought, her mobile rang in her hand and Cassandra saw it said, Lorna Calling on the display.

She took the call and put it to her ear.

"Hey, mate," she greeted.

"Lach and I are on our way. Lach figured something out and—"

Cassandra cut her off. "The woman."

"What?" Lorna asked.

Without being able to escape for privacy, she said simply, "Vision, Lor. I've seen it. You and Lach need to get down here. *Now*."

"We're both on our way," Lorna assured then disconnected.

"What vision, Cass?" Yasmin asked into the car softly. "Is something wrong?"

"Just go faster, Yasmin," Cassandra answered and the car speeded up, racing through the dark, wet night shrouded in thickening-by-the-second fog.

And Yasmin went fast. Very fast.

Too fast.

"*Yasmin, in the road!*" Cassandra screeched just as the Audi's tires hit a big log that was resting across the road.

Yasmin jerked the wheel automatically even though she'd already hit the log.

The car rolled. Then it rolled again. It rolled another half and a banged-up, unconscious Yasmin Delacourt and Cassandra McNabb in an Audi TT coupe ended upside down on the side of the lane a quarter of a mile away from The Point.

Baron, Gretl and Shadow

The intelligent eyes of the gray horse watched as his turned-back ears heard the two German Shepherds clawing and whining at the stable doors.

They'd been drawn in then locked in.

The big, darker dog gave up to step back and bark as the blonder, smaller dog continued to claw and whine with increasing alarm at the door.

Backing up, the gray stallion lifted up on his powerful hind legs and used its front hoofs to hammer at the stall door.

Then he did it again.

And again.

And Baron barked, Gretl whined and clawed and Shadow beat at his confines as the other horses whinnied and shifted and the rain poured down outside.

Belle

Exiting the bathroom on the way back to the drawing room, four things came to Belle.

One, there still was no Baron or Gretl.

Two, the children had not arrived. They couldn't materialize in front of Jack but they could be there in spirit and find their moments to show themselves to Belle and the others when Jack couldn't see. She knew this, they'd done it before. Not often, they were powerfully fearful of Jack catching a glimpse of them, but they'd done it.

Three, Miles was picking up Olive from the airstrip and due to the weather had called some time earlier when he'd learned her small commuter flight had been delayed. But still, even though the weather was worsening, they were later than expected and no call had come to explain why.

And four, Angus had not come down to have drinks and regale them with stories past of "wee ghosties."

Baron and Gretl could be napping somewhere.

Myrtle and Lewis might be there but since Jack was, they hadn't shown themselves.

And the weather *was* bad. Maybe Miles just assumed they'd understand this and didn't want to interrupt the festivities with an unnecessary call.

But Angus didn't often miss a chance to imbibe. He left a month ago, promising, like Cassandra had, to continue researching and looking for someone who might be able to assist them in getting Myrtle and Lewis home. That didn't mean he hadn't been around, mostly to check in, check Cassandra's protection spells, eat their food, drink their booze and regale them with stories past of "wee ghosties."

As quick as her strappy sandals would allow her to do so, she moved to Jack's study to look for the dogs.

When she got there, she flipped on the light.

No dogs.

"Strange," she whispered, turned off the light, closed the door and was about to retrace her steps to go to the staircase and Angus's room when she heard a noise come from the other end of the hall.

That was probably Elaine, Gemma or Carrie. Elaine was cooking. Gemma and Carrie were serving.

Belle smiled to herself. A dinner party at home with family and friends and the women were all in gowns, the men in formal attire and they were being waited on.

"I suppose I'll eventually get used to it," she murmured, thinking it wouldn't be hard.

She liked to dress up, especially since Jack so obviously appreciated it. She also liked to see Jack dressed up. He was beautiful always but criminally attractive became (nearly) unbearably attractive when he was in his well-cut tuxedo.

She began to move again toward the stairwell but another noise came from the other end of the hall. She stopped and looked that way.

"Elaine?" she called and there was no answer.

She took one step in that direction.

"Gemma?" she tried and when she got nothing she tried again. "Carrie?"

She took two more steps then suddenly the hall was plunged into darkness as the lights went out. A nanosecond later, the space was lit by a flash of lightning that was followed by a deep, bellowed roll of thunder.

"The storm," she muttered. "The electricity went out because of the storm."

She had no idea why she was talking to herself. She only thought it best to get back to Jack. He was protective, she'd been gone for a bit and there were no lights in the house. He'd want to know where she was. She'd go to him and ask him to find Angus and the dogs.

She turned back toward the drawing room just as another flash of lightning lit the hall.

And right before her stood a woman, her wide eyes bright with an unnatural light, her lips curled into an evil smile.

Belle opened her mouth to scream and braced to flee, and in her terror missed the fact that the woman's arm was raised over her head so she also missed that arm slamming down.

She didn't miss the pain that radiated throughout her skull when something crashed into it.

However, this lasted nary a moment before all went black and Belle Abbot collapsed to the thick carpet covering the stone floor of one of the many halls in Chy An Als Point.

Jack

The feeling seized him, so fierce he was paralyzed for a split second.

Then he moved and spoke, the piercing pain in his gut intensified to such an extreme, it was nearly debilitating.

But he didn't hesitate.

"Jensen," he barked, "come with me. I'll get you a torch. Then you find Angus. Mum, Lila, Rachel, you stay here."

He was striding to the door as her heard his mother start, "Jack, what on—?"

And Lila's, "Is something—?"

As well as Rachel's, "Where's Belle?"

He stopped at the door and saw Jensen close. The man didn't ask a single question. He was a man. He was also a father. He felt Jack's mood and he wasn't wasting time.

"None of you leave this room," Jack ordered.

"Jack, darling, what—?" Joy began.

"Do not...*leave*...this room," he clipped, jerked his chin up to Jensen and prowled out.

He was stalking down the hall, Jensen on his heels when Jensen asked, "Dude, you gonna fill me in?"

Jack didn't tell him that he knew. That he simply, for no reason that was sane, *knew* that Belle was in danger.

Instead, he shared, "The lights are out. The phones are out. Both Belle and my mobiles have disappeared. The dogs have disappeared. Angus has not joined us. Cassandra and Yasmin have not yet arrived. And Belle went to the bathroom too fucking long ago. None of this is a coincidence. Something's wrong."

"The storm—" Jensen started.

"The storm does not explain *two* missing mobiles, Angus's unusual delay in taking the opportunity to drink whisky and my dogs disappearing."

"Cassandra's protection—"

"Is magical," Jack finished for him. "If the threat to Belle is real, human, in this fucking realm, it doesn't..."

He turned into the kitchen, trailed off and stopped dead.

This was because he found the kitchen dark and deserted. No Elaine. No staff.

This was also because his mind's eye brought up a picture of Belle.

Always but always she wore Cassandra's protection amulet around her neck. Even to bed.

Tonight, she was wearing his diamonds around her neck.

No amulet.

"*Fuck!*" he hissed then strode to the drawer with the torches.

"Jack," Jensen whispered, his concern heavy in his tone.

He handed Jensen a torch and tagged one for himself.

Then he issued orders, "Find Angus. As you try to find him, find your mobile or *any* mobile. Get it to Lila. She calls nine nine nine. She calls Cassandra. She calls and checks on Yasmin if Yasmin is not with Cassandra. Then she calls Lachlan and Lorna and she tells them to get to The Point as soon as they can. In that order. You don't wait for her to make these calls. You keep searching for Angus and my fucking dogs."

"Right," Jensen whispered, didn't hesitate and Jack saw the torchlight bobbing as the older man raced from the kitchen.

Taking a deep breath even as he moved swiftly, Jack turned on his own torch and strode to the door he'd exited months ago with Belle the night they met when he was guiding her out to show her the stables.

He moved into the dense fog and pouring rain as lightning lit the night, bouncing against the looming fog, making it eerie, threatening. And he moved through it as the flash disappeared and the thunder rolled.

But he wasn't headed to the stables.

He was headed in a sprint to Belle's cliff.

The site of Brenna Addison's murder.

Mickey

"We have to land, mate. This storm, this fog—" his pilot friend said into Mickey's earphones.

"We're over Devon," Mickey cut him off.

"We won't make it to Cornwall in this weather," his friend retorted as the plane bounced alarmingly in the storm.

"Try," Mickey bit out.

"Mick—"

"*Try*," Mickey growled.

The pilot growled back but it was merely an angry, worried sound, not an intelligible word and he flew on thinking if they got out of this alive, Mickey Dempsey was going to owe him big.

Huge.

Lorna

Lorna, driving too fast on the rain-slicked roads through the fog so thick she could barely see past the headlamps on her car, took her life in her hands (further) when she snatched up the ringing mobile sitting on the seat beside her.

She didn't look at the display. She just took the call and put it to her ear.

"Talk to me," she ordered.

"You close?" Lach asked in her ear.

"The good news is, no one but me is stupid enough to be on the roads tonight, even the police, so I've got a straight shot. The bad news is, I've called Cass three times since I connected with her and got no answer. I've called The Point, no answer. Belle, Jack, Lila—"

"Me too," he interrupted her. "And I've called Uncle Angus six times. Nothing."

"I don't have a good feeling about this, Lach," she warned, her voice low.

"Me either, love," he whispered. "Can you think of anyone close we can send there?"

"Nope," she answered.

"Fuck," he muttered then, louder, he ordered, "Drive but be safe. I'll see you there."

"See you there."

She disconnected, tossed the phone on the seat beside her, concentrated as best she could and drove.

Fast.

Jack

She wasn't there.

Belle wasn't on her cliff.

Brenna's cliff.

Breathing heavily, soaked to the skin, terrified out of his mind, he looked up at the dim shadow of The Point looming over him in the fog.

Lightning rent the air followed by thunder and he saw them.

He saw them.

Two children in the window at the landing on the stairwell in the eastern turret. Two children who looked to be shouting and banging their fists against an invisible barrier.

Myrtle and Lewis.

Jack Bennett blinked.

And when his eyes opened, he was no longer Jack.

He was Joshua.

And his children were up there.

So without hesitation, his long legs moved, racing toward The Point.

Racing to his children.

Caleb

Caleb Caldwell's body swayed violently and he blinked.

Then he felt it.

Rain pummeling his skin.

Earth beneath his feet.

He looked down.

Earth beneath his feet, solid, real, *right there*.

He was not in Bennett's brother.

He was real.

He was himself.

He was *back*.

His head shot up and his eyes focused on the drifting fog, seeing James Bennett racing through it toward The Point.

Caleb smiled.

Then he raced after him.

Angus

"Dude, you okay? Dude? Angus? *Angus*?"

Jensen was shaking him. Angus, head foggy and killing him, blinked, feeling thick moisture on his face as he pushed up.

"God, man, *God*! I can't find any fucking phones, and dude, you totally need an ambulance."

Angus heard his voice, saw his shadow but it penetrated that the room he was in and beyond was dark.

Then he remembered.

"The other," he whispered.

Jensen ignored his whisper and ranted on, "Something's *whacked*, man. *Whacked*. I found those girls, the woman, you know, the servants. They were asleep, dude. *Asleep*. All piled on top of each other in a corner in a room off the kitchen. Nothin' I could do would wake 'em, Angus. They...were...*out*."

"The other," Angus repeated on a whisper.

"What?" Jensen asked.

He tried to focus on the man's shadow. "The other."

"You're fucked up, dude. You got a head wound. Sit tight, I'm gonna—"

His hand darting out, with fierce strength he latched on to Jensen Abbot's forearm.

"There is another," he declared, his voice getting stronger. "A partner. A woman. A *witch*. Belle's in danger."

"Tell me something I don't know. My baby girl has disappeared. The dogs—"

Swiftly, ignoring the lightening in his head that caused him to sway slightly, Angus got to his feet.

"Let's go," he stated, moving toward the shadowed door.

"Dude, you need to—"

Angus whirled to him, his kilt twirling. "Jensen, let's *go*."

Then he turned back and ran to and through the door, not waiting to see if Jensen followed.

Belle

"Please turn that off," Belle whispered, pressing into a corner of a room, her head foggy and killing her, blinking against the light from the torch being shined into her face, feeling thick moisture dribbling through the hair on the side of her head.

"Yes, you're pretty. Very pretty," she whispered back, and it was so dark, her head muddled from the blow, the torchlight blinding her, Belle couldn't see her. She couldn't even see what room she was in.

"I need to—" she started.

"I knew, of course. I saw your pictures in the paper, *all of them*. But he told me. Again and again and again and *again* how pretty you were. Prettier than me. Better than me. Your eggs were the best in the world. Your hair was so soft, such a pretty color. Your eyes, so gray, so beautiful. Your clothes so fashionable. And you designed them. *You*. The Tiny

Dynamo. His beautiful Belle. His beautiful, sweet, *perfect* Belle who could do...no...*wrong*."

"Who are you?" Belle whispered, knowing, whoever she was, she was insane.

She shined the light in Belle's face, Belle blinking at the light and the throbbing in her head, and this went on for long moments before she finally whispered her answer.

"I'm nobody."

Baron, Gretl and Shadow

Having beaten down his stall door, Shadow galloped through the stables and proceeded to hammer at the stable doors with his hooves as now both Baron and Gretl barked loud and howled louder.

The latch no match for Shadows powerful blows, it gave way and both doors swung open.

Without hesitation, all three animals burst into the dark, stormy night.

Jack/Joshua

Joshua raced up the turret taking the stone steps two at a time. He rounded the curving stairwell to the landing and both of his children's eyes came to him.

But there was something wrong with them.

He could *see through them*.

"*Jack, no!*" Lewis cried, his son's eyes on him, wide and horrified.

But he didn't falter as he charged to them. They floated, yes, *floated* away from him, across the landing, their young bodies slamming into what appeared to be an invisible barrier behind them so when he raced across the landing they were easy to catch.

And catch them he did. Dropping to his knees, he swung his long arms out to the sides and curled them around their wee bodies.

Bodies that solidified instantly at his touch, coming real, forming flesh, so when Joshua held his children to him, he felt their warmth against his frame and more, *they* felt the power of his.

"Oh my gracious, Lewis," Myrtle breathed.

"You're safe," Joshua whispered, pulling them closer.

"Belle," Lewis whispered back, Joshua's head came up and he looked to his son.

"Lewis?" he questioned.

"Belle," Lewis repeated in a whisper then louder, "Belle." Joshua watched his son's eyes dart over his shoulder and he shouted, "*Poppa!*"

Joshua released them, got to his feet and whirled just as Caleb Caldwell hit the landing, his arms swinging out, both his hands wrapped around a thick, heavy candlestick, and he struck.

Belle

"Sick of it," the madwoman whispered as Belle pulled herself together, and it occurred to her hazy brain she should get the heck out of there. "Sick of hearing it. Sick of *feeling* it. *Sick of it!*"

"I—" Belle started just as she started to edge along the wall to escape, but suddenly of its own accord, her body locked.

Then she blinked.

And when she opened her eyes, she was no longer Belle.

She was Brenna.

And her children and Joshua were in danger.

So without hesitation, her mind clear, the pain in her scalp dulled, her legs moved to start racing toward the door.

She only got two steps before she was caught, shoved back and she hit the wall.

She stared at the shadowy woman who stood before her.

"Let me pass," she demanded and for her words she felt the sharp sting of a slap on her cheek and her head jerked violently to the side as the woman struck her.

"You've spoken enough over the years, Belle Abbot, and you weren't even *there*. Now, *I* get to do the talking," the woman said to her.

Brenna ignored this lunacy, one thing on her mind, and started again toward the door but did not get very far before the woman again was upon her. She shoved, she pushed, they grappled and kicked.

"Why are you doing this!" she cried as she struggled. "Let me pass! My husband and children need me."

"*I don't care!*" Came the demented shriek in response as Brenna was viciously shoved away.

She lost control of her limbs and reeled back, but with effort she remained standing only to see the woman had grabbed hold of something and was coming her way swiftly, arm raised.

She was close, there wasn't time to escape so Brenna cowered and lifted her arms to deflect the blow.

The woman didn't make it because Joshua's two Alsatians came barking and snarling into the room. Baron leaped through the air and landed on the woman, knocking her sideways. The dog kept at her as Gretl came darting to Brenna then retreating quickly to the door, darting back to Brenna and to the door again, whining.

"You know where they are," Brenna whispered.

Gretl woofed softly.

"Take me," Brenna urged, Gretl took off out the door with Brenna racing after her.

Racing to her husband and children.

Angus

With Jensen at his heels, Angus turned the corner to the stairwell of the eastern turret and he slammed full body into Jack Bennett.

He wheeled back two feet and stared at the shadowy figures.

No, not just Jack.

Jack holding Myrtle firm to his hip with one arm, his other hand engulfing in a strong grip the hand of Lewis.

Both the children were real. Not phantoms.

Real.

"Now this is one in all my years I've never seen," he muttered, eyeing the apparently alive and breathing children.

"Holy fuck," Jensen muttered behind him.

"Caldwell's on the stairwell," Jack informed them and Angus shook off his surprise as Jack strode forward, through and beyond the two men. "I need to get my children to safety and find my wife."

"Your children?" Angus asked, following him and looking at him closely, or, more accurately, looking at his broad, soaking wet, dinner-suit-jacketed back.

"Your wife?" Jensen asked, following Angus.

Jack stopped and turned with the children.

"I need a safe place for the children so I can find *my wife*," he clipped.

"Uh, right, lad," Angus muttered.

Wife, children, they were not dealing with Jack.

They had Joshua.

Well, at least he'd seen *this* before.

Angus turned to Jensen. "Where's Lila?"

"Drawing room," Jensen answered.

Angus looked back to Jack or, he was guessing, Joshua. "Lila will keep them safe."

"Drawing room," Jack murmured, turned and strode swiftly through the house to the drawing room, taking the children with him.

He opened the doors and Angus had the chance to see the women had lit candles so there was dim light. He also had the chance to see the faces pale and hear the gasps.

But this was all he had the chance to see.

They all turned when they heard a dog woofing and saw Belle racing behind the dog on her high-heeled shoes, her hands in her skirt holding it up.

"My love," Angus heard Jack murmur.

"My sweet!" Angus then heard Belle cry.

Then Angus and the rest watched Belle race directly into Jack, throwing her arms around him, Myrtle and catching Lewis up in her embrace.

Well, it seemed Belle was Brenna if the presence of living, breathing Myrtle and Lewis didn't faze her.

This also didn't faze Angus but it fazed Jensen.

"Holy fuck," Jensen muttered.

Still holding on, Belle arched her upper body back and caught Jack's eyes.

"Something's amiss," she declared at the same time Jack announced, "There is danger."

"Am I seeing what I think I'm seeing?" Rachel whispered.

"If it's what I'm seeing, you're seeing what I think I'm seeing," Lila whispered in answer.

"I think I'm seeing the same thing too." Joy was also whispering.

The entire room stilled and braced as a commotion came from the hall, there were running footsteps and then a dripping wet, formally clad, shoeless Yasmin and an equally dripping wet somewhat formally but definitely eccentrically clad Cassandra skidded to the halt at the doors.

"*Caleb Caldwell had a partner and she was a witch!*" Yasmin shrieked.

"You stole my thunder, mate," Cassandra muttered.

But Yasmin's eyes rounded, her torso swayed back and she cried, "Oh my *God*! Myrtle and Lewis are *real*!"

Cassandra took in this fact and her eyes cut to Angus. "Have you ever seen this?"

"No' ever," Angus replied, shaking his head then concluded, "Best part of the job. Can have years in it and still be surprised."

Cassandra looked back at Jack, Belle and the children, murmuring, "This is going to be the talk of the Winterfest Coven meeting, seriously."

Jack cut in at this point and Angus's eyes moved to him to see his on Angus.

"I know you but I do not. I do not understand this. I also do not care. Caleb Caldwell is in my home. I was able to incapacitate him to get my children to safety although I doubt he will be unconscious for long. I also doubt he has left this house. He is still here. He is, as usual, intent to do mischief. And we cannot delay in finding him and dealing with him."

"There is a woman," Belle put in quickly. She was now at Jack's side, one of her arms curling Lewis close, the other arm holding Jack and Myrtle. "She's in the west wing. One of the bedrooms." Her head tipped back and she looked at Jack. "My beloved, I fear she's demented."

"Caldwell and his partner," Cassandra said and moved into the room, pulling Yasmin with her and closing the doors behind her. She turned to face the congregation that automatically gathered together. "Right, I had a vision," she announced. "Past and future. Caldwell allied with a local witch. He did this on the hush-hush. No one knew about it. Unfortunately, he did this in the only way he knew how. He beat her into submission, forcing her to help him. From what I gather, she's been reincarnated too. And to make unhappy matters unhappier, she's been reincarnated into Calvin Cole's wife."

"Oh lordy," Rachel whispered.

"Shit," Jensen muttered.

"Great, just great," Lila snapped.

"She's also here," Cassandra added. "Both of them are. The spell Caldwell forced her to cast was that Brenna and Joshua would never be together, never happy, never living their lives to their fullest. In order to do this, if they were to be reincarnated, it would happen at a time where Caldwell and his partner were also reincarnated so that they could stop Brenna and Joshua or, in our time, Jack and Belle from living happily ever after."

"So how do we stop them?" Joy asked.

"They both have to be destroyed," Cassandra answered. "If he's taken out, he won't come back. And if she's banished to hell, that's it for her. But there's a complication just because Caleb Caldwell was a full-blown ass. As we know, the children are ghosts, or um," she eyed the wee ones before she went on, "they *were*. And this was at Caldwell's behest because, seriously, this guy was one major dick. He forced the witch to put a spell on the children to tether their spirits here after she smothered them. They could appear before anyone *except* their father or any master of this house. If they did, Caldwell would return to this earth, alive and breathing, so he could have fun." She eyed Jack and the kids and finished, "I'm guessing this happened."

"Indeed," Jack answered and pulled Belle and the children closer to him.

"This means, I'm afraid," Cassandra went on, "that all that work I did protecting against magical mayhem was for nothing. We're dealing with two humans here. And that means anything goes."

"Shit," Jensen muttered gain.

"So why are the children real and Jack and Belle are, um...not exactly Jack and Belle?" Lila asked.

Cassandra shook her head. "I'm not sure but my guess is, love's a powerful thing."

"What?" Belle whispered and Cassandra's eyes went to her.

"Love's a powerful thing, mate. It holds a magic all its own that no one can control. When there's love, and a lot of it, anything can happen."

"Oh my," Joy whispered.

"So we must destroy Caldwell and this witch," Jack brought the matter to hand.

"You got it," Cassandra answered.

"And how do you propose we do that?" Jack asked.

"Well, him, he's not supposed to be here so we can do whatever we want with him. Her, she's real, from this time, but she's got the reincarnated bitch witch attached to her soul. So we need to get it out."

"Perform the same ceremony as you did on Miles?" Joy queried.

"Exactly," Cassandra replied.

"Then that's what we'll do," Jack stated, bending to put Myrtle on her feet.

"Uh, we kinda need the bitch that's got the bitch witch in her to do it," Cassandra informed him as Jack straightened then pinned his eyes to her.

And his voice was a low rumble when he replied, "Then let's find her."

Cassandra grinned.

Belle wet her lips.

Angus began to move to go get his whip.

The doors to the room opened and Lachlan and Lorna, dripping wet, strode in.

Upon arrival, Lorna announced, "Lach should give up the family business and become a race car driver."

At the same time Lachlan spied the children, his red brows shot up and he muttered, "Bloody, fucking hell."

Caleb

"As before, you take care of the children, I'll deal with Brenna," Caleb ordered.

She shook her head.

"I want Belle."

"I get Brenna."

"I want *Belle*."

He raised his hand and brought it down hard on her cheekbone. So hard, her head whipped to the side and she staggered.

"*I'll* deal with Brenna. Then I'll dispatch Joshua. *You* take the children."

Righting herself, hand to her cheek, instinct caused her to agree, "Oh-okay."

"Let us go," he stated, lifting his hand toward her.

Instinct again forced her to lift hers to him, he took hold and dragged her from the room.

Jack/Joshua

"I do not like this," he growled.

"I do not like it either," Brenna whispered, and with his arm already around her, he pulled her closer.

"Trust us," the Scot he did not know, but still did, assured.

Joshua stopped at the door to the outside that was in the kitchen and locked eyes with the Scot. "My wife and I should be with our children."

"We have to lure him out there and we also have to lure her to the children." The Scot got close and his voice dipped low. "We'll no' steer you wrong, lad. Trust us."

Joshua held his gaze but he already knew, though he didn't, that he could.

Without time to unravel it, he nodded, turned to the pegs by the door and snatched up a rain slicker. He helped his wife into it then he turned her to face him and settled his hands at her neck.

"All will be well, my love," he whispered.

"I hope so," she whispered back.

He bent his head to touch his lips to hers, gave her neck a reassuring squeeze then he turned and led her into the stormy night with three men following.

The Other

She opened the door and saw the candlelight immediately just as she smelled the incense.

And she also instantly spied the children huddling together in the middle of the room.

The little girl let out a short, stifled scream before she turned her face into the boy's neck, and she watched the boy's arms tighten around his sister as he stared at her defiantly.

She grinned her manic grin as she entered the room.

She got four feet in, noting the children didn't retreat right before the doors swung shut behind her and five women jumped her.

She struggled but only briefly.

She'd long since learned when to give up a fight.

Joy and Rachel

Holding down one of the flailing woman's legs, Joy turned her head to Rachel who was holding down the other one and whispered, "You didn't have to pull her hair."

Rachel looked to her friend. "Yeah I did."

Joy fought back a grin, considering it might be rude, and continued, "Well, then you didn't have to pull it so hard."

"That's debatable," Rachel muttered and shifted aside but kept hold on the leg that Lorna had moved to in order to tie it down.

"By the way," Joy began and Rachel looked back at her, "have I told you your dress is lovely?"

Rachel grinned a big grin. "Hey, thanks. Belle designed it. And, also by the way, yours is too."

"Bloody hell," Lorna muttered, yanked the rope tight and the woman cried out.

Joy bit her lip but it was in another effort to try not to grin.

Rachel didn't bother.

She just smiled.

Belle/Brenna

Arms tight around each other, they stood together on the cliff, the lightning and thunder gone, the fog surrounding them, the wind whipping at their hair and clothing.

"We must go home," she whispered into his neck, pressing deeper, and his arms got tighter.

"When this is done, we'll get the children and go home," Joshua whispered back.

"I've missed them." Her voice was a throb and his arms got even tighter.

"And I too," he murmured but the low sound was harsh.

Her head tipped back and she caught his beautiful, striking green eyes. Eyes Joshua Bennett shared down the line with his heir, James.

"I've missed you too, my beloved."

One of his hands came up to cup her jaw and his face dipped close, his voice was low and rumbly when he replied, "And I you, my love."

Before he could do what she knew he was about to do, what she loved, what he did so very frequently in their time together, touch his mouth to hers, she felt him.

Joshua did too for the pads of his fingers tensed into her skin, his eyes narrowed angrily and his head came up.

She turned in the circle of her husband's arms and watched as the figure formed through the fog.

Her heart clenched, her stomach lurched but her hand itched.

And, not knowing what came over her, she tore free of her husband's hold, strode forward, and before he could begin to know her intention she pulled back a hand and slapped her should-be-dead, former husband across his face so hard his head snapped to the side.

His burning eyes slowly came back to her but she did not cower.

"Tonight," she whispered, "you burn in hell."

Then she put her hands to his chest and pushed, her feet moving, shoving him back, going with him, straight toward the cliff.

Myrtle and Lewis

Myrtle's head snapped up and her eyes found Lewis's.

"Mumma," she whispered.

"Poppa," he whispered back.

The witch spirit tore free of the woman arched on the divan keening a mighty, frightening keen, and it exploded in bright white sparks that flew all over the room.

The children didn't see it.

They were racing to the door.

Racing to their parents.

Racing to the cliff.

Lachlan

"Belle! Brenna! Whoever the fuck! Stop fighting!" Lachlan gritted in her ear as he struggled to keep hold of the madly fighting woman in his arms as the clash of Bennett and Caldwell played out on the edge of the cliff with two German shepherds barking their encouragement.

"Let me go!" she cried, wrenching her body sharply but he held on.

"Guide him to the cliff, lad! Throw him over!" Angus boomed, he and Jensen both circling the combatants, keeping the arena small, shoving Caldwell back toward Bennett's fists anytime he tried to escape.

"I'm..." Bennett grunted on a punch landed on Caldwell's jaw. His fist curled in Caldwell's shirt jerked Caldwell straight again and he went on in a grunt, "Having..." and he landed another brutal blow, this time on Caldwell's cheekbone. "*Fun!*" he finished, delivered another vicious strike, Caldwell's legs gave out from under him and Bennett let him crash to the ground.

"Dude, seriously, it's cold, raining and I'm hungry and wearin' this fuckin' stupid suit. Can you just throw him over the cliff so we can get inside and I can fuckin' *eat*?" Jensen requested just as Bennett pulled back his leg and landed a powerful kick to the prone man's gut.

"Not done," he replied.

"Laddie, your woman is also out in the cold and rain and hasn't had dinner," Angus reminded Bennett, and Bennett's head came up, his eyes going to Belle.

"Are you all right, poppet?" he asked considerately.

"Keep going," she encouraged.

"Fuck me," Lach muttered.

Bennett landed another kick.

"Mumma! Poppa!" The cries carried through the night then the two children formed out of the fog, racing toward Belle.

Lach let her go so she could crouch, arms wide, and both of them slammed into her body. Her frame rocked with their colliding weight but her arms curled around the children and she stayed strong.

"It's all right, my sweetlings. Everything is fine. Poppa is taking care of the bad man and then everything will be fine," she assured them as

Lorna, Cassandra, Lila, Rachel and Joy raced after the children and stopped at the cliff.

"The witch?" Bennett asked sharply, turning away from Caldwell who was prone and groaning on the cliff edge.

"Well, the bitch witch, dispelled and sent to hell," Cassandra started her update. "The just plain bitch, tied to the divan in the drawing room, and I zapped her with a sleeping spell so she'll wake up, hmm...I'm guessing...Wednesday."

"Excellent," Bennett muttered at the same time Joy shrieked, "*Jack!*"

And all eyes turned to see Caldwell had pulled himself up, he had an arm reaching out toward Bennett and just when he would grab hold, out of nowhere, a huge, gray horse came galloping to the cliff, on its back was Miles Bennett and in front of him, Jack's PA, Olive Mayfair.

Jack threw his body one way, Miles and Olive leaned forward, the horse reared back on its hind legs and struck out at Caldwell with its front hooves.

Caldwell reeled back, one step, two then he fell over the side of the cliff.

"*Breeeeeeeehhhhhhnnaaaaaaaahhhhh!*" he shouted on his way down, the name stopping abruptly.

Everyone stood still, unmoving and not speaking.

And they did this until Lorna muttered, "Well, that was a bit of an anti-climax."

At the same time, some man Lachlan had never seen came jogging up, stopped dead and stared at the two children in period clothing being held in Belle's arms.

"Fucking hell," the man Lachlan didn't know was Mickey Dempsey whispered before his eyes shot to Bennett. "Jesus, mate. It's true."

And after the man uttered these stunned words, Miles, incongruously sitting bareback and drenched to the skin on top of an enormous gray steed with a middle-age woman held in his arm, said drolly to Jack, "Sorry we're late."

And at that, Lachlan burst out laughing.

Lila

"I'm not sure," Rachel whispered, huddled with Lila and Jensen at the bottom of the stairs that Belle, Jack and the children just disappeared over the top of.

"It'll be fine, baby," Jensen soothed, holding her in his arms.

"But—"

"Rachel, my darling," Lila stated, tearing her eyes from the top of the stairs and smiling at her beautiful, beloved daughter. "It'll be fine."

She watched her daughter draw in a breath.

Then she watched her nod.

Lila drew in her own breath.

Then she turned toward the drawing room, muttering, "I need a drink," and thinking, as was her wont, dramatically, that not in all of history were truer words ever spoken.

Jack/Joshua

"Sleep," he murmured to the three beings he held in his arms in the big bed.

"But—" Lewis started, lifting his head from Joshua's ribs to look at his father.

"Sleep, son," Joshua whispered.

Lewis held his eyes. Then he nodded and settled in.

Joshua pulled his family closer.

The storm outside had settled. The rain now fell in gentle, calming patters as Joshua Bennett held his family close.

Lewis's head grew heavy on his ribs, and Joshua, as well as Brenna, felt their son drift to sleep. He knew his wife knew this when her head lifted from his shoulder, her neck arched back and her eyes found his.

Joshua bent his neck and touched his mouth to the sweet one of his wife. And when he did, he noted it tasted no less sweet than he remembered, even centuries later.

As he pulled away, he felt Myrtle's head had come up from his stomach and he looked down at his daughter.

"I knew, I just *knew* I always loved you, Jack."

Joshua smiled through the shadows and whispered, "Sleep, Myrtie Mine."

He watched his daughter smile.

Then she whispered back, "All right," and settled in.

His eyes went to Brenna and he also happily took in her smile.

Then she settled in too.

Their weight heavy and beautiful on his body, he felt his girls drift off, the youngest first, the older second.

Not long after, Joshua Bennett's eyes closed.

Hours later, the sun shining bright against his eyelids, Jack opened his eyes and found himself and Belle alone in their bed, Belle snuggled close in his arms.

Dog tags jingled on Belle's side of the bed and Belle stirred.

His arms tightened.

She lifted her head, looked down the length of his body then her head swung to him. He noted her eyes were sleepy but that didn't mean they didn't hold wonder along with sorrow.

"They're home," she whispered.

"Indeed, poppet," Jack whispered back.

He watched the tears fill her eyes.

When the sob hitched in her throat, he pulled her over him and caged her tight in his arms as she burrowed her face in his neck and cried.

Jack sighed.

Last one down.

EPILOGUE
THE PERFECT PLAN

Jack

Mostly as guard, Jack stood on the steps of his ancestral home beside the relatively attractive, definitely pale woman who stood at his side but she still appeared to be shrinking away.

"My PA will contact you," Jack stated. "Her name is Olive Mayfair. When she does, you'll need to give her the number on an account that's in your name only. Once you do, she'll deposit money into it. It will be enough that you can comfortably set up a new life in a place of your choosing. However, if you're with him, in contact with him or if this account also bears his name, you'll be on your own."

"I won't leave him," she muttered to the steps.

"That's your choice," he replied. "It's the wrong one but it's yours."

She was silent.

Jack turned his eyes to the lane, willing the taxi to come down it.

That was when he heard the whispered, "He'll come after me."

Jack looked back at her. "He won't."

She pulled in breath and he actually noted the effort it took her to lift her chin but she didn't catch his eyes.

His heart clenched when her gaze came to rest on his shoulder and she declared in a soft voice, "He will."

"Trust me," Jack stated firmly. "He...will...*not*."

Her head jerked at his tone, her eyes flashed to his then she looked away.

Jack turned his gaze back to the lane and waited.

"Tell your Olive person to call." He heard her mutter and Jack sighed with relief he felt for a woman he didn't know, a woman who had harmed his Belle but still a woman who was broken.

"I will."

"And tell...tell..." she hesitated then said quietly, "tell Belle that I didn't...I'd had enough...last night, I wasn't exactly my—"

Jack looked down at her. "If there's anyone on this earth who understands your behavior of last night, it's Belle. Don't worry. Heal and live your life. But I will say do it elsewhere. I will give you money to start a new life but that's it. There will be no more. Further, I never wish to see you again. And you will not like the consequences if you ever see Belle again."

She nodded immediately.

Jack sighed again, turned his head and finally, thank God, he saw the taxi coming down the lane.

Softly, he said, "You will heal. She did."

"She found a good man."

"She found her strength and it did indeed come from love but not simply mine. If you're smart enough to surround yourself with people who care about you, genuinely and healthily, you'll do the same."

He looked down at her to see her eyes on his face.

"I'll try," she whispered.

"Good," Jack whispered back.

She pulled her lips between her teeth but still, even with that, the ends curled up in a small smile before she quickly looked away and Jack watched her run to the taxi, throw open the door and fold inside.

He watched the taxi drive away.

And after it was gone he realized he didn't ask her name.

He turned and walked up the steps as he looked up them noting that Lila was standing at the top, arms crossed on her chest, head turned, eyes aimed at the now-empty lane.

When he arrived at the top, he stopped close to her and her head tipped back so she could catch his gaze.

"You're a kind man, Jack Bennett," she said quietly.

"She's been living enough of a nightmare. I saw no need to add to it," Jack replied.

"As I said," Lila began, "you're a kind man, Jack Bennett."

"My thanks, Lila," he muttered, feeling his lips twitch, and he threw out an arm to the door for her to precede him.

She didn't move.

Instead, she informed him, "I came out to watch, of course, but I also came out to tell you that beyond those doors lies drama."

Slowly, Jack closed his eyes.

He opened them and asked a question he didn't want to ask, "And that would be?"

"Yasmin," she answered.

"Again, that would be?"

Lila grinned. "Yasmin of the, she's come to the realization after the events of last night that Quincy is the love of her life and she doesn't want to let him go, so the first thing she did this morning was inform him of this fact to which he told her to go jump in a lake variety of drama."

"Fucking hell," Jack muttered, his eyes moving to the door.

"It's full blown and she has Cassandra, Joy and Rachel in attendance in the morning room so, advice, avoid that room," Lila told him.

"So noted," Jack replied.

"Personally," she went on in a conversational way that made Jack look at her, "I'm considering finding Miles and sending him in to comfort her. I've heard he's at the stables. That's my next stop. What do you think of that idea?"

"I think that if Quincy Delacourt is too stupid not to forgive a good woman who did something misguided and emotional because of demons she's grappling with that he should help her to fight and not leave her on her own to fight them, then he deserves to lose that good woman," Jack answered then finished, "And that, Lila, is what I think."

"I'm in complete agreement," Lila stated through a smile, her eyes dancing.

"Do you think I can go and find my fiancée now?" Jack asked politely.

It was Lila who threw her hand out toward the door this time and offered, "Have at it."

"Thank you," Jack muttered and headed to the door.

"See you at lunch," she returned and headed down the steps.

Jack didn't bother to tell her she wouldn't.

It was Sunday. He was on his way to find Belle, gather his dogs, load them all into his car and head to her cottage in St. Ives. This was after he found Olive and told her to clear his schedule for the next week. Her head might explode but after it did, she'd pull herself together and do it.

He was two feet from the door and deciding to ask Olive to clear two weeks when it was pulled open and Angus raced out, eyes wild, kilt swaying madly around his knees.

"Ghosts in Leeds!" he boomed. "Nasty beasties! Must dash!"

Then he darted down the steps to his beat-up white van in the drive.

Jack watched over his shoulder as Angus's white van coughed to life, reversed on a trail of exhaust smoke that gave testimony to the fact that Angus didn't waste precious ghost hunting time by bothering with MOTs, and finally he watched the van speed down the lane.

He did this noting that Angus McPherson never said good-bye. And he did this thinking this was likely because Angus McPherson might leave but he was never gone for long enough to make the unpleasantness of a farewell worth it.

Jack strode through the door Angus left open, closed it behind him and had taken four steps into the hall before Jensen prowled in, spied him and instantly started in.

"Dude! The party last night, a bust. And if you think I'm puttin' on another monkey suit, think again. Not...gonna...happen. Once in my life was enough and I did that when I married Belle's momma. Against my will, I did it again last night, and seriously, Jack, I relive another last night, I wanna be wearin' my ol' standbys. Jeans and a tee." He came to a stop at Jack and announced, "So, tonight, engagement party take two. And I'm takin' care of the *whole* thing. And there won't be a bowtie or a high heel anywhere near this fuckin' place for *my* shindig."

"Belle and I are leaving in approximately half an hour and we won't return for two weeks," Jack replied and Jensen swayed back, his eyes getting big.

"Two weeks?"

"Maybe three," Jack stated.

"Dude," Jensen muttered.

"After that, when we return, by all means, throw a party. Do whatever you wish. The only thing you *can't* do is invite people around with whom Belle isn't completely comfortable."

Jensen threw his hands up in the air, shouting, "Right on!"

Jack shook his head but grinned doing it.

Jensen took in his grin, dropped his hands but socked Jack in one arm and declared, "You're all right, Jack."

"I find your acceptance somewhat disquieting, Jensen," Jack shared honestly but, as expected, Jensen took no offense.

Instead, he burst out laughing, turned and shouted to a woman who was nowhere near, "Rachel! Baby! Party!" And he strode swiftly from the hall.

But in the wrong direction.

Jack didn't inform him of this.

He moved through the hall but only managed to get five more steps in before Mickey Dempsey, who was descending the stairs, captured his attention.

Jack stopped, crossed his arms on his chest and waited.

Dempsey approached him and stopped three feet away.

"Called a taxi," he announced. "It'll be here in a minute."

"Safe journey back to London," Jack replied and Dempsey nodded.

"You'll tell Belle good-bye?" Dempsey asked and Jack noted he only wished his farewell was known to Belle, not any of the others currently under his roof.

"Of course," Jack muttered.

At that Dempsey strangely whispered, "Killing me, mate."

"Pardon" Jack asked.

"This is the story of the century. Fuck, the *millennium*."

"Dempsey, do you honestly believe, even if you could write it, that anyone would believe it?"

Dempsey grinned. "No way in hell. Probably why all the shit that Scot spouted last night over whisky never made the papers. It happens, no one says shit because, if they did, anyone listening would think they're round the bend."

"Precisely," Jack agreed.

"Still pissed off I missed all the action. The end was good but the rest of it sounded phenomenal."

"As an onlooker, perhaps. As a participant, trust me, it wasn't that fun."

Dempsey grinned again.

Jack held his eyes and said quietly, "Your assistance is appreciated."

"First, you paid me. Second, I didn't help much."

"You helped and it was appreciated," Jack reiterated.

Dempsey's gaze stayed locked to Jack's and he nodded.

"Good-bye, Mickey," Jack said.

"Cheers, Jack," Dempsey replied then Jack turned and watched Dempsey walk across the entryway and out the door.

When he closed it behind him, he turned and caught Olive striding down the hall toward him.

"Good," he called, "I don't have to find you."

"Oh Lord, I don't like the look on your face," she observed.

She was going to like what he was going to say a whole lot less.

"I need you to clear my schedule for two weeks," he told her and her eyes bugged out. "For the week after that, maybe two, make it light in case plans change and Belle and I remain on holiday."

"Jack Bennett," she started, "are you telling me, on a Sunday at eleven o'clock in the morning, to clear your schedule for a holiday you've given me exactly six working hours on a *non*-working day to clear?"

"That's what I'm telling you."

She looked to the ceiling but told Jack, "You'll be the death of me."

"Cut the drama, Olive, you'd be bored stiff if I didn't hand you a challenge and do it with frequency and increasing difficulty."

Her eyes snapped back to his face. "Yes, but you aren't supposed to *know* that."

He ignored her statement and ordered, "Clear my schedule."

"For two weeks?"

"Make it a month, just to be on the safe side."

"Death of me," she muttered.

Jack ignored that too, grinned at her then went in search of Belle.

It took him some time but he eventually found her in the easternmost turret, leaning a shoulder against the wall by the window, her eyes aimed to the view of the Cornish cliffs and sea.

He approached her on quiet feet thus she jumped and her eyes shot to his when he got close.

"Hey, honey," she whispered and Jack moved in.

Rounding her, he fitted his front to her back and wrapped his arms around her, one at her chest, one at her ribs. He pulled her close and turned his eyes to the window.

It was late autumn. The air was chill. There wasn't a cloud in the sky. The deep blue of the sea and bright blue of sky was unobstructed except for the rich browns and vibrant greens of the rocky cliffs and their grassy knolls that made up what Jack, with some experience through his wide travels, felt was the most beautiful coastline on the planet.

"Why are you up here, poppet?" Jack asked quietly after she settled into him.

"I don't know," she answered quietly. "I miss Myrtle and Lewis, I guess."

"You want to be near," he surmised and she shrugged. "Love, they're home," he reminded her.

"Yes," she whispered.

"Finally home, Belle."

He felt her chest expand with her breath, she let it go and nodded. Then she fully relaxed into him, her hands gliding along his arms to hold him where he was holding her, her head falling back to rest against his collarbone but the uninjured side pressed lightly into his neck as she kept her gaze trained out the window.

After they stood close for a while, she queried, "So, what's happening down there?"

"Yasmin is having a drama in the morning room. She's decided she wants Quincy back, she told him and his response was that he's refused to take her back."

He heard her swift intake of breath and her hands convulsed on his arms but he kept talking.

"Lila is off to the stables likely on the ruse of working but definitely with the intent of matchmaking. Miles, she reports to me, is there. And Miles, she explained to me, is the person she intends to send in to comfort Yasmin."

"Oh my goodness gracious," she breathed and Jack smiled.

He also continued.

"There are ghosts in Leeds, nasty ones, and Angus and his white van are currently to the rescue."

Her body started shaking gently and he knew she was laughing silently.

He couldn't hear it but it certainly felt good.

"And last," he carried on, "your father is planning his version of our engagement party for when we return in three weeks from wherever it is we're going. We'll start at your cottage and I don't know where we'll end. Perhaps Australia. And perhaps we'll extend our time away to a month."

She turned in his arms and raised shining, happy gray eyes to his.

"A month?"

"Maybe two," he muttered, lost in her eyes in which there was no storm. Just amusement.

And happiness.

And seeing it, Jack decided, he'd be happy to be lost in those gray eyes for a lifetime.

Though, this was a decision he'd made ages ago.

Approximately a millisecond after he first saw them.

"If we're gone two months, we can't get married next month," she reminded him and he grinned.

"Right, then, a month away, come back, get married then go on our honeymoon," Jack declared, and a giggle burst from Belle even as she pressed closer and wound her arms around him.

"That sounds like the perfect plan," she whispered, coming up on her toes.

"Bloody right it does," Jack agreed, dipping his head to hers.

"Love you, Jack," she whispered when his lips hit hers.

"And I you, poppet," he whispered back.

Then in the place over two hundred years before, the ghost of a terrified, newly dead, young boy witnessed the murder of his mother, a man in love kissed the woman who loved him back as the sun shone on Chy An Als Point.

Lachlan

Through the misty dark, Lachlan McPherson walked to the house he left too early the night before.

He was hoping she was home.

Emma.

Except during obvious times when he had to think of other things, like driving like a lunatic and not killing himself or holding a struggling Belle-slash-Brenna so she wouldn't topple over the cliff in her drive for vengeance, he hadn't been able to think of anything else.

Anything.

But Emma.

This was unusual.

Never, not once in his twenty-nine years, had a woman preyed on his mind.

And Lachlan McPherson had had a variety of women who could do it.

It was just that none of them did.

Be careful, he heard her words in his head said in that sweet whisper, the like he'd never encountered before, as he moved up her front path deciding, if she wasn't home, he'd go to the pub he'd found her in and ask after her.

One way or another, he'd find her.

Absolutely.

He stopped dead at the door.

It was ajar.

"Fuck," he whispered.

He looked to the left, to the right and up.

The house was dark.

Then his neck grew tense and his eyes narrowed when he sensed it.

Putting his hand to the door, slowly, he pushed it open.

Slower still, he walked into the dark house.

Even in the shadows he could see it was in disarray. It looked as if an almighty battle had been fought throughout the front rooms. And a sense of deep unease stole through him as he saw the dark splatters in the shadowed rooms that looked disturbingly like blood.

He stopped dead in the entry, his gaze slicing to the hall where he saw the large, brawny male ghost hovering and smiling.

"You want 'er," its eerie disembodied voice sounded all around then for some reason the ghost lifted its forefinger to its nose before dropping it, leaning jeeringly forward and hissing, "*Catch me if you can!*"

With that it disappeared.

Lach stared down the empty hall.

Then he pulled out his phone, engaged it, slid his thumb on the screen and tapped it.

He put it to his ear.

"Seriously, Lach, what the fuck?" his sister said in his ear.

Lach stared down the hall.

He smelled her perfume, his gut lurched and his heart squeezed.

"I need you," he replied.

Belle

Loved Up in Holy Matrimony.

Europe lost its most eligible bachelor this week when James Bennett married Belle Abbot-now-Bennett, The Tiny Dynamo.

The ceremony was small, family and close friends only. Surprisingly, no details were leaked but eye witnesses outside noted that Miles Bennett, James's brother and once a competitor for his now wife's affections was seen entering and exiting the Registry Office, and on his arm was the stunning, recently divorced socialite Yasmin Delacourt who was wearing a very attractive but very large hat.

Photographers were able to catch this photo of the pair exiting the Registry Office this past Saturday after the short ceremony was complete.

Although the couple is known to be on their honeymoon, details of where that is are unknown. Spokespeople at Bennett's conglomerate have shared only that the couple will be away for some time, this on the heels of their disappearance of the month prior to their wedding.

Calvin Cole, Belle Bennett's estranged ex-husband, was unattainable for comment and it is thought he's left the country.

Lila Cavendish, renowned artist and the new Mrs. Bennett's grandmother, was at the ceremony and will be unveiling her highly anticipated Cornwall series next month in a small gallery in St. Ives.

When asked if the couple will settle in London or Cornwall, Mr. Bennett's spokespeople simply but confusingly answered, "But of course."

Clearly, evidence is suggesting intriguing, handsome James Bennett and his beautiful, mysterious new wife intend to keep going as they have throughout their stormy courtship, quiet and private.

Belle's eyes drifted from the article to the photo they were able to get.

It was mostly of her mom and dad's back, Dad's head turned, his profile laughing. But through them you could see Belle, her hair pulled up in a soft, feminine updo threaded with strings of tiny pearls, her head tipped back, a big smile on her face and that smile was aimed at Jack.

Jack's handsome head was tipped down, his grin aimed at Belle.

She remembered that moment.

It was the best in her life.

And since then, they kept getting better.

And because of this, every day, several times a day, Belle Bennett thanked her lucky stars.

Suddenly, the magazine was pulled from her hand and tossed to the floor. She was pulled from the bed and found herself back in it, but atop Jack's body.

"Stop reading that rubbish," he muttered, lifting a hand to smooth the hair back at one side of her head.

"There was a good picture of you," she protested.

"Really?" he asked.

"Jack, every picture of you is a good picture," she told him and watched him grin.

She took in a breath.

Then, too casually, she wondered aloud, "I wonder if our child will be photogenic."

Jack's arms got tight around her and his grin faded from his face but his eyes grew intense on hers.

"Pardon?" he whispered.

"You know, when we were away the first time, how we decided—?"

Jack cut her off and asked in a low, rumbly voice, "Belle, are you carrying my child?"

Belle answered immediately and she did it in a soft, breathy voice, "Yes."

Half a second later, she found herself on her back, her husband on top of her.

Beside the bed, Baron and Gretl settled in on a jingle of dog tags.

And out the window, winter rain fell soft on Cornwall.

The End

This is the final book in the
Ghosts and Reincarnation Series.
Thank you for reading!

NEWSLETTER

Would you like advanced notification about Upcoming Releases? Access to exclusive content? Access to exclusive giveaways? The first to see a new cover reveal? Sign up for my newsletter to keep up-to-date with the latest from Kristen Ashley!

Sign up at kristenashley.net

ABOUT THE AUTHOR

Kristen Ashley is the *New York Times* bestselling author of over one hundred romance novels. She's a hybrid author, publishing titles independently and traditionally, with books translated into fourteen languages and millions of copies sold.

Kristen's novel, *Law Man*, won the *RT Book Reviews* Reviewer's Choice Award for best Romantic Suspense, her independently published title, *Hold On*, was nominated for *RT Book Reviews* best Independent Contemporary Romance, and her traditionally published title, *Breathe*, was nominated for best Contemporary Romance. Her titles *Motorcycle Man*, *The Will*, *The Hookup* and *Ride Steady* (which won the Reader's Choice award from *Romance Reviews*) all made the final rounds for Goodreads Choice Awards in the Romance category.

Although Kristen is super proud of all those accolades, she's just happy that—after years of writing with no publisher or agent interested in what she did—she now has a loyal readership who, on social media, she can share recipes with and regale with stories of her bent toward being a klutz.

Kristen was born in Gary and raised in Brownsburg, Indiana, but since leaving her home state (Hoosier by birth, Boilermaker by the grace of God!), she's lived in Denver and the West Country of England. All of these places were home, and she's put them in her books with all the love she still has for them.

Now, after years of cold, misty days in the UK (that she still misses, along with cream teas, custard and battered sausages), Kristen resides in almost constant sun. She writes at her desk in Phoenix or among the deer and javelina in her little cabin up in the Arizona mountains, regretting often that she forgets to put the sunshade over her windshield, thus her car often doubles as a human oven. Even so, she loves calling all the sun, saguaro and beautiful mountains home.

You can read more about Kristen and her books at KristenAshley.net.

facebook.com/kristenashleybooks

instagram.com/kristenashleybooks

pinterest.com/KristenAshleyBooks

goodreads.com/kristenashleybooks

bookbub.com/authors/kristen-ashley

tiktok.com/@kristenashleybooks

ALSO BY KRISTEN ASHLEY

Rock Chick Series:

Rock Chick

Rock Chick Rescue

Rock Chick Redemption

Rock Chick Renegade

Rock Chick Revenge

Rock Chick Reckoning

Rock Chick Regret

Rock Chick Revolution

Rock Chick Reawakening

Rock Chick Reborn

Rock Chick Rematch

Rock Chick Bonus Tracks

Avenging Angels Series

Avenging Angel

Avenging Angels: Back in the Saddle

Avenging Angels: Tenderfoot

Avenging Angel: Bad Medicine

The 'Burg Series:

For You

At Peace

Golden Trail

Games of the Heart

The Promise

Hold On

The Chaos Series:

Own the Wind

Fire Inside

Ride Steady

Walk Through Fire

A Christmas to Remember

Rough Ride

Wild Like the Wind

Free

Wild Fire

Wild Wind

The Colorado Mountain Series:

The Gamble

Sweet Dreams

Lady Luck

Breathe

Jagged

Kaleidoscope

Bounty

Dream Man Series:

Mystery Man

Wild Man

Law Man

Motorcycle Man

Quiet Man

Dream Team Series:

Dream Maker

Dream Chaser

Dream Bites Cookbook

Dream Spinner

Dream Keeper

The Fantasyland Series:

Wildest Dreams

The Golden Dynasty

Fantastical

Broken Dove

Midnight Soul

Gossamer in the Darkness

Four Realms Series:

Night's Fall

Ghosts and Reincarnation Series:

Sommersgate House

Lacybourne Manor

Penmort Castle

Fairytale Come Alive

Lucky Stars

The Honey Series:

The Deep End

The Farthest Edge

The Greatest Risk

The Magdalene Series:

The Will

Soaring

The Time in Between

Manor and Mysteries Series:

Too Good to Be True

Mathilda, SuperWitch:

Mathilda's Book of Shadows

The Rise of the Dark Lord

Misted Pines Series

The Girl in the Mist

The Girl in the Woods

The Woman by the Lake

The Woman Left Behind

Moonlight and Motor Oil Series:

The Hookup

The Slow Burn

The Rising Series:

The Beginning of Everything

The Plan Commences

The Dawn of the End

The Rising

River Rain Series:

After the Climb

After the Climb Special Edition

Chasing Serenity

Taking the Leap

Making the Match

Fighting the Pull
Sharing the Miracle
Embracing the Change
Finding the One

The Three Series:
Until the Sun Falls from the Sky
With Everything I Am
Wild and Free

The Unfinished Hero Series:
Knight
Creed
Raid
Deacon
Sebring

Wild West MC Series:
Still Standing
Smoke and Steel
Smooth Sailing

Other Titles by Kristen Ashley:
Heaven and Hell
Play It Safe
Three Wishes
Complicated
Loose Ends
Fast Lane
Perfect Together

www.ingramcontent.com/pod-product-compliance
Lightning Source LLC
Chambersburg PA
CBHW051424190726
48289CB00001B/40